Fixing Shadows

Fixing Shadows

Shadows

Susan Barrett

review

First published in Great Britain in 2005
by Review

An imprint of Headline Book Publishing

10 9 8 7 6 5 4 3 2 1

Cataloguing in Publication Data is available from the British Library

ISBN 0 7553 2175 8

Typeset in Bembo by Avon DataSet Ltd,
Bidford-on-Avon, Warwickshire

Printed and bound in Great Britain by
Clays Ltd, St Ives plc

Headline's policy is to use papers that are natural, renewable and recyclable
products and made from wood grown in sustainable forests. The logging
and manufacturing processes are expected to conform to the
environmental regulations of the country of origin.

Headline Book Publishing
A division of Hodder Headline
338 Euston Road
London NW1 3BH

www.reviewbooks.co.uk
www.hodderheadline.com

For Richard, Grace and Ned

In memory of Robin Bradshaw 1939–2002

Secure the shadow ere the substance fade,
Let Nature imitate what Nature made.

Early daguerreotype advertising slogan,
sometimes attributed, erroneously, to Shakespeare

Prologue

For gone two years now we'd left off dreading the nights. No need to decamp to the Underground every evening with Thermos and blankets. Mind you, after that direct hit burst the sewer and the gas and the water mains and did for the six hundred sheltering down there, we'd felt safer staying above ground. Of course, since those terrible nights of the Blitz, they've dug two deep-level tunnel shelters by the Tube with all facilities laid on – bunks, canteens, toilets. Safe as houses, and everything you could want just when it wasn't much use to anyone. Snafu, as per. No warning with Jerry's new bomb, you see: no chance for Wailing Winnie to tune up. So Duke and I had no time, no time at all, or we might have got into the place under the stairs or gone down to the Anderson. But – it's a funny thing – nowadays I can't stand to leave my bed at night, can't bear the cold any more, and no more can Duke. If you've got to go, we reckon it's better to die at home, comfortable in your own bed.

The choking smell of ancient brick dust and soot is visible: it smokes out of the smashed building. Vic, the ARP warden, sucks it in like he'd draw on a fag. He's trying to catch the whiff of coal gas under the smell of soot, smashed lilac bushes and scorched paint. These old houses are the worst: even if the gas-lamps have been swapped for electric, they're crawling with piping that can still hold gas. After a direct hit like this, a house is like a traumatised body – no matter if the mains have been shut off, the mangled tubes and pipes will dribble and seep. All quiet and then the whole thing goes up in your face.

Vic is cautious as he treads the crunchy roof slates. Respect must be paid to the dead house, lying with its innards out, a huge, slumped, murdered thing, with all its raw humanity now brazenly on show. It made you think, though, seeing what was spilled into the street. All those relics of lives, preserved for what, for whom? Faded girls' plaits, laid up in drawers; milk teeth from children who'd long grown, hoarded in the corner of a sealed envelope; bundles and bundles of anonymous photographs; wrapped tablets of pale soap; unused linen kept for best, all tucked in with lavender bags gone to dust. Why did people keep these things so carefully never to look at them, stow them away like secret treasure, only to forget they had them? War or no war, eventually all the hidden archive of ordinary lives would be turned over by the next generation and thrown, unceremoniously, away. But bombing's indifferent display of the dead and their effects never fails to offend against Vic's sense of propriety.

Mind you, he's seen some sights in his time. A woman dead – quite nude – in a bath lolling heavily upon the brink of her violently opened-up bathroom. Over-full pots slopping under frowsty beds, chilled by uninvited outdoor air and eyes. Once he'd been called to a direct hit on a funeral parlour and found coffins slithered out on to the high street, as well as fish from the next-door fishmonger's and boots from the shop on the other side, all muddled up together. And there'd been the old man, trousers around ankles, who'd found his last resting-place in the outdoor carsey. But he isn't one to join in the sniggers, or the looting. When he's on duty he's the professional mute, attendant at a funeral where vulgarity and lunatic laughter keeps breaking out. The everyday exposure to the absurdities of life and death had made snorting buffoons or indifferent souvenir hunters of too many. It's the smell not the sights that gets to him, the smell of human flesh and blood. That's what stays, afterwards, makes you realise the horror.

Vic keeps a weather eye on the photographer from the local rag who is snapping a kiddy's teddy he's placed among the rubble: sob-stuff to sell papers. He looks out, too, for the labourers who are sorting through the debris for anything that can be slipped profitably into back pockets. Some even have the cheek to carry collecting sacks. It's a poor show. Like degenerate Father Christmases, they clamber about on the roof, trying to find a way in to snatch the booty. Picking at the house corpse. Plundering its secrets.

'Over here, Vic.'

It's his mate, Barry, standing up high on a part of roof that has not yet collapsed because it is keyed into the chimney-stack, which stands rigid, like a brick backbone thrust up through the centre of the house.

'I think I've got a whole room under here.'

'Know who we're looking for?'

'Which number's this one? Any idea? I've lost me bearings.'

Vic treads his way delicately across the road, where the buzz-bomb has dealt a casually thrown hand of bricks and slates. He finds the front door, somehow left standing unsupported, its blackout curtain still drawn. On cautiously looking round it, he sees the reason the door has not collapsed: it's supported from within by bales and bundles of old newspapers. The whole hallway is stuffed with them, and only a narrow passage left between the stacks, like a secret rabbit-run worn through tall grass. Just inside the door, where you might step if you could force it wide, stands an old-fashioned plate camera, tribute to an age in which joinery and engineering could beautifully co-exist. Vic reaches round and picks up the camera. It's so solid, so heavy; he weighs it in his hand for a moment, then looks up at the door.

'It's number thirty!' he shouts to Barry, on the slumped roof.

'Oh, I know it. Was two old girls living here when I was a lad. All manner of queer visitors in their day, comings and goings at all hours – sent my mum hopping mad. Then, if I remember, two nephews came to stay permanent. Old girls died, old boys stopped on – used to see them toddling up and down the road together arm in arm, like Darby and Joan. Nice old chaps, the type you'd call proper old-fashioned gentlemen, but terrible ones for hoarding.' He picks up a newspaper. 'I remember, they used to show us kids how to cut out those paper boys and girls holding hands all in a row. We were devils for that. Then we'd paint them up, each one different, to look like all the kids in our street. Funny how things come back to you, ain't it?'

Vic joins Barry on the roof where two workmen are beginning to pick up slates and toss them down to the street.

'Anyone down there?' Vic calls, through the gappy roof. 'What d'you say their names were?'

'Don't think I ever rightly knew. Just used to call 'em Mr G. and Mr D.'

With a rush, a patch of slates cascades and cracks open the space within. Sudden vertigo, as the rescue party of Barry and Vic is now balanced only on a roof beam, looking past the toes of their boots into that giddy gap below. They gaze down into a peep-show bedroom, lit by a sudden shaft of outdoor light. A gush of warmed bedroom air bursts upon them, carrying away the last breath of George and Duke.

Through the hole in the roof, they see down to where smashed slates, plaster and laths have splattered on to the broad, bare back of a wooden wardrobe, which, in turn, has toppled like the mighty mahogany tree it once was upon the double bedstead. Vic kneels at the precipice edge and uses his torch to peep inside. His is the big eye that looks through the doll's-house window to spy on the dolls' private lives. But he does not catch them out, though it is palpable that the instant before he looked there was life in this room. Now all is still. The only sound is the trickling of plaster upon the wooden wardrobe and the mundane ticking of the bedside clock.

'Is anyone down there?' Vic calls again.

The clock ticks back.

'The floor looks solid enough. I'll go in and see if anyone was asleep down there,' says Barry.

They lower him, a rope round him, until his feet meet the floorboards.

'There's definitely somebody in the bed. I can see a foot.'

Then they send down a rope to tie round the wardrobe's waist. Vic jumps into the room to help manoeuvre it off the bed, as the labourers above haul on the rope. The heavy piece of furniture pirouettes upon one leg, uncovering the bed.

Here we lie, Duke and George, so peaceful, next to each other in our bed, head by head and hip by hip in striped winceyette pyjamas. We are holding hands. Overall, a powdering of ash-soft plaster dust has whitened the tableau. We seem to lie, the 'sculptur'd dead', like carvings upon a monument: twinned dead sons of a noble house. All that is lacking is the patient little dog at our feet.

Vic cannot take his eyes from our hands. They are beautiful old men's hands, one plump and soft, the other lean and smooth. Not gripped but loosely held, one by the other.

Two old pals each giving and receiving the hold.

Barry leans in to have a look. 'That's them – poor old so-and-sos.'

And the press photographer's Leica flashes in our dead faces.

Book One

1873

A Portentous Birth to The House of Fainhope

The billow of curtains brings Stevens over to the window. She looks out into the increasing night, silhouetted against the lighted room beyond, the very tip of her nose and a slice of her forehead pressed pale against the pane. She brings down the lower sash and cuts in two the cool ribbon of evening air, which has been insinuating its way over the sill and swelling the curtains.

As the window is closed, the bedroom door opens, causing her to turn away from the night into the lit, warm room. Dr Oliver nods to her, puts down his medical bag and removes his coat. 'How often have the pains been coming, Stevens?'

The lady's maid replies, in a guarded whisper, 'Oh, my goodness, sir, they just seem to run one into another. I've never known it so bad before. I'd swear this one is a boy – it's making such a business of coming into the world.'

'Hush, woman. I don't want to hear idle speculation upon the sex of this child!' While he is talking, he moves to the bed in the middle of the room where a woman is panting and wild. Heels dug in, knees braced, grasping for a sure handhold, she fights and resists, as though an inexorable weight will drag her down towards the foot of the bed and extinction. Pain is sucking at her. Pain wants her to let go and fall; it wants her to bite hard on the abscessed tooth, to dance on broken ankles and plunge burnt hands into flames. Pain demands that she surrender and do the very thing that will hurt most: push.

Dr Oliver moves to the bed and assesses his patient. 'Your Grace, I think the time is near. May I?' With that, he unceremoniously flings back the bedclothes and inserts his fingers between the straining thighs. This abrupt invasion is met by animalistic bellows from the woman on the bed. 'Pray calm yourself, Your Grace, we don't want to dissipate your generative energies in noise instead of effort.'

'Get off me, you fucking man! I will scream if I want!' The woman glares at him and opens her mouth to roar and roar again.

Up in the night nursery, a little girl who is having her hair brushed loses her place in counting out the hundred strokes. Her sister's unauthorised head pops into view above her high-sided cot.

In the library, Lord John Harpur clamps his son Harry to his side and looks at the pale, tired boy.

Mrs Beam, in her subterranean kitchen, sighs and clips the scullery-maid round the ear as she knuckles bright a copper pan, with silver sand, salt and vinegar.

The new nursery-maid, eleven-year-old Lucy, her face shiny with steam from her can of hot water, pauses at the governess's door. Timidly she knocks and enters. Here is another woman upon a bed, like a pathetic inmate of Bedlam, with a knot of linen clamped between her teeth and her nightdress pulled, unheeded, to the waist. A cautionary illustration of 'the deranged female lunatic in the full spate of her insanity', wanting only straw and chains. The madwoman turns her eyes away from the dark-red, skinned thing that has spilled out upon the sheet and looks on Lucy. And with that, innocent Lucy runs from the room, an iron taste of blood in her nostrils, unsure of quite what she has witnessed in that dreadful chamber.

By the time Lucy reaches Dr Oliver, he is fastening his cuffs and wiping clean his hands upon his coat tails. He the professional servant; the Duchess of Fainhope his gracious patroness. On looking into the wheezing, folded face of the wrapped infant that has been handed to her by her maid, Stevens, Her Grace quizzes it languidly, 'A boy? So you are a boy. A poor enough sprig, but you will do.'

Lucy is unsure whom to approach. She shouldn't really be here, but that there is a doctor in the house at the very moment when one is needed is surely licence. At last she decides upon Stevens, as the nearest in rank to her own.

Stevens conveys, with genteel embellishments, the request to Dr Oliver. 'If you please, sir, Miss Mantilla, the governess here, is taken ill. She begs pardon to ask for your assistance.'

Dr Oliver follows Lucy down corridors unaccustomed to the confident tread of male feet. Into this domestic female domain, only Tom Kitten may stray. Dr Oliver is not insensitive to the deliciousness of penetrating these forbidden realms. Tongue-tied Lucy shows him to Miss Mantilla's door and stands back for him to enter. He is a gentleman and a doctor: all his science and his masculinity will see off the shameful, womanish mess within.

A horrible sob of suppressed pain and fear is released as he enters. Lucy, outside the door, crosses herself at the exorcism.

Inside, Miss Mantilla modestly pulls down her nightdress and says, in a most shockingly ordinary voice, 'I'm so sorry. I appear to have had an accident.' She begins to sob plaintively, and Lucy knows that Dr Oliver has made the world straight and sane again.

On the short return journey to the Duchess's bedroom, Dr Oliver has time to consider what he has been privy to this interesting half-hour. Without knowing exactly what hand his opponent holds, he must play these fortunate cards to maximum advantage. It looks so like a flush that he suspects he is being bluffed. These reflections mean his leave-taking is somewhat preoccupied.

'Your Grace, a happy outcome and my hearty congratulations on it. So I bid you farewell.'

When she detains him to enquire about the domestic commotion that called him away to the servants' quarters, he is taken aback that she refers to it. Does she know, or does she not? He must play his trump with care indeed. For now, let the nursery-maid be the one unambiguously to name what happened there.

So, with unusual alacrity in leaving his noble patient, Dr Oliver is graciously nodded from the room and the mistress of Fainhope Hall can address herself to the brother-in-law and nephew who attend her downstairs. She turns to her maid, who is arranging the baby's linen before the fire to warm: 'Stevens! Pay attention, woman! You must carry news to Lord John. Tell him only that our uncertainty is over: the future is secured. It is enough. He will understand.'

With the compressed lips and cautious tread of one bearing an overfilled jug, Stevens sets off down the principal staircase, careful not to slop any particle of this coded communication. At the instant she makes the library, anxious to decant, a shriek is heard from behind the door left ajar by her exit.

After hours spent straining to apprehend any sound coming from that particular chamber, his ears have been sharpened to so painful a degree that the suddenness of Stevens' arrival, and the cry, cause Lord John Harpur to start from his chair as though scalded. 'It's come at last! Which is it, boy or girl?' This he amends, regaining some sense of decorum, and indeed of the sequence of events, to the more civil proposal that Stevens should 'hurry away upstairs and bring back reports of a safe delivery, please God'.

Stevens, discovering that the vessel brimming with great tidings has been upset by all this palaver and that she and it are equally dry of sense, hesitates to reconsider what the Duchess's exact formula might have been. Having arrived at the conclusion that she no longer has the slightest notion of what her mistress told her to say, she heads off further confusion by simply delivering the facts of the matter, as they appear to her. 'Oh, sir, the child is delivered already, this twenty minutes and more past. Her Grace sends that a son is born to her.'

After hours of suspense, this sudden, unequivocal thrust deflates Lord John's expectant smile and hopeful heart on the instant. To hide his fallen face from the servant he turns it upon Harry, whose hair he ruffles. But the ruffle becomes a cuff and is rather more than the sleepy boy can endure without giving way to wails.

'Come, Harry, you must be a brave boy. My compliments to your lady, Stevens. Now I shall deliver this young man home after his long wait upon his cousin, the heir, eh, Harry?' says Lord John, with grim levity, as he buffets the boy out of the library before him. Stevens has left the room, so does not hear Lord John Harpur's parting comment, addressed it would seem to howling Harry, and spoken straight from that deflated heart: 'So this is your destiny. A destiny that came out of my brother's grave, God help us all.'

Lucy is panting, a livid red slap on her cheek. She had put into words what she saw, but she seems to have been tainted by the telling and has made Her Grace very angry. And Her Grace is more than usually angry. Though she should be confined to bed she has picked up the loosely bundled baby and is walking about her room distractedly. Lucy is tempted to fold the baby's little dangling leg safe under his shawl, but she is frightened to come near so bobs a curtsy and runs away to cry in private.

The First Departure

Now that she is alone the Duchess sits with the baby on her knee and explores his still face with her lips to test for the merest breath, the vaguest warmth. She brings his chest close to feel and listen for any fluttering, turns her finger in one lax palm, trying to awaken in him the reflex to grip on to life. She has curbed her compulsive pacing and brought her ragged breathing under control; finally she is still enough and quiet enough to understand that her boy does not move or breathe. The alarming shout that Lord John mistook for the crow of triumph was in truth her howl of recognition that what she held in her arms was nothing but the corpse of a great hope. Now the shrivelled complexion and straight black lips confirm that here is just the clay of life, unanimated, cold, dead.

She holds his body before her at arms' length to give it a brisk shake. The little head nods to her and she throws it back upon the bed, only to take it up again, leave go, and then, gathering it up, carry it out into the corridor. She walks through the house with a caution composed in equal parts of pain and concealment, leaving a speckled trail of blood spots like the breadcrumbs that traced an escape route back through the woods. The scattered, rusty change doesn't remain long to mark that journey between the Duchess's bedroom and her governess's –

scrubbed out, just after dawn, by a nameless woman on her knees.

Now she finds Miss Mantilla's door and enters. Dressed all in white, with long dark hair hanging loose and the wizened changeling child in her arms, she appears like an elf-wife come from inside the fairy hill to meddle and mismatch. The governess, surprised, scrambles in her disordered bed to conceal her shame, all the while whimpering in alarm.

'I hear that we are doubly blessed, miss. Show me – do we have a Jack or a Mary? Will he be sweeping crossings, or she carrying slops once Mama has thrown herself on the parish?' asks the Duchess, her face impassive.

Miss Mantilla still cringes as she lays the baby on the bed, where its wrappings fall away and it seeks blindly for comfort in the cold air. The disproportionately large, purplish sexual organs of a newborn boy are displayed between sinewy, jack-knifed shanks. He writhes and wrings his long-fingered hands, as though in despair at the prospect of the life that lies ahead.

His movement and scent draw the Duchess near, like an animal instinctively attracted and excited by that reflex struggle and the deep, earthy odour of the newborn. She looks on the baby with fascinated, hungry eyes and her servant steps quickly away from the bed, surrendering him to her. 'Oh, Your Grace, forgive me. Look, I disown him – I relinquish him. I will do anything to maintain your good name.'

Sitting upon the bed, her clumsy bundle heavy in her tired arms, the Duchess looks at the governess and muses: '*My* good name? Yes, my illustrious name must be preserved at all costs. But, then, the cost will not be so very high for me, will it? I shall suffer inconvenience, true, but merely the inconvenience of replacing a servant at short notice. Names such as mine will tend to retain their splendour whatever ordure is flung at them. But what of yours? I understand that for a person in your position a spotless reputation is her dearest possession. Something so precious, and yet so easily spoiled. So how, do you suppose, may the miracle of social decontamination be expedited for your *good name*, my dear?'

The governess fails to meet her mistress's black eyes, which are turned, unblinking, upon her.

'To begin,' continues the Duchess, as though patiently repeating an ill-learnt lesson, 'you might indeed cast him off, but then where shall he be cast and how shall his origins be disguised? Shall some simple childless couple from the estate be found, both mute from birth? Will the wild beasts of the woods take on his care, or shall some cold doorstep receive this anonymous bundle tonight? It would seem he must gather his tatters around him and take charge of his own destiny. And what of your destiny? Can there be future comfort, or peace, or employment for a friendless woman who brings a bastard into the world, however repentant she may be?'

Miss Mantilla understands that her mistress is challenging her, and that if she can only match her hard logic, she will arrive at the correct answer to the problem and please icy teacher. 'I do disown him, deny him. I am firm in this. And I will do anything to wipe myself clean again and retain my position here.' Even as she says this, Miss Mantilla tries ineffectually to draw together his loosened wrappings against the chilly air.

'Good. Then why cover him from the cold? Life is cold for him and ever will be.'

Miss Mantilla, desperate to demonstrate her resolve, picks her naked baby out of his nest of bloodied scraps and deposits him upon her marble nightstand. His back arches and his limbs extend in shock, and he starts a rusty, spasmodic cry, blue lips quivering in a comic exaggeration of anguish. But Miss Mantilla holds firm and turns away her head. On this signal the Duchess springs from the bed to catch up the vital, naked boy, letting her own stiff bundle drop. 'It's done, then,' she says, tugging away the shawl from that dead creature so that it rolls across the bed towards the governess, then greedily parcelling up the writhing baby within it. Miss Mantilla begins to understand that the only workings needed to solve her conundrum were addition and subtraction, yet still she is at a loss to comprehend how this solution was arrived at and what it might mean. The living child's cry of distress makes her look to the Duchess who has him held slightly away from her, his little, searching fingers and toes entangling in the cobwebby shawl as he seeks for warmth and the security of a firm hold.

'Lie still. I will warm you a little,' she says sharply, to the struggling child in her arms, and then, looking back to the woman on the bed, 'You see, how simply your problem is answered, Miss Mantilla. My name can easily bear what yours may not.'

Beguiled and dazed by the sudden lifting of her burden, Miss Mantilla lets the Duchess reach the door before stirring herself to form the question: 'Why?'

'It's a substitution, a swap, Maria: for I have need of the thing you must cast off. A very fine swap indeed,' says the Duchess briskly, as she opens the door. She pauses on the threshold. 'But I know that you cannot be perfectly comfortable until you have done your job thoroughly and left all clean and orderly behind you. Therefore, before we may continue again as we are accustomed, you may take a short holiday to dispose of . . . what remains.'

Miss Mantilla, her eyes fixed by those compelling black orbs, places her hand upon the dead infant beside her in confirmation that this is what must be disposed of, and the Duchess answers the gesture with her own, bringing one finger to her lips for an instant. Then the door closes upon her mistress and her bartered baby.

She sits upon the bed and looks at the poor dead thing with which the pact was made, the bargain struck. For so long she had wished for her own baby's death, that it should be dissolved away in the blood she had looked for every month, or that it should just wither and die like this one had. But when the blasphemous prayer, 'Lord, get rid of it', which she had repeated with such passion every night, failed her she had resorted to even greater crimes. She had plotted his elimination: tried to scald him with hot baths, strangle him with tight lacing, poison him with gin and Beechams pills and murder him with falls. Always she had denied that it was a child that quickened within her, picturing the thing that squirmed in her belly as the muscular spasm of a monstrous fish leaping towards life. She had never imagined him into being with the face and form of a human child. He was the secret bruise made by sin that ached in the night, the hard stone of inescapable and gathering doom she carried about with her all day long. But now that she has voided the stone and somehow survived, now that she has indeed 'got rid of it', as though it was borne away by a dark angel summoned by her sacrilegious prayer, whence comes this new agony of loss and defeat? She turns to the little mummy on the bed, but his is not the shape that her arms need. This little graven image of a baby is not meant to be held. Miss Mantilla puts it inside a pillowcase and hides it away in her bottom drawer. 'No use crying over spilt milk,' she says sharply to herself.

And then she goes to sleep. For the first time in seven months she can sleep without dreams of devils and wake without the certainty that something terrible must happen today.

In her bedroom, Her Grace, the Duchess, is awkwardly cradling the baby that struggles for life. He is naked under the shawl, his little belly packed tight under thin skin, surmounted by the stump of the umbilical cord: the snapped stalk from which he might have dangled ready to drop into her waiting lap; overripened fruit; mottled, dinted and smelling high and sweet. With her milk she will make him hers. She puts him to her nipple with a slight shiver as he begins to suck, whether from the coldness of his hard gums or from some other cause we cannot know; her jaw is set firm.

When Miss Mantilla wakes the next morning she wonders at the close smell in her room: a rank mustiness something like yeast and sour milk. Lying among her stained bed-linen she cannot curb the idiot smile that has attached itself to her face or the nervous energy that prickles to find release despite the stiffness of her limbs. Perhaps it is the pain and loss of blood that make her feel so airy – so light-hearted and light-headed. It is as though the core of her has been scooped away, leaving her so hollow she could float right up to the ceiling. She wonders whether this was how the early martyrs felt after their own agony – this high, puffed-up, precarious bliss that exists at the other side of mortal suffering.

Although gladdened by this sense of absolution, she knows it cannot last. The blood and the mess and the ache in her empty centre are what bring her back to herself. She resolves to think only of what is to be done now and how it should be done, and goes about the business of cleaning herself and the room with practised efficiency. Like a child who dares not look under the bed in the certain knowledge that, should she do so, the monster curled there will be brought to hideous life, she cannot look back and bring the events of last night fully into being. She will permit herself only to remember that she was violently purged of that clotted sin for her own good and was made new and clean again. She cannot allow her imagination to reach out for him. Instead she will marshal her determination and intelligence, as always, to do what has to be done, and turn her back on that which cannot be mended and so must not be mourned.

This early morning Lucy, too, is awake: she is struggling with the heavy coal scuttle, ash-pan, brush, tinder-box, spills and day-old newspaper to mend the nursery fire when she is intercepted by Miss Mantilla. The little nursery-maid looks up from where she kneels, startled to find the governess standing over her. The narrow costume, narrow boots and narrow face above the tight white collar exemplify absolute self-control.

'You may inform Nanny that I shall be unable to attend to Lady Georgina today as I am called away by family illness.' For a moment she confronts Lucy with eyes full of stone-hard denial, then releases her to glance at the clock on the nursery wall. 'You are ten minutes behind with this fire.'

When Miss Mantilla looks back down into Lucy's face she reads nothing other than submission there. Lucy is not trained in intelligence and determination: she has had little use for either. Certainly they are not qualities expected or welcomed in a nursery-maid. What she has had abundant tutoring in, however, is unthinking obedience. Miss Mantilla continues to hold the nursery-maid's eye as she takes from her hands the pages of yesterday's newspaper that Lucy was balling up to build the fire. So secure now in her dominance that she isn't even tempted to explain why she wants them, the governess dismisses the girl peremptorily: 'Miss, you have a smut on your cheek.'

Lucy really does live in the present, and as her hand leaps to polish away the smut her imagination is wiped of the hallucinatory events of last night by the reality of today's routine drudgery. And her flatly automatic 'Yes, 'm,' is eloquent enough for the governess.

Back in her chilly room, Miss Mantilla hums a hard little hymn as she efficiently wraps and turns, wraps again and ties the newspaper bundle that she is assembling upon her nightstand. She muses that by the time the young lady whom she drills in the schoolroom and the younger miss whom Nanny alternates between spoiling and scolding in the day nursery have awoken, the rest of these sheets will have been consumed by fire and she will be half-way to London. It occurs to her that for all Lady Georgina, seven, and Lady Euphemia, three, know of the real world that lies beyond the park gates they might be well-born apes living in a luxuriant tree in the jungle – where the air is always warmed, the food to hand and there are numerous females, such as herself, employed to cuff them into becoming proper grown-up ladies. They do not consider who lights the fires; they barely know that fires need to be lit. For them food grows on trays to be taken in the day nursery, and clothes will always find themselves freshly folded in drawers. Like all well-brought-up children, they are so beautifully adapted to this rarefied environment that, were their tree to be shaken, they would fall from it into a hostile foreign land in which they would certainly perish. Miss Mantilla considers grimly that, down here on the forest floor where the common or garden animals roam, the civilised niceties she schools them in, such as compassion and forgiveness, are the characteristics of the weak. It is the fiercely self-interested and the predatory who thrive where she must dwell. They don't know they're born, two pretty hollow-headed china dollies, she says to herself, as she fits the newspaper package snugly within her small cardboard suitcase. She snaps it shut and leaves her room with never a backward look.

As she steps into the early-morning air and sets off down the crunchy carriage drive, with a determined tread, the household's steam is already up and the great engine is beginning once again its diurnal journey along accustomed tracks. Down in the kitchen Mrs Beam is putting all her frustrations into pounding dough, while the usual recipient of her menopausal fury, Kathleen the kitchen-maid, is scrubbing carrots. Out by the stables the lad is forking horses' muck into a reeking pile. The housemaids are pattering above and below stairs with brushes, brooms and dusters, Stevens is sponging clean one of her mistress's many black crêpe costumes, and Miss Hart, the housekeeper, is counting the sheets in the airing cupboard. What a splendid phenomenon is the big country house, travelling sublime through each well-ordered day, its noisy, unremitting engine hidden but ever hungry, powered by the human fuel of domestic service.

As Miss Mantilla strides down muddy lanes, she offers up as penance the bloody, aching spasms made by her body as it closes back in upon itself. Her head is up and her grip is tight on the small case. She is passed by Dr Oliver, mounted on horseback, off to attend his aristocratic client. He tips his hat to her and surmises that she has been banished. No more sport to be had there, then.

The yard dogs, along with the indoor pet dogs, are now being fed by the stable lad in the courtyard. He is trying to exchange a word or two with Kathleen, who has brought out the meat scraps from the kitchen. She has been told to stay away from boys by Mother and is shy of them, so she sinks her chin into the collar of her uniform to hide her shamefully blushing neck.

Miss Mantilla waits on the platform of the railway station, where milk churns are being unloaded from the home-farm cart, ready for the London train. The farm man nods to her in recognition and she turns away, irritated at his presumption. And has to sit down. On the train, she puts the suitcase into the string luggage rack where it is just too wide to be completely secure: every time the train jolts, Miss Mantilla looks up involuntarily at it, lest it should fall.

By the time brick walls have replaced rushing trees and fields outside her carriage window, the whole household is gossiping about Miss Mantilla's unexpected departure. There is even some speculation in the servants' hall that she has cheeked the mistress and been dismissed without a character. Despite the pleasure to be had from painting this picture of impending ruin and misery for the uppish madam cast friendless on to the streets, Louisa Stevens grudgingly puts an end to the fun. She herself had had the pleasure of informing Her Grace of Miss Mantilla's defection and that lady was disappointingly unmoved by the news.

Once the topic of unexpected departure has been chewed dry, the next item on the conversational menu is the long-anticipated new arrival in the house. To be sure this infant son will secure the succession by giving the duchy of Fainhope its new heir at long last. But what is to become of the Fainhope estate until he comes of age? The masculine faction takes the view that all will be scattered to the winds, for how shall the inheritance be kept of a piece if entrusted to the unsafe hands of a babe and a widow woman? However, the senior females see their future in a sanguine light, being more familiar with the firm grip of the widowed lady and therefore sensible of quite how assiduously she might hold it all together. But it is to Mr Law, butler and domestic Solomon (himself clinging on by his well-pared fingernails since the tenth duke's death), that all turn for judgement. Mr Law's wisdom rests upon a talent for snooping, and his ubiquity when port and brandy are served and weighty matters discussed by his betters. He is also the senior male servant and therefore in theoretical line of descent, however distant, to those illustrious men who decide other people's lives for them. And, as it pleases him to remind the lower servants, true to his name, his word is indeed *law*. So being in full command of the facts, to wit that a posthumous boy-child has been safely delivered, Mr Law is able to pronounce his verdict. His Grace's will took into account this as yet unborn heir and directed that Her Grace, the Duchess, should be the legal guardian of her children. There are gasps at the heterodox nature of this provision. As for the estate, two respectable trustees have been nominated: a banker and a solicitor. It will fall to them to administer money and properties until the young duke comes of age. But Her Grace will continue upon her throne for the next twenty-one years, at which point the eleventh duke of Fainhope will, no doubt, banish her to the dower house.

This judicial pronouncement excites lively speculation upon the Duchess of Fainhope's luck and perspicacity at having arranged affairs thus to her advantage.

'Can you credit it? Near as dammit seven months to the day since the old duke's death,' comments the first footman.

'And she only goes and pops an heir – how's that for pulling a rabbit out of the hat?' adds the second footman.

But it is the groom who best sums up their admiration with his long and vulgar whistle, which Mr Law chokes with a look. Then, speaking up for the female faction, a parlour-maid remarks, 'She didn't even have a settlement when she married the old boy and look at her now, sitting pretty!'

'Would have been a very different matter if she hadn't've pulled it off, though. That Lord John would have been through the door so fast she'd be spinning like a top,' speculates Stevens, who had been privy to the look of punctured ambition on Lord John's face when he had received the disappointing news that Her Grace had indeed got off safe.

At the thought of that near calamity averted, a more sombre tone descends upon the company until Miss Hart, the housekeeper, rallies them: 'I propose that we raise a toast. Here's to Her Grace's continued prosperity and to ours!' And those that have tea-cups raise them and those that have none mimic the action in hearty assent.

'More properly, we should drink to the new duke of Fainhope,' corrects Law, although his platitude is lost in the general relief that Her Grace, the Duchess, has her heir and that, at least for the present, the status quo will be preserved below as it is above stairs.

As the great engine of the house eases its way into evening rituals, Miss Mantilla is walking down a south London street of terraced houses, the case banging heavily against her leg.

Through the Forest
and Home Again

Miss Mantilla pauses to compose herself for a moment at the brink of home, then raps hard upon the door. A smaller, younger version of herself answers, smoothing black hair away from an unconsciously smiling face. 'I thought you had set off for home— Oh! Maria, is it you?'

Miss Mantilla, in the effort to hold off sentimental collapse, is snappish in her reply. 'It is me and I may be admitted to my own house, I hope. Or shall we fold our arms across our aprons and gossip here on the street?'

The two enter the narrow passage and sister Aurora attempts to relieve her of the little case. But Miss Mantilla cannot let go so an impasse is reached in which neither gloves nor coat can be removed and the two stand face to face in the hall, both trying to prepare an opening remark. At last Aurora reaches for her sister's hat and the clumsy contact between them unfreezes Miss Mantilla sufficiently for her to let go of the case and unbutton her mantle.

'Who is it, Aurora?' the other sister, Teresa, calls from the back parlour. She is cutting out material for a blouse upon the table. She stands up from her work, the long dressmaker's scissors hanging down loosely in her hand, Atropos with her life-cutting shears, her hand halted by the unannounced visitor. 'Is it you, Maria?'

'Have I changed so much that both sisters are reduced to gaping ninnies?'

Indeed, she has not. For it is just this sharp tongue and the prerogative of her seniority that she has long employed to make silly girls of the two women. It suits her well, in her present plight, to assume the role of the authoritative older sister: it robs her interrogators of the ability to ask intelligent questions. She is so well used to it that it requires little effort to sustain and it reinforces that iron self-restraint with which she must overcome her welling emotions.

The back parlour presents a homely domestic scene interrupted: tea things have been pushed to one side of the table to make way for the blouse material and the kettle is still smoking on its trivet by the fire. Mrs Evans, the cat, is comfortable on the best parlour chair, paws folded before her ample bosom, on her square of velveteen offcut. On the other a scrapbook has been thrown down, spilling picture postcards, pressed flowers and theatrical programmes. Miss Mantilla picks up a postcard. It shows a West End actress, one finger raised in an attitude of coy salute; under her feet is written, 'Please, dear, post letter on chest of drawers for me, T.' There is something so cosy and carefree about this inconsequential message that the load she carries at last brings her to her knees.

'Have you lost your situation, Maria?' Teresa asks timidly.

This is the worst eventuality that these giddy girls can imagine and it makes Miss Mantilla smile her tight, controlled smile. 'No, I do not believe that I have, my dear Teresa. To the contrary, I am quite indispensable to Her Grace.'

She pulls herself upright while Aurora is quick to shoo the disgruntled cat from her throne so that Maria can sit there. 'Are you to stay long, sister? Will I take your case to your old room?'

'I must stay one night only. My duchess cannot spare me for longer. I shall take the case, Aurora. And I must see Papa.'

But she makes no effort to move from the chair where she sits somewhat sprawled, as though she has been thrown there. Both sisters stand uncertainly in the wreckage of their relaxed, companionable evening. Aurora finds courage and kneels by her eldest sister to take her hands and gently peel away the gloves she still wears. 'You must take something to eat, dear Maria. You are exhausted by the journey.'

At this cue, Teresa is happy to hurry away into the safety of the kitchen to butter bread and empty the slops from the teapot.

'Please excuse the disorder, Maria. We did not expect visitors. Teresa and I were to have spent a quiet evening together, employed in making and mending.' Aurora sees the room through her sister's eyes; what was homely disarray she now perceives to be a slovenly affront.

'Where is the girl?' is Maria's only reply.

'Oh, Bessie had such a cough we could not bear her in the house any longer so we sent her home to deafen her own family with her barking. Papa will be so pleased at your unexpected visit. He does nothing but talk of you and wonder about you.' Aurora is beginning to gabble in the face of this grave, silent sister. Whenever she has wondered about Maria it was with a pricking sense of guilt and queasy obligation that made her gladly turn her thoughts to impossible butcher's bills and Papa's bedpans, and away from her hard, dutiful eldest sister.

When Teresa ventures back into the parlour, Aurora has nervously restored some respectability to the room, tidying around Maria as she sits immovable in her coat, tipsily lop-sided. She looks awkward as a stiff-legged doll, bent into a sitting posture upon its doll chair, while the two big girls fluster about the room.

'I will take some tea and then I must go to Papa,' she says at last, but makes no effort to drink from the cup that has been placed by her elbow.

Upstairs, the old man in his big bed frets in the gathering gloom. The fleecy beard, combed out upon his eiderdown, is like a pile of soft white feathers in the dusk. It must surely be time for his tea. He fumbles for the walking-stick that leans against the bedhead and knocks on the floor. Ah, here someone comes. Silly article, with tea and a lamp.

The expected female shape is framed in the open doorway but, for a moment, he doesn't recognise the face lit grotesquely from below by the oil lamp she is carrying. Alonso gives a gasp and cries out, '*¿Quién es? ¿Quién va?*'

'*Soy yo*, Papa. Oh, my papa . . .'

'*¿Maria, eres tu mi niña?*'

She puts down the lamp and goes to her little father, marooned in his double bed, stoops to take his hand and places it on her forehead in benediction.

'What can this be? Has my eldest child who went out to seek her fortune come home to me? Has she journeyed through enchanted forests and over seas of forgetfulness to get back to us?' Then he sees her face more clearly, and says, 'What ails thee, my dear? Not ill – or ill-used, I hope?'

'No, not that. But, Papa, life is so hard.'

Alonso tries to raise his drooping daughter from her knees, but his hands are ineffectual as a bunch of twigs. He cannot get a grip on her, but must clumsily buffet her upright with dry, unruly fingers. 'Papa is here. I will look after my little girl. Give me a kiss, my darling, and wipe your tears.'

When she dabs unthinkingly at her eyes with her pocket-handkerchief she is surprised to find they are dry. As she leans over him to receive her kiss, his body feels like a loose bundle of umbrellas under the feather quilt. She is careful not to put too much of her weight on to his frail ribcage, supporting herself awkwardly with a hand upon the bedframe.

'Tell me everything, and I shall make all right again.'

'Papa, it's nothing. I am so tired, that's all. And I may not stay long.'

'Long enough to lick your naughty sisters into shape, perhaps? I thought they were sending to China for my dish of tea this evening!'

'Papa, shall I come home?' she ventures, with a plaintive intensity she hadn't intended.

'No, no, Maria darling. We really manage quite well without you. Though I miss my aide-de-camp.'

'Well, let this visit be a surprise inspection of the troops and catering corps.'

'That's my brave, good girl.'

Her voice and her smile are firm and reassuringly resolute again, and it is with surprise that she notices the stream of tears that now course down her face and off the point of her chin. 'Papa, there is one thing I must do before I send for the foot-soldiers.' She picks up the little case that was left by the door and, balancing awkwardly upon a bedroom chair, she hoists it over the carved top piece of her father's huge Spanish wardrobe to sit on top, like lumber, hidden from sight.

'There, that's done. Everything is all right again.'

That night the three girls sit in the old soldier's room as they had been used to do before the eldest, Miss Maria Mantilla, turned mercenary to earn a wage for the little household. She sits by the bedhead, reading in a steady voice to Papa, while the two other girls find what places they can and endeavour to sew by the dim light of the single oil lamp. A tableau of mutual filial duty and respect before venerable old age.

Alonso has been snoring for a good quarter-hour and the two younger sisters have pricked their fingers into numbness in the dim light before Maria finally lays down the book and glances over to release them to their beds.

On her return, the dog-cart is sent to collect Miss Mantilla from the station and the household is alert to her homecoming. Miss Hart is anxious to quiz her over a missing bedsheet, Lady Georgina is waiting to show her the pot hooks she has been practising, and

Her Grace, the Duchess, is attentive for her arrival. Since she has been away, the Duchess of Fainhope has felt the thread that binds Miss Mantilla to her attenuating to the point at which she worries it might snap and let the woman free. She must re-establish the mutual ties of obligation and fear that will keep her servant tightly ensnared in their scheme.

Now Miss Mantilla is returned she stands before Her Grace empty-handed, her eyes downcast. The Duchess sits in her bed, nursing the substituted child on her lap. 'Miss Mantilla, I do not anticipate that this interview will be an easy one for either of us. However, I believe a bargain has been struck – to our mutual advantage—'

'Your Grace—' Miss Mantilla interrupts.

However, the Duchess is quick to continue to weave the words which will secure her and keep her tethered near. 'You may keep your position and your reputation. What I offer you is a most comfortable nest in which to place your cuckoo. However . . .' And here Her Grace, the Duchess, with a gesture of calculated self-confidence, appears to reveal the weakness of her own hand: 'However, my complaisance may lead you to believe that you have influence.'

The feint pays off and she knows that Miss Mantilla is hers when it is the servant and not the mother who replies, 'Your Grace, my influence in the nursery and the schoolroom will be that of governess and no more. I have no ambition, no vainglory, no sentimental attachment.'

'There, now, we are in complete accord.'

The two women are silent for a while. It is in the attempt further to reassure her mistress that their business has been concluded that Miss Mantilla, affecting disinterested conversation, asks, 'Will he take his father's name?'

Her Grace – who, during this interlude, was dwelling upon quite who the other parent of the baby might be – is startled into thinking that she is referring to the real father. 'It was His Grace, my husband's wish that, should he have an heir, he would bear the family name,' she replies, with a little too much vehemence.

'Could a second or third name be of my choosing . . . just to honour my own father?' Even as she speaks, Miss Mantilla knows that she has overstepped the mark.

The Duchess delivers her last, definitive blow: 'Miss Mantilla, here I think your ambition does o'ervault itself. For what is in a name? Why, everything is in a name. What is this scrap of humanity but a name? His *only* job in life will be to immortalise this name and no other. The single syllable that makes him "George" creates him, and when I named him I made him mine.'

She looks fixedly at her servant as she deliberately plucks the baby from her nipple. Quick as a tick he darts at the pulsing breast to renew sucking, cheeks working urgently, eyes intent upon her stern face.

'Yes, Your Grace.' She can stay no longer. That luxuriant look and the indecent noise of his guzzling are more than she can bear.

'Now, I hope we really do understand each other. You should go to your charge in the schoolroom – one who bears many wholly legitimate syllables, all of them merely decorative, unfortunately for her.'

Lady Georgina, pink and expectant in the schoolroom, finds she cannot humour Miss Mantilla today. She lisps out the lines she has been set to learn and finds that they are not to her satisfaction. The long line of pot hooks is all to be done again and considerable fault is found with her hair, which evidently looks as though a bird has made a nest there. Even though Georgina is charmed with the idea of a bird wanting to nest in her hair, she is cross not to have pleased bad-tempered Miss: she marches to the day nursery to tease her little sister into such a fit of howling that Nanny doesn't know what she is going to do with the pair of them.

On the other side of the park, alone in his smoking room, Lord John Harpur is finding fault with seven-year-old Harry. However, it is not the ugliness of his pot hooks that makes Lord John despair of him. Harry will come to nothing because he has become a cousin, just as he himself remains an uncle. While he was the sole boy cousin of girls he had prospects. He was a boy of substance, of whom his father could be proud. But look at him now – just plain Harry: a seven-year-old boy with his mother's curling hair and his father's fine eyes. Whatever is to be made of him?

Lord John whacks his wife's spaniel, which has misguidedly come up to his chair for petting. The creature runs off, whimpering, leaving Lord John to consider again how badly Harry has let them all down.

It is now night-time. Lucy has carried away the nursery tea-trays and the expensively tall footmen are making their rounds of doors and windows. All are safely gathered in – children to their night nursery, junior servants to their garrets, the mistress lying in and no master or guests to service. But all is not right in this well-regulated universe. The servants gossiping in the servants' hall are fidgety with too much leisure. The necessity to stoke and polish and maintain, which keeps the great, glorious engine of the household machine running smoothly, has lost its urgency. With no real push to get the steam up, the pistons pumping at full tilt, daily forward motion is becoming largely a matter of habit and momentum. And, like the Hall itself, the estate farms and forests seem to carry on by themselves, somehow.

Since there are no guests Miss Hart is considering whether to close up some bedrooms. Mr Law has ventured to tipple from brandy and whisky bottles, for which his late master will never again call. Mrs Beam has relaxed into being a good plain cook, and Kathleen is astonished to notice that her fingernails are growing back, so little elbow grease has been needed these last weeks.

All the bustle and business of the house has contracted around the little world of the nursery, the schoolroom and Her Grace's chamber. With no husband's needs to accommodate, no society to suit herself to, her job as dam to the next heir done, she may devote herself solely to the business of wet-nursing him, her nocturnal familiar, who sucks life and legitimacy from her. Lucy, Nanny, Stevens and Miss Mantilla maintain the illusion that this is a well-run ship, and how is Her Grace, the Duchess, to know any better? Enclosed in her room, they are the only people she sees. Her dominion has shrunk to this. But what does it matter to her if the cook leaves off making a savoury course, since she has taken her ordained destiny by the throat and throttled the dull, dependent life that lay ahead? By sleight of hand she achieved it: made herself mistress of her own future, outside the laws of God and men. Everything her new kingdom needs is here in this room, personified in this changeling baby that she is fattening.

In her own Spartan room, Miss Mantilla retrieves the pillowcase from her bottom drawer with its stuffing of stiffened cotton sheet still inside. She bundles it into a ball and presses it against her to relieve hard, hungry breasts.

Illness

It is now January, and Lady Euphemia's fourth birthday. A tea party with games has been arranged for herself and Georgina with those neighbouring children who might be depended upon to behave like little ladies and gentlemen in the teeth of activities that juggle naked infant ambition with insupportable disappointment. However, Master Harry, discovering himself excluded from the scramble to find chairs from the ever-decreasing number lined up in the middle of the room, does not choose to acquit himself with dignified restraint.

Lord John Harpur, brother of the late duke, uncle to the present one, and the Duchess of Fainhope are positioned some distance from the mêlée, she draped completely in black crêpe (as indeed are the birthday girl and her sister). Lord John is talking in a low voice, his glass of sherry held upon one knee. 'My wife does well enough during the summer months. It is during the dark season of the year, such as now, that she declines and becomes vapid.'

'Caroline was ever thus, Harpur. But you both have consolation in your fine boy, no doubt?' she replies, looking at the red-faced, grimacing Harry.

Lord John does not feel it necessary to remind himself of his son's charms and says, without looking up: 'Harry is as robust and bonny as any yeoman farmer's son, but I fear he has not the same fine features as your boy.'

'George is such an ugly baby. However, even the prettiest is a very nasty object when undressed, to my mind!'

They sit in contemplation of this engaging image for a few moments. Then Lord John says, as though the thought has not been constantly upon his mind, 'May I suggest that since nearly a twelve-month has passed since the death of my poor brother, and four since the birth of his heir, you should perhaps meet the trustees of the estate?' When she does not answer, he prepares to go further down this dangerous path of enquiry – choosing a jocular tone to light his way. 'There they sit, warming their backsides at our expense, and for what? Nothing has been decided or can be decided until the estate business is properly handed over to them.'

'My husband's will, which you witnessed, John, makes me guardian of my children. He saw me fitted to that duty. How, then, may a ninny and a booby, whose business is in banking and in law, know better than I about the world I was born to?'

The path that Lord John has embarked upon proves a steep and thorny one, but having ventured upon it he has no choice but to struggle onwards and upwards. 'Quite simply it is the law.'

'It may well be the law, but I defy it. While I have custodianship of the heir, I nominate myself as trustee of all he will legally inherit. Who could hold his interests in greater care than me?'

Lord John perceives that the gradient increases, but he knows he cannot now turn back as this thicket of spines closes behind him. 'But do you not lack the guiding hand of a man on the estate now that your husband is gone?'

'I find that I manage quite remarkably well without someone to tell me what to do and how to do it. Indeed, a husband would not allow me an opinion, let alone control over my own and my son's affairs.'

'You must know I had some ambition to fulfil that role.'

She laughs, although at first he cannot guess why, and he finds – as if by magic – that he has passed through the thorny barrier of the woman's hauteur. However, it seems now that his way is perilously smooth.

'John, you are still married, I believe, however vestigially. And I am out of bounds, being your dead brother's wife!' His feet are sure to slip on this slope of ice.

'Oh, I did not mean that . . . I meant only in the unworthy capacity of senior member of the family and parent to the next heir, but for—'

'But for George. Your brother's posthumous tap on the nose,' she says playfully, hitting him upon that aristocratic prow a little harder than required to make her point.

'Of course, nobody could be more pleased than me that the land will be safe in George's hands. The old family name must live on . . .'

'Really, John?'

'I'm sure he'll grab a tight hold when his time comes.'

'You must know that I am not to be pensioned off either now or then. George must not expect vapidity from me.'

So this is the summit, the point, the clincher. He is finally close enough to see her as she would be seen: an ice queen immovable upon her chilly peak, directing all below her.

Less than a week later, at wintry midnight, there is once again 'musical chairs' in the house. Many are out of their beds and all rushing to find their places. A groom is galloping away through the park, Nanny is sitting, head in hands, in the nursery corridor, and Miss Mantilla is banging upon the Duchess's bedroom door. 'Your Grace, do rouse yourself! Her crisis is come! Your Grace – oh, do wake up! Rouse yourself, your daughter may die!'

The door opens and Miss Mantilla glimpses George's cradle far away from her in the dark room. Her Grace is struggling to close her nightdress.

'Is Dr Oliver sent for?'

'Yes, but Nanny thinks it might be already too late.'

'Too late!'

The two women in their billowing nightdresses run down corridors and up stairs to the night nursery where Georgina is lying on her sickbed. Nanny springs from her place upon the floor to bar the way. 'You must not enter, Your Grace. The air is full of contagion.'

'Idiot woman! I have had the inoculation – out of my way.' With that, the Duchess bursts through the door to look upon her sick daughter. She is followed by the two servants, who are not similarly protected. 'What can I do? What can I do? God, what must I sacrifice?'

This last anguished cry echoes in the cavity of Miss Mantilla's own heart, but she must contain the rejoinder that is in her mouth, ready to be spat out: 'What, make your own sacrifices, ma'am?' But duty has taught her sex and class to swallow rather than to spit.

'The physician will tell us what is best for her,' says Miss Mantilla, bringing her a chair to sit on by the sickbed.

'If she, too, should die!'

'If she should die, then may I have her pony, Mama?' It is Euphemia, padding on warm round feet from the corridor towards her mother.

'Get out of here! Get rid of this interloper!' screams her mother. Lady Euphemia is carried away, largely unmoved by this witchy mama, in the arms of silly Nanny.

Miss Mantilla tries to restore sanity. Her own supreme self-constraint recoils at this uninhibited emotion. 'The nursery-maid is looking out for Dr Oliver. As soon as he arrives I will bring him to her – I have been most in contact with her. If I am to fall ill, then I am to fall ill,' says the loyal governess.

'I will wait in my sitting room. You must bring him to me as soon as you are able.'

⌒⌒

37

Three of the principal protagonists of that other cold, wild night are now assembled in Her Grace, the Duchess of Fainhope's private sitting room. Dr Oliver relishes the opportunity to see these women, servant and mistress, together and in delicious disarray. His manner, however, is that of the grave professional. 'When I speak of disfigurement, Your Grace, you must take this as an encouraging sign. I mean that she will recover. But concomitant to a full return to health must be some scarring and perhaps a reduction in her sight or hearing. Disease will leave its mark, I'm afraid, in these cases.'

'Then she *is* to live!' This, spontaneously from Miss Mantilla.

'You have seen several other such cases round about?' asks the child's mother without feeling.

'Hers is the fifth. Two little brothers in Deanchurch died only yesterday.'

'Whyever did I allow all those filthy children in here, bringing their foul diseases with them?'

Since there can be no reply to this, without seeming to confirm that in some way Her Grace, the Duchess, might be at fault, the doctor and Miss Mantilla remain silent.

'You say she will be scarred. She was always one who would require artifice to raise her from plain to merely pretty. Now I am to have an ugly, weak-eyed daughter?'

'You are to retain a child when others have lost theirs!' rejoins Dr Oliver, before he can think better of it.

Miss Mantilla rushes to cover his indiscretion: 'And what of the other children at the birthday party – our own Lady Euphemia and baby George? What can be done to protect them now?'

Before the doctor can answer, there is a knock on the door and the missing fourth protagonist peeps round it. 'Excuse me, Your Grace. Nanny sends that baby George is crying to be fed, and that I am to tell you Lady Georgina is sleeping peaceful now,' says Lucy.

'Miss Mantilla, you will be in sole charge of my daughter. I will, of necessity, quarantine myself and George until her contagion is passed.' The Duchess stands to leave. She is no longer interested in the conversation. 'Since you have matters to discuss and I have no more to add I will excuse myself. My thanks for your ever-loyal service to this family, Oliver. I bid you both goodnight.'

And, with a nod to both, she is gone – leaving Dr Oliver, still in his muddy riding boots, and Miss Mantilla, clothed only in her nightdress, alone together. Miss Mantilla springs up to follow her mistress, but Dr Oliver continues blandly on with hygiene regimens and convalescent diets, which at last bring her back to her chair. She has quite forgotten that she is a woman and he is a man, when she is suddenly returned to vigilance. He has moved from his masculine pose, standing by the fireplace, to a chair near her own. Leaning conspiratorially towards her, he says, 'I know you will make an excellent nurse, Miss Mantilla, such is your devotion to the children in your care . . . although this night does recall another such.' He raises an interrogative eyebrow.

Her reply is like a warning shot across his bows: 'I think neither of the girls has been so ill before, Dr Oliver. However, it is late . . .'

'I mean that night when I attended a childbed – or was it two? Yes, I recollect two infants born that night. And yet . . . and yet by daybreak one seemed to have quite dissolved away. Like dew upon the morning, one might say.'

Since this man ignores her polite circumlocutions and will not withdraw, Miss Mantilla must be more blunt and unambiguously dismiss him. 'He died. Now you must go.'

'That, my dear lady, I might be credited with having surmised. What's more, my powers of divination extend to a notion of how he might have travelled to his last resting-place – I also recall a trunk or suitcase in your possession the following morning . . .' He continues, close enough for her to smell cigar on his breath, 'Where my educated guesses betray me is how you brought it off, eh!'

She shrinks into her chair away from him. 'He died. As infants do. He is buried in a far graveyard.'

'Quite. The world was ever thus. The oddity in this matter is you, my dear. What, ruined and yet retained your position here?

You must hold the very secret of Her Grace's heart.'

He is panting a little with excitement at the chase. She, like a wounded doe, turns her big brown eyes on him. She is so soft and vulnerable that he would very much like to hurt her more. The beseeching eyes inspire in him the urge to debase and bully. 'Did the old man blast away with both barrels to make sure he hit home? Found the mark both times with one on either side of the blanket, did he? Got himself an heir as well as an abishag – a little "mother's error"?' He tilts up her chin to make her face him and show him those wounded eyes again.

'Control yourself! The child's father is not known to Her Grace and never shall be. There is no need now. There was a child . . . He died, leaving nothing behind him. My mistress is gracious enough to forgive. And I will be ever grateful to her. Now you must leave!'

However she twists and turns before his pursuit, he must press her to the last reserves of her endurance to overmaster her. 'My dear woman, larger society does not nod at such slips – whether evidence remains or not. There are consequences for women such as you. If Her Grace's leniency has bound you to her with bands of adamantine loyalty, then how shall my silence be rewarded?'

Dr Oliver kneels at her cringing feet and, before she can guess what he will do, he pulls her sharply forwards, by both ankles, on to the floor. Her nightdress rides up behind her as she sits down heavily, feet pulled to either side of him, so that he is now kneeling suggestively between her opened legs, ankles still firmly held.

As she opens her mouth to scream, there is a knock on the door. Miss Mantilla scrambles to her feet and Dr Oliver calls, in as steady a voice as he can manage, 'What is it?'

The groom puts his head round the door, surprised to see the stuck-up Spanish miss in here too. 'Dr Oliver, I've gave your horse a good rubdown and he's tacked up ready for you at the front door.'

Miss Mantilla and Dr Oliver leave the room at the same moment. Neither looks at the other.

Cryptic Conversations

It is Sunday afternoon and Miss Mantilla and the housekeeper are taking tea in Miss Hart's parlour. Miss Hart is anxious to make more of a friend of the governess – she feels that, until now, she has been negligent in bringing her out of herself. To put it simply, she has learned from the groom gossiping with the footman, that the Spanish tart is carrying on with the doctor and she wants to know more. So a little tea party has been arranged.

But it is heavy going. The governess is clearly exhausted from nursing the girl day and night and it is hard to tempt her into confessions when her every sentence is punctuated with yawns. Miss Hart is at present trying to drum up a little animation over the virtues of folkloric cures and preventives, in the expectation that the natural dialectic of general conversation will inevitably lead them to the door of modern medicine and so to Dr Oliver.

However, the conversation persists in taking quite another course and has led them now into a stagnant tributary, where they are washed up on the subject of 'wise old women who live in the woods'. Miss Hart is telling her guest about a particular crone known to her mother, who could predict the coming weather by looking into badgers' setts, when she is struck by a magnificent idea. 'What do you say to the reading of tealeaves?'

'I only know that there are some who set great store by it, but I can't see that random dregs in a cup can be "read" with any method.'

'Well, I'm sure there can be no science in it, Miss Mantilla, but doesn't the poet have it that there is more in heaven and earth than we can dream about? I mean to say, more than scientific men can know of?'

Miss Mantilla acknowledges this point of view with a smile.

'Well, tealeaves and glass balls and whatever may be one thing, but my friends, the Misses Timms are something other.'

And so the master stroke has been effected. The Misses Timms have been introduced, and now that Miss Hart has them in the room, she will press them to her service. 'The Misses Timms are two ladies who have the God-given ability to see into a person's heart, and tell that person exactly what may lie ahead for them in questions of love – or any other matter,' she continues temptingly.

But her guest still seems noncommittal.

'Surely it is every woman's wish to know something of what her future may hold?'

'I would wish that my future was as unremarkable as it is possible to be. I don't want any shocks and surprises!' replies Miss Mantilla, trying to end this morbid conversation in dismissive jocularity.

'Really, Miss Mantilla, if you want to be warned of any shocks and surprises, then you must accompany me this very evening and you may judge for yourself. I can only say that you will see and hear such things at the Misses Timms' that may startle away this rationality of yours.'

'Miss Hart, I don't know whether you succeed best in tempting me in or in frightening me away!'

Leaving the two ladies to their tea, we set off across the garden, past the ha-ha and on through the park until the broad-leafed trees grow close with scrub and bramble and so reach the encircling limit of the Duchess's dominion in a muddy lane. You might trudge this lane in claggy boots, but Her Grace prefers to spank along it on slick sprung wheels, spattering you, no doubt, as well as the hedgerow as she passes. Not far now until another, shorter, drive, this one lined by sulky sweet chestnuts, planted by some forgotten squire for posterity's benefit. They first hide, then reveal the manor house, which goes with the title of second son, younger brother and, it would appear, mere brother-in-law. Ungrateful posterity, in the shape of the present incumbent, has plans to root out the lot, for Lord John has lately fallen out with tradition.

Even so, it is a good enough house with good enough stables and a gentleman's garden through which the gentleman gardener now walks. Lord John Harpur is pleased, at least, with his new specimen shrubs: there is nothing like them in the whole county for he retains a 'horticultural man' to forage for him in the attic rooms of Empire. As he walks he takes some comfort in the speculation that even if he isn't to be 'enriched from ancestral merchandise' then, like one of Isabella's proud brothers, he can at least send others to their peril to furnish his estate with the latest trappings. For if, unlike with Keats's pearls and pelts, no native diver's 'ears gush'd blood' or tortured seal 'lay full of darts', there had been some danger, not to mention expense, in the getting of these exotic tributes. With his specimen rhodo-dendrons and magnolias, he purchased celebrity among his neighbours, albeit as a sort of second-hand explorer and adventurer.

The gardener does not saunter alone: he is in conversation with his sister-in-law, who has no argument with the benefits bestowed by the dead hand of tradition.

'Harry has been asking after his poor cousin.'

The Duchess of Fainhope laughs, and replies, 'Then his kind concern should be a lesson for the patient's own dear sister. It must be confessed that Euphemia has yet to be cultivated into a reflex of sympathy for the afflicted. She complains that Georgina's face looks like a rice pudding with jam stirred in.'

'She does not mean to be cruel.'

'Indeed she does! Well, if not cruel then at least candid. I must confess, now she is regaining her strength, I lose patience with Georgina myself. And I was frightfully well brought up!'

The two turn towards the house where the face of Lady Caroline Harpur is fleetingly seen at an upstairs window. Lord John offers his arm to his sister-in-law, the Duchess, as they near the shallow steps that lead to the french windows standing open for their return.

'I need no support.'

'Such a blessing to be in robust good health,' he replies, directing a nod up towards the vanished figure of his wife.

'But I think you prefer the cooing of a matrimonial dove?'

'I could certainly not compare you to a dove, much too fierce for that!'

'Indeed, John! Then with which creature would you compare me?'

'Something very proud and independent – and feminine, of course.'

'Then I fear it must be something mythological. A chimera.'

'You do not think that Nature allows all these characteristics together in one beast?'

'I do not think that any known female creature is allowed to be both feminine and fierce.'

'Surely all mothers can be roused to exemplary acts. Even a hen can be, when she is defending her young from the sparrowhawk.'

'I don't call that fierce. I would say that was an instinct towards good housekeeping, into which Nature has tricked her. As she counted each one from its shell, now she gathers them all in. I would rather be the sparrowhawk than that tidy hen.'

'But I suppose both are motivated by the desire to protect and nurture their young ones. The sparrowhawk is driven to kill the hen's chicks to feed her own.'

'I say to you, then, both are poor things that have no free will but are bound in involuntary chains of maternal impulse. Whatever it is, it's not truly independent action,' replies the Duchess of Fainhope, shooting a challenging look at her brother-in-law.

'If you mean that Nature, rather than intellectual choice, is solely what drives that female propensity to nurture and protect, I would say that might well be true in the lower species . . .'

'. . . but not in that most elevated among all humankind, a woman. For is not she nearer to an angel in the house than a hen in the yard?'

Lord John chooses not to reply to this teasing. Not for the first time he feels the ground turn treacherous beneath his feet. There really can be no conversation with her, for she doesn't talk like a woman at all. She is forever leading him into some quagmire of slippery allusions, all the while seeming to jeer at him over her shoulder as she bounds lightly to the other side.

'We seem to have come full circle in our argument, John. For, you must agree, an angel can never be described as "fierce". And so I win. You must concede that my like exists neither in the animal kingdom nor out of it!'

He must concur with a nod, and she is fired to press home her point: 'I am not the victim of circumstance and my sex, but turn both to my advantage and reinvent myself according to my own design.'

'Then you have evolved into "new woman", with cigarette in one hand, daring novel in the other, sitting astride a bicycle.'

'Brother-in-law, do not compare me to some girl wobbling about without the use of either hand. I am something much older and more enduring. I come closer to one of your metamorphosing Greek goddesses, Artemis or Hera.'

As they re-enter the house, and subjects more suited to a domestic setting, Her Grace does not hear her brother-in-law's glum rejoinder, 'Or Medea.'

In the narrow London house, sisters Aurora and Teresa have been taking advantage of the lengthening evening, even though it is a Sunday, to work upon their miniature painting. It is a craft they can pursue from home and, unlike the meaner piecework of assembling matchboxes, button-stitching or fitting bristles into brushes, one that, they can deceive themselves, errs on the side of dilettantism rather than mere sweated industry. The ever-diminishing returns they win from it certainly reinforce this notion. Since the mania for '*carte de visite*' photographs, with their ability to 'please the heart and satisfy the memory' at an ever-reducing cost for unlimited reproductions, the girls' clientele has shrunk. Like that of hand-loom weavers and lacemakers, their anachronistic handiwork has had to give way to the ease and economy of mechanisation. So, apart from those Luddite traditionalists who still want to see their relatives' features reproduced in kindly pigments and on a base of forgiving ivory, there is little call for their slow skill in producing portraits by hand. In fact, by degrees, they have become 'outworkers' for the new industry: copying from photographs has evolved into the artifice of painting on top of them, which has, in turn, given way to hand-tinting and retouching, so that the Mantilla sisters' arcane talent with a brush allows them still to occupy a tiny niche in the inexorable industrialisation of the portrait.

Alonso Mantilla's girls had acquired those accomplishments proper to their status as dependent, delicately raised daughters, polished to ornament another man's middle-class household, when theirs *was* a proper middle-class household. But none of this expensively accumulated skill, in playing musical instruments, painting a Highland scene, the embroidering of footstools and the singing of sentimental ballads, has yet charmed either girl a husband. Thus it is to bolster Alonso's dwindling capital and army pension that they employ, to order, artistic facility and squirrel-tail-hair paintbrushes. Nevertheless they consider this respectable drudgery to be a boon in comparison with poor Maria's fate. They earn polite pin money but she must find a wage sufficient to keep their heads above water. As the cleverest of the three, it is she who must go abroad and exploit her thwarted intellect as a servant among strangers: one of that army of respectable, if impoverished, middle-class maidens of England who go for a governess.

Aurora and Teresa might have considered that Maria had the best bargain of the three, having read their fair share of that extensive genre of romantic literature, 'The Governess Novel', from which the meek but discreetly beautiful one contrives to be rescued by the end of the book, usually by advantageous marriage. However, judging by the real-life experiences of their sister, they know it to be an inauspicious situation. Far from guaranteeing a brilliant match, the position of governess apparently demands qualifications high enough, wants few enough, looks plain enough and spirit humble enough to satisfy the fickle demands of any lady and consequently to render her unattractive to any gentleman suitor in the land.

And quite apart from finding no friendship, let alone romance, above stairs, the governess finds no solace in the servants' hall either. Let us refer to Maria herself upon the uneasy subject, in one of her early letters: 'At the Hall I am neither honest fish nor fowl, let alone good red herring. My dears, I am the duckbilled platypus of the serving classes, neither one thing nor the other, but impossibly constructed out of odds and ends, part superior servant, part indigent lady. Neither *them* nor *us*, so I am never in my element, ever mistrusted or condescended to, always alone.'

These poignant dispatches from Maria's exile, when she was still astonished by her surroundings and homesick for the familiar hearth, had gradually been replaced by more preachy communications, harking upon the sacrifice she has made for them and the duties they owe her and, as a result, are less eagerly anticipated. Nevertheless Maria's *Friday Letter* is still a document to which ceremonial is attached: first carried to Papa with his morning coffee, then read aloud, after a discreet interval, by Aurora, since Papa's eyes can no longer be relied upon to decipher handwriting, and subsequently scrutinised in private by both sisters as closely as though they searched for hidden messages. Finally she is pressed between the pages of the family Bible. Since Maria has been away from them for five years, they have been forced to remove the oldest stratum of her letters, which threatened to burst the book's binding. Those first brave home thoughts from abroad are now stored in a hatbox on top of Papa's wardrobe. They are nearly due to open a second hatbox archive for a deposit of middle-period letters.

Aurora wipes her paintbrush on a rag, and picks up the most recent letter, saying to her sister, 'Poor Maria. She seems to be largely employed in dressing the young ladies' dolls for a living. Apparently Her Grace doesn't value intellectual stimulation – at least, not for her daughters.'

'I think Maria's duchess has not the least interest in her daughters' intellect. In fact, I'm sure she considers that learning and curiosity only "spoil" a girl's prospects.'

'Perhaps she's right. When she takes her wares to the marriage market, an ability to parse Latin verse and dissect frogs won't be what attracts the buyers.'

'You make the poor girls sound like a hundredweight of potatoes, not flesh-and-blood young ladies,' says Teresa, moving to the window to peer outside.

'They might as well be, for isn't that what all the balls and coming-out parties are for? The young gentleman must pick over the girls and see which are "sound" and which are rejects before he makes his choice. And opinions in a young lady are generally considered a blemish.'

'To continue your potato analogy, he must also pass over any who have "eyes",' Teresa replies, with a smile. 'Anyway, however she may be marred by beauty or brains, I think you forget that the most attractive thing she brings to this marriage market is her fortune.'

'Oh, I don't deny that.'

'What chance do I stand, then, doubly disqualified – rather adept at dissecting and naming the parts of any number of amphibians and with absolutely no money to my name?'

'Why, none at all, Teresa. You will have to stay with me, an overheated intellectual with more opinions than is strictly polite, contented in her spinsterhood.'

Aurora pulls the pursed lips and pious, upturned eyes of a bookish old maid. Having demonstrated the wonderful independence enjoyed by over-educated middle-class maiden ladies, living on a pecuniary knife-edge, over unfortunate heiresses, she turns back to her palette.

Teresa turns again to the view from the window. She sees a working man shambling along the gutter, shoulders hunched and hands sunk in pockets. He pauses to pick up something from the road and in that moment looks up to find her face at the window. Teresa starts back as though she has been complicit in seeking this contact. 'To be sure it is hateful to have no life of one's own, to exist just to be some man's wife. And yet, Aurora, don't you long for something more?'

'What more?' replies her self-sufficient sister.

'I hardly know... A prospect of delight, perhaps.'

'I find my delight in a "flask of wine, a book of verse – and Thou", of course.'

'You forget the private income, Aurora.'

'That goes without saying. How else will I purchase the wine and the book? But, really, to enjoy the simple pleasures of the wine and the book one must have the "Thou" too, my dear.'

'You mean me?'

'Of course. Who else?'

'Do you think *she* has anything outside the little girls? I mean a connection with another.'

'What? Romantic suitors? You forget that Maria is a very common species of tuber, my dear Teresa. Gentlemen bearing potato trugs will not be truffling around our plain, good, poor Maria.'

'You goose! I mean the opportunity to think, and discuss her thoughts. Such as we have with each other,' says Teresa, regaining her composure and letting go this hesitant attempt to introduce the impossible notion that the purpose of their lives might be found in romantic love.

'Don't you recollect her writing that there wasn't anyone with whom she could talk freely at the Hall? Probably because her own intellectual accomplishments are so hard to match!'

'Quite. Still, it must be . . . she must be lonely.'

'She never complains of it, these days. And, you notice, she never writes that she misses us or our silly conversation. It's all "I was introduced to charming Lady So-and-so", or "the park is splendid at this season", and that kind of showy-off nonsense now.'

Teresa stands behind her sister's chair and begins to make tiny plaits of the escaped hair at her nape. Aurora, compliantly, lengthens and bows her neck better to expose this grove of dark softness, feathering the vulnerable neck cords. 'You must not mind her, Teresa.'

'For the most part I think I do not mind her half enough. She is so far away and her life is so very different from my own. I only seem to worry about what will become of me. Isn't that dreadfully selfish?' replies Teresa, twisting the tight plaits up into the heavy overhang of thatch from where they spring free with vegetable vitality, unfurling little fists.

Aurora pulls away from her sister, annoyed by the pricking of pulled hairs. In the effort to rid herself of the plaits, she teases and riles her neck hair into angry hackles. 'Life just seems to come down to making do and mending – to boots, boots and more boots. Oh, Teresa, do stop it!'

'You joke of us ending our days as defiant spinsters. But, really, what will become of us all, Aurora? Where will we find our delight?' Again Teresa looks out of the window, but still finds no answer there.

What indeed is to become of intelligent, educated young ladies who lack a duchess's talent for overturning convention? How shall they live happily ever after with no prospect of magical riches, fairy godmother or handsome prince?

An Epiphany

At just this moment Miss Maria Mantilla and her new-found friend Miss Hart are making their way through the hallway of a tiny claustrophobic cottage where Teresa might have found one future scenario for herself and Aurora. For here, too, live spinster sisters in quiet impecuniosity: the Misses Timms, Amelia and Cecilia – they are Aurora and Teresa grown older, the one stouter, the other narrower. The cottage industry that buys the increasingly inferior cuts of meat and week-old eggs in this establishment might also be called an artistic one, although the Misses Timms operate in the noble sphere of performance art.

The less talented of the two, Miss Cecilia has grown into the role of 'showman' to her sister Miss Amelia's superior theatrical abilities. It is she who must set the scene, furnish the atmosphere with the appropriate suggestion of mystery and menace. In this case, her preparations are largely superfluous as, in the interval between the drinking of tea and the coming of occult night, at least one of her clients has already done a fine job of agitating herself into susceptibility.

Cecilia Timms has cultivated a low, sinister tone appropriate in the gatekeeper to this chamber of secrets where the elder Miss lurks. However, despite the ominous sound of her voice, she cannot hide her girlish excitement at welcoming two such lucrative pilgrims into her parlour. 'My sister will be so pleased to receive two ladies from the Hall.'

Miss Hart, as cicerone, condescends for them both: 'Miss Mantilla and I have left a very agreeable fire for our expedition tonight.'

'Shall I tell the coachman to wait on you?'

Miss Mantilla's blunt reply confounds the housekeeper: 'Indeed, we did not come by coach. We walked.'

With that, they enter the darkened front room where Miss Amelia is only a moment ahead of them in hastily repositioning herself to be discovered looking, with myopic intensity, at some picture cards on a small muffled table. She is a clumsy hummingbird to her sister's delicate ox, with a voice as high and inconsequential as Miss Cecilia's is ponderous with meaning.

'Oh, gracious! Do enter the chamber, ladies. Miss Hart, my dear, I was only just saying to my sister, there are vibrations tonight such as I haven't felt since the last time you was here.' She rushes at the two visitors as they enter the darkened room, like a moth blundering towards the light; Miss Mantilla experiences an urge to bat her away. Then she pauses in front of the governess and peers up questioningly into her face while standing upon her toes. Miss Mantilla can't help but behold a small, aged girl in sore need of a subduing slap.

Miss Hart attempts to regain her proprietorial advantage over her fellow servant: 'Miss Mantilla, may I introduce Miss Amelia Timms, spirit mistress? Someone about whom I have told you so much.'

The parlour that the ladies have entered is fitted out according to that mode of decoration apparently inspired by the chapel of rest: it is largely dedicated to the contemplation of death. Appropriately the corpses displayed in this room are artfully suspended in idealised attitudes, which suggest rather than reproduce life. For here we find that stuffed birds roost within domed-glass coffins. If large, they stand forever predatory among spongy moss, grown brittle on plaster rocks; if tiny, they perch on tipsy nests, perpetually at the point of spilling their sugared-almond eggs. Brittle butterflies and lustrous beetles are framed like snippets of gorgeous fabric. And the lessons of the inevitable transience of youthful bloom are confounded by '*immortelles*': felt flowers and shells, protected from air and sunlight for all eternity under more glass domes. A dusty bowl of tin fruit, fleshed with coloured wax, can neither wither nor decay. And overlooking all from their elaborate frames, Timms relations are fixed for all eternity in the stiff, mannered poses of the recently alive. Even the cut-paper pattern in the bleak, shining, empty hearth grins through the bars like a skull.

The Misses Timms belong in this sanctum of death in life and life in death; it is an unconscious metaphor for their business enterprise. For this is a half-way place where the membrane that seals off the dead from the living may be broached. And it is the preserved-girl Miss Amelia's job to lance it.

'We have high hopes of you, Miss Timms. As I said to your sister, my friend is anxious to communicate with the other side,' continues Miss Hart, with a shiver of pleasant anticipation.

Miss Mantilla shivers too, but this is from the tomb-like chill in the fireless room.

'We can only hope the spirits are going to co-operate, ladies. They can be dreadful sulky when the mood takes them,' says Miss Amelia, ushering them to upright chairs set around the shrouded circular table. 'But we'll just have to do our best, shan't we, my dears?' Whether she addresses herself to the two ladies from the Hall or to the recalcitrant spirits isn't at all clear. She nods the visitors to their places at the table, and Miss Cecilia backs deftly into the shadows.

For a while the ladies sit uncomfortably silent and unemployed. Miss Mantilla muses how close this stale, cold and deathly gathering comes to her notion of the Protestant religion. Her own Church's lively smells, bells and depictions of sumptuous death and agony are so much more effective in conveying one into a mood of spirituality.

She is so wrapped in this speculation that, at first, she doesn't notice the slow fall of a single quite large white feather. Miss Hart must nudge her in the ribs before she sees it idling down to slip stop on the table before Miss Amelia.

'I see we are in luck this afternoon, ladies – no naughtiness. Please to place the hand nearest to me in my own. Cleanse your mind of everyday thoughts and open your heart.'

Miss Mantilla places her right hand in Miss Amelia's dry claw. She finds that now her mind is filled rebelliously with thoughts of embroidery hoops and pudding recipes.

Miss Amelia looks suddenly vacant, then starts like a hunting dog and, like a hound scenting its prey, she even appears to 'point': her eyes suddenly turn upon Miss Hart, who jumps and looks apprehensively behind her.

When Miss Amelia talks it is in a changed, stentorian voice and her brittle handhold has become a fierce grip. 'We welcome you, Bright Feather. Track you through realm of heath and forest to bring Miss Mantilla . . .' Here Miss Amelia suddenly drops her ominous manner and leans toward Miss Mantilla to ask, 'Could I have your given name, dear? He gets so touchy about that sort of thing.'

'It's Maria, but who is "he"?'

Miss Amelia replies hurriedly, in her normal voice, 'Red Indian chief, dear – died in such a dreadful battle it's a wonder he'll talk to Christian folk at all. He does like his ladies, though, so we should be in luck.'

Miss Amelia composes herself once more and resumes the booming voice, the masculine clasp: 'She was given the name Maria – the chief among women to our people. O noble warrior, have you anyone there who has departed this vale of tears and would pass back again to comfort her?'

Everyone sits in charged silence. The creaking of Miss Hart's stays, as she shifts about on her hard chair, seems amplified to comic levels. Miss Mantilla again finds refuge in thoughts of pudding basins. Indeed, such is her detachment in the face of the others' morbid anticipation that she can even assemble a recipe from pantry leftovers while simultaneously wondering that her private fancy should be so prosaic. It returns her to the thought that something is fatally amiss with the scene-setting. It is this poor little parlour, bravely attempting gentility, that suggests thoughts of domestic economy rather than the profundities of mortality. She smiles as she notices the telltale taint of over-boiled milk on the air. Yes, she can smell out the straitened means and desperate respectability of these two old maids. No money for a parlour fire, no money for a servant-of-all-work to catch the milk pan in time; but they probably still have their few groceries delivered and tip the boy.

Miss Mantilla sneaks a glance at Miss Hart, who looks as though she is trying to quell an imprisoned belch, or something worse. If there had been a fire in the grate, she would surely have dozed off comfortably by now. Yes, the smell of spoiled milk.

It is at this moment, when she is most deeply unselfconscious, that she apprehends the sensation of something warm and heavy in her lap. She thinks, A cat, and cannot make her brain understand that there appears to be nothing substantial there when she looks down. She lowers a hand hesitatingly, and cautiously dips it into the thickening air above her knees. With a little cry she pulls it away and, although impelled to jump up and run, finds herself unable to move. It is as though she is shrinking away, appalled, from her essential self.

'Oh, my goodness, somebody's here right now. I can see something hovering right by you, dear. Is it someone you recognise?' says Miss Amelia, eyes bright and predatory as a sparrow's. Miss Hart lets out a pale shriek.

'I think I feel something quite small on my lap. But this cannot be – see, there is nothing here.' Again she tests the air tentatively above her heavy lap. The thing that lies there feels so substantial that she involuntarily presses her knees together so that it will not fall through them to swing in her skirt.

Miss Amelia is now chirpy, as though she has a beakful of

worm. 'A beloved pet perhaps, now departed? Do you suppose? Although I was set on getting a dear loved one this time.'

All the while Miss Mantilla has been making bolder and bolder forays into her lap, each time flinching away from what she finds there. At first it was just the sensation of a puddle of weighty warmth; then her fingers began to mould a form. But where she felt for fur she found smooth, naked skin. Now she does not seek it out with her eyes but trusts wholly to the sensual feel of the thing. Each time she looks with her fingers she describes more of him. She finds limbs that reach to her, lips that search out her little finger, fists that open to her as unfolding buds seek the sun. They discover each other through hungry touch.

The two other women at the table look askance upon this upturned, unknowing face, transfixed by rapture. Miss Hart finds the wanton, naked sensuality too intimate for her to bear. She coughs discreetly and thinks that the foreign woman is making rather too much of a meal of things.

Miss Mantilla consumes a deep, slow breath and closes her eyes in an ecstasy of sensory fulfilment. Yes, yes: yeast and iron and sour milk.

'Can this be quite safe?' Miss Hart says, privately wondering whether the governess has gone mad.

'I hardly like to say, dear. It must have been a very beloved pet. Did she have a little doggy or a cat?'

Miss Mantilla tries to raise him in her arms but finds that this burden cannot be held close: limber, he leaps from her, elastic with life. As she scoops, so his body filters through her hands with a flowing sensation like that of emptying sand. He slides through her as she slides through him until her catching fingertips are left with only the memory of touch, the roundness of a cheek, the spring of new skin; then a dropped handful of limbs, firmed by bone, and all gone.

Even though she still delves in her lap for him, the warm weight has all run away. She opens her eyes and the internal light is gone from her ardent face.

'Departed already, dear?' says Miss Amelia. 'They can only stay such a short time before they're called back. Still, you had the chance of one last stroke, eh?'

'He grasped my finger.' Miss Mantilla holds up her little finger to look at it with wonder.

'Nip you, did it, dear? Never mind, meant affectionately, I'm sure,' continues Miss Amelia.

'His round head. And his little feet, two such little feet, with toes. So warm. And the weight of him.' Miss Mantilla looks into her lap and tries to shape again what is no longer there.

Miss Hart leans conspiratorially over to Miss Amelia and whispers, 'She must be talking about an infant. *Two* feet and with toes!'

'My little man. On my knee like warm new-baked bread. But he is taken from me!' Miss Mantilla presses her hands to her bodice to relieve a sudden welling pressure there.

Miss Amelia inclines to Miss Hart and confides wearily, 'Oh dear. Dead babies are always finding their way through. Can be quite a nuisance. I had a scalded boy once, wouldn't leave off howling for gone on a week, right there by the coal-scuttle, stubborn as anything. Even the mama tired of it – got quite sharp with him about crossing back over in the end.'

'But she can't be the mama,' ponders Miss Hart, her mind racing.

'Doesn't have to be. These babies are shameless things. Any port in a storm, you understand. The bother I have trying to get rid of them . . . Although she is very affected by the visitation.'

Miss Mantilla begins to be aware of the conversation being conducted above her head and struggles to surface into cold, thin reality again.

'You must excuse me, ladies. I am much overcome by what happened here. I thought I felt a baby, although I could not hold him. Poor little thing! Poor little baby, alone in the cold world with no one to love him . . .' She is overtaken by tears at the thought of that chilled body seeking warmth and a secure hold.

'I wouldn't worry so, dear. There are plenty of lady angels and suchlike to care for them, you can be sure. Now, Miss Hart – Florence. You next, I believe. Are we hoping for a departed uncle or will it be that seafaring brother this time, dear?'

Really, thinks Miss Amelia, turning to her next client. These dratted babies just bring out the worst in people, and so hard to send back once they've wormed their way through.

Miss Mantilla cannot bear to stay in the room, but leaps up to reclaim her mantle and overshoes.

Miss Hart is torn between her desire to pump the governess on their homeward walk and the pleasant prospect of her own cathartic grief. In the end, she settles for a cosy chat with the dead.

As Miss Mantilla hurries into the hall, aware she is committing an injury to the common practices of friendship that will require much mending after Miss Hart has trudged home, alone, through the rainy night, she is met by the stealthy bulk of Miss Cecilia and is startled into saying, 'May I return alone? I would so like to hold him again.'

'I'm sorry to have to tell you, Miss Mantilla, that my sister finds babies the most quixotic of all her spirit visitors. She can but try. However, it's a perplexing business to sort out any particular one from the press on the other side. We wouldn't want to disappoint you.'

Miss Mantilla nods briskly, buttoning as Miss Cecilia continues to low, 'So many get carried off every year, you know. A hard winter is guaranteed to swell the celestial ranks. And we find mamas and papas can become unreasonably pernickety about getting just the right dead infant.'

'Oh, he is not dead!' She says it without thinking and is glad that it is only this slow, gentle beast who heard, not the sharp little bird in the parlour.

'Not dead. Oh dear me,' replies Miss Cecilia, as though this were a not-quite-respectable condition. 'But you must come again,

Miss Mantilla. Is there not a dear departed one with whom you long to communicate just once more?'

'Thank you so much. Will you thank Miss Timms for me and convey my apologies for leaving with such haste? I really must . . .'

Since Miss Mantilla cannot immediately contrive an end to her sentence, Miss Cecilia has a chance to intervene. She is anxious not to lose this new client so she conjures the first thing that enters her head: 'Oh, we think you really must visit us again. I should mention that we see a dark man with a black bag standing behind you. I would beware of him – he looks as though he wishes you harm.'

Miss Mantilla pushes past her to rush for the door and the enclosing night.

Three Interviews by Which We May Know the Duchess Better

Now, in the course of our narrative we must conduct a series of interviews during which we may draw out our villain and show a little more of Her Grace's stratagems.

Dr Oliver's footstep has become familiar along the public and private ways of the Hall, he and his black bag having been in regular attendance on the young patient there. For Georgina's recovery from the smallpox has been protracted, not least by the doctor's minute instructions as to her convalescent regime. Now he has been summoned to Her Grace's sitting room where he lolls with an easiness that alerts our subtle Duchess: people are not easy in her presence. She must sniff out the meaning of this impudence.

'She does well enough but, I suspect, she will never recover her old vivacity or looks. She will grow to be one of that species, "delicate spinster dependant",' she says unemotionally, while his casually nodding foot provokes her inner fury.

'I'm sure that Lady Georgina will fulfil her mother's highest expectations,' replies he, with conventional servility.

She is damned if he will be easy with her. 'Dr Oliver, do not attempt to flatter me or my daughter. You and I must know that she will be of most value to you. What? A rich, young lady in regular need of her physician for many years to come? Such expectation must be worth a new carriage and pair of bays at the least.'

At last the foot has stopped its jogging and hangs, as though itself stunned into attentiveness. 'Your Grace! I am a loyal servant of this household, and have been from the time of your late husband. My professional oath compels me to act only for the benefit of my patient and not my purse.'

He blusters. Good, she has him upon the high horse of his professional respectability. Since he has remembered himself, she may defuse his bombast with that unchallenged superiority that is the advantage of her class. 'Let us have plain language, Oliver. You know enough of this household and its inhabitants to drop the "emollient" manner.'

'I would rather describe my manner as "delicate", Your Grace. Certainly, I have privileged knowledge. I might, for instance, have wondered aloud, but for my delicacy, about Miss Mantilla having met with a misfortune.'

He has been stung into revealing more than might be sensible by the misapprehension that he and this fine lady have been for some time engaged in a conspiracy of silence over the vanished baby. She, however, is shocked to discover the source of his vile self-confidence. 'Hush, man!'

Having fatally misinterpreted her confusion as yielding weakness, he is emboldened to press her hard: 'Is my speech now become too plain for you, Your Grace? Or must I speak in that roundabout vernacular of "letting cats out of bags", or perhaps of finding the "goose that lays golden eggs"?'

'What can you mean?' she answers coldly, trying to stem this hot spillage with hauteur.

Just one more thrust and she must acknowledge his advantage over her, he thinks. 'Doctors must be men of the world, to be sure, but when I see a fallen woman maintained in the bosom of a respectable family I must wonder. Such incontinence leads me to suspect the existence of a special circumstance, one that outweighs the shame of illegitimacy, a secret perhaps?' He ventures a wolfish smile.

So, he will not be quelled by icy disdain. A direct offensive must crush him. 'We come to the source of your impudence, do we? The "golden goose"? It is always the same with your type. You may be assured that no gain is to be had from persecuting Miss Mantilla and certainly none from provoking me with your vulgar digging and delving. I do not talk of such things to people such as you.' She has guessed right that unambiguous words from her, his noble patroness, will set him back on his heels. She notices that his reply attempts to cover his earlier slip.

'Excavation, rather than mere "digging", Your Grace. It is socio-scientific curiosity, not prurience or greed, that leads me to uncover these old bones.'

And now that she has the measure of him and his feeble stab at blackmail, she will nail him to his professional 'delicacy'. 'Respectable circumlocution again, Doctor? Why not let your words match your purpose and make them to the point? I'll use them for you. You smell out fucking and with it dirty money. You are dismissed.'

'Your Grace, I did not wish any offence. Consider that it might have been your own harshness that stung me into this ill-advised outburst. I shall never mention this matter again,' says Dr Oliver, leaping to his feet as she signals that she will stand.

She smiles on him. 'When I say "dismissed", I do not mean from my lucrative employment but from my presence. Now that we understand each other I expect you to put away your "socio-scientific" trowel and continue to drive comfortably and dine well. Believe me when I say that a gentleman should not relish feeding from dung-heaps.' She speaks almost kindly, but it is the benevolence of the tyrant who idly fondles the last snivelling child left upon the battlefield. 'Then go, man.'

Dr Oliver leaves, involuntarily ducking his head as he passes her, as though expecting a slap. As he calls for his horse, he wonders how he has managed to lose every masculine advantage of strength and intellect over this witch woman. What is more, he still hasn't uncovered the tantalising secret that must lie with this vanished infant.

That same evening the Duchess of Fainhope is closeted in her husband's old office with the estate manager, Mr Gouch. The vanquishing of impudent Dr Oliver has left her with the taste for blood and she is anxious to subdue this other assailant upon her citadel, for the man is grumbling and angling his way towards telling her that she has no business with giving him his instructions. 'Your Grace, without the yearly shoots, we're quite overrun. Young birds eating their heads off. And it does nothing but encourage poaching when men see the number of pheasants on our land and no one to clear them off it . . .' He continues nibbling away at her, minute after minute. '. . . and so I advise we put the greater part of the woodland under mixed arable farming and be done with the lot of them.'

'These last years agriculture does not pay. Do you assume I know nothing of the price of wheat? I will not be bamboozled into greater reliance upon the freakishness of the weather and the capriciousness of the market. And I will not have a view of mangel-wurzels from my window. Thank you, Gouch, our principal crop will continue to be game and you will deal with the poachers.'

She stands but, although he must rise too, the injustice of his situation rises hot in his broad farmer's face, so he speaks on: 'There is also the matter of the repairs needed to the home farm and the rents owing on some of the cottages—'

'And the foot rot in the sheep and the arthritis in Mr Coombs – and whatever shall we do about the drainage in the big field? I know, Mr Gouch. I could wish that I didn't, but I do. You must know that I am not my husband. I will not confer with you over breeding plans and agricultural shows. I pay you to take responsibility so you must take responsibility. Do as you think fit about sheep and tenement roofs, and as I will look over the game books and the estate accounts at the end of every month, don't think of swindling me. Do you understand?'

As Mr Gouch exits, the Duchess wonders when she will ever quell these importuning men. They cannot be in the same room as her without wanting to try her defences. From all sides come confident cannon- and sling-shots fired in the hope of hitting the feminine faultlines of stupidity or timidity that must bring her tumbling down and let them in. What they all underestimate is how, brick by brick, she has been constructing this fortress around herself for so very long. Foundations set in neglect and defiance, buttressed by single-minded resolve, fiercely armed with ambition and intelligence. In conjunction with these, she enlists as twin champions in the tournament her class and her sex. For men are shackled in combat by the chivalry owed to her as both a noble and a woman, and further confounded by her refusal to yield before them. Where they expect to exploit genteel sensibility or feminine submissiveness they find the brutish vigour and tenacity of a masculine intellect and are themselves unmanned.

A knock on her door signals her last interview of the evening, one that requires different, tougher rules of engagement from those skirmishes with stupid, envious men. The Duchess seems again, in that close room, to see the baby lying upon the nightstand, as though exposed upon an altar, and knows that theirs is a powerful alliance, founded on sacrifice and sealed in blood. The Duchess does not like balance or equality in her dealings: she is not an egalitarian. She regards the need for an ally as weakness and the practice of keeping female confidantes worse. But perhaps more dangerous than an ambitious ally is an unreliable one who cannot support the equal and opposite forces needed to hold the centre. For it is apparent in the way Miss Mantilla glances possessively about the room for the baby that she is still in emotional bondage to the child. Now, thinks the Duchess, the time has come to exploit that weakness, to tip the balance between benefit and debt and boldly seize the upper hand. 'I wonder would it do the child some good to go from here?' asks Her Grace, disingenuously.

The directness of the question fools Miss Mantilla into responding from her overburdened heart and not from her head. She, too, has the image of that baby on the nightstand, rather than the recently departed doctor's patient at the front of her mind. 'Sent away?'

'Would that distress you? You know that you have two others to keep you employed here,' the Duchess continues, in a tone that suggests concern.

'I would not presume to have an opinion about how Your Grace chooses to bring up her children,' the governess replies, careful to sound neutral.

The Duchess ignores this and pushes on with her interrogation, teasing out the truth. 'Indeed. But I have a notion that a change in scenery, in air, may be healthful. Do you not think?'

'Perhaps this is too soon?' Miss Mantilla responds, speaking as calmly as she can at the prospect of this calamity while her heart cries: 'Not now, not while he is so young!'

'When would be the right time?'

'Of course, one generally sends a child away to school, but perhaps when my little knowledge of such things is exhausted a master might be engaged to replace me in the schoolroom. A university man, I mean, for the Latin and Greek.'

'I had meant only for her to leave us to restore her looks at the coast or among mountains. However, you recommend that there is no hope for her but that she becomes a blue stocking?'

'You mean Lady Georgina?'

'Whom else? So you consider that poor, benighted Georgina has a strong enough intellect for Latin and Greek?'

'Not at all, Your Grace.'

'Of course not. If she can't be beautified then she must stay by Mama and sew a fine seam all her days. We must rest all our hopes upon a brilliant match for her sister. If anyone is to be sent away to school, it should surely be George, don't you think?'

Her relief that George is not in imminent danger of banishment now emboldens Miss Mantilla to angle unwisely for his future security, under cover of the Duchess's terror of disease. 'I have no opinion. But perhaps we should remember the danger of contagion and the other vile influences to which a child sent away to school may be exposed. Besides, I'm sure that in him a carefully regulated home education may produce as fine a mind as you could wish.'

'I hardly think so,' says Her Grace, her ear attuned to the pitiable scheming.

'Oh, I am sure George will do us credit once his intellect has been carefully cultivated!'

The Duchess is now thoroughly alert to that whine of maternal ambition, only greedy for the gratification that filial success brings, and is quick to smack it upon its unwisely craning head. 'What use has my son for a cultivated intellect?'

'But he must learn to be a gentleman,' Miss Mantilla replies, heedless now, assuming that the Duchess's expectations as a mother, for the boy, and her own must concur.

'He is not required to be a *gentleman*. George, Duke of Fainhope, does not need to learn to charm in polite society: polite society must suit itself to him. It will be sufficient that he knows how to command, to appreciate a good horse and that he breeds within his tribe.'

'These are things that he might learn from the master of hounds!' Miss Mantilla is rash with indignation at this slur.

'Quite possibly. But then, why should I suffer as a hurt to myself the prospect of my son turning into a country bore, like his father before him, since I consider he reflects neither credit nor disgrace on me personally? And beyond fulfilling your duty as his governess to my satisfaction, why should you care? If I were to say that he shall be dispatched to school or confined in a cell like the prisoner in the iron mask, you should help me pack him off, or turn the key, with no greater feeling either way.'

'Oh,' Miss Mantilla replies, in an agony of conflict, 'he must certainly follow your plan and pass every day in healthful exercise with the outdoor servants – but there will be no need for an iron mask, will there?'

So here it is, betrayed by that reflex of compassion, worse even than the need to find fulfilment or identity through another: the wretched need to love! The Duchess despises love: love that yearns to sacrifice itself, love that reduces its sufferers to dependence, ridicule, disappointment. 'I think you have not yet hardened your heart sufficiently,' says Her Grace, sounding almost benevolent. 'Let me tell you, Miss Mantilla, what life has taught me: the only things that should really matter to a woman are control over money, and freedom from sentimental enslavement. Human connections are useful only in so far as they bring her more money or greater influence. I have found that love alone brings neither.'

It is as though she stoops to raise the other woman to stand shoulder to shoulder with her upon the summit, looking down upon a conquered empire.

'I would turn the key. I would throw it from me,' Miss Mantilla says. And the two take hands briefly across the divide. 'I have no other choice. I am as much your thing as he is.'

And then the Duchess of Fainhope understands that perhaps it is not too much love but too little money that truly separates them. For if it is money that gives the Duchess her freedom to act, freedom to live outside the constraints of her time and her sex, to defeat these men (even if it was money that brought them near), then it is fear of poverty, not love for her child, that truly keeps Maria Mantilla dependent.

But, then, what if this strong, resolute woman should realise that she, too, could take control of her own fate? What if she, too, learned to live the larger life, to root out parasitical love, stamp on it, use it as a stepping-stone for her own, personal ambition? What if she, too, forged a connection with a more powerful man and used his money to buy her freedom to act? Might a governess then become a match even for a duchess? With a stab of fear, she remembers her recent interview with Dr Oliver and that nasty dissemination of guesses and innuendo. Could they have agreed some kind of alliance against her?

'One last matter, Miss Mantilla. Has Dr Oliver sought to befriend you?'

'He has . . . certainly been indiscreet,' replies her servant, remembering those muddied riding boots.

'Has he offered you anything? I mean, has he tried to buy your confidence?'

'I hate that man,' Miss Mantilla flashes back. 'I would rather burn than give him any satisfaction!'

'I know you to be as impenetrable as marble in this.' Reassured, the Duchess relaxes. 'At present I think it wise that we keep him close, better to know his intentions. But, believe me, his fascination will be what draws him to his eventual destruction. Endure, Maria, endure.'

'Endurance is my greatest strength. I endure all.'

'Perhaps for not too much longer. But you may be sure that when the time is ripe I will swat him and be done with him.' With that, the Duchess unconsciously flicks at Miss Mantilla's set, emotionless face as though to demonstrate the swatting of a gnat. She notes, with approval, that her servant barely blinks. 'Marble, indeed!'

The governess bows to her and leaves the room.

So many little lives batten upon the Duchess, both men and women, from the meanest servant to her noble brother-in-law. They scramble after the things that matter, power, money and influence, but are all the while hobbled by their little vanities and pin-pricking needs. Only in this woman does she recognise the potential for ruthlessness and the self-restraint necessary to wider ambitions.

Perhaps, for the present, it will benefit her to keep Dr Oliver as the focus of Miss Mantilla's hatred rather than let it be turned loose where it might do more harm. If not an ally, then how much more useful, and secure, it was to share a common enemy with this resolute woman! Like three tigers each biting hold of the tail of the tiger in front, they race in a circle of hatred, ambition and fear, enclosing George so that he stands secured in the middle. But if one of the tigers should be removed from the race, may not the two left turn and rip each other to shreds?

The First Seven Years

George grows in the space created between these two unnatural mothers. Like high, parallel walls, they secure and defend, but little light and less warmth find him in this narrow place.

One chilly March day, as Lucy is about her business of repairing the nursery fire, eighteen-month-old George, late in everything, ventures his first step. He has been pulling himself up on a chair, to be returned to the floor, time after time, by knees that subside under his baby weight. At last he lets go with one hand and reaches across the room to his sisters, working their samplers under their overseer, Miss Mantilla. Her Grace, the Duchess, is there also, to issue instructions, but since Nanny is away from the room the little boy is in no one's direct care. Lucy is not sure whether she may touch the infant without being bade by her superior. She would instinctively have taken his fat hands in hers, had he been any other baby, but there are strict rules about the care and control of this little princeling so she fights back her need to reach out to him and yet, such is the kindness of her heart, can't repress the glad tidings: 'Oh, do look! He's taking a step.'

The domestic group at the other end of the room looks up to see George's heroic stagger. Georgina and Euphemia jump up, clapping their hands, and, equally impulsively, Lucy gives way to instinct and bends to support him as he stumbles towards his sisters. Her Grace glances up and then away, having looked on the nullity called George reared up on forked limbs.

Miss Mantilla remains unmoved in her chair, as though seated upon a monument. Like some Spartan matron, she observes with stoic detachment the triumphal march of crowing girls and unsteady George, knees pumping, hands gripping, and sees something vulgar about his strut.

And so the walls grow taller and the space between them narrower. George grows, too, he grows tall and spindly, stretching for the light in this steep gully. By stages he is divested of petticoats, his gums are painfully furnished with sharp little teeth, and his curls cut. Thus breeched, weaned, shorn, he is evicted from his baby cot in the nursery to sleep alone in a big bed. These brisk deprivations which mark the passage from infancy to boyhood are so like punishment that it is perhaps unsurprising that he never takes to it. Nanny knows that every morning she'll find him curled on the floor and not tucked in as she left him. Perverse George says he is more comfortable out of bed, he likes to feel the cold and hardness of the floor. Certainly he is a queer, unlovable child, not one you could coddle in front of the nursery fire: he'd just sit there, stiff as a poker, trying not to let any part of him touch you back. No, a proper little man, with no use for Nanny's cuddles.

George likes to watch. He will play with his toys, but he lacks any real talent for it. He would rather watch his sisters' unselfcon-scious role-play with dolls and tea-sets than expose his own inner world to outside view. Being watched, in turn, he finds unbearable. But when he is the one to observe, particularly when he is undetected, he feels powerful and calm. Perhaps like every other child, he still believes that he is the only one in the world to have an interior life. For it is hard for us to understand that there is room enough in the world to contain all these striving, conscious individuals who make up the human race. George likes to read the expressions on his sisters' faces – the turmoil of prodigal emotions. Hidden himself, he wallows in their intemperate surface display and finds inexpressibly poignant the way they make themselves vulnerable to his gaze. It is as though he took in the arts of concealment and emotional caution with his mother's milk.

Miss Mantilla finds George wilful and gross. Like a phantom limb, he grows huge, unwieldy and grotesque in her estimation. She considers that he walks shockingly and holds himself worse. He always appears dirty to her, and to have a perverse attraction to filth. She feels that it is her duty to rear him, train him, make him into a gentleman, but is overwhelmed by his faults and defects.

Once, when he has been helping the stable lad with his pony, she comes upon him. He appears to her besmirched with the ordure of the stable. She wrestles a bowl of warm water and soap and scrubs at him until any trace of this low occupation is gone and with it a layer of skin, such is her zeal in making him pure. 'Oh, Miss Mantilla, you are too rough with me!' he cries, tasting the rancid kitchen soap she is using on him.

'I will not have you looking like a blackamoor.'

'But how can I still be dirty? How can my neck and my ears be dirty when it's my hands I use out of doors?'

'You should not mix with such people. I do not know why you are so attracted to these low types. You must learn to keep to your own kind.'

'I wish I'd been stolen by the gypsies when I was born.'

'How dare you even think such a thing?'

'I'd rather be an orphan and live my own life, free and happy.'

Miss Mantilla slaps him then, one of the few times she has made involuntary contact with George. 'Never forget, you are one of the luckiest little boys alive. You were born to be an English nobleman and there is no higher position on God's earth.'

'I hate you! I will tell Mama you must be sent away.'

Miss Mantilla smooths upon her dress the hand with which she slapped, both to wipe away the imprint of his firm, child's cheek and to soothe its sting. 'George, I am hard with you because life is hard. You must be tempered as the blacksmith tempers iron, to make you strong and unyielding. We must all be made to the shape for which life has fitted us so that we may serve God's purpose for us in the world.' She has hold of his hand now in order to keep him from running away. At the same moment both realise that they are touching. As George's hand seems to come alive in her grip, she hastily gives it back to him. 'Enough of this. You are clean as I can get you.'

And indeed he was clean, clean to the point of being raw. She even gave him a large dose of rhubarb and soda so that he should be purified in and out. But if she could have fed him lye and scrubbed away at his skin until she hit bone, she would have done it. For Miss Mantilla there is something about the look of George that brings to mind the poor little sweep who must wear his mask of soot, no matter how he applies salt water. But, alas for the governess, there is no sparkling river of forgetfulness in which to dip him and cleanse away all the sooty sins and misery of the world. For her, the mark of ineligibility he wears is indelible and calls out to the world, 'Unclean. Unworthy. Fraud.'

George finds his comfort in the chill asceticism of his bedroom's bare boards, and Maria Mantilla hers in the rancid rags that once held the form of her lost baby. There exists between the two of them the force of a magnetic repulsion. It is as though mother and son were turned wrong end on to each other by the topsy-turvy contract of denial and renunciation by which she kept and lost him. Thus inverted, their love repels with the fierce energy with which it should attract and join together. Miss Mantilla knows her cuckoo is an anathema. In him milk and blood were brought together to curdle and stink. And yet her mistress was right to suspect that, even though her mother-love for him was denied, her need to identify herself in his successes would be a hard tie to break. She is disappointed – and not merely as his governess – to find that George inclines to be a dull boy. So she looks for the growth in intellectual curiosity and good manners that she believes will reveal his mark of quality. What she does not understand is that a propensity to lark and spit with the stable lad and a baleful mistrust of book-learning might be considered even more authentic proofs of impeccable breeding.

Every day she attempts to grind him sharp against *Mangnall's Questions* and *Blair's Preceptor*. And every day she cuffs him into cultivated literary taste as he stands by her knee, pointing along the lines of another children's edition, intoning in a dull, unmodulated voice what he finds there. Lucky child that he is learning to read at a time when authors are learning to write for children. But for George it makes no difference whether the words sparkle with the brilliance of genius or merely reflect the dull glow of self-improvement – from Lewis Carroll's *Alice* to Frederick Farr's *Eric*. Little by little, George crawls through the children's library of Sir Walter Scott, Charles Kingsley, Hans Christian Andersen, Harriet Beecher Stowe, Charles Dickens, Thomas Hughes, G. A. Henty, George MacDonald and much else besides, since Miss Mantilla is avid for the latest publications. They are her escape into a world of fantasy and dreams that soothes and comforts her, and seems to make her own life easier to bear.

It is only when they adventure into the exotic realms of those serpentine stories within a story that Scheherazade tells, *The Arabian Nights*, to learn of Sinbad the Sailor, Ali Baba and Aladdin, of viziers, genies, lucky fishermen, stupid husbands and clever wives that, like King Shahryar, George becomes engaged. When they come to the last of the thousand and one nights, they read together of the beautiful daughter of a commoner, who is overheard by the new Sultan to gossip with her two sisters about whom they dream of marrying. After the two elder sisters speak of their wishes to be wives to the Sultan's baker and the Sultan's chief cook, and always have full bellies, the youngest, and wisest, sister aspires to marry the Sultan Khosrouschah himself. Of course, the rules of magic, and story-telling, demand that audacious wishes, spoken aloud, will always be fulfilled so all three get their heart's desire.

When it is time for the common-born Sultana to give birth, her two jealous sisters act as midwives. However, they substitute the legitimate baby prince, 'bright as the day', with a dead dog, which they present to the Sultan. Twice more the Sultana gives birth – to another son and to a daughter – only to be cheated of her beautiful babies. Each time the child is put into a basket and floated away on the waters of a stream that runs near the royal apartment, and the Sultan is given a cat and a piece of wood as substitutes. Of course, the cast-off children, being royal, come to no harm and are discovered by the childless intendant of the Sultan's garden who unwittingly raises them to be the perfect princes and princess they were born to be. But by the time of the third unnatural birth, the Sultan has lost patience with his wife and decides he will rid the world of this monster. However, he is prevailed upon to let her live as she cannot be blamed for these grotesque offspring. He proclaims that she will be kept alive, but in such a manner that she will desire to die more than once each day. Dressed in the coarsest habit, she will be immured in a palace at the gate of the principal mosque, with iron bars at the windows. And everyone who goes to prayers shall spit in her face, on pain of the same punishment. As George reads on, he leans into the side of the governess's leg, finding anchorage there against the passionate swell of the story that casts away the wronged queen upon her tragic shore, bereft, betrayed and benighted.

Miss Mantilla's eyes fill with tears at the injustice. Hadn't the Sultana given the king his heir, and one to spare, and a beautiful, dutiful daughter as a bonus? Yet he seems to find it so plausible that this low-born wife should give birth to domestic animals.

George reads on, fearing what further tragedy he might uncover with each new sentence but impelled to continue. Once the wife has been banished to her cruel cage the essential point of the tale is discovered in the fate of the 'real' protagonists, the lost children. Nature and nurture combine to make them beautiful, educated, well mannered and wise – like all those European displaced noble children, lost in the woods, their inherent '*gentillesse*' cannot be extinguished. So George stops worrying over the fate of the cruelly treated mother and becomes embroiled in the reassuring symmetry of a noble quest of threes, in which the princess, being the youngest, is destined to succeed. George knows the 'rules' – he understands that the first two must go before so that the third will triumph. He understands the importance of treating with respect the old and loathsome soothsayer, who will be met at the side of the road, and he understands the significance of alterations in magical objects, through which we may learn of the fate of an absent one, like the Princess Parizade whose knife would drip with blood and whose necklace of a hundred pearls stop running upon their string to tell of the fate of beloved brothers far away. He knows about trusting to magic and showing no fear, he knows about the necessity of following instructions absolutely, so that the princess's return with the three magical prizes, the talking bird, the singing tree and the golden water, is a predictable triumph.

Miss Mantilla might have put a more conventional gloss on the story. Her moral might have been, as all good children must know, that the meek will inherit, patience will be rewarded and the humble must suffer on this earth before they deserve their reward in some other. Or even, bringing the story right up to date, she might have used it to illustrate the travesty of 'marrying down'. But she is anxious to release that poor woman from her shameful prison. Inevitably the Sultan accidentally meets his children and wishes that they might be his own, which, of course, they are, wishes always being fulfilled. The mother is duly released from her prison palace, reunited with her children and her sisters punished.

So we reach a thoroughly conventional conclusion of wrongs righted and parents reunited with their natural children. Indeed, King Shahryar must have thought so too, since this was the last tale he made Scheherazade tell. But Miss Mantilla finds she is not to be so easily satisfied. As George reads to the end of the last line and closes the heavy book with the sigh of a huge task completed, she says, querulously, 'What was her name?'

'Who? Parizade?' he asks.

'No. Not the princess, the mother. What was her name?'

'I don't know. I've forgotten,' he says, sullenly.

Miss Mantilla searches back through the pages for the name, but finds none. It makes her obscurely sad.

The book is finished. George has enjoyed discovering how guile, beauty and good fortune will always beat a lucky path through every trial or danger – for the infidel heroes and heroines of *The Arabian Nights*. It never concerns him that the tales should also be true to everyday human emotions. They are only fairy stories, after all.

Now George is seven, an age when he could fairly be said to have formed the boy in temper and character. Born with a silver sea around him, splendidly isolated by his privilege and expectations, he is an island. Or perhaps he is nearer to the religious recluse kept upon his isolated rock to endure so that others may enjoy the earthly life. Now that he is seven, Her Grace could well wish that she could keep him as her personal hermit somewhere upon her estate, to hand but not too close. For she sees that he will grow into a sly and disagreeable youth. He holds himself as badly as ever, his manners are dreadfully awkward, as well as his speech, which is horrible. But whatever his personal shortcomings, he is valuable above all else to her for he embodies her stake in the ducal estates – he is her hostage against personal ruin. Not the creator of great wealth or privilege but its convenient conduit.

But perhaps George would prefer to dwell on his lonely island as a Crusoe, for ever in the expectation that one day he will be rescued: that, rather than an austere Arsenius, his Friday will find him. While he waits, he has one other living soul to keep him company. Like Robinson, who endured for long years with only his cats' friendship, George has Lucy. She is always associated in his mind with grates, just like a cat – a kitchen cat, grey with ashes, flitting through the house on quiet paws, or crouched before the fireplace.

Once, when he is alone in the day nursery, sent away from the rest for smacking his lips in a vulgar way while eating, she comes upon him. 'What are you doing here, Master George?'

'I'm not fit to be seen downstairs.'

'Oh,' says Lucy, kneeling to genuflect with pail and brush before the fire. 'What have you got there?'

'Just some paper men.' He holds up the linked paper figures he's cut out only to crumple them up and throw them to the floor.

'Don't do that,' she says, smoothing them out. 'They're lovely.'

'I sometimes think Mama would prefer me if I was made of paper and she could fold me up and forget about me until I've grown.'

'How would you grow up, Master George, if you were only made of paper?'

'Well, you could wait a few years, flatten me out and draw on a moustache and top hat. Then Mama and Miss Mantilla would think me very pleasant company, no doubt.'

'You would make a funny man, though, Master George,' says Lucy, feeding the fire. 'You'd still be mad to climb up trees and eat puddings.'

'Well, then, it wouldn't matter. Once you're a man you can do whatever you want and the women must let you.'

The two pause to consider this statement, for their experience in this kingdom of women has proved rather the opposite.

'Let me show you how to make your little men into fire angels,' Lucy says, taking George's scissors and snipping each man free of his brother. She stokes up the fire to make it blaze and offers it the sacrificial figures. They feed them to the flames and watch the paper fly away up the chimney on a draught of hot air.

It is a rare, bright memory of his childhood that George keeps close ever after.

Progress

Let us now journey to London and discover how our enterprising sisters, Aurora and Teresa Mantilla, have fared these last years. Here they are, just as we left them, busy with their retouching work, in the south London attic room with its good northerly light. See, Teresa stands by the window apparently still looking for something, or someone to provide her with the answer to her vague romantic yearning. But listen, too, for the prosaic enquiry upon her lips tells us that time has indeed wrought changes in that precarious household, and that the wearisome topic of the domestic economy has, for now, chased away girlish hopes and dreams.

'Bessie must manage with what is left in the larder. Really she must. I cannot spare more money for groceries this week.'

'Can't I give Mrs Bartholomew's little son brown eyes instead of blue? I have more burnt umber than I know what to do with and none of the lapis,' says Aurora, as she contemplates that glum boy's photographic portrait upon her desk and takes the opportunity to warm her hands around a little charcoal-burning device.

'I wish I could swap paint for food, as easily as you do eye colour. Anyway, you may not give him brown eyes. Mrs Bartholomew's little Alf is an angel of goodness, with *blue* eyes, and she most certainly will notice – whatever the state of our household accounts.'

'But, Teresa, I *can* convert paint into a meal, and directly,' says Aurora tartly, and with that she makes a quick sketch of a plate, blocking in some grapes upon it. 'Now, would you like your meal in the old French style – a well-hung hare, with viola, or some other delicious musical instrument, or cherries and a pocket watch? Or would you prefer some Flemish milk poured from an earthenware jug? Or perhaps we might have something in the modern English manner – split-skinned pomegranates from Christ's own table and a couple of mackerel in a dish? But, no, I would have to include a naturalistic fly upon those, which is sure to make us ill,' she says, choosing an expensive purple for her grapes.

'I see you have finished your work for the day, my love,' comments her sister, looking back to the window.

'It would seem that I have,' says Aurora, giving each of her grapes an unsubtle highlight, which turns them into a plateful of lustrous purple eyeballs. 'Anyway, my hands are so cold I would be sure to give Mrs Bartholomew's Alf a dreadful squint should I continue.'

'Is that Father calling? I'll go to him, you tidy the things.'

Teresa runs from the room, leaving Aurora, who wanders to the window with her cleaning rag and brush, perhaps to take over her sister's watch, like a virgin in her tower looking out for her rescuer.

From that window, what is to be seen but sleepy London stirring and stretching herself? Lately she has outgrown her too-tight skirts, which crack open at the seams to let off the pressure of this burgeoning nineteenth century. Roads lined with new houses have poured out at every side, scaling hills and flooding valleys to muffle and blur contours. For progress scores a new, rational pattern upon the land, leaving just a palimpsest of those shapes and forms that Nature made. Every outlying village, with its green and dusty lanes, is now a new suburb, smart under tarmacadam and bisecting privet.

Never was there such a scramble to assemble and accumulate, never before such a call for little workshops, set humming to the tune of the times, turning out stair spindles, staining glass, smoothing marble, splitting slate, moulding porcelain; for a hundred thousand new staircases, new-glazed front doors, new mantelshelves, new roofs and gleaming new sanitaryware. Forest, mine and quarry are all hollowed out to swell the great overflowing Wen. Construction and manufacturing weighs heavy on the new-claimed land. Slapped down hard above ground, red brick pushes out stiff fingers to burst through the old frontiers, while thrusting beneath grow the secret arteries that fetch and carry for the new, outflung London limbs. Water and gas arrive, and ordure is carried away by stealthy pipe. And in this modern world people also are conveyed by pipework. What Aurora surveys from her window is the above-ground evidence of all this burrowing and excavating. An untidy cutting is being opened into the artery, which runs direct to the city's heart, so that veins, which will be coloured maroon, yellow, green, brown, red, black and blue, may branch in all directions to transport the suburban workforce – flesh and blood pumped to power the great city.

She notices that the navvies have brought up spoils from the sour tank into which they dive deep with picks and shovels. They display the earthy treasure upon the exposed London clay – grave goods from an underworld tomb. She can see pieces of old metal and broken pottery, higgledy-piggledy around the hole. Maybe these pots and pans, rags and bones are evidence of a Bronze Age, Roman or Elizabethan London – or maybe they are just pots and pans, rags and bones: history become junk, or junk become history. Aurora sees that an old woman is picking them over. Whatever does she expect to find of use among these hand-me-down artifacts when everything you might possibly need is to be had by the bushel, machine-made and spanking new? Old lamps for new, perhaps?

As she watches, she sees the old woman slip and scramble upon a moving tide of soil that is sucked back into the hungry hole.

The sound of her scream and the rumble of satisfaction the earth lets out as it rushes back to reclaim itself come to Aurora a split second later and make sense of what she has seen. Now she watches as an elderly cottage, nearby the excavation, shudders and shakes off some gusts of thatch. Like the sudden whisking away of a curtain, the façade drops into the street and the building slouches by degrees like a dying beast collapsing to its knees.

Shouts come from outside for everyone to leave their houses and get away to safety. Aurora and Teresa bundle old Alonso into dressing-gown and slippers and, half carrying him, stumble out to where the excited neighbourhood has been disgorged.

For the first time ever Mrs Evans, the cat, and Peter, the elderly canary, have sole possession of the house. The cat recurls herself upon a cushion, the canary cheeps and Alonso's bedside clock ticks like the reassuring heartbeat of the house.

Like refugees with Cossacks at their backs, the people scramble away from their dangerous houses, carrying Teresa and Aurora with them. Alonso is seated unsteadily on a handcart belonging to an enterprising neighbour. He has to share his litter with those essentials immediately to hand, rescued to sustain life, which include a gilded pier-glass and a piano accordion. At least they shall have music wherever they go.

All around, other household trappings are swept along by this tide of moving people. Here bobs a family Bible, there the family pet. Aurora notices one distracted woman, who appears in her apron, still holding the bowl and spoon with which she had been engaged when the call to evacuate went up.

Aurora wonders what else she should have saved. What about the half-finished commissions, or the precious paints, or her second-best corset? Without this press of people forcing them along, she can imagine herself and Teresa tripping in and out of the house, conscientiously stripping it bare, so that their lives would be laid outside on the street. But then what? She would still have to select only the things they could carry. Alonso, looking back anxiously from his hurtling pallet, calls, 'Teresa, my love. May I have my cap?' Of course! That is what she should have taken. And Aurora finds herself, *whoosh*, in her father's deserted bedroom looking at the velvet skullcap that she herself embroidered and left hanging, forgotten and forlorn, upon the bedhead.

A huge tremor passes through the house as more debris roars into the cutting, animating the cap tassel, which begins to swing. There is another rush of earth and masonry, and the house groans to itself. Sparrows erupt from the roof slates and a fine layer of plaster dust and soot is sifted into the air. As the tassel tolls, the great carved Spanish wardrobe totters, then staggers upon feet too dainty for its bulk, and the great trunk of furniture is felled as though the mahogany tree that went into its making plays out again the memory of its death. It crashes down, straight and true, to meet the resistance of the massive wooden bedstead, which sprang from that same Spanish forest.

With a slither and a rush the hatbox lets slip upon the bed the cache of Maria's carefully chosen thoughts from exile. Also delivered on to the counterpane is the dusty suitcase she had hidden there nearly a decade before. Here it lies, solid and benign as a loaf of bread, risky as a powder keg.

Evening comes on, and the refugees upon the hill settle into a dislocated domestic routine. Some people have brought bedrolls upon which they now sit, drinking tea made from water boiled in everyday kitchen kettles upon bonfires. Children play, parents scold, and each family group arranges its possessions around it in a semblance of normality. There cannot help but be a lighthearted cheerfulness about people gathered in the open, and there is almost an air of carnival as these people sit among their household chattels, gossiping with their neighbours. And, indeed, the piano accordion is put to good use to justify its salvation.

In Alonso's house the plaster dust and soot have settled as though, while they were out, some perverse housemaid had gone about scattering and drifting where she should have swept and dusted. It silently coats the back of the wardrobe with lint and dulls the velvet of Alonso's lonely cap.

The clock continues to tick-tock, the cat stretches and mews for her supper, the canary fidgets without his night-time cover and floorboards creak under feet. The cat and the canary are no longer master and mistress of all they survey, for there is another live heartbeat in that house. There is careful, heavy breath, too, that seems to test the air for danger or discovery, like a sixth sense. As he mounts the stairs, the sensual cat rubs around his legs, marking him with her scent. He wants to kick her away, but is constrained by the utter concentration it takes to tiptoe in work boots.

His eyes cannot make sense at first of the graveyard of toppled furniture looming in the dim light of Alonso's bedroom. On putting his hand upon the bedpost to lever himself over the broad back of the cupboard, he finds sliding softness where he had expected unyielding support. He brings the detachable thing up close to his face, as though to smell rather than see it in this gloom would be his best method of identification. The tassel swings against his hand and he throws the cap from him on to the bed, where it thumps, as though it were a horribly live thing. The drum-breaker feels before him, skimming the surface of the counterpane, to find that hard landing place. His hand fits instinctively around the familiar feel of a suitcase handle and he pulls it too violently towards him, unable to judge how heavy or light it may be. Apparently deciding that it is quite sufficiently weighty with possibilities, he thumps down the stairs, pursued by the cat. He picks up a tablecloth swag-bag of gleanings from the parlour, then leaves the back door ajar to the evening air.

In Fainhope Hall George has been settled for the night. As soon as Nanny has taken the lamp he slides, as always, from his bed to his habitual place on the floor. There is a fire in his room tonight because he has an aching ear and a hot forehead. Her Grace, the Duchess, alert to the sudden depredations of childhood illness (the one sly opponent over which she has no control), spares no expense in warding it off with blazes, doses and other proven charms. On the whole George would prefer to be cold. He curls in around the hot, buzzing infection as though to protect and nurse it. He surrenders to the ringing in his ears and the heavy sensation of kapok-stuffed limbs as though they brought delightful relief.

The crib-cracker has scraped his way over the wall of Alonso's garden, into the little back alley that connects the terrace of houses. He finds a stone with which to strike open the lock on the suitcase. What will this bran tub hold?

The newspaper-wrapped parcel tumbles out at his feet so that he must crouch in this gloomy passage to open his prize. He juggles it in his hands, unsettled by the dried-out, hollow feel of the thing. As he strips away the brittle newspaper to reveal another layer underneath, and then another, he encourages himself with the thought that at the centre there must lie something small, light and valuable. He imagines it as a birthday present, teasingly disguised beneath layer after layer of wrapping, each meant to increase anticipation and magnify surprise at the treasure hidden within. He has yet to unpeel the last page of stiffened old paper when a spasm of disgust for what he might finally disclose makes him throw the horrid, rigid thing from him into an open dustbin, for the ambiguous feel and musty smell of that package suggest something that was once alive. He runs up the alley with his cache of candlesticks and teaspoons, as though pursued.

As the bundle hits the bottom of the metal bin, George in his bedroom looks up startled by a hollow clang. The noise comes from the top of his wardrobe, and when he looks there he sees a light that pulses strongly enough to throw a distorted shape of the wardrobe top on to the opposite wall. Eyes distracted by this shadow show, he fails to notice at first that another, independently moving shape has been cast there. So the first time George sees him, this night visitor is a trembling shade, come to reclaim the real lost boy. Only then does George turn to seek the solid form that cast the moving shadow of itself upon his wall.

He sees him sitting on the wardrobe top, naked legs dangling, still wet from his shell, in a nest of scraps and tatters, peelings from his tacky, newborn skin. 'Painless tooth extraction, chimneypieces of all descriptions, how to restore the walking powers, left-off clothing, Cocke's Compound anti-bilious pills,' sings the radiant boy, in a high, ecstatic voice.

The visitor stands and his outer windings unwrap around him to flutter down upon George. The boy on the floor turns up his eyes to this bright being and recognises him as his own, like a lost twin. His one friend come at last to this lonely, island kingdom.

'The cheapest and best Indian carpet, just ready! Discover for yourself the best-kept secret of Society's brightest beauties, Harrington's pure milled soap.'

It is as though he is singing the poignant song of all humanity.

George holds up his arms to the ethereal boy standing above him, and says, 'Oh, do come down to me!'

The twin tilts his bright face to George and smiles at him. This time the beautiful words are sung as a question: 'Steam to Italy, regular line of screw steamers, loading in the London dock?'

'Just jump down to me. I'll catch you,' replies George, standing and reaching up to his saviour.

The boy sings back, '*Minerva*, six hundred and seventy-six tons, for freight apply . . .' and, on the dying fall of his last phrase, leaps to George. He lands light as a spirit cat and, although George goes to him, he is attracted towards the dying fire whose coals give out the same pulsing glow as his own pale skin. 'Coal-scoops – plain, black, open scoops, from two and fourpence, ditto zinc lined. For reasons above mentioned . . .' He turns to George, pulls one of his newspaper peelings from his chest and hands it to him.

George turns it to the fading light of the fire and reads aloud, ' "Teddy Cox. Boy – come back, fool! All is settled satisfactorily. The old bull pup is heartbroken. From Harry and Cobbett." ' He whispers, 'You went away and now you've come back?' He looks to his twin for endorsement and finds exultation there.

The twin takes the strip George read from and holds it face down over his heart, all the while looking at George.

'Where were you? I mean, where did you come back from?' George says, and the twin tears another strip from his body and hands it to him, smiling his encouragement to read there. ' "On the fifteenth inst. at Bellagio, Lake of Como, the wife of John Robert Wright Esquire, of the Inner Temple . . ." ' Here George cannot decipher the print as the newspaper is stained and torn. He continues to read aloud what is still legible. ' ". . . prematurely, of a son, who survived his birth only a few hours . . ." '

Looking into George's eyes, the twin sings the reprise, 'Only a few hours, only a few hours, only a few hours.'

The boy and his bright twin sit together on the floor before the fire, not touching – although George is aware of the subsiding heat that is still generated from his body. Strip by strip they reveal more and more of that sticky pearl skin, each taking it in turn to read what they find there. George takes comfort from the beautiful sad words, which tell of comings and goings at Court, admirable inventions and patent cures. At last they reach the very last strip of hanging newsprint. The twin peels it away from himself and sings with particular emphasis, as he looks into the nearly extinguished fire: 'Friendless and Fallen – London, female, preventive and reformatory institution – est. eighteen fifty-seven – contributions are earnestly solicited.'

When Lucy goes to wake him, as she does every morning, she finds the feverish boy asleep, as usual, upon the floor before cold cinders, surrounded by a pile of stale yellow newspaper scraps, which she sweeps up into her ash-pan.

When George wakes he looks around, as though startled to find himself on the floor. 'Where is he?'

'Chilled to the bone again. No wonder you fall ill, Master George,' says Lucy.

George sees the waste newspaper and scrabbles it into his arms. The desiccated embalming strips crackle as he holds them close.

'Who is it you're after? You don't want them nasty things, give them here.'

'I need them . . . to keep me warm,' says George.

The Arrival of the Suitor

Time has moved on since that momentous day when George found and lost his one true companion. The three years since last we were at the Hall have seen little change there: none of our protagonists has come and none has left. However, it is on this day that the spell of stasis will be broken by a new inmate.

Lucy is in the kitchen assembling a tea-tray for Miss Mantilla and the young ladies. Mrs Beam, the cook, and Miss Hart are in conversation. Since their little trip to converse with the dead, Miss Hart has lost all patience with the Spanish miss. She ruined a good pair of kidskin boots on that little foray, and even though a decade has passed she will not forgive in a hurry her wet walk home.

Mrs Beam is only too happy to stoke the housekeeper's sense of injustice connected with the nursery regime. 'All I want to know is, where is he going to be taking his meals and who with? Because I can tell you now, this household is getting more and more peculiar. All these little bits of meals, what with invalids' special diets and nursery teas,' gesturing with her floury elbow at Lucy with her tea-tray, 'and comings and goings and I don't know what else. I'm just saying, it's not what I call an aristocratic kitchen no more.'

Miss Hart takes the opportunity to interrupt this helter-skelter of grudges when Mrs Beam pauses to swipe the sweat from her indignant brow. 'You're not pining after the old duke's shoots, surely? All that hanging and gutting . . .'

'Well, all I'm saying is, you knew where you were with pheasants and gentlemen with gentlemen's proper appetites. It was what I was brought up to.'

'As far as I know, he is a gentleman. But he's a very young one. So let's hope he'll do as he is bid.'

'A young one, eh,' winks the cook.

'The Duchess and I will just have to watch out that he doesn't develop a taste for hot Spanish onions,' shoots back Miss Hart, and the two middle-aged virgins nudge each other with concupiscent glee. Since the Dr Oliver question, the kitchen/housekeeping axis has kept itself amused by disseminating propaganda concerning certain disgraceful characteristics known to prevail among the Latin races.

'A drop o' warm and wet, Miss Hart?' asks the cook, without a hint of irony.

'Oh, I shouldn't, but I will.'

The two turn to glare at Kathleen, the kitchen maid, to attend to the teapot.

For Aurora and Teresa, too, time has moved on since that momentous evening when the world slipped. And although their domestic arrangements continue much as we left them, here, too, an arrival is imminent.

It cost them their second to last remaining silver coffee spoon to persuade the enterprising owner of the handcart to deliver Papa safely home and, so that he could reoccupy his bed, to right the toppled wardrobe.

The scattered letters were returned to their hatbox on the top and Alonso's cap re-established upon his thinning locks. Bessie was summoned to take a hand with the cleaning operations that then ensued. She paid herself, unofficially, for the extra inconvenience of that unseasonable spring-clean with the last remaining silver coffee spoon, so then they had none.

Before the brawny man could replant the wardrobe in its accustomed place Teresa, her head wrapped in a tea-towel to denote the seriousness and scale of the work to be done, set about whisking away the powdered plaster that coated the broad back of that piece of furniture. As she leant into her work, in the very instant that she wiped them away for ever, she thought she saw the imprint in the fine dust of tiny footprints. From then on she mused to herself that it had been mischievous elves who had broken into their house that night and carried away the candlesticks. She never told Aurora of this theory.

Perhaps not elves but malevolent goblins – for in the months dating from that unfortunate landslide, some unpropitiated house god seemed to be at work, letting china slip from wet hands, paint dry in unstopped bottles, botched commissions lie unclaimed, and over-wound clocks stop. And so, by these unremarkable degrees, Alonso's household appeared itself to be slithering ever nearer that other abyss: of insolvency. At last, when they really did not know where they would find the shilling for Alonso's sleep medicine, desperate measures were resorted to: they would let out the master bedroom to respectable lodgers. Aurora decided on this scheme in a rush and Teresa conceded in a flurry, so the implications of deposing Papa from his bedroom to install him in Maria's boxroom, thus reducing themselves from the status of lady artists to that of landladies, were blurred by their giddy enthusiasm for the plan.

So the two girls sit in Alonso's bedroom comparing the newspaper columns wherein accommodation is offered and sought. Teresa is reading, increasingly mirthfully, from *The Times*: 'Look, here's another one. "Wanted in some cheerful suburb in London a kind household of experience, to receive a Gentleman (a Chancery lunatic), who would require genial companionship and amusement with as little restraint as his case will admit of. No other patient must be taken." Oh, and look here – "A qualified attendant would be indispensable," it continues!'

Alonso fidgets in his bed. 'I must say, my dear, I would object to a lunatic. Cannot we have some nice young person, or even yet an infant?'

'Oh, Papa, for me it isn't so much the lunatic but the qualified attendant – *where* would we find for him to sleep?' answers Aurora, suppressing a guffaw.

'In the spare bedroom, of course. The poor lunatic would expect to be housed in the attic, on dirty straw, as appropriate to his case.'

'To howl at the moon and disturb the neighbours. How deliciously melodramatic! I'm sure he is not a lunatic at all, but some poor wronged handsome boy – heir to a fabulous fortune.'

'You are forgetting that we live in prosaic reality and not a book, Aurora. We must send the lunatic and his attendant off to some other, outer suburb,' says Teresa.

Aurora takes the newspaper and scans the columns. 'Here are several concerning the placement of children,' she says, and reads, '"ADOPTION – A person wishing a lasting and comfortable home for a young child of either sex will find this a good opportunity. Age no object; if sickly, would be gladly accepted. Advertisers having no children of their own and about to proceed to Canada. Premium fifteen pounds. Respectable references given and required." What on earth do you think that could mean?'

'Some kind couple who want to start a new life with a poor unfortunate child,' says Teresa, blandly.

'Odd, though. Why mention infirmity? It's almost as though, reading between the lines, they are offering to take unwanted children off their guardians' hands and dispose of them . . .'

' . . . in Canada?'

'Perhaps "Canada" is just a code,' says Aurora, with a shiver. 'Let us confine ourselves to the straightforward columns of lodgings offered to adults. I think we should compose something along these lines: "Refined and comfortable home for lady invalid or delicate girl, in quiet, convenient London suburb. Terms moderate. Care of Mays' advertising offices, one hundred and sixty Piccadilly . . ." Dum de dum de dum.'

'That certainly sounds prosaic enough, not a hint of melodrama. But don't you think we should stretch to a respectable married couple? All these other convalescents and consumptive girls seem to expect accommodation in the homes of medical men and their wives,' says Teresa, all the while industriously feeling for and plucking out stray feathers that tickle or bristle through Papa's leaky eiderdown, as though it was not depleted enough already.

'I will grant you the married couple, but I do insist on keeping our minds open to my ailing ladies. They are bound to be quiet and discreet,' replies her sister. Teresa continues to run her hand over the quilt to feel for the pricking of little quills.

'But, Aurora, if we must put up with tiresome invalids drooping about the place, coughing like bargees and calling for beef tea, quite apart from the "medical man and wife",' Teresa blows featherdown from her fingertips and picks up the newspaper, 'we can't pretend to offer: "delightful locality", "warm but bracing air" or, look here, "a fine sheltered sandy beach" or this, "pony carriage and boat kept"!'

'In that case, we must simply conclude our advertisement with "Situation equals Torquay"!' Aurora observes.

The two girls look out of Alonso's window at the gloomy London street and burst into howls of laughter loud enough to bother the neighbours.

A week later, on the very afternoon that Teresa and Aurora sit, nervously occupied, in the kitchen awaiting the arrival of the respectable couple who replied to their forlorn notice in *The Times*, the new occupant of Fainhope Hall makes his entrance. He is Mr Briggs, the young man whose possible dietary requirements put the cook into such a bad mood when last we saw her.

If Mr Briggs is going to be difficult about his meals, he is going about it in a cunning way. If it is his plan to subdue this female household beneath his tyrannical heel, then his anxious servility and deferential blush, when directly addressed, suggest he has chosen to play a long game. A very long game indeed.

Here he sits with his young pupil in the schoolroom. They are about the business of breaking the twin codes that keep secure the door between the classes and the sexes. Straight is the gate and tortuous the way to that bright upland occupied by the gods and English gentlemen. 'No, George. That is the gerund.'

George is not very good at deciphering the codes but this matters little. That he may never compose a beautiful line after Virgil matters less, but that he has been exposed to the complicated brain-teasing that is parsing Latin and Greek matters greatly. Like a painstaking riding instructor with his yearling, it is Mr Briggs's tedious task to break the boy in to the classics.

Rather than a beakerful of the warm south, Latin gives George the taste of the dust of ages in his mouth. It must be added that Mr Briggs, gerund-grinder, has hardly more enthusiasm for the work. He himself had scraped through the classics at school by resorting to the purchase of exemplary translations, exercises and sample work sold on by more talented boys who had passed through those groves of academe a year or two before him. And so there existed, within the school, a formula for the redistribution of wealth – that is, as is natural, from the dull to the bright, from the young to their elders, from the weak to the strong. The masters winked at these transactions. We may take as illustration of an illegal trade allowing for stable conditions the importation of opium into Shanghai, which kept the British traders buoyant and the natives subdued. Just so, in the School Empire the strong triumphed, the weak paid their taxes so that they would not be punished for being weak, and the governing body looked on benignly at the exercise of free trade.

As one weak in body and intellect neither aspiring to sporting honours, as a wet bob or dry bob, nor distinguishing himself as a scholar, the boy Briggs's experience of the school economy had been that of the lowly toiler. For him no cups or prizes, only an endless cycle of chewing over and regurgitation so that what knowledge he did manage to acquire grew into a much-worked, tasteless, fibrous lump. Now, having become a learning-shover himself, he dutifully does his best to remove any savour that George might have found in study and create for his student a similar bolus of dry facts.

Quite apart from causing annoyance among the women below stairs, the inoffensive Mr Briggs is also making an impact above stairs. Lady Georgina, now sixteen and not at all improved in her looks, has become violently fascinated by the man in their midst. Each time he turns his vacant eyes upon her she reads whole stanzas of ill-suppressed longing in his every unengaged glance. In the brief weeks since he first came to the Hall she has galloped ahead with their unspoken relationship. Hardly bothering with the introductory interlude of reverent admiration, she has pressed her imaginary suitor all the way to a barely sustainable peak of burning desire, by way of hopeless fascination and ardent appeal. Now she hardly knows what to do with him further. The narrative of their mad, impulsive romance is so advanced that she aches for its culmination. The urgent attentions she has imagined for him have stoked her hot bed every night now for a week and all she needs to utterly deliquesce is that he should speak one actual word to her.

For Miss Mantilla, too, he is an irritant, although she is made hot by imagined slights rather than imagined ardour. Now that the two young ladies and their younger brother have outgrown Nanny, Miss Mantilla is the undisputed head of that minor dependency, the nursery. Yet having succeeded to the title, she finds herself wishing that her sphere of influence had extended beyond the restricted realms of the upper storeys. With the introduction of this schoolmaster, she must harbour yet another body within the borders of her fiefdom and perhaps one with expansionist ambitions. She hates to feel besieged. A sentiment, you might remember, she shares with the mistress of the Hall.

At their mealtimes, the whole nursery entourage is now obliged to squeeze itself round the single table. Mr Briggs, herself, George, Georgina and Euphemia all dine together. And Her Grace, the Duchess, or Mrs Beam, makes no effort to provide them with elegant eating. They sit over soup, brown and transparent as beck water, and as full of flavour.

'The salt, if you please, Miss Mantilla,' is Mr Briggs's ingenuous request and she hands it to him, bridling at his tone. She may have had no formal education but she fails to see why the man should patronise her.

Meanwhile Georgina's heart is pierced by a dart of ecstasy. Clearly he means to lead the old biddy away from the true object of his ardour by this slight attention. She smiles covertly at him – and he wonders at the ugly girl's evasive eyes, which, startlingly, are naked of their lashes and never seem able to meet his own but must slide off his face towards his lap. He tries, unsuccessfully, to catch her with his own weak smile before her glance can slither downwards.

'George, you must tell us the correct chemical name for this condiment before you shall have any,' says Miss Mantilla, taking hold of the salt cellar and holding it temptingly before the boy. She is not completely ignorant of the sciences, whatever Mr Briggs may think of her.

'It's sodium something, but I can't remember the other part,' replies George, who would happily eat the whole meal unseasoned so long as he is not made to perform for it.

'It is sodium chlorine.'

'Chloride, sodium chloride,' interjects Georgina, before she can think better of it.

'Indeed, sodium chloride. Have you learnt that well now, George?'

Georgina's blush of triumph before her godhead is met by her governess's own flush of annoyance at the forwardness of the girl. An unsubtle man, Mr Briggs hears but the few, unremarkable words they exchange and misses the unspoken conversation raging across the dining-table. As Miss Mantilla and Georgina clash over the soup spoons, he notices that the governess's raised colour enhances her looks – and, even sitting, how tall she is.

Georgina is giddy with the certainty that the amorous dialogue between herself and her lover, so loud and insistent in her head, must have betrayed their secret infatuation. Those looks, with eyes too hot to hold each other, across the dining-table, his sensuous way of stroking the side of his water glass, his special attentiveness towards her – all this must surely discover them to their enemy, the old woman. Unable to contain the rising gush of words that threatens to burst in her throat, Georgina throws down her napkin like a gauntlet and exits the room.

Miss Mantilla purses her lips to wipe them and, looking after the girl, wonders whether this erratic behaviour has been caused by the training corset being tightened too far. Like foot-binding among the Chinese upper classes, this method of quelling a girl, rendering her docile by constraining her active nature, is often hard to bear at first. The girl is certainly pale – perhaps this passion is, rather, a symptom of that unmentionable anaemia, Miss Mantilla muses again. Is Nature turning the girl into a woman quicker than the corsets can shape her into one? Pity the poor thing, the good it will bring her.

The eventual agitation of the bell-pull at Alonso's front door thrills through the house. It causes Teresa to jump to her feet, letting the peas she was podding fall to the floor, and nervously smooth her hair, as though it stood on end with the shock. Both sisters run to install themselves in the more appropriate setting of the parlour, while Bessie whips off the sackcloth with which she protects herself when wringing out the linens in the back garden, and hurries to open the door. The household is all at sixes and sevens, unprepared for these prompt callers.

For Albert and Carrie Flynn, the door opens upon a young woman-of-all-work, her face bright as a steamy plate, hands rough and reddened from the wash.

For sweaty Bessie it reveals a no-longer-young couple got up to look more respectable than comes natural, she with well-darned gloves and an unfashionably plain-dressed hat, he in boots with soles too thick for a proper gentleman. Nevertheless they have a card – which he hands to Bessie with his hat and gloves. Hoity-toity! If those two great girls expect her to be the drudge in a common lodging-house they've got another think coming. She only agreed to come to them because the old man was bedridden and no trouble. And now where were we, letting out rooms left and right and wanting cooked tea every evening? Bessie ushers the callers into the parlour to discover the expectant landladies poised upon the threshold hand in hand. If they can't contrive to put these two shabby individuals in their places, then she'll be buggered if they can expect her to play along. Bessie carries the card between fastidious forefinger and thumb and hands it to Miss Teresa. 'Mr and Mrs Flynn, 'ere about the old gent's room.'

She'll not be obliged to stand for this. She'll be out of there. In the very near future. You can bet on it.

Miss Mantilla is spending a fruitless afternoon pursuing the subject of a girl's coming to womanhood with the recalcitrant Georgina. Eventually she discerns that all her talk of the monthly suffering of women and being 'unwell', her discretion over the domestic affliction, the curse of Eve, and even, in last resort, the schoolgirlish talk of 'holy week', has not yet been necessary – evidently the silly girl remains a silly girl. However, she now appears to be a confused silly girl, with a half-formed notion that her governess is trying to accuse her of something. Georgina seems to be under the misapprehension that Miss Mantilla is talking to her of her innermost thoughts. Miss Mantilla sniffs a secret and has a notion that it springs from bodily embarrassment. Certainly the ravaged girl appears self-conscious in front of the interloper in the schoolroom. Perhaps it is no more than vanity, then.

The Servant Question

It is evening time and George is at his lessons when Miss Mantilla comes to send him to his bed. Or he should be at his lessons. She finds him sitting on the fireside rug smoothing out tatters of newspaper old enough to fray into dust as he flattens each jagged fragment upon the floor to make a yellow archipelago floating on a red sea. 'What is this?' she asks, indicating the paper islands.

George does not reply but attempts to hide them away.

'You must throw this rubbish upon the fire. Your mama will be angry – who knows what diseases it might harbour? Come, now, I have given you an order. Throw these nasty things upon the fire.'

The newspaper tinder catches easily in the flames before it flies up the chimney, like Lucy's paper angels of long ago. We might speculate that this rapid flight had been the fate of the mysterious disappeared boy, who sang so poignantly from these mouldering song-sheets.

'You are a very disappointing boy, George,' says Miss Mantilla. 'It's time for you to go to your bed.'

'I know I am a bad boy. I do try to make myself better. I think I once had a guardian angel who tried to help, but I lost him and can find him no longer.'

Miss Mantilla's reply is brisk: 'You may be sure, guardian angel or not, that the Lord God is watching over you, unseen, even now. He sees everything and feels every bad deed that you commit as a blow to His own body. As I do. Although you cannot see Him He is always present, so you must live your life as though you were always under His gaze.'

'But I *did* see him. He is a naked, blazing boy who looks just like me!'

'You are to run to your Mr Briggs and ask for two stripes on the palm. You may explain to him that you are a liar and a blasphemer.'

Despite her preoccupation with George's moral and physical development, it must be remembered that Miss Mantilla still has responsibility for the welfare of her original charges. Alerted to the possibility that her delicate young lady might be ailing, and finding that indeed she droops and pines more than usual, Miss Mantilla sends for the doctor. It has been many months since he has attended patients at the Hall, such has been the governess's unwillingness to find herself alone with him again. However, his desire to discover the mystery that these two women guard has not abated these last years, even though he has had few opportunities to persecute the governess and now knows better than to provoke his chief aristocratic patroness with further enquiry. Nevertheless he is excited by the prospect of being able to sniff among these petticoats again, even if he, a household dependant at bottom, must keep his hot curiosity on a short rein.

He gives Lucy a fright as she emerges into the corridor, down which he stalks, from the concealed door on to the servants' staircase. Like a startled bird rising up in the path of the gun, she draws him away from his intended quarry. So he, instinctively, lowers his sights to this lesser game, the bird in the hand. Taking her by the wrists, he steps with her back into the obscurity of the servants' stairway so that they are half-way between two worlds –

standing in close shadows but looking out at the bright uplands of the quiet hallway.

'You're a nice little girl, eh, miss?' He contrives to hold both wrists secure behind her back so that he may have her face to himself. She tries to hide it from him, but he still has one hand free to tilt her by the chin so that he can graze her lips and smear her cheeks with his wet moustache.

'Oh! No, sir, I would rather not, sir, I'm much obliged to you, sir, but I would rather not sir – oh! Let me go.'

Dr Oliver now secures Lucy in position by trapping her against the wall with his body, so that he can free one hand to bring out some loose change from his pocket. 'Come, now, don't whine. This will pay for you to be a good girl.'

He knows he has her completely contained and secure. Her very feebleness, together with the possibility that he may be discovered in this half-way place between upstairs and downstairs, fuels his excitement.

'I will tell, sir!'

'Tell? You will not tell, little tweeny, little cinder-grubber. Little cinder-grubbers never tell of such little liberties.' He holds one of her hands in front of her and forces a sovereign into it. 'There, the deal is done.'

Lucy introduces the hand holding the purchase price back into his pocket and he is quick to hold it there, pressing it in deeper until it meets with his erection lying under the thin material of his trousers. 'Quite right, what do you need with money? Don't your class belong to mine already? Bought and paid for?' He begins to move her hand rhythmically over his concealed member, thrusting it backwards and forwards, all the while talking fiercely to her, telling of her sad, limited existence. He fucks himself using her – using her as she was born to be used: a utensil for the effectuation of her betters' dirty work. And as he diminishes her so he becomes more excited with the splendour of his unassailable superiority.

'You are a mule, drudging in and out of kitchens, running

upstairs and down with coals and cans of hot water, or down on your knees before a grate. You are a mule – there is no sense in you. You are a beast of burden, a slave too dirty and ignorant for anything but toil.' As he reaches his moment of climax he calls out, 'Mule!' and flings her hand away from him. 'Don't cry, be a good girl. Now, take the money. You've made your conquest, but I don't want you boasting all over the place about hooking a gentleman admirer.'

'Oh, sir, I must go.'

'But you'll be back, my merry little mule. Now you've had a taste, you'll begin to itch for more of the doctor's medicine. And I'll be obliged to tickle you better again.'

Half collapsed before him, she is a bird laid at his feet by a soft-mouthed gun-dog. Not broken but somehow crushed; something that once flew but is now just a meaningless bundle of feathers. He is faintly repulsed by her: was the utensil made dirty by his use of it, or he contaminated by its uncleanness? Nevertheless, he knows his duty. He chucks her under the chin and spins a coin for her before he resumes his perambulation of the corridors, wiping his hands upon the tails of his coat.

Mr Briggs and Miss Mantilla are together in his schoolroom. Despite the incommoding presence of the governess, he cannot delay that delicious consummation of breaking open the cases of equipment, which have been forwarded and arrived, that morning, from his home. As he reveals each artifact of wood and metal, she circles him, attempting to engage him in a contemplation of the serious shortcomings of their joint charge, George.

'While, I agree, he may never make a scholar, still I propose that science, rather than the classics administered with the birch, holds the answer,' says the master, distractedly delivering a bulky instrument from its nest of wood chippings.

'And these,' she indicates the devices, 'may be the engines for his improvement?'

'I think, dear lady, that the birch will keep him at the level of brutish ignorance and these may light the spark of an enquiring mind.'

'Do you really believe him to be a dullard?'

He mistakes her tone for affront at being identified as the one responsible, as his governess, for slack George's want of intellectual brilliance, rather than hearing in it the anxious hurt of an interested party. 'Not at all. I see, rather, a young man who may be helped to become much finer than we find him at present. He is one who might be said to have grown flabby – lacking the company of boys of his own sort, as he has. Our duty is to contrive a way to build those intellectual muscles that he might have developed in the course of natural competition with his peers.'

'And this intellectual exercise will come from taking photographs?'

'I think it will be a beginning. The scientific study of photosensitivity as well as the precise practicalities of preparing plates and mixing chemicals may well do the trick. Who knows where it may lead?' says Mr Briggs, gleefully dusting down his bellows. So the tutor, concealing low self-interest behind a mask of enlightened pedagogy, rids both himself and his pupil of the drudgery of the classics, to insinuate into the daily regimen his own, true love, photography.

'And shall my two young ladies also benefit from learning to make photographs?'

'I would say that it is an occupation that will do them no injury. The technique of wet-plate collodion photography may teach them patience and a good eye for a composition, in much the same way that still-life painting or embroidery might.'

'So it is all things to all people, then? A panacea?' sniffs Miss Mantilla.

'There are certain miracles it cannot bring about. Much as I am a devotee of the plate camera, I cannot claim that it will work the miracle of transforming our ugly duckling, Lady Georgina, into a swan.'

Now he has gone too far. She has put up with the wheedling criticism of her academic skills, but she will not stand for this bumptious fault-finding in her remaining sphere of influence. Miss Mantilla resorts to a sharp slap upon this puppy's nose: 'Really, sir! You should not talk so of Lady Georgina – even in jest. We would both do well to remember that we are servants in this house. We may be educated above our station, but we are dependants here. I cannot afford to lose my situation and I guess that neither can you.'

Mr Briggs is stirred by the haughty rebuke in a way that makes his ears pink with emotion. 'I beg your pardon, madam. I meant no offence to you or to your unfortunate, disfigured charge. For you have surely worked your own miracle with the poor girl. You are quite right to chastise me. I am in need of regular admonishment, I'm sure.'

Taken aback by his eager submission, Miss Mantilla has no choice but to be gracious in victory, although she is puzzled that he should put up such feeble resistance to her counterblast. There's no fight or sap in the man – he's like a rotten, bendy reed, she speculates. However, the glad prospect of gaining command over him is now in her sights. She proceeds to further illustrate her point with a nicely chosen aphorism to demonstrate the proper difference between knowing one's place as a servant and being servile. 'Mr Briggs, I consider that we are the educated Greek slaves in the Roman household. Below us, to be sure, are the barbarians who toil and serve. But "though we wear sandals upon our feet" and walk with our masters, still we are like strangers in a strange land. And we must bow down in our captivity for fear of the chaos that reigns outside these city walls.'

'I quite understand you, Miss Mantilla, and you must believe that I consider you to ennoble all beneath your feet.'

She is gratified that he serves her metaphor back to her, but obscurely troubled that he should have been quite so breathlessly pleased with the overblown imagery she had employed. It seems to have lit a strange new fire in the funny little man – who now stands before her, knees slightly bent to make himself lower than she. How curious: apparently she has indeed risen in his estimation.

Since we were introduced to the two new lodgers, the evacuation of Alonso and his furniture to Maria's old room has been effected and Mr Albert Flynn and his pale Carrie have been installed in the superior front bedroom. Bessie continues to be affronted by the common pair. From the very start her disapproval for these two has hung in the air, gathering and solidifying, until it becomes a quite tangible snub. So her vendetta built, from the merely sullen (sniffing audibly at their inferior luggage as she conveyed it to their room) to mutely provocative (she leaves on her slovenly apron when serving them their tea) to downright disobedient. The interval between their pulling of the bell and her answering it has now grown so noticeably long that Teresa and Aurora are in fear of their lodgers leaving in a huff.

However, Mr Flynn has no aspirations to the well-bred condescension that Bessie finds lacking in him and his lady. He not only doesn't notice her campaign but he and dear Carrie feel passing concern at causing the poor girl extra work. Lucky for her, Carrie reined in her first feeble impulse to help with washing the crocks, which minor kindness really would have scandalised the magisterial drudge.

There is another, larger, reason that Bessie's insolence fails to put the couple in their place: quite simply, she occupies a blind spot in the noble vision of their joint destiny. For the most part, Mr and Mrs A. Flynn have their sights either elevated to the celestial heavens or cast down so low that they look upon the depths of godless depravity. In neither of which spheres do they find her to dwell.

Mr and Mrs Flynn have a mission, a mission to save the world, and Bessie's individual need for salvation isn't pressing enough to make her in the least bit interesting to them. During the day, Mr Flynn is engaged as clerk to a firm of shipping agents and

Mrs Flynn improves each hour with study and pamphlet-writing. It is only after dark falls that they become their true selves. Transformed into the instruments of the Lord, they go about their vocation in and around the stews where London's poor roll in filth and ignorance. They are a two-pronged weapon in the good fight, cleansing wherever they go with soap and the spirit.

Teresa and Aurora wonder at the endurance of their lodgers, who return every morning, still blazing from their nightly tussle with the devil, only to reinvent themselves, with a wash and breakfast, as little grey mice set upon the treadmill of the daily round. Aurora knows that, during the afternoons, Mrs Flynn often naps upon her bundled leaflets, but what of Mr F., seated at his tall desk? Does he never nod over his inkpots?

Aurora speculates to herself that their lodgers might, with justification, claim back six-sevenths of their weekly rent as presumably they only occupy the bed on Sunday nights, this being the day of rest for super-humans just as it is for ordinary mortals.

On Sex and Photography

Is not this nineteenth century the very cauldron of artistic, industrial, social and scientific advance? And of all those patented inventions that increase the comfort and convenience of everyday life is not photography a most wonderfully ubiquitous addition? For now we may, with ease, choose to commemorate ourselves in every location, attitude and garb. And even if we do not choose, who nowadays can promenade innocently about the park or take a punt upon the river without being waylaid by some opportunistic man with a tripod, keen to capture the moment? In just a half-century of photography, consider how these marvellous pictorial reminders of all that is banal have multiplied. And how the weight of all those family snaps presses upon us to clutter our lives. Isn't this miracle of invention, which allows any fool to point and click, an exemplar of the wonderful democratising effect of progress?

Not so for Mr Briggs, for although he is a photographic zealot he is also a primitive. His heart was early lost to the arcane wet-plate collodion process invented by Frederick Scott Archer of England, and he abjures, even despises, all that is innovative, efficient and modern. For Mr Briggs, the wet-plate process, the exacting rite into which he was first initiated, is the one, the only true photography, its practice like the observance of an older, sterner, purer religion. Mr Briggs, a man of little imagination, is humbled by the precise method and chemical cookery, and excited by all the possibilities for failure in this unwieldy technique. Already thirty years behind the times, he wrestles with second-hand antiquated equipment, while the rest of the world is merrily taking snapshots.

Having insinuated the venerated devices into the Hall, our photographic prophet sets about installing a dark laboratory in which to initiate his disciples, George, Georgina and Euphemia. Here he demonstrates how each clear glass plate must be coated with a very thin layer of iodised collodion (made from gun-cotton dissolved in ether and alcohol, mixed with potassium iodide), how the coated plate must then be dipped in a silver solution, making it light-sensitive. After this, all is rush and hurry, since exposure to the subject matter needs to be completed before the chemicals on the plate have had time to dry out. The wet collodion process waits for no man, so the corridors of the Hall are alive to the sound of scampering feet hurrying between laboratory and subject matter.

Although they must run with their wet plates, there is less urgency over the exposure time, which depends on a still subject and an adequacy of light. The measure of both of these constraints is tricky to judge as success, or otherwise is only apparent upon fixing and then not properly until a print has been produced. Mr Briggs experiments by using a cat to calculate whether conditions are light enough; he has a theory that one can gauge from the contraction of its pupils the quantity of available light. But the experimental animal, seated in a warm ray of sunlight, proves an unsuccessful portrait, since it takes fright and runs away, leaving only a ghost of itself on the plate, the blurred remainder of one of its lives.

Thus Mr Briggs and his charges gallop around the Hall looking for subjects to immortalise and are bewitched by the most mundane of compositions. The etching of ice upon a pane of glass, moss on roof tiles, the silk of a spider's web, or dust in the hollows of a monumental carving, all are recorded and rendered with such devastating finesse that they seem to open the eye afresh to the wonder of the ordinary. They have less success with human subjects. Stevens will persist in leaping up from her pose to look quickly beneath the camera hood to check on her appearance, only to be confounded with the sight of her just vacated chair. Miss Hart was attempted: she was seated in a shaft of sharp northern light and told to keep her eyes open. However, the tonal distortions that plague this antiquated technique made the finished portrait an unpleasing composition: the red of her cheeks and the purple of her nose being inaccurately translated as black. Photography may fail to flatter through faulty technique, inadequacy of materials or practitioner just as more traditional forms of portraiture, but with photography the subject cannot accuse the disinterested lens of malicious inaccuracy. So Miss Hart saw that she was incontrovertibly stouter, older and wartier (quite apart from blacker) than she had hoped herself to be.

The most successful image of a living being was one captured by ten-year-old George. He found Lucy sitting in the kitchen garden, plucking a chicken, and made a portrait of her, which in its broad and soft tonal effects and the ordinariness of subject mimicked a Rembrandt. He called it simply 'Working Girl'. Of course, since he had to still her fidgeting fingers for the length of the exposure, the composition was more suggestive of dreaming than of working. But he caught on her contemplative face a look of such unlikely dignity that one might almost have imagined fine sensibility there: the capacity to feel and suffer.

Despite his disingenuous rationale for George's study of photography being wholly self-interested Mr Briggs had unintentionally succeeded in lighting a spark in his inert pupil. And others, too, within the Hall were stoked up during that first incendiary season of the new tutor. For a fascination with photography took hold of the children and they persuaded Her Grace to buy them more up-to-date dry plate equipment, marvellous in its speed and efficiency. Photography and sex, then, were the pursuits that sped the summer days, many of the household dabbling in both – indeed, one seemed to feed upon the other, both occupations having in common the need for darkened seclusion and that exclusive concentration upon the object of interest exerted by photographer and lover alike.

Only the Duchess failed to catch. She contrived to ignore the general passion for photography, and never sat still long enough for any of her suitors to fix her in their sights. For during this time, like a princess in want of a prince, she was beset by appellant suitors from far and wide. Luckily for Her Grace, she had no ancient parent or foul fairy to set the impossible task that would secure the fair one's hand. She alone imposed the trials that these swains must undertake, ensuring that there never would be a chink through which some third son or clever tailor might slip to win his prize. She made the rules, she held the key, and she alone knew the answers to all the riddles. What chance, then, did her pursuers stand with the hind in control of the chase?

The Duchess of Fainhope knows that she will not have to parry these fortune-hunters for many years longer. Her own daughters, now seventeen and fourteen, must soon step into the ring themselves to be courted by suitable petitioners. She considers that someone may be 'bought' for Georgina, and that Euphemia will have to make shift to win her own match-made fortune. Perhaps then the eligible Duchess may relax her guard and graduate to the more interesting character role of mother-in-law.

Georgina, of course, has her own ideas about whom she will marry. This being the long summer of developing passions, she has become adept at wooing, with the well-composed composition and the carefully prepared plate. Her favourite subject is the object of her desire, Mr Briggs. Over and over she holds him captive – suspended upside-down in the viewfinder of her camera – so that his image may be exposed upon her cringing, bared heart. But the light and heat that come from him are so intense that instead of imprinting upon her they shrivel and blast. In her agony, she does not understand that this fierce love is her own, reflected back on her from his indifferent, dull hide. It is a damaging irradiation that she stands before in the effort to get a little warmth.

Apart from supplying herself to be 'still-life', Lucy is the sorcerer's apprentice who must help with the alchemy of photographic chemicals. She now exudes a top 'note' of ether, which bothers Mrs Beam. What bothers Lucy is the secret stench that she alone detects: of sticky-sour willow buds, which her own skin heats and releases from fumbled underclothes. Dr Oliver continues to seek her among the ashes and cinders, but it is not to sweep her away in his magic coach and four. The hasty journey they go on, when he can seek her out, is a short, rollicking ride, which tumbles her back into the hearth at its end and leaves bruises behind.

But it is the coupling of sex and photography in Mr Briggs and Miss Mantilla that makes that giddy season whirl. It was by degrees that Mr Briggs brought into focus the true nature of his interest in photography, and majestic women. And it was by degrees that Miss Mantilla allowed their photographic sessions to become more elaborate and clandestine. She has grown to have expectations of Mr Briggs just as he has singled her out, found her at last — his muse, his goddess, his nonpareil. So we find them at night, in the schoolroom, engaged in a little illicit photography, more advanced equipment allowing experimentation upon the human subject in a low light. She is dressed in a loose Greek style, with draped robe and bare feet. He is flitting round her, a little brown bee to her statuesque flower, adjusting her robe and tilting her chin to a more imperious angle.

'So queenly! Like one of the "angels" sold in the Roman marketplace. But perhaps the attitude ought more to be one of elevation — above the ordinary rabble, as it were.'

'Should I stand upon something to raise me up?' enquires Miss Mantilla, in a matter-of-fact voice. These sessions have become so familiar that she is quite accustomed to standing here, in the cold of evening, wearing almost nothing. The game requires it.

'Yes. I think so. And I should lower the tripod and crouch

down. Like this,' says he, pointing the camera lens up at the underside of her proudly jutting chin. 'Yes. Now we have the right angle of lofty condescension. I wonder . . . I wonder whether we should add some shackles . . . to emphasise your nobility?' he introduces cautiously. This is something new and he waits, without breathing, to see how she will react to this modification.

Miss Mantilla decides that she must plunge on, she must make this into grown-ups' play now. She holds out her arms for Mr Briggs to fasten slim chains, from his props basket, around them. The two stand in contemplation of each other. If he will not take the initiative then she must. 'Should I not disrobe to be more exactly like Mr Power's sculpture?'

The image that flashes upon his brain of looking up at that cool nude, raised upon her pedestal, serene in her degrading chains, makes him flush.

She sees the repressed excitement that courses through him and knows she has him. Imitating the modest, downward glance of the Greek slave in her pure white marble, she artlessly pushes down the robe from either shoulder with her shackled hands to reveal real naked breasts and then, with a wiggle of her hips, she causes it to slip to the floor entire, leaving her exposed. If that isn't giving it to him on a plate, she doesn't know what is. But from the corner of her downturned eye, the next movement of which she is aware is not the expected passionate lunge. Instead Pygmalion hurries away from the corporeal woman to duck under the cloak that envelops his camera and gaze at the blurred, inverted image of his perfect statue. His voice comes to her from beneath the protective carapace of the muffling cloth: 'Oh, that is very fine. A fine feeling of . . . artistic elevation.'

Miss Mantilla knows from experience the bitter truth that a man cannot resist vulnerability in a woman. 'You have me entirely helpless, what should I do now?' she says, in a pliant whisper.

Mr Briggs, who can wait no longer, finally opens the shutter and lets go. In the flash made by a small amount of magnesium powder being blown through a spirit flame, sex and photography come together. And the incandescent image of an undressed governess in a classical pose is fixed in an explosion of fire, smoke and ash ready for developing and printing. For a moment afterwards there is a subdued silence between them and then he asks, still behind the camera, 'Are you cold?'

'Cold as marble. Oh, warm me,' comes her appeal.

He approaches her, ritually raised up yet humiliated upon her dais; a commodity in the marketplace. She holds out her arms to him so that he may bury her shameful body in his pigeon chest, the contract between them struck at last. But she is startled as he falls passionately at her cold feet to kiss them, sighing, 'Oh, you make me feel so small!'

George has come to find Lucy as she folds the nursery linen away in a cupboard. He has printed a copy of his composition, 'Working Girl', for her.

'Is it me?'

'You moved. Look how blurry your hands are.'

'No one in my whole family ever had a portrait took before. Isn't it fine? Only I would have liked to be wearing a cleaner apron. And not had that chicken on my knee.' She takes the print and scrutinises it closely.

'It's not a portrait, Lucy,' says George. 'It's a photograph. The whole point is it shows you how you are, not how you want to be. That's why Mama and Georgina will never sit for one.'

'Oh, my! Just imagine if I was coloured in.'

She hands the photograph back to George, but he returns it to her. 'Here, you can colour yourself with my inks. Put rouge on your cheeks and decorate your apron with butterflies. You could make that chicken into a bunch of roses. You can make yourself as ladylike as you want.'

'Well I should like to do all those things,' says Lucy, 'but it doesn't feel right to. I'd reckon I was making myself out to be better than I am.'

'I'd say it was only surface colour and decoration that does the "bettering". Look at it the other way round. If I took a photograph of 'Phemia sitting on the step in your apron, don't you think she'd look just exactly the same as you?'

'Oh, I'm sure she never would. Her lovely hair and her nails . . .'

'That's what I mean – don't dress her hair and let her scrub a few floors and you two would be like sisters,' concludes George.

That evening Lucy distracts herself from the friction in her knees by thinking on the conundrum of the interchangeable lady and her maid: sisters under the skin. But the mental substitution, of that unquestioning right to live a life dignified by comfort and leisure for this sordid scramble after existence, is beyond her. In her present situation, the groaning doctor thrusting away at her from behind, there can surely be no comparison with what the young lady might have to expect from her future suitors.

As he efficiently rebuttons his trousers and chucks her under the chin, she thinks that she could more easily imagine herself as one of the patient horses in their nearby stalls, voiceless, waiting to be used, than as the young lady in the Hall. Dr Oliver hands her a large linen handkerchief as her reward and goes out, refreshed, into the yard to find his gig.

Since that night when she turned into a statue and Mr Briggs adored at her feet, Miss Mantilla has rather fallen out of love with photography. It begins to seem to her a silly and childish occupation. It served its purpose in bringing him close, but now? Now they are involved in a more adult game and one, she is distressed to realise, in which she has more experience than he. For it is she, not he, who knows how best to arrange assignations in her cramped little bedroom. She who is adept at wheedling and pleading, using that secret, potent language on him that was once used to coax and flatter her into forgetful compliance. And thus it is she who feels the urgency that overcomes prudence, who must take the masculine role – holding his hands and whispering words into his pale face as he sits chastely upon her single hard chair. 'You must know I have some influence with my mistress?'

'Even so, we could not exist upon a sole salary. You could not continue to be employed here as my wife.'

'So you may marry and yet I may not – one and one does not make two?' She smiles, trying to make of him an ally, a co-conspirator in their relationship rather than its dour chaperone.

'I hardly think that I may. I mean, I never expected to be able to afford to. I looked only for a comfortable place to live and enough to support my surviving parent,' says he, piously.

Eleven years ago, in this same room, another man had called her a flirt and a tease, had made it seem that she had used her arts to excite and overwhelm him. *He* had buffeted her on to her back on this same little bed, with the weight of his words, telling her how it was she who had woven this trap, sticky with her desirability. It was a trap that had only one release mechanism, and when he had used it, sure enough he had escaped, leaving her behind, soon bloated by that sin. Yet she didn't remember that she had said more than two words to him. She certainly had never looked him in the eye before that night he first wooed her. She had been surprised and flattered by his attention. Amazed that she could have worked such strong magic without ever having intended it. And it had been so lovely, so lovely to be loved by a man.

Then she had been conquered by the idea of romance – that fairy story spun to please all little girls. She yielded because he said he loved her and she had learnt, at her mother's knee, that the love of a man is woman's ultimate fulfilment. And after she had yielded, then, of course, she had loved him – hadn't that act bound them together for ever? Now she was more pragmatic. A man was still what was required but not to fulfil some sentimental dream: she needed a man to save her from being a spinster servant with limited prospects of supporting herself into her old age. She needed a man to escape her financial bondage to the Duchess.

To catch this one, and make sure he remained caught, she must learn to use words and looks in earnest. And she has studied which words will work their amorous trick on the curious little man. She knows just which wriggling morsels to place before him, to lead the near-sighted chicken, unwary, into the pen so that the sneck may drop to trap him.

'Oh, Edgar, you must know how this makes me feel. Like a captive queen, I am proud and tall. The unworthy may grovel at my feet and yet I cannot be free.'

'Let me look at you, Maria. Let me look up at you.' Eagerly he gobbles the bait she scatters before him. 'I must stoop before your humbled nobility.'

She has his attention – the singular absorption that she saw in her first lover she now sees in him. But this time she won't submit before the fierce intensity of masculine need: she must harness and use it. It makes her feel powerful, like a maiden who leads the drooling ox by its nose, its head lowered, its red eyes rolled up helpless in their sockets.

'Kneel, then,' she says simply. And he does so, blushing fervently. They remain like this for some seconds, the governess standing imperiously over his crouched back. Now she has him, baffled, subjugated, but can she unremember her femininity sufficiently to seize the moment and act?

First she raises him to his feet, although he keeps his knees slightly bent, with the words, 'I may be noble but I may also stoop to conquer.' Keeping hold of his hands, she dips her knees now so that she may look up into his face. 'Yes, I would stoop to fulfil any woman's, any wife's natural duty to her husband.' She takes his awkward arms and tries to place them round her, moulding herself to him. 'Edgar, I am only a weak woman and you are a man. It is I who must give way to you.' She raises her abashed eyes to him and tries again to bury her face in his chest. This manoeuvre requires her to sink even lower, causing their knees to knock against each other uncomfortably, each competing to be the smaller and more yielding before the other.

Perhaps it is the ridiculousness of their toppling stance that brings Mr Briggs to his senses, perhaps the realisation that Miss

Mantilla is only a mortal woman, and not an inviolate queen, that scares him. 'Maria. Miss Mantilla, you must know that I would never – never! You must trust my decency as a Christian and a gentleman.'

At the last moment the chicken lifts its head, sees that it has been drawn to the pen and runs, squawking. She tries one desperate last ploy: 'Edgar, are not we outside the common morality? Am I not raised above it?'

But he has leapt to his freedom and the door. 'Miss Mantilla, I, we, cannot afford to be.'

And he is flown, leaving our failed seductress to weep.

The London Poor

Rather than despair of using Miss Mantilla and her uncertain suitor to illustrate what it is to love, we would do better to examine the *amour* of another, better-matched couple. For the union of Mr and Mrs Albert Flynn is one as securely founded upon love as it is tempered by a shared interest: their mission among the rookeries and stews of London. This worthy work is a vocation that they have been engaged upon all their married life; they are wedded to it as much as to each other.

Mrs Flynn, a pale undernourished woman, appears to need support from her robust and vital husband. But it is really she who stands firm as an iron rod, anchoring them both against the winds of despair and doubt that might, nightly, shake their resolve. For Mrs Flynn knows of what she preaches. She grew up in a godless household: her father drank and squandered, and her mother drank and aided him, until parents, children and some items of salvaged bedroom furniture found themselves standing together on the street with nowhere to go and no one to turn to.

Mrs Albert Flynn, who was then only li'le Carrie, walked away from the stranded bed and its hopeless occupants into a struggling, barely respectable life using her wits and her needle to stay safe in a world that found her chastity and her ambition for self-improvement a challenge and an affront. She knew herself in dire need of being 'saved' and was indeed 'saved' by several competing religious and philanthropic organisations until she was gathered in at last by the Fisher Folk and by A. Flynn Esq., her Albert.

How Albert came to be at that fateful East End meeting was perhaps an example of divine intervention. He admired a young lady tambourine player, 'an alleluia lass', and would devote his half Saturday to gazing at his 'happy Eliza' and to handing out texts. But once he set eyes on Carrie, saved again and full of grace, that other lady could rattle and strum ever after unappreciated. Albert was attracted at first to Carrie's luminous spirituality, which seemed, to him, to make her peaked little face give off an ardent, greenish tinge. Then he grew to admire her pale nape and button boots. Next he noticed her narrow shape and unremarkable brow, and so, by degrees, he progressed in his appreciation until he finally looked her full in the face, saw that she had two eyes, a mouth and nose and realised he loved her.

It was only, naturally, after they married that Albert delighted to discover the passionate nature of his new bride. Her passion matched his and their marriage bed became a bower of continual carnal delight. He thanked God for the sanctity of marriage and learnt to offer up every pleasure his inventive wife could contrive as she explored her way over and around him, testing and tasting as she went. Albert was so utterly satisfied with Carrie that he never doubted her devotion to the cause. Because Carrie loved the Work, then out of love of Carrie, so would he.

This small, wan woman, ever meek, drew strength like lifeblood from the Work. She fattened on the needy, inflated herself with the dying promises of the hopeless. Two characteristics had grown to giant proportions within her: her belief in her humility and in her superior goodness. Whereas Albert sometimes doubted the calling and often despaired in the Work, Carrie, ever fortified and warmed by these two inner convictions, was strong enough for both of them. She drank at the wellspring of 'do-gooding' and he drank from her. Well coupled indeed, this 'converted Jane' and her 'ink spiller'.

Their lives as lodgers in the household of Mr Mantilla continued following the same pattern: each morning he went to his work and each night he followed her to hers. And every Sunday night, and whenever else they could contrive it, they made enough use of their bed to more than justify the rental his daughters charged for it.

As you might have divined, the amatory life of Mr Briggs and Miss Mantilla does not proceed as happily, their forays into the plastic arts having stopped abruptly after that last assignation in Miss Mantilla's room. Since then they have been formally polite with each other. However, the governess has grown to suspect that Mr Briggs's particular interest in reproducing classic poses has not withered on the vine as has his interest in the finer details of the wet-plate technique. One evening she surprises him in the darkroom, where he is processing prints. Her entry causes him some confusion: he drops behind him in the sink the negative image he was processing and turns to face her.

'Ah, another of me as "defiled Christian",' she says, casually picking up the negative image.

'Miss Mantilla! You must know more of photographic technique than to enter the darkroom when the door is closed.'

'I do apologise. But I think no harm has been done.' She holds out the negative plate to him, then takes it back, looking again, more closely. 'But this is not of me, is it?' Holding it closer she studies the shadowed face of the model. 'I thought that I was your ideal subject, Edgar. Your *non plus ultra.*'

'My interest does not depend on any particular model. It may as well be her as you – it is the lighting effects and composition that create the mood I look for.'

'And she that sits to you understands this artistic detachment, does she?'

'I always behave towards her with complete propriety, Miss Mantilla. She inspires noble thoughts in me and nothing more.'

'Oh, I can believe that! But her mother may not be so complacent about her daughter sitting half naked to her servant.'

He flinches at that last word and stands dumb as Miss Mantilla paces about the darkroom still holding the negative image of Georgina upon her pedestal.

'I think I have become something more than a servant in this household,' he says.

'Do you?' She turns on him, alert to the alteration in him. 'The Greek slave has ambitions, does he?'

Mr Briggs's response is a smirk, which tells her more than he had intended.

'I knew it! Georgina is damaged goods so she just might be within your scope. Ah, Edgar, you could have had me, I was willing . . .'

'I think that there never was an understanding, nor yet a formal connection between us, Miss Mantilla,' he replies stiffly.

'No. I have no claim over you, have I? Not even that of a proper mistress − if that ever counted for anything.'

Mr Briggs says nothing but continues to rearrange bottles of chemicals in the darkroom. Miss Mantilla, leaning against the wall, slowly slides down it until she is sitting on the floor, her knees up, face in her hands. She begins to sob, not for that silly, vain little man but for herself. For needy Maria, who so wanted love, and romance, and a life lived happily ever after, but couldn't even catch this sapless gelding.

The next morning, Miss Mantilla observes Georgina with preternatural attentiveness. A girl who looks like a 'fury' in the morning isn't to be trusted. 'Please go to your room and attend to your hair, Georgina. And properly this time,' she dismisses her, briefly enjoying the tiny consolation of being licensed openly to belittle her rival, who flounces from the room. After this she measures the girl's every sigh and gesture against her own heavy heart to gauge the weight of pain and longing that love might have loaded there. The incontrovertible evidence that her charge now looks at her stolen suitor and he never at her confirms that there is something to uncover. For in her experience, while a man will ogle a woman before he has possessed her only to ignore her once the deed's done, a woman will do the opposite: first coy, then betraying herself with jealous eyes. But she is still dubious that the eunuch can have been debauching in the seraglio.

When one evening she suspects that the girl has gone to him, she pursues them both, looking from room to room. Passing down a corridor she detects a sound that drums out a rhythm as familiar as the pulse of her own heart. At first she cannot work out why this muffled beat should make the hair on the back of her neck stand and cause her to hold her breath so that she may listen to it more closely. Then she knows it – the gathering rhythm of that old, old dance that is in all of us. He led her in it but, deep in her bones, she had known it already – could keep up with him, moving with him faster and faster, fluid and adept.

So he *has* learnt to love live flesh, has he? She will interrupt their jig. Miss Mantilla slams open the door to the linen cupboard to discover Dr Oliver leant over Lucy, looking directly into her face. Neither says a word. He does not stop but winks salaciously at her, tapping his finger to his nose to signal complicity. She closes the door on the scene, as though upon a too-bright memory, and scurries away.

Lucy stands before the governess. This is an interview that Miss Mantilla has most vividly imagined herself receiving rather than giving. 'Shameful behaviour. You cannot expect any kind of a character.'

'Yes, 'm,' says Lucy, not listening to the spoken words – only hearing her own inner voice repeating: 'What shall I do, what shall I do?'

As though she too has heard, Miss Mantilla answers, 'You may pack your belongings and go immediately.'

'Oh, madam, where shall I go?'

'You have parents, I suppose?'

'Mother has so many of us. She wouldn't take me in, and a baby.'

The old familiar story – the inevitability of it all fatigues Miss Mantilla. 'Stupid girl. Do you never learn?'

'I didn't know, 'm,' says Lucy, 'until it was too late. Couldn't I just stay on and send it away, as you did?'

Miss Mantilla has so thoroughly absolved herself she had forgotten that the girl had been a witness to the bloody events of that night. Thank God, her own sin is dead, a dead bundle in which she had wrapped up all the guilt and pain to be simply disposed of. No fuss and no consequences – apart from what this stupid girl may choose to blurt.

'How dare you? Wicked, wicked, wicked!' She slaps Lucy on the face at each repetition. 'You must go away from here.'

Lucy stumbles from the room, 'What shall I do, what shall I do, what shall I do?' throbbing through her head.

Miss Mantilla follows behind and, turning her by the shoulder, hands her some coins, saying, 'Take this and go far away.'

Between them, Dr Oliver and Lucy have stoked up hot memories in Miss Mantilla – she feels naked. No, worse, she feels flayed. The dull complacency she had grown used to, while Lucy remained in the Hall, turns to pins and needles of vulnerability now that she is gone. For Dr Oliver remains, and that conspiratorial wink surely anticipates exposure. There had existed a kind of harmony while the three who knew had remained in orbit around the strong magnetic pull of the Duchess – each balancing the others. But Dr Oliver's influence has waxed as Lucy's waned and the safety in symmetry is gone. He must be got rid of. Now is the time for the Duchess to burn him up.

Her mistress is hardly surprised by Miss Mantilla's call to action. She has been waiting, waiting for this moment. He has served his purpose as their joint enemy, but if this picking insect thinks he may feed on her blood he will find it too full of bile for his stomach. While her governess frets over how a scandal is to be avoided she knows that, given a little encouragement, Dr Oliver's own ambition will do for him.

The only one to notice Lucy's departure is George. He watches her trailing up the drive from a high-up window, already too far away to hear his shout: 'Don't leave me here, alone!'

As she follows the country lanes that lead to the railway station she sees Dr Oliver approaching on horseback and hides in a hole in the hedgerow. Thirteen years have now elapsed between Miss Mantilla's departure and this second. The third woman will not have so long to wait before she, too, sets out upon that same path to meet her fate.

That very evening Mr Briggs and Lady Georgina are standing in front of Her Grace, the Duchess, he in a semi-permanent stoop of obeisance, she writhing in defiance. He has been hurried, untimely, into this difficult interview by the dangerous suspicions of his last, deposed, paragon.

'Mr Briggs, what you call love, I must call betrayal,' says Her Grace.

He knows that this must be the moment when all is lost or won. He feels as though he is speaking for his very life. 'Your Grace, my regard for Lady Georgina is sincere and disinterested. And, I humbly suggest, mutual—'

'Do you really believe that schoolmasters win noblewomen – even frosty-faced ones? Mr Briggs, this is life, *not* a romance.'

'We would live very quietly, far away . . .'

'We only want to be together, Mama,' interjects Georgina, trying to stiffen the resolve of her cringing lover.

'My dear, you may live as noisily as you will, but not under my roof, and not on your dowry.' She turns to bendy Briggs and says, 'Is your resolve as firm to take her on now?'

Georgina ventures, hardly believing that they may yet escape without being eaten alive, 'So, we may be married – but we are to go away somewhere and ask for nothing from you?'

'Georgina, if it pleases you to be Mrs Briggs and live in a back-street I will not prevent the match. But I think you were not raised for "love in a hut, with water and a crust", and I think you may find that my conditions may prove to be of material interest to your intended husband. May they not, Mr Briggs? I think he knows more of what a fixed income entails than do you.'

Georgina looks on him and he seems to sink even further under the weight of the Duchess's contempt. She sees that he has snapped and blunders on, in the misapprehension that they have found an escape route: 'Edgar, dear, we may be happy! We must live simply but we shall be forever together.'

'That is settled, then. Mr Briggs, you are, of course, dismissed from your post. I will give you your character as a wedding gift. Do not expect more. Georgina, it only remains for you to pack what you can carry. You may take the rubies bequeathed by your grandmother. They will find you a start in a suburb,' smiles the Duchess. She is so sure of him that she doesn't even pause to read the look of perturbation on his face. The skill with words he so needed in bringing the mother round must now be turned upon the happy, glowing daughter.

'You never loved me!' Georgina calls at her mother's departing back. 'Even my name was on loan, waiting until a son came to claim it. He's the only one who matters to you! If you don't need me, then I don't need you any more.'

He tries to shush her but she turns her triumphant face to his, saying, 'We have each other and that's all we need. Edgar, dearest, you have rescued me from the tyrant who held me in chains!'

He stands unhappily upon one leg and then the other. Does she not realise that these chains were golden ones and without them she is but a commoner, and a short, ugly one at that?

The Third Departure

Next morning Miss Hart has joined Mrs Beam in the kitchen to await the upstairs maid's return with dirty crockery and slops from breakfast as well as fresh scandal with which to feed their conversation. Mrs Beam favours her with a conspiratorial smirk, hungry for the latest, which is quick in coming.

'Well, 'e was missed at breakfast,' Miss Hart reports. She exchanges a meaningful look with the cook.

'So that makes it certain sure! I had it from Dora Stevens – she saw him skedaddle it last night. Looked like a dying duck in a thunderstorm. How did our Miss Dago take it?' says the cook, anxious to make the most of any other leftovers yet to be had.

'Cool as you like. It's our Lady Georgina as won't be consoled,' replies the housekeeper, 'crying in 'er room, and Mantilla requests, if you please, that she is to 'ave all 'er meals sent for the present.'

'My oath!' is Mrs Beam's concise reply to this fresh imposition.

Unfortunately for the weird sisters of the kitchen, the only source of reliable intelligence from above stairs is Miss Mantilla, and she is a freelance spy in this household. She herself carries the luncheon tray to Georgina in her bedroom. When her knock goes unanswered she enters the room to find all in confusion and disarray. The girl obviously has no idea how to pack for a journey. It looks as though she has simply thrown all her worldly possessions into the air to let them land where they would about the room. 'What are you doing?' she asks tartly.

The girl picks up two odd shoes and, holding them to her like stiff little dolls, wanders around the room. A sudden chill thought strikes Miss Mantilla: surely this scene of haste and high drama signifies an elopement. 'Where are you going?'

'I don't know – I must just leave. I can't bear to stay here any longer.'

'But you don't go to *him*, do you, Georgina?'

Georgina is stopped in her pointless pacing by the ludicrous idea that that shallow play-*amour* could be misconstrued as something as grown-up and dangerous as real carnal desire. 'Do you really think he left a forwarding address?' is her forlorn reply.

Miss Mantilla almost laughs with relief at the anti-romantic notion of forwarding addresses. Now she sees that the scene before her is not one of passion and self-sacrifice, just this silly miss in a pet, throwing her clothes around. That disappointing cold fish had given them both the slip.

'Oh, Miss Mantilla, I can't remain here.'

'Of course not, of course not. Poor girl, never mind,' she says, with considerably more sympathy now that she knows this hot blood is stoked by nothing more than shame. Miss Mantilla knows more about real shame and, apparently, more about real fleshy passion than this hot-house bud could ever guess at. High-bred and delicate, a forced, speckled bloom yearning upon the still indoor air without even a scent of her own to draw the idle bees. Yes, it would do to remove the trusses and supports that display the flower. Perhaps then Lady Georgina would discover that she could hold up her own head in the turbulent breezes of the outside world.

'Maybe your mama will open the London house for you. She really might consider launching you,' muses Miss Mantilla.

'You know I could not bear it! I want to be nobody, nothing – no family, no name. Just private and alone somewhere.'

'Of course, the Season would not be the place. But, my dear, I can really think of no way that a young lady may go off by herself unprotected.'

'I will not have a chaperone!' She flings the shoe babies from her on to the bed.

'Where, then? Are there respectable houses where you may board without comment? I simply don't know. Perhaps seaside lodgings that cater for lady invalids?'

'I don't want to convalesce. I want to escape!' shouts the flower, and it strikes Miss Mantilla, yet again, how utterly alien she is. She longs to be cast out, made anonymous and friendless. These things seem like comfort and balm to her. And money will ensure that she can never understand what banishment might mean to the truly friendless and alone. Ah, the luxury of running away to sulk.

'Ungrateful girl! I really don't know what you want!' she says, in exasperation.

Georgina drags the old trunk kept in the nursery into the middle of her rug and begins to sling into it necessities for her flight. Miss Mantilla watches as the ivory hairbrushes, a beaded slipper and a china shepherdess hit the bottom of the trunk. Lining the bottom is a layer of yellowed newspaper, thick enough to save the shepherdess from losing her head as she lands. Miss Mantilla sees a vivid tableau of slack Aurora uncovering the milk-jug in the pantry in her own drab kitchen at home. The evocative smell of sour milk is once again strong in her nostrils.

'Home, you can come home,' she says, without meaning to, and then, 'I know a house. I can vouch for the respectability of the family, and it is ideally anonymous and unremarkable. Somewhere to hide and regain your strength.'

The idea of that dingy, south London bolt-hole having been introduced, Georgina constructs in her imagination a sanctum, a hermitage, a temple of peace and untrammelled simplicity. Miss Mantilla is now anxious that the trainee nun's mama should approve her going to these new orders.

~∽~

'I would not give her my father's address before I had informed you of her proposal,' says Miss Mantilla.

'Then let her have it,' is the short reply.

Miss Mantilla feels herself impelled to make more of a meal of this interview, which, after all, concerns the future happiness of Her Grace's oldest child. 'I guess it will prove a temporary restorative.' She adds coaxingly, 'My sisters are sensible, educated girls . . .'

'If she chooses to go then she must go for ever.'

With a start Miss Mantilla looks into her mistress's eyes.

'Not "cut off without a shilling", Maria, I am not that harsh. She shall have her settlement, but there shall be no way back once she has made her choice.'

'Shall I send for her?' says Miss Mantilla, shock evident in her now downturned glance.

'To have firm charge of destiny, mothers must be hard, must we not, Maria?' answers the Duchess. 'As you will see, a sacrifice is called for to secure the future, and this time I will be the one to make it. Please, send her to me.'

That evening Dr Oliver's new carriage crosses paths with the Hall's brake, which has blinds down and is going fourteen to the dozen towards the London road. He is still wondering at the significance of this departure as he is shown into his most constant patient's bedroom. Here he finds his patroness sitting among the turmoil of Lady Georgina's hasty exodus. Before it can be suppressed, a smile of understanding opens his pensive features. Evidently a fox has come plundering again among these aristocratic chickens. He greets the Duchess of Fainhope with confident familiarity, sure of the situation and ready to turn this privy knowledge to his advantage.

'I was expecting Lady Georgina. Is she gone from home?' he insinuates, smooth as a snake.

'You might have passed her on the road. As you see, she left in haste.'

'My professional services are not required, then?' He half glances behind him as though to reassure himself of the exit. He begins to sniff a baited trap: what can these revelations signify?

'The only complaint my daughter suffers, at present, is that of a damaged heart.' Peremptorily the Duchess seizes for herself the character of the waiting and watching reptile, hypnotising with her level gaze and forcing him into the role of a small, foolish creature awaiting the strike of fangs.

'She perhaps has business in London?' he ventures warily, all swagger and puff gone.

'To tell the truth, since her lover deserted her she has run away there.'

'Not eloped, then?' He cannot stop himself blurting out his initial assumption, since the Duchess seems so determined to have all out in the open.

'No. The "lover" was more an invention on her part than any real man, but that is what the servants will be given to believe.'

'You would let the servants scandalise over your daughter? To what purpose?'

'I have a purpose, Dr Oliver, you could say I am ruthless in pursuit of it. It is self-preservation: a natural drive that, I believe, freezes out even mother-love.'

Dr Oliver is both fascinated and appalled. He should know that the only time the weak are indulged with such candour by the strong is just prior to their elaborately plotted elimination.

'The servants will also be let know that it is you who are her seducer,' she continues.

'Me? You would defame your own daughter to ruin me?'

'You? You have no idea what I would not do. She has served her part and you are an irritant I would be rid of. I live on to play the game.'

So the Duchess struck and the doctor knew he was done for. A clever and intricate trap she had sprung on him. And, by the very ruthlessness of the stratagem she employed to protect that secret, he sees that his exploratory digging and delving had threatened to uncover something really tremendous. Now, a Tantalus, he will remain forever thirsty, forever hungry to satisfy himself with the buried secret of the governess's baby.

The squashing of this man is little more than a matter of expedience to the Duchess. Ever ruthless in seizing the upper hand, it is nothing to her to cut him loose. But she is made uneasy by that other consequence of expelling him from the little circle of witnesses, for his departure might signal the unravelling of the strategic alliance that has secured her secret until now. Tied to her by bonds of mutual ambition, hatred and fear, doctor and governess have been unable to act independently. But to cut that knot will unhobble governess from doctor and perhaps set Miss Mantilla free to look full into her own face and find there the reflection of a well-matched opponent.

Book Two

Of the Well of Life to Taste

If Georgina's exit from her mother's house left confusion behind, it caused even greater chaos in the house to which she was bound. Here you may find her sitting among her trunks and cases in the parlour as Aurora and Teresa rush about upstairs tipping the contents of one room into another in an effort to redistribute the growing residential population of Alonso's narrow home. They have had to remove themselves from their own shared bedroom to make way for this latest incomer. Now they are improvising beds in their attic studio and the cat, not to mention Bessie, has been put in a hissing temper by all this nomadic wandering.

Teresa, with the workmanlike headpiece wrapped round her hair, fights the heavy straw mattress into submission then sits upon its vanquished body to study her broken fingernails.

'This is too much, isn't it, 'Resa?' whispers her sister. 'Do you think she's to be a paying guest, or just guest? I think we really must know.'

'Paying. I think she must be paying, mustn't she?' says Teresa, slapping at the lumps in her mattress, which seems to have some spirit left in it yet.

'All this is going to be the death of Papa,' says Aurora, dropping on to the fubsy little sofa she annexed from the parlour to make her own bed.

'And what must the Flynns think? Do you suppose we might lose them?'

Aurora reaches over and pulls off Teresa's tea-towel to flap it ineffectually in front of her glowing face. 'Ah, the Flynns. Well, I think the dear Flynns will be quite fascinated with our new PG – is she ruined, fallen or just misused? Whichever, she must be deliciously ripe for salvation. It's my opinion that the blackened soul of our lady visitor will attract the Flynns like flies to a dead dog.'

'Aurora Mantilla! Mrs Flynn is in the house!'

'Such a tasty morsel and conveniently installed here for them to experiment upon. She will be their homework,' continues brazen Aurora.

'Well, if the Flynns don't leave us, I'm sure Bessie will. I've never seen her look so black.'

'She's just jealous that Carrie'll devote herself to the purifying of this new sepulchre.'

'Aurora, *you* are the wickedest person I know,' laughs Teresa.

'Just the rudest, dear,' replies her sister, throwing a paint-stiffened brush at her sister.

That evening the whited sepulchre is seated at the head of the table, a saviour at either hand. Albert and Carrie, as Aurora predicted, are delighted with the new inmate. Bessie has been bribed to stay on and distribute the dish of savoury rice, which has been contrived from the heel of the strong cheese and some leftover mutton broth, and must be made to stretch round the now overcrowded dining-table. Mrs Evans has deserted for next door.

Albert, as the only man present, has the floor; he is addressing the silent, pocky Georgina, while Carrie looks on adoringly and presses his foot under the table with her own.

'Our "Skipper", as we call him, bids his "Fisher Folk"—'

'As we call ourselves,' interjects Carrie, sliding her foot a little up his ankle.

Albert smiles at her and nods, perhaps in equal approval of her devout prompting above the tablecloth and covert stimulation below it. 'Our Skipper enjoins us, his Fisher Folk, to cast nets into the very sewers of human depravity to bring in our catch for the Lord.'

'It is the lowest of the low that we are bidden to raise up. The worse the sinner, the bigger the prize, as our Skipper says.' Carrie smiles upon the new occupant.

'You must be getting only mud worms and eels in then.' Teresa passes off the glibness of her remark by smilingly handing round the bread as she makes it.

Aurora, though, picks up her sister's tone and continues, 'And is there much filleting and gutting required when you empty your nets?'

Teresa bites down hard on her bread to gag her rising guffaw, and Carrie's exploring foot finds the crook of Albert's knee. Albert returns to his theme. 'To continue with your analogy, when the mud of sin clings thickly to our "catch" a great deal of spiritual scrubbing and cleansing is necessary.'

As Albert's discreet hand finds her little foot, Carrie almost shouts out, 'Oh, the triumph! The glory in one such, who has been thus well shriven! So sweet and fresh.'

'I do like a nice fresh sole,' says Aurora to her sister.

'Particularly with a little slice of lemon,' replies Teresa, who is obliged to jump up and run, red-faced and crying with suppressed mirth, from the room to the concern of the little dinner party.

'Is assistance required?' asks Albert, his thumb caught briefly inside Carrie's slipper, in the cleft of her big toe.

'Oh, no! She only chokes upon a bone,' is Aurora's deft reply. The three other occupants of the table look into their plates of over-boiled rice and there is a little silence, which Aurora breaks by turning to Georgina with the rhetorical remark, 'Lady

Georgina, what do you think of the splendid work of our fine Mr and Mrs Flynn?'

'I think that I should very much like to see for myself. I have had very little exposure to the world at all, let alone the world these people inhabit,' she replies, startling them all.

'It is perhaps not a world for a young lady such as yourself, Lady Georgina. It is another England, a dark and heathen land that we seek out,' says Albert Flynn, in a theatrical voice full of prurient relish. He raises his thumb, discreetly, to his nose and sniffs the savour of Carrie's foot there.

'But "another England" that you find on your very doorstep, is it not?'

'Let us say not quite on *our* doorstep!' says Aurora, jumping up to ring for Bessie to clear the plates. She has the unpleasant sensation of having found herself, the quick and clever one, somehow on the outside looking in on an exchange, spoken and unspoken, that is moving too fast for her.

'You would be surprised quite what foul nocturnal trades are conducted within a yard of your front door,' returns Carrie.

Aurora notices that this conversation has lit the pale, damaged face of the hot-house flower with a blush. The three lean forwards over the table as Teresa re-enters the room, having evidently splashed cold water on her face leaving dark spots on her costume.

'What do you say, Albert? Shall she come?' asks Carrie.

'I truly feel called upon to go with you and open myself up to life as it is lived,' says Georgina, catching at her sponsor's hand.

'You would be a welcome addition to our missionary work among the rookeries of that hidden London, I'm sure,' continues Albert.

'This very night, then!' says eager Georgina.

Teresa, who has been barely listening, looks quickly at Aurora in alarm. 'Oh, I don't know. We were charged by our sister to protect you, Miss Georgina – I mean, Lady Georgina. I don't think your mama would forgive us if we allowed you to roam the streets at night with strangers. It cannot be respectable behaviour for a lady. Aurora, support me in this . . .'

But Georgina's reply comes the quicker: 'Do you suggest that Mrs Flynn's conduct is not respectable, then?'

Whatever tart reply Aurora had readied remains unsaid and Teresa, losing her nerve, blusters, 'Indeed, no! But she is a married woman and has her husband to protect her.'

'Then I will have the benefit of both Mr and Mrs Flynn as guides and chaperones. I always wear my veil when I go out so there is no danger that I will be recognised. I think I have outgrown the need for governesses. Let my true education start.'

That night, Aurora on her sofa and Teresa on her crackling straw pallet, the sisters whisper.

'*Governesses!* She might as well just join *old* with *spinsters* and be done.' Aurora is buzzing with indignation.

'We've only ourselves to blame. We should have been stronger. Do you think we should have? Will Maria be angry with us, do you suppose?'

'She's certainly a slippery article. Swam straight into their waiting net and not a thing we could do.'

'Well, I shall say we only agreed to provide bed and board. And at extremely short notice – or no notice at all, really—'

'Teresa, please do shut up. Maria isn't in charge of little spotted miss any longer. Or of us.'

'I just worry that those two are going to gobble her up. Poor little girl.'

'"Poor little girl", my eye. It's those two should be watching out. She can't have been exposed to Maria since infancy and learnt nothing.'

'Just as I say, there's no speaking to her. Is there, Aurora?'

Perhaps the weight of responsibility might not have pressed so heavily had they known how few home thoughts flew after Georgina. If anything, Her Grace, the Duchess, regretted the absconding schoolmaster more. He had caused the greater inconvenience by leaving the boy uneducated and, worse, unoccupied. She could not contemplate the risks of introducing a new tutor into her pristine kingdom, but to send George down off her mountain and into the everyday world of school and other boys' society might be even more dangerous. How, then, was the boy to be kept safely busy but also isolated from the contagion of new ideas and expectations?

She takes George on a visit to his uncle Harpur, whose own son, Harry, is just returned from school and from other boys' improving companionship. The influence these have had upon him is quickly seen, and heard, as the two sons walk behind their parents along Lord John's new fern gully.

'George, good old chap. Here am I, fast as you find me. I mean to say, I'm at a low watermark at present – you couldn't help me out, could you?' whispers Harry. There being no ready offer of relief, he continues, 'You know how it is: I'm dusty, I'm completely gritty, down to my last penny. D'you see?'

'Oh, you mean money. I haven't any money of my own, Harry. I'm sorry.'

'Not that you won't have more than you know what to do with when the dog's lady, up front, leaves go,' says Harry, gesturing towards the Duchess. 'I wish I could change places. You know, vicie-versie.'

'I will swap. I'd much rather be you than me.'

'You wouldn't like it,' says Harry, looking at his father.

'I'd really like to be anyone else but me. I'd rather be a horse,' says George.

'Bob it!' says Harry, giving George a friendly box on the ear. 'Horses can't be heirs. I say, *horses can't be hares*, d'you get it?'

Her Grace notices, with distaste, the acid-yellow waistcoat that her nephew has affected and the way he converses with George, out of the corner of his mouth, as though placing a bet. '. . . I can't think what is to become of him.'

'That young man's future could be said to be secured,' ventures Harpur, with a rueful smile. 'The same cannot, unfortunately, be said for my lad. I had hoped he would become somebody but . . .'

'But for George.'

'Not at all. I meant I had hoped he would go to the university and find himself a liberal profession.'

They pause and glance behind them to see the two scions of their house rolling in the dirt play-fighting.

'Really! That school has made him little better than a butcher's boy.'

'A butcher's boy with a taste for silk waistcoats,' amends the Duchess.

'Quite. But he is not the one who must be raised to fit the rank of duke,' replies her brother-in-law, testily.

'Still, lucky George must be civilised somehow and I have lost patience with schoolmasters and their coquetting.'

Lord John gives a sly little laugh. 'There was a time when I would not have said the same of schoolmistresses and theirs.'

The Duchess of Fainhope betrays nothing of her surprise at this casual remark, though he might have felt it quickening her step had not the memory of that old, delightful conquest made his own stride down the earthy path the more sprightly.

'But why not send him to us? The two lads could be raised together here, in their own country under a father's masculine influence.'

'Of what would this "father's influence" consist?' says the Duchess, her steps chasing to mark time with her running thoughts.

'Healthy outdoor exercise would be the ticket: swimming the lake in winter, practising with Indian clubs, boxing with the groom . . .' Lord John replies, inspiration exhausted.

'And these alone may cure pernicious character traits?'

'I don't say only these. There'd be riding and shooting – I could see to that – or escorting the ladies . . . that sort of thing,' he replies, beginning to pant.

'Raised like brothers?' she says.

'Yes, just like brothers,' he reassures her. And they stop so that he may subdue his noisy breath and she her sardonic laugh.

'A well-rounded education for a young, country gentleman to be had just the other side of the park. I do agree,' she says, resuming his arm as they walk again. 'And one with no room for books at all! But when taking them shooting you must take care not to shoot yourself in the foot. Again.'

'Why, I'm sure I never did. But you're quite right, perhaps the shooting should be left to the gamekeeper,' comes the genial reply. This time there is no mistaking her hearty guffaw.

'You're a lucky piece, don't you know, George? No pa to stand in your way and the expectations. My, the expectations.'

'I *have* got a mother, though,' says George, as though this should qualify him for sympathy from badly-done-by Harry.

In Darkest England

London, waxing old and vast at the century's end, has drawn Lucy to it, a great compost heap of teeming bodies that generates its own sour warmth and bustle. But Lucy gets no comfort and no companionship buried in this thriving, striving nest. What she took for busyness she finds to be struggle and toil. Where she looks for the kindness of strangers she finds indifference or duplicity. The population, which feeds upon this rich, reeking town, seems to her to be divided into only two sorts of people, predators and their prey. The predation may be conducted at the highest or the lowest levels, the rape of whole continents or the theft of a beggar-child's supper. For class, education, fortune do not signify in the hasty assimilation and redistribution of the lucre, which pours in, smoking, from all corners of the globe only that the appropriation practised by the lions and the tigers is sanctioned and dignified by the name of commerce, whereas among the scavenging rats and dogs below them it is just plain theft. And below even these, drawn by the heat that wealth generates, exists the lowest category of all: the fleas, lice and other bloodsuckers that must feed where they may.

Lucy is not made to stalk with the predators, and as a species of prey she is shunned even by her fellow unfortunates as worthless to the point of parody – what, ruined and penniless and deserted?

My stars! But while there is a limited living to be had off her by opportunistic feeders she has value and is offered token protection and friendship, as well as not a few pocket-handkerchiefs. For she is soon made to learn that she has something of her own to sell. As 'fresh greens' and while her pregnancy remains not much evident, Lucy is marketable, if perishable, goods in the buying and selling game of live flesh. Having left domestic work, and the ranks of the county's greatest employer of female labour, Lucy is thus embarked upon service in its second: harlotry. But she is not the only amateur whore in town – generally known by the convenient sobriquet of 'omnibus' on the understanding that there will always be one along in a minute or two to take on boarders. And before many weeks the kid in her basket is so apparent that the concerned woman who would be her 'landlady' in a dressing-house, protection, lodging and clothes for a fee, and the friendly man who would be her Cupid with a cosh, again for a fee, and all the benevolent men who would be her dance partner in a four-legged frolic have moved on to feast elsewhere.

Now, like a little toiling beetle with no purpose other than forward motion, we may spy her as she goes down narrow brick-walled canyons and cobbled gullies, the smell of spices and reeking Thames mud in her nose. At her feet is the stew made from wet ashes, animal dung and night soil, and by her side, almost close enough to touch, within these blank hulks of warehouses, is stored up the wealth and tribute of nations.

She finds herself in that part of the city known as 'Tiger Bay', which lies along the Ratcliffe Highway, between St Katharine's Dock and Limehouse. This is the haunt of those harlots, known as tigresses, whose main prey are the sailors who spill on to land looking for a drink, a smoke and a fuck, and will find all three but maybe lose their pay, their good clothes and even their lives in the transaction. This is where the opium-masters peddle oblivion to those who can pay, but where anonymity is free to all. Here is a place where immigrants might be offloaded, or smuggled ashore, never to gain a clear understanding of what country they have settled in: whole thriving communities can lose themselves to speak, eat, live, work and die as natives of another place, clinging together in ignorance of the land where now they dwell.

Lucy passes one of the many shops selling animals and birds, which, like the human population in its strange plumage, have come from every part of the globe. A gnawed window-sill is lined with a file of white cockatoos, which jostle upon their perch for a better view of the outside world. In front of the shop, among the cages of painted finches and loud parrots, there sits a row of round-shouldered owls, incongruous country things, with their sad, evasive eyes. Aliens in an alien land.

An overloaded cart passes, carrying tea-chests from wharf to warehouse, pulled by a straining horse. Children hold on to the back of the cart, which drags them along striking sparks from the studs in their boot soles. Those without boots stand and jeer. The horse falls abruptly to its knees and the carter lashes it with his long whip. The pitiable sight of the animal plunging and struggling in its shafts in the effort to get up causes the children to cheer even louder. Lucy stands in the street and weeps in common sympathy with the poor, hopelessly entangled beast.

But there is another spectacle rounding the corner, which draws the children to it like a travelling circus. And, but for the sombre grey dress of the 'showmen and -women' in attendance, it might as well be. Drums and cymbals call the crowd and sound the storm as a paper and sealing-wax representation of a boat is jerked upon strings for the watchers' delight. The clamorous instrumental rises to a crescendo as it is agitated violently enough to empty it of its passengers – little shadow puppets cut from black crêpe paper, which are tossed out for the dour-faced mummers, one wearing a veil, to scoop up with enormous butterfly nets.

'It's ve story ov Grace Darlin'!' calls a cat's-meat woman, stopping to take a look.

'No, sister. It is the story of your immortal soul in peril,' replies 'Skipper' Charles Heever.

'Watch out, girls, they want us all fer knee drill,' calls the woman, picking up her barrow of cagmags. Her departure signals a general exodus and some throwing of pebbles. The denizens of the Ratcliffe Highway are well used to God's travelling showmen.

'Stay, good people. Hear our word. We bring you the Kingdom of Heaven itself! My fishers of men will come among you with solace and good news.'

'D'you lot do cocoa?' asks one who has lingered.

Carrie nudges Georgina to advance and address the woman. 'Madam, we offer food and drink for the soul . . .'

'Vat don't do me no good, lovey,' replies the old woman.

Carrie again pushes Georgina forward, whispering, 'Fish for her, Lady Georgina. Go on.'

Georgina reaches for the shoulder turned from her by the departing woman, and the reek of human flesh long stewed in old clothes makes her blink. But she is quick enough this time to say, 'We do cocoa *and* buns.'

'Why di'n't you say, dear? Vat'll do nicely.'

Another woman, drawn to their little party by the fear of missing out on anything that might be on offer, grabs on to Georgina's arm to steady herself. On looking up into that veiled face, and seeming to find disapproval there, she wheedles, 'Bless me, lady, it's only 'unger makes me drunk.'

Carrie puts her arm through Georgina's and squeezes it to her as the two hurry after their unwilling congregation, to hand out leaflets promising eternal salvation with buns.

Carrie, Albert and Georgina venture together down an alley that leads into a blind court around which low buildings, closer to kennels than houses, slouch. This enclosed space is like a fetid tank, its bottom coated with mud and slime from which the foul miasma cannot escape. The ladies, despite their missionary zeal, are aware of the seeping filth into which they step so their thoughts go down, rather than fly upwards, as they pick a route.

Georgina sees a small urchin carrying a tinier one upon her hip and, impelled by headlong bravado, approaches, Carrie's encouraging hand upon her back. She is excited by the prospect of getting close to one of this tribe, as well as driven by her desire to impress her mentors, and so she kneels to the child in self-proclamatory abasement. Thus one who has fallen from that ever-replenishing tree of civilised comfort, warmth and plenty to the forest floor below looks for the first time into the face of the natural, unadulterated human child, who contrives to find its living there.

'Come here, my dear, for I have something for you.'

How is it that a dog, a cow, even a farmyard pig can live its life through without benefit of soap and, despite the usual eructations, evacuations and excretions, will mostly smell of its own animal self (and if it should become fouled then it will contrive to get itself clean again), but these same natural processes left unchecked for only a little while in the species *Homo sapiens* will accumulate into loathsomeness? As she stoops awkwardly in the mire, Georgina not only smells the vileness of unwashed, feral human but sees, too, what indeed a piece of work is man when he is found in this raw state. Formed by God, but unimproved by artificial intervention or nurture, the child's hair is lank with human grease, a crust stops its nose and its little sharp teeth are rimmed with brown. It has that preternaturally sharp-witted and vicious look of the street child. But she will not be revolted. She leans towards the child and raises her veil to reveal her own rough, perfectly clean, pocky skin. The infant yells with fear at this transformation, which sets off such a squall in the baby that it brings out a half-dressed, stumbling man into the yard, on the lookout for someone to hit for waking him.

'Wot yu want?' he says, closing the buttonless army greatcoat over his chest. He sees first that this is a lady beneath the midge net, second that she is, unfortunately, dressed for philanthropy.

'I wanted to help you and your little ones,' says Georgina, standing up to face him, despite the blast of the raw alcohol that he seems to be distilling in his lungs. She drops her veil in order to muffle the smell and for something to hide behind.

''Elp away, my lady. But is it bread or paper you'll be 'elpin' us wiv taday? Poor li'le kiddies can't read and vey be *ever* so 'ungry. Yu need money fer food ter put in yer bellies, don't you, my li'le bread-snappers?' He talks in the affected wheedle of a professional beggar but his muscular build and lantern jaw belie the artificial stoop and supplicant cringe.

Georgina replies, trying to be brave, 'I could offer your children three meals a day and a bed at night if they had been orphans . . .'

'Now, did I ever say vey was mine?' he interrupts, with more vigour.

'Oh, but I thought—'

'You can 'ave 'em, an' good riddance, if you 'ave a notion to it, lady.'

'Is their mother living?'

He is stopped in the action of shrugging off the transaction and turns back to say, 'She may be, or she may not. I've a powerful strong notion vat she's not and their pa's died of a lung disease too. Poor wee mites.'

He takes the older child restrainingly by the shoulder. Georgina stoops to them again and says, encouragingly, 'Would you like to come with me and drink soup?'

''Old it, miss. You an' yer friends can't be just 'avin' vem away like vat. I've bin lookin' arter vese poor mites since Mammy and Daddy died. I won't let 'em go fer less van a tanner. A sixpenny piece, miss. Each.'

Before Carrie can stop her, Georgina reaches into her purse for the coins, which she hands over to the man who promptly spits on them before securing them behind each ear. She is anxious to leave this horrid place and tries to herd the unwilling children before her.

'Vose two'll wash up very pretty,' says the man approvingly, giving the little girl an encouraging shove. ''Member me, miss, eh!

I can get you any number a chickens like vese two. Sixpence a time an' all shapes and sizes, all very obligin' and every one a genuine orphin.'

Georgina now leads the grizzling child, by its filthy paw, to the mouth of the alley, which serves as a sewer, where the Flynns have preceded her. She is breathing out hard through her nose, trying to rid herself of the cloying smell of poverty that she seems to have taken deep into her body.

'Lady Georgina, we are not traders in human flesh. You should not offer people such as these money,' reproves Albert.

'But aren't they souls just the same? Two more to add to our tally?' she replies, with spirit.

'Of course, dear. But our work must not become a mere round-up of bodies,' says Carrie.

'But haven't these two been saved from a life of sin? Isn't there greater rejoicing in heaven over the salvation of even one soul who was lost and then brought to Him than those who were never in peril?' says Georgina, holding on tight to the struggling child.

'Certainly. But our orphanage is already overflowing and it cannot be practical for us to bring in every indigent child off the street. And such behaviour may be misconstrued. Our Skipper says we must lure with bread but cure with the Word. We must think of ourselves as missionaries in Albion's own Gomorrah.'

But despite the Flynns' caution Georgina has found her enthusiasm in life. Appalled and fascinated in equal parts, she is like a fearless lady anthropologist who, with an inward squeak of repressed excitement, recognises some lost and barbarous tribe it will be her life's work to anatomise.

Rosy dawn is reaching fingers stained with soot over the city by the time the Fisher Folk converge on the headquarters of their Wapping mission from their night's work. Here, in a warehouse rented for the purpose, men and women from the street are taken to sleep on leather mattresses stuffed with dried seaweed, each fitted into the framework of a wooden bunk bed. The rough wooden structures inevitably bring to mind the paupers' coffins for which these dispossessed men and women are bound and keep thoughts of mortality nicely to the fore, in the bleak watches of the night.

As befits this scientific age, the evolution from moral darkness must follow a method. Each man receives food and shelter for the first four weeks, then must work in a job provided for him to earn his meal tickets and lodging. So the men gleaned most recently sleep on the ground floor, women on the next and as each sex progresses in godliness so they progress ever upwards within the building, elevated by signs of increased personal cleanliness and deportment combined with hard labour. And as they evolve so they are rewarded, with new titles and privileges, until they reach the airier bedrooms of the attic, sprung mattresses, sheets and blankets, a hat – and emerge blinking into the pure light of Christian day.

However, this heavenward ascent is by no means a smoothly untroubled progression. Just as a man may ascend, so may he slither back down to land again, with a bump, in his wooden coffin bed. But, however recalcitrant, while a man or woman continues to ask for help, it will be given even if that means they must spend months confined to the crates on the ground floor. For Mr Heever, the Skipper, maintains the sanctity of free will: when a soul calls out for salvation it must be answered. However, the soul must be ripe for it, for it is no use harvesting the hard and bitter unripe fruit. And so these men and women lie like carefully stored apples in their basement boxes, waiting to mellow in the muffled dark.

Georgina and the Flynns have had some difficulty placing their street arabs. There is no provision for them at the warehouse so they traipse from house to house, knocking up the benevolent volunteer women who might take them in. Mrs Rendell is one such: the widow of an army officer she has three children of her own, but makes shift to accommodate these two extras for what's left of the night, pushing together chairs to make beds and using coats for blankets. In the morning they will be removed to the overflowing house in the country that the Skipper's two grown daughters run for cases such as these.

Georgina and the Flynns stride home, three abreast, arm in arm, happy with their night's work. Georgina is wearing with pride the little silver fish brooch that was given her tonight by Skipper Heever. She has never before felt so alive or so valued.

So the pattern of life shifts at Alonso's house. Teresa and Aurora surrender any notion of being melancholy lady artists with a side-line in paying guests, and become full-time lodging-house landladies and nurses. No more time for standing and looking out from windows. Since Bessie left in a huff they have been forever running up- and downstairs with hot water, dusters and bedpans. Teresa is rarely seen without her tea-towel headpiece and Papa becomes daily more confused about where he is and who they are. He is inclined to reassure himself with the explanation that Aurora is his mother, Teresa a disliked aunt, and addresses them in childish Spanish. However, this drudgery is helped by the fact that, generally, the other occupants of the house, apart from Albert, are asleep during the day and, apart from Alonso, absent during the night.

Georgina thrives on this nocturnal existence. She has become known, among the ranks of the Fisher Folk, as 'Angel of the Small Fry', such is her particular concern for the heathen children of the street. Indeed, she has grown so bold, even predatory, in her rag-picking work of philanthropy that, when the Skipper calls for a census to be taken among the rookeries and common lodging-houses (where the 'lower third' dwells), she has no shame in enquiring minutely after the squalid circumstances of those to be numbered. She and the Flynns are indefatigable in enumerating the inhabitants of every room where, crowded together in immorality, couples, children, itinerant relations, their lodgers and their lodgers' lodgers sleep, sometimes in rotation. They chronicle the income and expenditure of the bandbox and lucifer-box makers, the cane-workers, clothes-peg makers, shoemakers and tailors, who earn just enough to keep themselves from starvation. They interview the slop-workers, brush- and artificial-flower-makers, who don't. And they delve among the unemployable ex-soldiers, alcoholic doxies and deserted mothers who can contrive to stay alive only by vice and begging. But it is always the children who draw her. And it is this enthusiasm for harvesting these waifs and strays, quite apart from exasperating the overstretched Heever daughters, that leads her into difficulties.

Once, on spying a little girl wrapped in a sack shawl, topped by a tipsy straw hat, outside a tap-room door, she swooped, only to be chased off by the child's enraged parent, a slipshod, angry, shrill woman, who emerged, drooling from the mouth and bearing a jug of beer, which she emptied over the head of the child-snatcher.

On entering a foul, tilting tenement room where brown paper and rags stopped the empty window-frames, and fallen plaster revealed the ceiling laths, she had knelt reverently at the side of a child's sickbed. As the crone, who was the infant's teenaged mother, lifted the child into her arms, Georgina heard her say, 'Yu may 'av' vis un, miss. I can't afford ta lose it. It costs too much ta bury it.'

Another time, Georgina left the Fishers' mime show with her net still in her hands to investigate a bundle of rags and newspapers huddled in a doorway. Here lay a little child with the ethereal look of an undernourished angel, but one who had lain so still, so long, that crystalline rime outlined his exposed ear and highlighted the folds of his rags. The beautiful child opened his heavy eyes to see the veiled lady with her net and, gathering his rags around him, sprang up, calling, ''Elp! 'Elp! It's ve lady, she ain't got no fice an' she's arter me!'

Georgina was very upset by this and it was a while before she was quite so muscular in her work, limiting herself to light duties – handing out leaflets and tending the tea urn. This afternoon she is so busy gathering up the crêpe-paper puppet souls, missed by the busy nets, that she doesn't even notice the group of children turning a thick ship's rope in the middle of the road.

'I'll tell Mother when I go 'ome,
The boys won't let the girls alone.

They've pulled me 'air and broke me comb,
I'll tell Mother when I go 'ome.

I'm goin' ta London next Sunday mornin',
I'm goin' ta London at half pas' ten.

Give me love ta the dear old doctor,
Tell 'im I can't stay any longer . . .'

They sing, the tarry rope thwacking on the cobbles.

Lucy, who is watching the game, puts her head in her hands and begins to sob. One of the Fisher Folk ladies is quick to gather her in.

'Hi, hi, 'ere we go,
The driver's drunk and the 'orse won't go.
Now we're goin' back, now we're goin' back,
Back to the place where we get more grub.
When we get there, when we get there . . .'

The skipping girl stumbles and the rope stops, banging against her ankles. The next little girl takes her place in the cycle.

Georgina's eyes are downcast beneath her veil so that she does not even notice Lucy as she hands her a leaflet. In fact, even had she looked Lucy full in the face she might not have recognised her after her dark months alone in London. But these two, having followed their separate paths to London, were perhaps fated to meet again.

Suddenly a shoal of little pests wheels through the crowd, pushing and shoving as they pass.

'Miss, miss, show us yer fice. G'on ven,' challenges one daredevil, standing in front of Georgina on dancing feet. Another child pushes him closer, saying, 'Miss, give 'im a sixpence. 'E *wants* ta go.'

'Not bloody likely,' says the first boy, jumping back out of Georgina's 'range'. 'I'm stayin' wiv Ma!'

The children run off, chanting as they go:

> 'Hide-a-hood, baby snatcha,
> A tanner if she ever catch ya.'

Georgina's reputation has gone before her.

Fallen Girls

Lucy and another pregnant girl, gathered in by the Fisher Folk, have been brought to a tall damp house in Clerkenwell, run by Mrs Flood. For the Fisher Folk have expanded their activities into the specialist field of Fallen Girls, and this mildewy house, overseen by Mrs Flood and her squad of hardened philanthropist ladies, is to be the first in this new initiative. Lucy, now swaddled in her coarse cloth uniform, is brought before Mrs Flood and Mrs Bentley for her interview. Mrs Bentley has taken the role of 'book-keeper' in the new enterprise, recording information regarding the circumstances, habits, capabilities and disposition of the fallen. She opens her ledger upon the desk and smooths out the second sheet. Here she inscribes, in a beautiful hand, first the date and then the mundane circumstances of Lucy's tragedy. Each fact is pinned to the page by her precise nib. Name? Age? Any religion? Parents' names, address and circumstances (living/dead, together/apart)? Brothers/sisters? Previous employment?

When Lucy replies to this last question, 'Domestic servant,' Mrs Flood looks up at her and smiles. 'If you have been a domestic servant, then you will be well used to hard work. Believe me, your work will be hard here. But you will find salvation through it and through humble prayer. Every clean shirt will help to pay for your keep and bring you closer to God.'

Once she had established that this sorry creature was a domestic servant come to London from the country, Mrs Bentley's experienced pen could quite easily have flown on and marked the rest of Lucy's short history by itself – the only outstanding detail of the drab little story of her ruin being 'master, son or fellow servant?'.

There is one last question that Mrs Flood must ask, and she does so with the directness of a busy, self-assured woman. 'My dear, do you know yourself to have the disease – in your throat or elsewhere? If you do, there is the female lock hospital at Westbourne Green and another at Paddington where you may get treatment.'

Mrs Flood strides towards the far horizon, eyes levelled at her distant, if incontrovertibly attainable goal of personal salvation, hardly aware of the slime through which she must march. Her question hangs in the air over Lucy's shameful head. 'Never mind. You are a good girl, Lucy. Nothing vicious. You must go to your bed and rest. Tomorrow we will make an early start with our work.'

Lucy will be housed in an upper room with four other girls previously fished from the streets. By the time her history has been taken, the lights have already been extinguished, and she is obliged to feel for her bed, at first finding only those occupied by lumpy, sleeping bodies lying underneath their blankets. She undresses in the dark and lies down without properly seeing the others who breathe quietly around her. Just as she closes her eyes a peal of laughter breaks out.

'You're awake?' says Lucy.

'You bet.'

'Well, you can all shut up and get some sleep. I'm charvered,' says a grumpy voice.

''Arken to 'er.'

'How far a you gone, love?'

'Me?' says Lucy.

'You got a dumplin' on, 'aven't you?'

'We've all got bay windows in this 'ouse, dear.'

'My, she's got all 'er buttons on 'er. Does yer mother know you're out?' says one voice, sardonic in the dark.

'Mother thinks I'm still living in the country . . .' Lucy says, not knowing which voice to answer and choosing to respond to the one question she thinks she understands. However, this reply seems to provoke even more cross-examination.

'Oh, my! Dorothy in Daisyville.'

'Lovely an' snug in the country. All cosy in the same bed – sisters *and* brothers – was it, dear?'

'I was a nursery-maid in a big house in the country,' Lucy answers, trying to get an idea of the location of each voice in the dark.

'Well, you're not the only one 'ere works for a livin', love. I'm a needlewoman by trade,' sniffs a carefully cultivated voice.

'Very respectable, I'm sure. Ended up taking in fancy work, none ve less, di'n' yu?' jeers raucous Cockney number one.

'I reckon you been on the loose this two years, Olive Planner,' follows up the second, milder, Cockney.

'I have not indeed! I only went a bad way when my husband died. Jus' the one time, and only to pay off his medical bills,' the respectable voice snaps back, in its tragic dignity.

'Lord bless you if there's a single girl in all England doing work with a needle and can afford to keep hersel' virtuous,' replies a conciliatory Irish voice close by Lucy.

The belligerent Cockney shoots back, 'Jus' listen to 'em carryin' on, Dorofy-fresh-from-the-country. "To be sure we're all good girls 'ere," ' she says, putting on a pious Irish brogue. 'It's a mystery to me 'ow so many of 'em landed in 'ere up the spout, seein' as none of 'em niver done it but the once, and then kep' their legs crowsed, eh, Norah?'

There is an affronted pause in the quick-fire bickering and Lucy wonders if she dare close her eyes and attempt sleep.

'I can tell you, as soon as I've kittened it'll be straight back up West for me, girls,' comes the louder Cockney, breezy now she's shouted down the others and won the floor.

'I should say the nearest you'll get to the West End is Green Park. Nice and dark, eh, Beatrice?' says the disgruntled respectable voice of Olive.

'I swear, I'll swing for you!' bold Beatrice hisses back.

''Old your whiz!'

'Needlewoman, my arse!'

'Ssssh!'

'Deadly nightshade,' whispers Beatrice.

'Whore,' replies Olive.

'That the best you c'n do?' says the quieter Cockney, and the other girls burst into laughter.

Again there is a pause. When it is broken by Beatrice, the questions are once again directed towards Lucy, who is beginning to make out the dark bulk of the other beds in the gloom. 'You'll be used to washing work, Nursery-maid. You'll need to be 'ere. They reckon the Fisher Folk is a great deal 'arder on their girls than the Sally Army.'

'I 'eard tell they's so popular wiv the girls you 'ave to sew your own mattress 'fore you get a chance ter lie down on it . . .'

'This lot'll 'ave you up to your pits in washwater dawn till dusk—'

'Or on your knees,' interrupts Olive.

'A kind a work you're well suited to, then, miss,' says Beatrice.

There is a scramble as Olive leaps from her bed towards Beatrice in hers. The other Cockney girl is out just as quick, holding back the combatants and urgently hushing them: 'Stow magging and manging!'

The other two return to their beds, breathing heavily.

'Daisy, they ain't goin' a turn us out. Not at this time a night,' says Beatrice, when she's caught her breath.

'You don' know they won't. Anyway, I'm goin' ta keep me card clean till I've dropped the kid and then my gentleman friend 'as promised to set me up in a little shop,' replies Daisy, the quieter Cockney.

'My chap promised 'e'd spring me this time,' says loud Beatrice.

'Where is 'e, then?' needles Olive.

'Don't you worry, 'e'll be 'ere. 'E's just bidin' 'is time. 'E got a good tellin' off last time 'e tried to call.' Beatrice laughs grimly.

'Have you been here before, then?' asks Lucy, despite herself.

'I wouldn't never keep the census down, Dorothy. What you take me for? I ain't never accounted for no kid of mine. I always come in to drop.'

'What becomes of the babies?' asks Lucy.

'Off to the farm wiv 'em,' says Daisy with some relish.

'You may guess they don't mean they're taken to the country-side,' says Olive.

Beatrice laughs at this, her teasing now turned upon Lucy. 'No pretty baa-lambs in our London farms, Dorothy. They rear other livestock. An' London mould is made of soot an' ashes and we got 'igh walls for 'edges here.'

'She means the kids are lodged all together with some kind "auntie", who raises this human crop for the good of the Empire,' says Olive.

'All happy as pigs in shit,' is Beatrice's subdued coda.

'Gawd save the Queen and Gawd 'elp the Empire!' says Daisy.

'More like a crop for His Divine Majesty and his celestial empire,' comes Norah's sad, Irish voice from the bed next to her. Lucy reaches protectively round her swollen belly.

Carrie and Albert Flynn are sitting in Alonso's parlour with their *protégée*, Georgina. Serious matters are being discussed between the three: Georgina appealing, the Flynns insistent.

'Isn't my mission to bear this torment? Can't I offer it up to the Lord?' says Georgina.

'Oh, my dear, my dear,' coos Carrie sorrowfully.

'We feel this notoriety is too much for you. Notoriety is not what a Fisher must seek,' continues her Albert.

'You mean that I hinder the work by my presence?'

'Dear Georgina, Georgina dearest. You are rather too successful in your work . . .'

'You must know that the devil does not waste his ammunition,' says Albert firmly.

'There, you see! Their stone-throwing and name-calling must mean something.' Georgina grabs at this flimsy line thrown in her direction.

'It is not just this, my dear Lady Georgina,' Albert appeases her. 'Our work in the streets is changing. Skipper Heever spoke to the elders about how the mission must evolve. He said that our first duty may no longer be solely to dredge the streets. We are simply skimming off the top of this bubbling cauldron, which is the capital of sin and vice.'

This information is obviously news to Carrie too, as she had only attended the women's meeting, hosted by Mrs Heever, where the conversation tended to revolve around the practical arrangements of their mission – the minor issues of how the hundreds of people to whom they had offered salvation were to be fed, housed and clothed. In contrast it was at the men's summit that the problems of real weight and importance, such as the philosophy behind the work, were discussed.

'As you know, the warehouse and factory are full of these transient lodgers taken from the streets and yet the numbers applying for shelter never diminish. As we reap so the crop increases.'

'But are we to leave the poor children unsaved just because they are too many?' says Georgina.

'No. You misunderstand me. We will not cease in our work of philanthropy and elevation. But we Fisher Folk cannot continue to scoop up dirt so that the complacent passers-by do not foul their feet. We should no longer depend upon the fragments from gentlemen's tables and broken victuals from hotel and restaurant kitchens to quench immediate need and salve a guilty conscience. We must grow more radical in publicising our work if we are to be effective.'

'Skipper Heever wishes us to change?' says Carrie, doubtfully. 'I really cannot chain myself to railings and march with a banner, Albert.'

'He does not require it of you, my dear,' he replies.

'What does he want us to do, then?' says Georgina.

'That is a matter for more discussion, Sister Georgina. We seek a way to force the upper two-thirds to look upon the submerged third and feel ashamed.'

'I don't believe you can ever succeed, then. Polite society knows well enough that life outside their tribe is ugly and brutish. God knows, they see it for themselves every day. What is more, they are quite happy to believe that this is so because the poor know no better and have brought it upon themselves,' answers Georgina, speaking from the privileged position of tribal membership. 'One could go further. For the rich, such evidence of self-inflicted misery is like exculpation. It teaches them that they themselves are good and deserving precisely because they are happy and comfortable.'

Albert interjects, 'You say that they do "see", but I say that they are in fact blind. They choose to avert their moral gaze.'

'Then we must hold their heads and make them look and look until their eyes bleed,' proclaims Georgina, in a voice loaded with oratorical drama. 'They must be made to understand that not to look, and really see, will bring them harm. They must truly understand that this is "the dangerous class".'

'You mean that they must be made afraid?' says Carrie.

'They must be made to understand that this sewer is spewing a tide of sin and sloth, which must eventually wash away at the foundations of all that honest Britons hold to be good,' says Albert, repeating the words of the Skipper from the last meeting.

'No, no, Albert. She doesn't mean that. Do you, Georgina?'

'No, I don't think I do,' replies Georgina, slowing for an instant to order her excited thoughts. 'I think – I know that shame among the upper echelons is a very weak muscle, rarely used and so almost atrophied. And yes, Carrie, the thing that will spur them to generosity is not a noble desire to do good but a hint of fear for their own safety and that of their property. It seems to me that, in great part, the comfortably off believe that their well-being is in direct equation with others' misery. My kind consider that all the wealth and plenty they enjoy will be threatened by social justice – give the Lancashire mill girls only a half-holiday, let alone be obliged to feed, clothe and educate the lower third, and the whole edifice of Empire will come tumbling down! We must force their noses into this tide of filth and make them see that by continuing to do nothing they endanger themselves.'

For a moment all three are silent. Georgina is as stunned as Carrie and Albert by quite how radical are her ideas. She stands up abruptly from the piano stool, where she had been perching, her hands clasped, her face uplifted and lit by the ecstasy of divine revelation. 'I believe I have found my mission!'

Upstairs, Aurora and Teresa are at Alonso's bedside each holding a hand. They hear and ignore Carrie's familiar, exultant 'Praise be!' from below.

'Should we send for her?' asks Teresa, shifting on her knees to ease the pressure.

'The letter would not reach her until tomorrow and she would have to get permission to come, and then there is the matter of train timetables,' answers her sister, wearily.

Teresa is aghast at this litany of obstacles. 'You think he will not last so long?'

'Oh, God! I don't know – I don't know what to do.'

Teresa stands, cautiously straightening her deadened legs and taking a heavy step towards the door and away from her fragile father borne up upon his big, solid bed. 'She should be here,' says Teresa, decidedly. 'I *will* write . . .' Blood fills her feet with sparkles of pain and she pauses at the door. '. . . if you will not. And even if she can't get here in time,' the firmness in her voice gives a little, 'at least *I* shall not be blamed for keeping her in ignorance.'

Aurora, at the bedside, rolls the thin bones of Alonso's hand beneath its onion-paper skin. He does not return her hold with any pressure so she must rest this ethereal bundle of twigs in her own, live grasp and remember not to squeeze too tightly. There is no sensation of vitality in what she holds and she looks at the down of his beard to see it is still feathered by breath.

She has the dreadful expectation that Maria will descend like an avenging fury, angry with them for not having taken better care of Papa. But she wasn't here. She hasn't been here for years: how could she ever know the days measured out in bedpans and cups of tea, or understand how she and Teresa have blundered around trying to keep this leaky old body anchored when it so wanted to float free? For years they have been here, handmaidens to this slow death. Trying to keep cheerful for him. Running the household around him. Responsible, self-sacrificing, disappointed. No life for them. All for him . . . No, for her! For her ungrateful sister who got away. It was Maria, cold, hard, merciless and unforgiving, who had pressed them to this hard, filial duty. It was unappeasable Maria who had denied them the opportunity to please themselves, tricked them into remaining captive so that she could live free in the wider world.

Aurora feels warmth in her cheeks. She has never before dared criticise Maria so directly, even in her thoughts.

That morning Lucy and the other fallen girls stand at the seething washtubs, each with scrubbing-board and harsh soap cut from a mother block by Mrs Bentley with a knife that hangs by a ribbon at her waist. The boredom and drudgery of their labour might certainly be deemed penance enough for their sins. But this good lady maintains that within the work of whitening lies a more symbolic atonement for the besmirching and besmirched female body. God has ordained that the female sex is the original portal of all worldly sin and so it is fitting that woman's duty should be to maintain cleanliness. But some, it seems, are required to scrub longer and harder than others, and Mrs Bentley often has recourse to that block of soap, for the girls' souls, as represented by the tally of dirty laundry they are set to cleanse, are very, very black indeed.

However, for the nursery-maid used to hard domestic labour it hardly seems a punishment at all, just more of the same. Soil and toil, toil and soil. And in Lucy, Mrs Bentley's philosophy concerning the propensity of the female to pollute is also confounded. For hasn't her whole life been dedicated to the simple equation of dirtying herself so that others should go clean? Just so, apparently, when it comes to morality, it is Lucy's job to be publicly marked by others' filth so that they should appear pure. What an altogether useful beast is the scapegoat. Patient and accepting, Lucy doesn't pause to wonder why it should fall to her alone to whiten Dr Oliver's black deed, as well as her own forced defilement. Instead, she diligently rubs and swills and takes the opportunity to look about her at the other girls at work in the laundry room. Here is Beatrice, the louder Cockney, going at her washing with the same vehemence as she attacks other aspects of her life including, it is now apparent in the light of day, her hair colouring. There, Olive, the melancholy once-married lady and needlewoman gone to the bad, who weeps as she washes – so that her face shines with tears as well as effort. Lucy notices that Daisy, the quieter Cockney, has got the pip since she was forbidden to entertain them all with a selection of current music-hall hits and won't answer Beatrice's sly whispers. She looks in vain for Norah, the owner of the Irish voice from the neighbouring bed, and wonders where she might be. Has she perhaps been removed upstairs to deliver her baby?

All morning they bash and scrub and boil, and then they eat and pray. Then it's back to work, rinsing and rinsing again, drowning the linen in boiling water, to be twisted, wrung and mangled. At this point Lucy thinks she might die with the effort of forcing round the handle of the giant mangle. At last the cold, wet lumps of linen, punished in their every fibre, are stretched, folded and hoisted up to the ceiling on drying frames to drip.

Airing, ironing and starching are considered work light enough for those in their last days before confinement or in the first few weeks after giving birth.

So the day ends and Lucy, at last, finds relief from standing, even if the agony is only transferred from her feet to her knees, as they are set to pray again before dinner. She is still silent and uneasy with these new workmates, but the work is routine enough. Indeed, she finds some comfort in it, for heavy physical labour has a lulling effect upon the active brain, and the repetitive nature of laundry work, which has its own unshakeable cycle of processes, occupies hands and body leaving a fretting mind to sleep if it needs.

And she finds solace in her suffering too. For isn't she a very bad girl? In fact, the heaviness of her arms and legs and belly seems a preferable pain to that thin, tightening wire of guilt and fear. The honest ache of sore, chapped hands and tired muscles is real enough to bludgeon away the insistent dread of a queasy heart.

When night comes Lucy, too, could well have been described as 'charvered'. And, since there are no newcomers to excite the other girls into arguments, they all sleep, immovable as a row of boulders, until morning comes, bringing with it more bundles of other people's dirty washing. And so she continues, week upon week, quite reconciled to carrying on like this for ever, an unknowing beast, blindfolded and yoked to circle the well without the distraction of hope.

While Lucy daily scrubbed at blots, Georgina had only to write and address a letter to affirm herself in the cause of the Fisher Folk. It was the simplest of communications; her only concern was that her instructions would be perfectly understood and promptly obeyed. As she placed the letter on the hall table to be posted, she was curious to see that the other letter already waiting to be taken to the box bore the same address as her own, in Teresa's hand.

The time has almost come, in steamy barracks and quiet home both, for birth and death to ring the changes. As for dancers in a lighted room, the side door to the dark corridor opens and shuts so that some may shuffle off as others enter to join the busy throng. So life and death mark time in the remorseless round, the giddy whirl of dancers as they gain and leave the floor. On with the music, then, and let us dance!

Birth and Death

This morning Beatrice is taken away upstairs, her pains having come on as they boil and 'dolly-blue' expensively soiled hotel linen. Her rupture adds to the general flux in that waterlogged basement and as she is carried aloft to the drier reaches of the attic to give birth, she swears a terrible curse on all men and all laundry.

At breakfast the first post arrives at Fainhope Hall and letters, both with the same London postmark, are handed to the Duchess of Fainhope and to Miss Mantilla.

As Beatrice's baby is born and dies, the Duchess of Fainhope is bad-temperedly engaged in directing the packing of various trunks, crates and boxes with the help of Miss Hart, Stevens and Maria Mantilla.

'Might I stow away some little items of my own among Lady Georgina's things?' asks the governess. 'I am at present in want of a suitcase.'

'No suitcase?' sniffs Miss Hart, as though this deficiency is no less than to be expected from a Spanish woman.

'Pack whatever and however you please. Whom could I better trust with the commission of this peculiar request of Georgina's?' says the Duchess, turning a smile upon her governess. Then, to her maid, 'Stevens, for goodness' sake, stop puffing and make yourself useful.'

Briefly Miss Mantilla feels the benefit of Stevens's mortification before the thought of that missing suitcase again weighs her with dread.

It is before luncheon that the task of loading the carriage is begun. Teatime passes unobserved as it continues. By dusk, Miss Mantilla and her reticule are finally themselves packed in, wedged into a fissure in the cliff-face of Georgina's luggage. So Miss Mantilla departs into the gathering gloom, leaving lady's maid and housekeeper both sensible that they are outranked, and Her Grace certain that when her governess returns, voluntarily, from this London sojourn she will be hers for life.

As Miss Mantilla sets off on that familiar London road, Dr Oliver is nowhere to be seen.

Now it is gone nine of the evening and Aurora and Teresa kneel by their dying father's bed, like those paintings of kneeling, two-dimensional children ranked by size, in eternal contemplation of their parent's noble tomb. The old man has no revelations for them about stolen inheritances or mysterious birthrights. He speaks only once in two hours and that is to say, 'Maria?'

'Not yet, Papa. Soon,' answers Teresa, pressing his hand to her mouth to comfort herself.

There is a jangle from the bell and both sisters start.

'I'll open the door to her,' says Aurora firmly.

'No, I will,' replies Teresa. 'I'm the eldest and I sent for her.'

As Aurora listens, she seems to accompany the noise of heavy feet down the stairs and into the distant hall. She strains to listen closer, and her hearing becomes like sight, baffled by pitch darkness, so that featureless sound presses upon her ears, buzzing and squirming. She stays crouched in the covert darkness, holding her father's hand, as her two sisters mount the staircase. Their footsteps scuff at the doorway to their father's old bedroom, now the Flynns', and she hears Teresa murmur, 'Not in there.'

The two women's candlelit shadows precede them through the door, and it seems to Aurora that Maria's first glance is for the monumental wardrobe rather than its twin, the bed, where rests the pale cocoon of the old soldier.

Aurora levers herself upright, supported by the bedpost, giving time for her numb legs to regain some life as Maria approaches, and says, 'Will he know me?'

'He remembers only you. It is Teresa and me he doesn't recognise.'

Now Maria takes her turn in kneeling at the side of the bed. She holds his hand, still warm from Aurora's, and whispers, 'Papa?'

Miracles! He opens his eyes and looks smiling upon her. 'Daughter,' he claims her. 'Is life still hard for my little girl?'

'So much harder without you, Papa.' Acknowledged and shriven, the motherless girl leans across his chest and weeps on to their mutually clasped hands while the two unworthy sisters wait in the shadows. Aurora has a notion of how a sister of Cordelia or Cinderella might harbour, with justification, murderous thoughts.

Downstairs the trunks that had been Maria's travelling companions have been unloaded into the parlour by the coachman under the direction of an animated Georgina. These boxes contain the tools of her new mission; they will be the means by which she will force the Fisher Folk to take her seriously.

When Mr and Mrs Flynn return early from their nocturnal ferreting they find her, armed with a kitchen knife, forcing open packing cases and pulling out straw insulation upon the Turkey carpet. 'It's come, at last,' she says, brazen-faced from the effort of breaking open the boxes and the excitement of what she has in store for them all. 'The whole thing came to me like a vision: I can use the attic room for my studio. I may even employ our Spanish landladies to be assistants to my work,' she says, lifting a beautiful box camera from its crate.

'Oh, my!' says Carrie, startled by the confidence with which Georgina handles these shining modern contraptions. 'But where shall the ladies of the house sleep, dear, if their bedroom is to become your photographic studio?'

Lady Georgina is not used to interesting herself in the sleeping arrangements of servants: she is much more concerned with the sordid glamour of the disenfranchised and destitute. 'The Lord will provide, I'm sure of it,' she replies dismissively, and Carrie feels she has no other recourse than to add, 'Praise be.'

What monster fish-gobbler have they created?

Let us fly eastwards now, as night deepens, to eavesdrop on our fallen girls, lying unsettled on their seaweed mattresses. Listen as they talk in the dark of Norah, the owner of the soft, Irish voice whom Lucy heard on her first evening in the home but never saw. The girls are whispering Norah's story among themselves quickly and quietly before she is brought up to occupy again the empty bed next to Lucy. Daisy has the latest: she had been helping Mrs Flood sort pocket-handkerchiefs when Norah was brought in. She has just this minute come to bed and is leaky with gossip and opinion.

'When was it she ran off?' asks Olive.

'You remember, the night Lucy come. Gone a fortnight.'

'Why did she 'op ve twig?' asks Kathleen, a new girl who is occupying Beatrice's old bed.

'Are you goin' ter let me tell yer? I was just goin' to tell yer all about it if you gives us 'alf a chance,' says Daisy. She begins, as though embarking upon a fairy-tale, drawing them all in with a dark and mysterious story-telling voice: 'They finds 'er up on the Whitechapel Road. Outside the 'ospital, sittin' right there on the steps wiv 'er shawl wrapped around 'er—'

''Ad she dropped?'

'I was comin' ter that,' replies Daisy testily. 'Anyways, there she sits like a boiled owl, wrapped all around wiv that shawl. And can they move 'er? No, they cannot, girls. For doesn't she sit tight, 'olding that shawl around 'er—'

'I bet the baby's inside that shawl,' interrupts Olive again.

'Stow yer whiz, won't yer? Wasn't I jus' comin' to that?' continues Daisy, fiercely protective of her role as romancer. 'When at last –

at long last – they gets 'er up, don't they fine out what she's bin holdin' so tight, underneaf that ol' shawl?' She pauses for dramatic effect, which has largely been forestalled by the prescient Olive. 'There's 'er baby. A day-old boy and 'e's froze fast to 'er side, naked as the day 'e was born, dead as a tent-peg!'

'Dead!' gasps Lucy.

'Law,' says Olive, gratifyingly shocked by this outcome.

Daisy continues, with relish, 'We 'ad to put 'er in the copper to warm 'er frough afore we could get it free.'

'How can she bear it?' murmurs Lucy.

'Says it's all a punishment for 'er wicked ways,' says Daisy the oracle.

'What about all the men? Ain't adultery wicked no more?' says Kathleen, loud enough to make all the other girls look over in her direction in the dark.

'I swear her bloke's been sniffing around here tonight, trying to get her back behind locked doors,' says Olive. 'I heard someone trying the shutters.'

'Poor, poor girl to lose her baby,' says Lucy, with a tremor in her voice.

All suddenly fall silent as the door opens and a figure is seen standing at it, illuminated by a candle. 'I call it a lucky break, my dears. Poor cow's never been so popular. I 'eard there was quite a tussle between this lot an' the soul fakers abou' who'd get their 'ands on 'er immortal whatsit first.' The figure moves closer. 'Don't Mrs Flood and the rest on 'em love a tragic story?' continues the instantly recognisable voice of Beatrice. 'That's the way to manage it, says I – done and dusted and no miserable little client for the angel-maker.' She sits on the edge of Lucy's bed and is seen to be fully dressed, in an assortment of clothes obviously liberated from the airing shelves, with hair as elaborately dressed as is possible without a mirror. 'Just dropped by ter wish you all ta-ta, ladies,' she says archly.

'Aren't you lyin' in?' asks Daisy.

'Can't abide to be caged, love. I'm like a big cat, got to 'ave me freedom.'

'Free? Free to get beaten up and knocked up again, is it?' fires back Olive.

'D'you want a fist in your face, madam? That was *my* anca you 'eard at the shutters and 'e's ready with a stuffed eelskin if anyone needs boppin' on the 'ead!' Since no one responds to this provocation, Beatrice continues, 'Like I was sayin'. Seein' I done what I come to do, I'll now be biddin' you all farewell and takin' the air. Anyone else want to come along for the ride? My Sidney's very obligin'.'

Lucy's pregnancy is now only weeks away from term and she has grown possessive and protective of it. Fear of the baby farm, which appears only to ripen corpses, contends with fear of the cold streets and what they may hold. But the fierce imperative to preserve her unborn child is enough to make her raise her head from the comfort of the selfless treadmill and take action. 'I will,' she says simply, jumping out of bed.

Just Another Day

Leaving Lucy to her timely escape, let us now hurtle back across London just in time to observe aptly named Aurora drawing back the parlour curtains upon the dawn. The first light of day reveals Lady Georgina sitting there, fully clothed, surrounded still by the half-emptied cases and boxes. Looking up as from a deep reverie she asks conventionally, 'How does your father?'

'Papa has departed. I mean he died. My papa is dead,' replies Aurora, startled by the apparition.

Georgina watches as, in the course of this unexpected reply, her landlady seems to evolve from immature adult to elderly girl. The smooth forehead is wrinkled by a childish grimace of sorrow and she scampers from the room on heavy, middle-aged feet. She must seek out Miss Mantilla if she is to establish what she needs to know.

Her governess is to be found making tea in the kitchen, dry-eyed as to be expected, and coolly efficient over the kettle. 'My condolences, to you and your sisters. I am sorry for your loss,' Georgina says, to which Miss Mantilla replies with a nod, as though in approval of the rightness of the sentiment and the manner in which her pupil has expressed it.

'Will you be staying on here, to help with the household?'

Georgina treads somewhat cautiously: she is aware that the enquiry may be indelicately direct, but she needs to know.

'I don't believe so. I shall be wanted back at the Hall,' answers the governess.

'So you won't be requiring a bedroom?' asks Georgina, making quite sure.

'No. I think this house is quite full enough, don't you?' The rhetorical question hangs for a moment before Miss Mantilla continues: 'Aurora and Teresa will be glad of my old . . . I mean my father's room. The attic makes a draughty bedroom on these winter nights.'

Now it is Georgina's turn to conceal her overflowing emotions with a nod. It is not until she has regained the parlour that, under her breath, she lets out a half-ironic, 'Praise be,' and sets about the unpacking and rehoming with renewed vigour.

At this very moment the newly liberated Beatrice and Lucy are swinging along early-morning Brick Lane, arm in arm, with Sidney of the eelskin cosh. His rusty voice, hoarse from calling 'apples', and his pearl buttons mark him out as a coster.

Even at this hour the market stalls are busy and many of the costermongers setting out their wares acknowledge Beatrice's triumphant progress among them with cries of, 'Whoy-oi!'

'Cool ta ve dillo nemo,' calls one from behind his live-eel barrow, where he encourages the more animated of the eels to draw attention from those that shall never be lively again.

'What's 'e sayin'?' she asks irritably.

'Lord, love – 'e's complimentin' you on your rigout. Where you get vem rags from, enyway? You wants to moult vem mouldies – looks like you jus' stepped out ve big 'ouse,' replies Sidney, pulling down his front lock to curl upon his cheek as she stalks among the stalls, proud as royalty returned from exile.

'I ain't never been in no work'ouse. An' never you mind abou' these rags, I'll soon be gettin' back me old finery.' She stoops to pick up a pigeon feather and, flinging her rusty bonnet over a wall, sticks it into her hair.

'An' yer 'ands is red raw,' he complains.

'Ah, we must 'ave delicate white little hands now we are ruined, Lucinda,' she says, holding up Lucy's chapped hand to look at it.

'I'm used to hard work,' says Lucy. 'I think I must be fitted to it.'

'You ain't going to 'ave to mind 'ard work, fine ladies. I ain't got a yennep to bless meself wiv,' says Sid.

After she has taken a moment to invert his coster-speak and gain its meaning, Beatrice expostulates, ''Arken to 'im, Dorothy! Turned out like the Duke of Seven Dials and says 'e ain't got even a single penny to stand us girls breakfast wiv.'

'I'll beg you some apples, an' I call vat gen'rous,' he grudges.

'Bastard,' she replies good-naturedly.

'I'll be in funds agin, this evenin',' Sid grumbles, and then, more sprightly, says, 'Yu can earn us a quick sov for immediate necessities. Go on, girl, you and your mate tagevver. I'll stan' guard.'

Beatrice gives her lover what is known as an old-fashioned look, which deters him not at all. 'Vere's plenty ov costers lookin' for a quick 'un on a cold mornin', ay?' he encourages, looking doubtfully at Lucy in her advanced state of pregnancy and then away. Having apparently decided that she is a cause not worth pursuing, he redoubles his efforts with Beatrice. 'Vere's a dove. 'Er and me's dyin' for want ov a cup a coffee and a coupla thins,' Sid continues, taking Lucy's arm and moving her in the direction of a coffee-and-bread stall.

'Sid! I jus' dropped a kid for you. Me crown and fevvers aren't up to it. An' you can keep your bloody apples. 'Er an' me want a baked potato, each!'

'I swear you're a reg'lar trosseno, Bea. Listen, ne'er mind yer tenuc, I'll get you a potato fer warmin' up vem talented 'ands on. An' ven, love——'

'Found 'e 'as got some brass, arter all, ven! An' you can talk propa English, when you're addressin' Lucinda and me, bastard,' snaps Beatrice.

After they have eaten their potatoes, piping hot from the can, Sid gives his paramour a little push, saying, 'Go it, my tulip, git ter work.'

And Beatrice, tossing her feather, sidles off to accost some idlers, repeating, 'Bastard,' under her breath.

The other two stand for a moment in silence, surveying the noisy, enterprising market where the necessaries to furnish a house, feed a family, clothe a community or plant a garden are all to be had.

'So, Lucinda . . . Dorofy,' he says conversationally, 'you ain't got a tib of occabot about you, I s'pose?' Seeing no vestige of understanding in Lucy's face, he continues, 'Yu bin leadin' a gay life long?'

'Oh, no,' she replies. 'I don't think I was ever happy.'

Sid looks at her with an uncertain little smile that doesn't quite reach his eyes, and lets his steering hand drop from her elbow. 'Ne'er mind, eh, love.'

Now it is the afternoon of that same, commonplace London day. Here lies Alonso aloft on his vast bed, hands crossed upon his chest, four tall candlesticks at each corner and a kneeling daughter at the foot and at either side. It is so cold in the room, with its closed curtains and dead fire, that Aurora has not thought it necessary to burn the incense in its thurible. The sisters conduct a conversation of whispers, speaking with hot, bitter breath into the counterpane where they rest pious foreheads. Aurora and Teresa had expected Maria to take charge in the organisation of Alonso's funeral. They had hoped that she would also be forthcoming with the funeral expenses. But she has mentioned neither, only requisitioning the place of chief mourner by the bed so that Aurora, on the other side, must squeeze herself between the nightstand and the wardrobe. Maria seems to be waiting irritably for her sisters to leave her alone in the room with Papa but Aurora is damned if she will give in to this. She and Teresa have plotted that Maria shall never be left unattended at her vigil. Maria mustn't be allowed to sequester herself here in noble, single attendance when Alonso had three daughters.

Now vigilant Aurora is desperate to relieve herself, and the urgency of a full bladder combines with the pressure on her knees to lend a sensation of acute, religious martyrdom. Herself released from knee drill, Teresa has preceded her downstairs to prepare lunch from what she can find in the larder and the meat safe so, when Aurora can bear the combined pressure no longer, Maria (as always) gets her way and is left alone. On returning Aurora is surprised to find that her sister has risen from the privileged position at the bedside and is balancing on a chair, trying to reach to the top of the wardrobe. She looks down over her shoulder upon her sister, saying, 'D'you know whatever became of that old suitcase of mine?'

'Goodness knows. Why are you worrying over suitcases?' she asks irritably.

'It is mine and I have need of it. Aurora, this is the only place in the world I may call "home", where I belong – even though it seems I must offer up my own bed to your domestic economy.'

Aurora squirms at this use of her name and the tone of Maria's voice: not so much angry as disappointed at a needless pain caused, yet again, by her and Teresa's prodigal behaviour.

'Don't you think I have the right to expect what little property I may call my own, that I have *entrusted* to you, to be respected?'

That voice makes Aurora want to shake the chair her sister is standing on until her supercilious teeth rattle – but for Papa, on the bed, whose heart would surely break.

'If you only knew, Maria, how 'Resa and I have struggled. Struggled to manage, to make ends meet, Papa being ill and us his only nurses,' she digs back. 'We've had so little time, quite apart from no space, to paint these last months. Lodgers were the only way we could earn an income and, you seem to forget, it was you who sent us Lady Georgina who had to be given our own, our only, bed. I don't know what became of your old suitcase and I don't care!'

At the moment that Aurora escapes from the room, in tears, Teresa returns with a tray of eatables. She looks up at her sister, still on the chair, with an expression of apprehensive supplication on her mild face. 'I did my best to polish up there, Maria, really I did, but I just couldn't reach right to the back.'

So we come to the end of that first long day of cold vigil in Alonso's house, and Georgina and the Flynns are talking quietly in the parlour. It was felt inappropriate to venture out that night and, somehow, Albert and even zealous Carrie appear to have lost some appetite for the Work. Maybe what kept them at home that night was the prospect of sleet striking on freezing streets, drunken abuse and the smell of unwashed bodies and vile exhalations – all that had once most pleased and elevated their senses. Or maybe it was the obscure presentiment that the creature metamorphosing before them, upon the Turkey rug, needed watching closely. For Georgina, standing by the empty grate, nose pinked by the lack of heat yet animated by an internal warmth that makes eyes and teeth flash, seems really to be growing larger before them. And it is poor Carrie who appears to be the host upon which this predatory splendour nourishes itself. As Georgina expands, so Carrie shrivels, sunk in her padded chair, like the thin green carapace from which this magnificent monster emerged. The sexual vigour with which she fed her Albert is all converted into growing Georgina.

'Don't you see? It is an act of divine intervention,' says the Amazon.

'I really think we must not call it that. A good man's life can never be the price asked,' says Albert, feeling small and scorched.

'Even when it is the Lord's own work?'

Albert demurs with a little cough.

'Well, I'm sure we regret our landlord's demise. But doesn't it strike you as strange that, on the very night we prayed for my mission's success, my photographic equipment arrived and the room we needed to use it was granted to us? Praise be!'

The empty shell of Carrie seems to collapse in upon itself a little more. Her feet now barely touch the floor and her head is sunk low so that her voice seems to come from somewhere deep and hollow: 'Death cannot be the price paid for earthly ambition.'

Comes unexceptional night and while all sleep in the overcrowded house Maria, with no bed of her own, wanders with her candle. Like an uneasy spirit searching for release, she opens drawers and empties cupboards to assemble that little pile of possessions she can lay sole claim to upon a japanned tray given her by an aunt. It's a collection of articles that even the housebreaker would have passed over – five unmatched napkin rings, a cruet set missing its salt cellar, a pretty teacup with a mended break running through its heart, and some long-folded pocket-handkerchiefs, embroidered with her initials by Mother and now spotted with rust marks where they were pinned together. Valueless, incomplete, spoiled. She sits on the floor with her worldly goods arranged upon the tray like a dolly's tea party. Tomorrow morning she will return to where she really belongs. Tomorrow she will manage the funeral arrangements and put some steel into Aurora and Teresa, who seem to have slipped into being nothing more than a couple of drudges. Impulsively she empties the tray into the coal scuttle, converting her sad treasures into trash and, once again, begins her unquiet wandering. Searching, searching, under beds and on high shelves – she even goes into the cellar, sliding over coal to delve among the old umbrellas and holed pots and pans that have found their last resting-place down there.

When all is settled she will be back at her home, the Hall, where everything is whole, matched, paired. Where there is none of this desperate vulgarity of keeping up appearances, no need to make do and mend. She could leave those silly girls to carry on burning holes in milk pans without a backward thought now that Papa is gone, but for that one, last, missing thing.

This same night another who is friendless and fallen wanders by herself. Despite her heavy body Lucy is compelled to keep on the move, as though fleeing before danger that threatens the child she carries within. She parted for good from Beatrice and Sidney when they launched into a violent argument, which put her in half-mourning with a black eye and sent him hobbling away in the opposite direction, as fast as bruised shins and flattened toes allowed. Since then she has wandered the streets of the East End, still wearing the uniform of a fallen girl hidden under a huge musty army coat donated by Beatrice, all the while taking care to stay clear of the freezing steps of the Whitechapel Hospital. Now she stops to warm her hands at a brazier. Even though it is bitter cold there are still people going about in the street, even some girls who stand shivering with their sewing under the street-lamps to gain a little free light by which they may continue their sweat work. And so all over London, in every court, alley, square and avenue, this ordinary, momentous day draws to its close.

Home

It is time for Maria to leave. Papa is buried (tucked in next to Mother), Aurora and Teresa have been bullied into a semblance of domestic order and have reclaimed their bedroom now that Georgina may occupy Papa's old room.

Maria has nothing more with her than she brought, packed among Georgina's salvation machinery, and this she carries in an old sewing-bag of her mother's. She has come to bid Georgina and the Flynns goodbye. On asking her former charge whether there is any message from her to be delivered to the Duchess of Fainhope, Georgina replies, with relish, 'You may tell her that I have found friends here and a purpose in life, which were denied me before.' Having been cast off, Lady Georgina's anger towards her mother might have had fair cause, but her antipathy has been founded more upon those passing injustices and unconsidered slights that Olympian adults hand down to children and which, beyond all other, pleasanter, memories of childhood, persist to stoke resentment. Georgina chooses to snub her mother because she has had time to reflect. During these months of separation and growing independence she has worked over sample evidence of the vivid abuse heaped upon her in childhood: the case of the unfair slap, when the broken doll had really been Euphemia's fault, the evidence of malice aforethought in the ill-considered birthday present of the magnifying hand mirror. All tended to only one outcome: guilty, as charged, of being heartless and unnatural. So Georgina herself sentences her mother to be banished.

At least one of the new-found friends, however, looks as though they could wish that Georgina had been reconciled to a life of idle comfort with Mama in the country.

Miss Mantilla reproves. 'I will bring her your compliments *and*,' she says, in the tone of the unreconstructed governess, 'I will thank her for the items you requested.' Just as she is about to leave she turns in the doorway and says, as though the thought had only then occurred to her, 'I left the Hall in such a hurry that I neglected to bring a suitcase, as you see. This is really not suitable for the train. I seem to remember that there was an old one stored upon the top of the wardrobe that once stood in your room, Mrs Flynn. Could it have been left there by my silly sisters?'

'Oh, no, there was nothing,' replies Carrie.

At this moment, it seems to Maria that she hears a cat crying somewhere in the house and she says so to Teresa. But no, for Mrs Evans is still fugitive. And even though they search the house, until the very minute of Maria's departure, no cat is found.

When train timetables demand she really must leave, Maria gives each sister a peremptory kiss and turns on her heel, the sewing-bag banging against her leg as she strides out. And as she goes, disappearing down the street, so the sound of crying fades, too, as though she carried it away with her. She is leaving, never to return. She is sure of that, for what had once tugged at her to return has vanished as though it had never been.

Half a day later she is back where she belongs, crunching up the drive in the chaise that had met her at the village station. She looks on the sweep of the façade as an old friend, its lighted windows beckoning. When her carriage draws up at the servants' entrance and the Duchess's own dog rushes to greet her she is warmed by a sense of her acceptance here. Of course she must use the servants' stairs to reach her own little room, with its fire in the grate and warm water on the washstand, but that is only right. And as she sits upon her bed to remove her bonnet, she lets out a sigh of relief at the homecoming completed. She may not have contended with the dangers of rocks and whirlpools but, nevertheless, she feels as though she has come through some ordeal to get back here, safe.

Should you happen to cross the park now to call upon Lord John Harpur you might surprise a stealthy shadow that flits about, like a lost boy shut out from the comfort of the family hearth, seeking a way home. He walks the night slowly, circling the manor house, disembodied, until his breath is made visible in the light still poured out by the few lit windows. At the first he views Lady Caroline, half comatose upon her sofa. The little dog that lies on her feet leaps up and advances across the floor, yapping, disturbed by the unheard presence that slides past in the darkness. Next is the sequence of tall dining-room windows through which the under-footman and a maid are to be seen righting the room. As he passes, each in turn reveals the next flickering picture in the zoetrope – the maid replacing an epergne upon the sideboard . . . a golden tangerine falling . . . rolling . . . dropping to thud unseen, and, in the last, the exit of the footman. Perhaps, like the circular picture sequence of the zoetrope, this scene, too, replays itself over and over. He does not stay to see, but turns a corner and comes to another window where, alone in the illuminated tank of his library, Lord John sits over his brandy glass, with lamp, fire and his rich rows of books. The scene of domestic benevolence glows within its frame. Warm light beams out to confront the cold and dark of indifferent night, which presses back, hard, upon the panes. This is where George dwells, on the outside looking in, vital in the freezing cold. Here he feels the illusionary power of the observer unobserved and relishes the energy of the concealing night.

But even night-stalker George must lay his head somewhere, though never upon his pillow. Creeping upstairs to his bedroom he's anxious not to disturb Cousin Harry, for he knows that Harry is practising smoking cigars at his window and will want to give him a puff and make him sick. He is anxious, too, not to be discovered with the bundle of old newspapers that he has under his arm. In fact, such an insubstantial figure is he, seeming rather to haunt than inhabit the rooms, that the mansion's other occupants act out their lives as though insensible that he is a player on the same lively stage as they. His room is cold, no one has remembered to make up the fire – they rarely do. But George doesn't mind if it is cold – he likes it. Neither does he care that he is ignored for he finds the glare of human society hard to tolerate. George has other ways of finding comfort and company. Strip by strip, he tears out the personal adverts from *The Times* and lays them upon the floor, smoothing each so that it will lie flat. Even though they are but simulations of the magical winding strips that were burnt up in the fire, they still represent the warmth that happiness and companionship bring. He lies upon the paper nest, positioning himself in the bleary mirror set in the wardrobe door, and seems to see there a pale boy in the candlelight.

Our poor Lucy, like an animal driven to find a nesting-place, is also searching for somewhere safe to lie down. Even though it is near midnight, and cold as charity, she feels hot and encumbered. The night air is a dense fog coloured deep red by flaring gas-lamps, sour and oppressive. She is sensitised to her body, yet feels alien within it. It is a dread feeling, familiar from those times she was about to be violently sick and longed for that explosive relief – willing to endure anything in order to cast off the feeling of pent unease and overwhelming physical consciousness. Even her bones no longer belong to her, for the tops of her legs feel as though they will come adrift from her hips, and her backbone crunches and jars as she walks. She undoes the coat, then the dress beneath it and would have continued to pull open her skin, so uncomfortable is she in this urgent, bursting body. But she cannot stop, driven to search down each reeking alley and in every doorway for that safe, dark, warm lair. It seems to her that she is looking for the place in which she must lie down to die, that it is Death who has possessed her body. She can feel the flex and clutch of his muscular fist lodged in her entrails.

It is the familiar smell of horses' urine that attracts her through the unsecured gate into the cobbled yard. So strong a sensation that, like smelling-salts, it distracts and numbs the devil inside her. When she pushes at the stable door, at the end of the yard, she finds that that, too, is unlocked. Inside, a horse, tethered in its loose-box and standing in deep litter, turns from its hay-net to look at her. Its eye gleams. It looks away and shifts from one back foot to the other, accepting her. This is the place, then. Death has brought her here so that he can push her out of this turbulent body.

For the rest of his life Frederick Goss, carter, would retell the events of that night as his East End Nativity. Of course, the tale of a birth, any birth, noble, religious or otherwise, is always a miraculous one. In most stories it is the beginning and, you may be sure, the baby brings with it, like a gift from a cruel or kind fairy godmother, a quirk or characteristic from which his life story will unfold.

When Fred had felt his way down the ladder from his lodgings above the stable, club in hand, he had expected to see some little toerag leading away his horse. What he found in his stable was a living tableau of mother and child in the straw, the grand old horse standing near, breathing warm sweet air over them both. Being a practical man he had found a piece of clean string to tie off the navel cord, and a sheet to wrap the infant in. But being also of a romantic turn of phrase, he never mentioned these details in the telling. Instead he pointed out the eerie glow that lit the stable that winter's morning and the ethereal beauty of the new mother. He never reported that his first words to Lucy had been, 'That's ve way, old gal. Well done,' spoken in the encouraging tone he used on horses.

But he always closed the retelling on a rueful note, saying, 'Remember now it was a cold, sere December morn. There's the mother an've baby and stap me ifen vere ain't even a manger full a hay to lay 'im in. And I can tell you, I 'ad to pinch meself more 'an once to recall what *exac'* day of ve month it were.'

At this point he would generally let his audience hang in suspense for a little while, before continuing, 'December the twenty-second. Yes, December the twenty-second – no call to put the kettle on fer shepherds an' wise men.'

His audiences always liked this return to reality, although on that famous morning he had checked his almanac with a trembling finger before he could be absolutely sure. And when he was sure, he had laughed off his childish fancy and made room for Lucy and the baby upstairs. But he would never cease feeling that he had been especially honoured and blessed and that he would, in the future, always commemorate 22 December.

Photography and Philanthropy

As Lucy found a new home, so Aurora and Teresa lost what little hold they retained over their old one: Lady Georgina's was an expansionist regime. She advanced and occupied in the name of progress, forcing the two sisters to retreat before her to the very limits of their domain. The photographic equipment was moved, under her direction, by the sullenly rebellious natives to the attic uplands: new territory, which she claimed as her own. Aurora and Teresa's primitive artifacts of paint, brush and canvas were superseded by Georgina's marvellous machinery, which, like so much in this modernising nineteenth century, did an old job in less than half the time with more than twice the accuracy.

And the natives could not grumble about lack of compensation for the loss of their traditional ways, for under Georgina's new governance they discovered that photographic assistants earned twice as much as did dabbling portraitists and inaccurate retouchers. They also benefited by being educated in the industrial technology of their coloniser – taught how to prepare the photographic plates, how to develop and process and print, and their outmoded talents as painters were exploited in the daubing of the suggestive backcloths needed to dress Georgina's photographic representations.

However, even as the natives breathed a sigh of relief at the regular income, they still felt stripped of the dignity of being gentlewomen, albeit distressed. As Teresa put it, 'I would feel myself happier as a lady artist,' turning over hands stained with chemicals.

To which her sister accurately replied, 'And hungrier.'

During this time Albert and dear Carrie were also squeezed by Georgina's drive to annex and assimilate. The disciple became apostle and the Flynns, too, were drafted to service Georgina's mission. Immured at home by her shameful veil, she sent them forth every night to trawl the streets for their most pathetic denizens. Their instructions were to seek out depravity and despair in all their most lurid forms. She would accept only that which had the power truly to disturb. Any substandard offering – picturesque pathetic or merely sentimental – would be thrown back upon the street. What fed Georgina's new mission were photographic subjects whose eyes could meet the gaze of those who looked on them with sufficient hunger, for revenge and restitution to send a lasting chill to the depths of their souls.

On many mornings the Flynns emptied their net to release their stinking night-haul upon Georgina's doorstep. She would sort through their offerings and direct her assistants as to which backdrop they should erect and which props should dress each set. Most frequently required was the winning combination of painted doorway, broken crate and dirty straw. While the set was prepared the model would wait most commonly in the garden, pacified with a jam-jar of tea and the promise of lodgings that night in the Fisher Folk's warehouse. Some co-operated, others did not. One practical man turned his hand to *snowing*: legging it over the garden fence with a bundle of washing pulled from the line. And a band of starveling, rat-faced kids murdered the chickens Aurora kept in a slummy hutch behind the privy. They were found, choked by feathers, having been under the misapprehension that chicken flesh was best enjoyed raw.

Teresa and Aurora's neighbours were less than charmed by these callers.

'Queerish, I call it. Your lady lodger may be sentimental about these low types but that doesn't excuse her entertaining 'em at home. Who's to stop these thieves and rascals from taking advantage of honest folk?' demanded the brawny man who had relieved them of the silver coffee spoon.

Aurora noticed that the complaints were never directed at Lady Georgina, who was much too intimidating in her oddity and her elevation. Even so, that she was an eccentric aristocrat only seemed to add to their affront. As the ferocious lady next door put it, 'She may come of good blood, but then so does black pudding!'

And so it was that our meek landladies had their ears bent by the fear and prejudice of the righteous and respectable. And what extravagant terror they anticipated – floodgates opened, tidal waves unleashed, all that was good and ordinary swamped: high expectations of people already brought to such a low ebb that they would weep with gratitude over a friendly jar of tea.

Ignorant of this opprobrium Georgina continued to assemble the armoury of images with which the assault upon the sensibilities of the elevated one-third would be launched. She photographed single subjects, both full-length and portrait. She composed group shots comprising from two to seven models – in the last case the seven were the defeathered rat boys, who were only constrained to keep their poses by the promise of a taste of the premature pie that those poor chickens made. Although Georgina did her best, through art and artifice, to fix the brutish reality that the Flynns found in the East End for her every night, she never could quite capture the truth of what was brought before her camera. She suspected that it was the fault of the painted backdrops and set dressing, the contrived look of the scattered straw and that ubiquitous crate. Away from those streets and tenements, which were their natural habitat, how could her subjects look real? Georgina saw a stilted artificiality in those photographs, which suggested, to her, mounted animals displayed in cabinets.

She knew that those photographs were failures. They failed, on her terms, because they could not be made to hold the reality of the moment. A connoisseur of the shocks she had found for herself in the streets, she sought to procure a similarly strong and immediate sensation for her viewer: to jar them into seeing properly. So the scrofulous, run-down, gaudy and grotesque were brought to her, all in the attempt to nail down, to fix the fleeting moment in the unfolding narrative of London street life. But it just didn't work. In the instant that the image was transferred to the plate she lost the immediacy of what really stank and shivered before the avid gaze of her camera lens, and made something immortal. These weren't vivid dispatches from the front line so much as poignant mementoes.

True, there *was* something unnatural about her poses – her very presence made her subjects uneasy – but the essential problem was that her photographs had an unaccountable nobility, which didn't so much terrify as transfigure. Quite simply, where Georgina sought fear and loathing, she found the picturesque. Even the grimy beak-chasers, looking malevolently out of their group portrait, in their cut-down jackets, ruffians' bowler hats and rag neckerchiefs were transformed by photography. The camera resolved their random grouping among the props into a harmonious composition. It discovered the soulful effect of pathos in their still, sullen faces, and gave grace to their sinewy limbs. Georgina's pictures did not repel so much as distance and soothe the viewer.

But Georgina did not understand this. She tried next photo-graphing 'details', in the attempt to suggest the vivid impression harvested by the nervous, horrified eye that darts about its subject, wary of taking in the horrid whole all at once. So she focused upon hands or feet alone. But it soon became apparent that the grimier and more distorted the subject matter the more eternal and dignified her photographs. There was something about the close-up etching of old dirt in creased skin, the marks of labour and old injury, that fascinated in an image, rather than disgusted as they did in real life. However hard she tried, Georgina could not achieve simple, nasty verisimilitude, but was condemned to elevate humanity as though to tell some eternal tragic truth.

However, locked as she was in her private obsession, she would not give up. Having at last decided that naturalism was impossible under the conditions in which her veil forced her to work, she began to experiment with making her representations unashamedly contrived. Her models were arranged in the poses of those characters more familiar from the painterly arts: a desperate alcoholic, ears reduced to stubs, fists to folded nubs by a thousand fights, became a Bacchus of the streets holding up his bunch of grapes, seated on the parlour chair. She attempted an Ophelia, using a young prostitute whose own circumstances (having been dragged from the River Thames into which she had flung herself that morning) inspired the 'personation. However, that young person could not be kept from shivering violently so she was done up as Mary Magdalene: another example of typecasting.

This fanciful detour into classical and biblical mythology didn't last long. Aurora and Teresa found it impossible to supply all the props and costumes to re-create these scenes from ancient Greece and the New and Old Testaments. There was only so much they could contrive out of a few embroidered shawls and costumes. And, grotesque as these portraits undoubtedly were, the overall effect was of looking through a kind of distorting lens that beautified what it saw and made the banal interesting.

It was this difficulty with scene-setting that suggested to Georgina what was to become her speciality, her 'voice'. She had noticed that, as items from the parlour were dragged upstairs to her studio to furnish sets, there was a strange and exciting dissonance between their everyday respectability and the tramps and slatterns waiting to be placed among them.

'Mrs Flynn, I have decided to transport my subjects to the parlour rather than bring the parlour to them,' she directed, in her usual autocratic manner. 'My new idea is that they shall be displayed in all their frightfulness, drinking from your porcelain, sitting at your fire. Literally putting their dirty, naked feet under the table. Think how effective that might prove. I'll call them my "Home and Hearth" portraits.' It was as though she, alienated herself by her oddity and ugliness, collected an alternative 'family' of photographic pariahs to keep her company in her outcast world.

For Carrie Flynn, though, it was the last straw. Without the knowledge of her husband she had approached Mrs Heever with a few smuggled prints. Within days a secret committee meeting of the Fisher Folk elders was arranged and Carrie appeared before them with her evidence.

'What message does she intend to broadcast with these photographs?' demanded one peppery gent. 'They're nothing better than curios – like those exhibits of stuffed kittens posed in sailor suits or frogs on swings, only more disagreeable.'

'Perhaps our daughter Georgina has strayed away from philan-thropic work into an obscure field of artistic expression?' queried the Skipper.

'Nonsense. It's nothing more than lachrymose twaddle!'

'Insanity's nearer the mark,' said a man known as First Mate.

'We must turn to our estimable Mrs Flynn for elucidation on this, perhaps,' said the Skipper, smiling on Carrie. 'In your view is our young lady unwell in the head or merely misguided?'

'My husband would have neither,' said Carrie, simply.

'He is a very muscular Fisher for the cause,' the Skipper replied encouragingly.

'And I would never normally speak contrary to him. However, I fear that a female given her head like this, using mechanical contraptions, delighting so in filth and deformity, must be unnatural, even ungodly.'

There was general assent at this very proper sentiment, and it was agreed that Sister Georgina should be vigorously prayed over.

Carrie snuck home that evening buoyed by the expectation that 'something would be done' to rid her of this succubus. However, she might have been less sanguine had she seen that, after she had left the men to their business, the elders' only action was boldly to file the prints in a box marked 'pending'.

Happiness

As we have seen, not many streets away from the Fisher Folk's East End mission there now dwells the East End Mary whom Fred had found and carried aloft to his lodgings above the stable. Since Fred is no carpenter and we know Lucy to be no virgin this is a biblical personification that perverse Georgina might herself have contrived.

Simple Fred, a never-married man in his mid-thirties, dedicated tea-kettle-purger, delighted in his new-made family, and Lucy, amateur whore, suspected that she must be the one to make payment for the shelter he offered her and her baby. But he asked nothing. He made up a bed on the floor for himself and wondered over her as though she was a mythical creature he had accidentally captured for himself. She waited for him to name his terms and he asked her, a hundred times a day, whether he might fetch her something to eat, or drink, or be allowed to rock the baby. He begged clothes and linen for the child from the families who lived around the courtyard where his own stable and lodgings were. He changed the baby and even washed his dirtied nappies and her female rags. Lucy was appalled and ashamed by this – it was, to her, an anathema for a man to do a woman's intimate laundry.

Fred delighted in the baby and, because he did, Lucy learnt

how to love her little burden too. At first she found that she could best see her baby as deserving of love when she saw him held by Fred. And when Fred was unintentionally rough with the baby – jogging him on his knee until the head bobbed on a sinewless neck – she felt the impulse to protect and nurture grow in her. She fell in love with them together. She loved Fred out of gratitude, and her baby because the instinct to do so was taught her. Hers was neither mother-love nor 'love at first sight': she came to love Fred and the baby by degrees, starting with the man's strong, kind hands and the beautiful ripe curve of the baby's cheek. Only when she was sure of these did she commit herself to loving a little more, until she fell in love, head over heels, with the baby and the man complete, in all their parts.

Simple Fred had no such dilemma about loving her, although he was cautious and very shy about showing it. When at last he got up courage to approach he did so with extreme caution, as though she might snap in two or flare up in a righteous fury – she felt she might scream with impatience. But as they grew more used to each other and he more confident, she recognised that he had learnt how to handle her with the same gentle assurance as he was accustomed to show his dear horse. He was not an inspired or particularly passionate lover, it was not in his nature to be so flamboyant or demonstrative, but he went about it in the same reassuring routine way that he did everything – considered, deliberate and steady. He did not use her as she had grown to expect from men, as though he were invading, but acted as though this was a dialogue in which an answer was expected from her. She did not, at first, know how to reply – the expectation of intimacy seemed like impropriety – but eventually, when she grew confident enough to respond, their love-making grew into a friendly and comfortable agreement between the two of them. And even though hers was not romantic love it was not any the less valid and strong. Lucy leant upon his broad chest, muscled as a stoker's, and relaxed into domestic love.

One particular evening, ten weeks after he had found her, Lucy and Fred sit, easy together, the baby's hot, damp cheek lying upon her breast; he has fallen asleep while feeding. They are in the middle of a debate over the right name for the boy. It is a decision that they believe, like others before and after, will have influence in shaping the rest of his life.

A well-chosen name must achieve two things, one temporal, the other mystical. First, it publicly signals the scope of the parents' expectations and ambitions for the child. The most modest choice is a name that is unexceptional and unobjectionable – a neutral signifier, promising acceptance in the class to which the child is born, and a quiet life. If the name is pretty or diminutive then the child is probably a girl and her parents think it appropriate that she should grow to manifest these baby characteristics. Pride in the family and its achievements is celebrated in naming for a parent or some other illustrious ancestor. Commemorating a king or queen is a broader expression of this satisfaction with the status quo, or simple lack of imagination. And if these mortal dedications are not thought powerful enough, then a biblical name or personification of a holy virtue is chosen. Most risky is the signal sent by a name that hankers after social advancement or predicts some future prowess. Of course, apart from revealing the parents' expectations for their child, the second, secret significance in public naming is to charm into being the child of their imagination. Choosing the correct name is like an invocation to the gods, or a temptation to Fate, for a name is a magical thing and must be handled with care.

So when Lucy suggests that he should be named Fred, she is not just proposing to compliment the modest carter but also to rededicate the baby – wipe away and obscure the pain and fear that went into his getting. Plain 'Fred' would make of him something normal, simple and plain – make him belong to her and him alone, make him lovable. But the carter can't bear that the miraculous baby should be burdened by his own disappointment of a name. He wants something splendid for him, like Topaz or Hero.

Lucy is frightened by these brave names. Their vainglory seems the wrong way to nominate the outcome of a hole-and-corner sin and it worries her that the loud pride with which they proclaim him may tempt Fate to come crashing down upon his head. Also, she is shamed to think that it is not this kind and generous man who has the right to name him but the one who fathered him and left him branded with the title 'bastard'. Lucy, choked by her anger and humiliation, crushed by gratitude for Fred's unjudgemental desire to celebrate a stranger's by-blow, cannot say that this is why she may not speak but weeps with eyes turned to the floor. Fred goes to stand behind her and places his hands on her shoulders, which makes her slump even more dejectedly.

'Ne'er you mind. The old 'orse may as well be 'is dad, for all I 'ave to say on the matter,' he encourages her, thinking she is crying for the real father about whom he has no notion other than to feel obliged to the chap – his loss being Fred's gain.

Lucy chews her lips angrily to bite away the remembered sensation that sly, wet moustache has left upon them. 'Then let the horse be his dad, and done with it,' comes her humble reply.

'Nah, ve old boy may 'ave a fing or two to say about vat – seein' as it's a geldin'.'

She nearly smiles at that. 'He was born in a horse's stable, so why not?'

'Luce, if 'e were born in an 'amper, it wouldn' make the boy a pork pie, would i', no more 'an a pickled onion, eh, love?'

Now she has the nerve to look up into his face. 'Fred, you are a specimen. I'm not saying he *is* a horse, just that he don't belong to the man that had the making of him. He don't owe home or happiness or anything to him. He found all of those in Duke's stable, in your stable. And me too.'

'Ven ol' Duke must stand as godfarver,' says Fred, somewhat moved by Lucy's vehemence.

'There couldn't be a finer one in all the world.'

'Duke'll be honoured, I'm sure.'

'And the boy is to be named after his dear godfather.'

'If you say so, love,' says Fred, plucking the warm, curled little grub from her arms and kissing its puckering forehead, so that it unrolls itself and wails in comic despair. 'Dear little Dukey,' he says, laughing at the cross face.

So both had their way. Lucy hid her boy, with gratitude and humility, behind that gentle horse's borrowed name and Fred used it to proclaim to all the world his pride in his adopted son.

The Life

Let us not forget that other absconder from the Fisher Folk home who, when last we heard of her, was sporting a black eye and borrowed finery. Cockney Beatrice remained on the loose after parting with Lucy and Sidney, but her luck has not been in. She has been trying to accumulate a little starting capital with which to launch herself back upon society, but the limited returns to be had from cruising poor neighbourhoods, combined with the need regularly to drown her sorrows, means that it has taken her nearly two months to get together money enough to buy herself glad-rags suited to a life up West.

She has come to Monmouth Street, where there may be found any number of chobey shops specialising in the supply of second-hand clothes to the desperate. Having stopped to look for an outfit at Abrahams Outfitters, she fingers through the mouldering wallflowers exposed for sale outside the shop before entering to seek a better class of rag. The lady proprietor makes a quick assessment of her customer and stands close by to see that nothing is slipped under her skirt and made away with.

'Give us some space,' complains Beatrice. 'It's enough like a bloody spice island in 'ere wivout you breavin' in me face as well.'

'Only tryin' to 'elp,' grumbles the old woman, backing off a little.

'What's this 'un?' says Beatrice, pulling out a stiff garment, the pattern, material and even colour of which has been obscured by the shine of wear and dirt. 'Preserve us, it stinks,' she says, throwing it down and making to leave. The shopkeeper picks up the rag with reverential fingers, as though she could make its merits apparent in the tender way she holds it.

''Tain't so far gawn but ve sides may be turned in ve middle and kiver a body comfortable, lovey. An' vis 'un only wants a bit of a rub frough,' she says, taking up and smoothing the largest stain on another garment as though this simple remedial action would be in the least effective.

Beatrice moves deeper into the shop, where the more expensive items are displayed, perhaps the brocade of a duchess, the satin of a courtesan: so many histories wrapped up in these old clothes. 'Looks like someun was murdered in this 'un.'

'Vere's some lovely riggin' 'ere. Straight orf ve backs of ve gentry. Look at this, dovey. Now, this'd look beautiful on.' The old lady holds a costume up to Beatrice from which racks of dingy lace are detaching themselves like guttering from a derelict house.

Beatrice steps away in mock horror. 'You should burn this stuff, I swear! Look at the light infantry on that. Gawd knows what you'd catch orf of it!' To emphasise her fastidiousness, Beatrice makes an elaborate show of wiping her hands on her own filthy skirts. However, her eye is caught by a box of decorative miscellany from which she pulls a droopy ostrich-feather fan, clumped and grey with dust. 'I want the costume altered and pressed – with a *hot* iron – and this fan thrown in and I'm not paying more'n a sov for the lot,' she says, fanning.

The old lady staggers back, hand to chest, employing the specialised gestures of melodrama that denote the wronged and exploited. 'What d'you take me for?'

Beatrice builds upon the dramatic theme, initiated by the old lady, with a performance of affronted heel-turning that would not have been missed up in the gods.

She is allowed to reach the very door of the shop before the old woman judges it right to supply her answering rally: 'A sov an' a 'alf and I'll frow in some ribbon an' a pin and vat's me last word.'

Beatrice pauses, and the woman adds quickly, 'I couldn' part wiv va fan alone for less van a shillin' – I swear vat's what it cost me.'

By now Beatrice is slowly making her way back into the depths of the shop, although still very much on her dignity. The shopkeeper knows that she must keep up the banter to tempt this customer back into a dialogue of negotiation. 'You'd 'ave ta slit me froat to get your 'ands on it for less, dear.'

Playfully, Beatrice raises her arm to the old woman, who cowers before her. 'Don't worry, Grandma, your scraggy neck's too tough to saw through.'

'Charmin', I'm sure, attackin' an ole lady,' she grumbles, rubbing at her neck as though she felt Beatrice's fingers there.

'What about this costume, with the ribbon and the pin an' this midge net? An' that's me last word,' counters Beatrice, picking up a veil from the assortments box.

'Vat'll keep the gen'lemen guessin',' says the shopkeeper, approvingly.

'Dead right it will!'

And so the transaction is completed, and Beatrice is suitably armoured for her assault upon the rich pickings of the West End.

Forewarned, Skipper Heever had blandly accepted Georgina's scenes of 'Home and Hearth, Through a Glass', when she had officially presented them. However, since the elders obviously intended to make no use of them, a month having passed and no word, Georgina at last determined that she must herself turn entrepreneur. She hired a hall in which to launch her manifesto to a crowd of disaffected, and curious, Fisher Folk, the well-to-do being somewhat over-represented, perhaps attracted by the prospect of gaining social advancement, by association, with this aristocratic young lady. She dragooned the Flynns as officers and paid, from her own purse, for the hire of the hall and the advertisement conveyancers, employed to parade the details of the meeting through the streets. She directed the construction of the stage on which she would stand, and the painting of the various exclamatory banners reading, 'THE NEW BARBARIANS?' and 'BEHOLD, I STAND AT THE DOOR AND KNOCK!' There wasn't a smell of a cut-out fish or pasteboard boat. Lastly she had to sell her personal jewellery to fund the printing of a stack of postcard-sized *carte de visite* prints of her latest photographs. These were to be the new artillery in the battle for God's Kingdom on earth: her street grotesques misplaced, standing and sitting at their insolent ease, in Alonso's respectable parlour.

Now she stands, burning with zeal behind her veil, watching the hall fill with curious members of the general public as well as Fisher Folk. A vision of female nobility, raised upon a platform – Mr Briggs would have been deeply moved by this personification of Georgina. And, she finds, she was born to orate. As she talks, the Flynns pass around the calling cards, which represent everyday degradation, malnutrition and disease in these new and disturbing forms. Several ladies leave but Lady Georgina talks on: 'Brothers and sisters, we must not shirk. It will be as though the rabble, which we find every day upon the streets, were introduced into the very bosom of our complaisant city. It is said that, "London is the epitome of our times, and the Rome of today." Rome, the greatest city the world had seen, fell because she had not eyes to see the dangers that lurked within. Are we not like new Romans, grown flabby and arrogant? With these picture cards filthy feet will seem to stand upon silk carpets and leave their mark behind. The glare of that wolfish hunger will lay waste to the tray of dainty eatables. Rag-pickers' fingers will fumble and tear at hem and cuff. The stench of the sewer will be savoured by delicate nostrils. Believe me, brothers and sisters in Christ, these portraits will shock and disgust but they will make eyes see that have here-to-now been blind.

We will engender fear. Fear, not feeble pity or a simple call to "Christian charity", shall win the day.'

At this point several of the crowd call, 'Shame,' and 'Blasphemy,' but Georgina is not to be interrupted: 'Fear moves to action where mere pity does not. You accuse me of blasphemy, yet did not Jesus Himself find His work among beggars, lepers and harlots, such as these, rather than among the rich? Are not these outcasts invisible in our new Rome? "That is so," I hear you murmur. Then it must be our duty to shine a light upon these barbarians of our times!' Georgina is really working her audience now: she sways as she speaks as one possessed, which her detractors maintain she is, by some diabolic force. Her address builds to its climax, carrying all who remain in the hall before her. 'Fear and disgust. Disgust and fear. Two mighty weapons with which we will win this war. Disgust might, at first, cause the drawbridge to be raised up tight against us, but hand in hand with fear it will work upon those sealed inside until they are driven mad and deliver themselves, and their money, tribute to our holy cause. For we *shall* be the victors, the moral victors, in this war.'

When Georgina steps back, drained by fervour, from the brink of the stage, it is Albert who moves forward and, reverting to the metaphors of his old leader, delivers the final exhortation: 'Go, then! Go among polite society and use these "hooks" well. Cast these picture cards with their message of the Fisher Folk mission upon as yet untroubled seas. Leave them where you would once have left your calling card. Place them within the pages of your lending-library books for others to come across. Post them through letter-boxes. Go, and return with your catch for the Lord!'

Several in the crowd are moved to tears and applause, and not a few to a delicious sensation of having found an exciting new prophetess.

However, Carrie, ever quiet and obedient, has her reservations. Was it only she who recollected that the Rome with which Sister Georgina compared their own capital had been a godless and corrupted place where true Christians had been persecuted by the ruling classes? Carrie has the uneasy sensation that they might win more lasting support for their cause by showing the poor as helpless and their children as deserving of sympathy – like the poet's wailing waifs and strays, 'orphans of the earthly love and heavenly', 'weeping in the playtime of the others, in the country of the free' – rather than this revolutionary rabble intent upon destroying the country of the free and pillaging their houses. It sounded to her more like the call to crush the dangerous rabble under heel than an invitation to solace them. Georgina's message had surely departed from the simple precepts of Faith, Hope and Charity that the Bible taught them. And surely simple Charity, not fear and loathing, was there proclaimed the greatest of all?

One other, seated near the back of the Fisher Folk hall, remains unroused by Georgina's martial splendour: he is interested in the prophetess, not her message. Attracted by posters advertising Lady Georgina Harpur's talk, you might recognise this particular member of the civilian audience by his untrimmed moustache and black bag. Having discreetly approached a Fisher man to enquire after the lady orator's private address, which he is unable to supply, this fellow appears shy of approaching the lady herself, surrounded as she is by the crush of other admirers. For Lady Georgina is a great success. Many go away into that night fired by her call to action. But as he disappears down the street Dr Oliver has no thoughts for Georgina's revolutionary new mission: her chance discovery has aroused in him the need to settle the old, chafing business he has with the house of Fainhope.

Not far away, and not long after Georgina's unusual meeting, our redoubtable Beatrice is also launching upon her new enterprise. Today she is to be found working Burlington Arcade – when she is not chased off by the regular whores whose beat this is by long tradition, or by the police whom the shopkeepers pay to do so.

Now we may find her as she saunters, dressed in a smarter costume than the original with which she had equipped herself from the outfitter's shop, with new gloves, hat and the veil. The veil has become a useful marketing aid: with it she is anonymous when she wants to be, and it attracts a particular type of 'trade', those gentlemen who like a bit of mystery or even danger in their sexual transactions. Since veils are generally worn by those whores with something to hide, there is a nasty thrill to be had in risking a ride with her. The veil marks her out as 'speciality merchandise', titillation for those jaded by everyday flesh. True, a client whose needs are moderated by inhibition is a safer option than this type of desperate thrill-seeker, but he doesn't pay as well. And Beatrice needs the money.

She takes care to vary her route between the arcade shops so that her purpose is apparent without being blatant. Her special target, in those trawling perambulations, is the tobacconist's shop window where gentlemen linger comfortably to appraise snuff-boxes or the female form. But she can only risk returning there every quarter-hour or so.

She is affecting interest in a pearl-handled penknife when up sidles a likely gentleman. He stands beside her with a look of triumph. 'Found you! Such dedication to a cause – do you never rest, Lady Georgina?' Dr Oliver is excited at having turned up this unexpected ace so soon after having sat down again to the game.

Beatrice is wrongfooted by this unconventional overture: she isn't sure what his banter means and is wary of launching straight into her terms and conditions. The gentleman obviously wants to talk first. She tries to keep negotiations open by effecting a musical, 'Sir?'

His mysterious reply does nothing to guide her – 'Can the mission be so short of funds, my lady? Or is this field work?' – but she recognises his tone, and this gives her the confidence to say, 'Ne'er mind a field. There's a 'otel we may use, close by.'

However, this saucy invitation is obviously not what he is expecting from her. 'So you *are* only a tart. How disappointing,' he replies contemptuously. 'Let me peep beneath the curtain, nevertheless, for I'd know that particular physog in my sleep.'

Then he tries, as punters do, to lift her veil and Beatrice slaps him away. He raises his hand to her and then, thinking better of striking a fashionably dressed lady in a public place, even if she is only a whore, wipes his palms on his coat and stalks off.

'Piss off yourself, nosy-parker!' If she is the barker outside this sideshow then the veil must stay in place. The trick of it is in gingering up the punter to do the work for you, letting mere suggestion arouse his imagination to supply whatever is his deepest desire, his worst fear, which alone will carry him over the threshold. All the charm of anticipation is lost if they are allowed a quick peep before the deal is done, the entry ticket paid for. The poor Lion Boy with his harelip and mane of backcombed hair belies the painted representation of chained savagery outside the freak show. Likewise the Remarkable Tattooed Lady, as advertised, is remarkable chiefly for the lack of frisson she produces in the crowd when they, at last, behold her inked-over naked hide. A wise whore understands this truth – she isn't in the business of just selling sex: what satisfies the customers, and keeps them coming back, is how tantalisingly she dresses up the *idea* of sex. Beatrice isn't a particularly wise whore – she wouldn't still be working the streets if she was – but she is enough of a show woman to know that she might have struck on a new way of setting out her stall. 'Lady Turned Whore,' the poster would shout. 'Pay up, pay up, to experience the depravity of Lady Georgina, noblewoman gone to the bad!'

Family Life

Time slips past in town and country alike, sweeping our dancers along with it. Some twenty months have elapsed since last we looked in at the room above the stable. Still together, Lucy and Fred, Little Duke and Big Duke have become a family and live, like everyone else they know, off, by and on the river. Ubiquitous river: black lifeblood of London. Always the reminder of river, even when it is hidden and silenced behind high wharf walls, the tang of tidal mud, and worse, is now so familiar that, when she is away from their part of London, Lucy is breathless in air that seems neutral and too thin. Malevolent river. A brew of pestilence, a sliding trap of hungry mud and thirsty water greedy for human lives. Lucy fears the summer's fevers that carry off the weak and young, dreads the everyday news of bodies that are gargled down that gullet, then coughed up to slop in its wash. Bountiful river, London's native source, that floats in the ships to be serviced by that multitude who teem along her margins. Today the river is a good, kind river that needs Fred and his cart to transport cargo from dock to warehouse. Today it brings their daily bread.

At last, twenty minutes after he turned horse and cart into the courtyard, Lucy hears Fred stamping up the wooden stairs to their room above the stable. Although he left before dawn she knows that he will never come up for his tea before he's seen that Big Duke is fed, watered and comfortably bedded down.

''Ow do, missus?' he greets her, as always, and sits down to unlace his boots.

She carries baby Duke over for a kiss from his dad, and as she stoops to place him on Fred's knee, he covertly slips something into her hand. 'Oh, Fred! What's this?'

'Carter's gleanings, gal. Tea clipper put in today loaded down wiv best China – a few leaves don' signify.'

She tries to give him back the package. 'You shouldn't, you really shouldn't . . . It's no more than stealing.' Fred laughs and tries to make her sit on his free knee, but Lucy has jumped up and is dragging a chair across the room so that she may stand on it to reach her hiding-place for such contraband upon the top of the storecupboard.

'Got somefin' fer me nipper, an' all,' says Fred, reaching into his pocket with one hand while holding Duke steady on his knee with the other.

'Fred, what if you were caught? What will become of us?'

'Never!' he says melodramatically. 'I will never be caught, my dear, for I am "a lucky man". I 'ad it from a gypper woman a-lookin' in 'er glass ball. Ain't vat right, Dukey?'

'I wish you wouldn't give him stolen things, Fred,' she says, coming a little nearer to see.

'Vis treasure won't be missed, love.'

He opens his hand just under baby Duke's little face to reveal a handful of dully glowing gems. Lucy gasps, her hands to her mouth, until Fred's laugh makes her look more closely to see that this is only 'river glass'. The rubies, emeralds, diamonds and jet are just glass pebbles made from broken bottles washed to opaque smoothness by the restless river.

Fred sets the boy down upon the rug by the fire to play with his finds, but Lucy swoops to grab them up and wash them. 'Fred, they're dirty. Just think how dirty everything from the river is!'

'Never did me no 'arm. Like muvver's milk to me. I were raised on the stuff and I ain't no weakling,' says Fred, crossing to Lucy and picking her up in his strong arms.

When Lucy had first arrived in this land, lassoed by the river and barricaded by docks, she came as a castaway. Indeed, this part of the river was popularly known as 'The Island'. Like the natives of Babel, they spoke in different tongues here, quick and spiced with odd words and expressions. A polyglot evolving mixture of thieves' code, back talk, rhyming slang, Parlaray crossed with Romany, and the slang and shorthand of all nations imported by sailors and settlers. And when Lucy wanted words with more punch and pungency than her pallid native tongue she learnt to borrow from the domestic Yiddish of her neighbours.

Like what came from their mouths, what the people of the Island put into their mouths was likewise highly flavoured and idiomatic. Their food was street food – nasty and lickerish and instantly gratifying, with its combination of high seasoning, fat and sugar: battered meat scraps fried in some nameless grease, hot penny puddings, Dutch cucumbers in barrels of brine, the brown and sweet butter cake, the flaccid 'bola', the 'Stuffed Monkey', and lolly-pops, boiled up from the molasses spills, scraped off the sticky West India warehouse floor. Lucy learnt to cope with jellied eels – with their nasty surprise, a razor-sharp bone – and mash, with bile green 'liquor', and to use a pin on whelks and cockles. Even the rabbits were different here: flabby white monsters with skin that slipped off easy as a loose glove. River dwellers swallowed prodigious amounts of liquid, porter and coffee, gin, rum, any number of other spirits that found their way off the ships, tingling, tooth-rotting lemonade that had never known a lemon and, of course, that universal comforter, sweet tea. They were all forever swilling down their gullets as though to loosen the grit and dust they took in with every breath.

And, like the thirsty mouth of the nation itself, there were the docks where the ships' masts bristled in a thick plantation of naked saplings so close, it was said, that you could cross the river from side to side without getting your feet wet. In all seasons the docks swallowed, bolted and gulped down the people and the riches of an Empire. And what an indigestible turmoil of things this was. And in such superfluity! Enough ivory and ebony to mend the smiles of a million parlour pianofortes and tiger-skins to place beside them. Twice as many cases of indigo as were needed to dye the Thames a lovely blue, and perfumes to scent it with too. Tea from China, its fragrance sealed up in lead-lined packing cases, oranges from Seville, fine cigars, allspice and sweet molasses, silk, cochineal and carpets. Such delicate smells, such refined flavours, such tropical splendour.

All was carried from the ships by those five thousand 'casuals' who must wait for a favourable wind to bring them in, then jostle and fight at the 'call on' to win the chance to haul the bounty ashore. Men with 'cat's paws' and hooks, men with strong arms and backs, men with handcarts and wagons ready to sweat and toil over cargo from every point of the compass, from straw-packed ice cut from Norwegian floes, to beaten-brass coal scuttles from Benares. All to be immured within those hulks of warehouses, blank and grim with the ugliness of utility. Apart from the odd pocketful of tea, precious little was let to slip from the gobbling mouth. And so, as well as having to learn how to talk and eat like an Islander, Lucy had also to learn how to live like a poor person. Although she had had nothing when she had been at the Hall, still she lived with the ever-present idea of limitless 'plenty' and she had never felt hungry there. No ingenuity had ever been expended on making the most of anything, be it food, fuel, light or clothes. That vast liner had steamed ahead night and day, blazing light and heat into the cool countryside and leaving a trail of waste, unheeded, behind it.

So she has had to learn how to shop often for tiny quantities, buy on tick and invent ways of combining what she has in her larder to make appetising meals. An active, contriving mind was required to get and cook food, ration fuel for light and heat, and keep clothes clean and whole. She was no longer required to do simply what she was told: now she must provide and improvise for herself, Fred and Little Duke. She learnt the practicalities of making the most of her resources – not to feed Big Duke with the carrots that had gone only soft, not to throw out the tealeaves after one brewing, never to let a live fire in the grate go uncovered by some slow-cooking pot or pan. She learnt always to save candle ends and soap, always to make hot water work twice – or three times – and always to help a neighbour in expectation of your own need. And as she learnt to think and plan so she began to live in the future as well as the present. She stored up what she could in the expectation of those lean times when the wind was in the east and the cargo boats lay trapped in the Channel and there was no work, or pay, for stevedores or carters. So Lucy learnt how to raise her head from the featureless toil of labour and see some dignity in the contrivance needed to keep her little family afloat each succeeding day.

And yet there was a price to pay for this independence: an impotent fear of what the future might hold, for herself and her family. It was as though she had been given freedom of choice, in the little ways she lived her life, to find that she was still chained to the malicious stratagems of Fate. She had only to look around her to see that all her resourcefulness could not guarantee her family protection from the tricks and snares of the unforeseen. A child slipped, broke his head and died in fits. A candle toppled, burnt out the family home. A horse kicked, broke the leg of his driver and lost him his livelihood. All around her she saw how chance mishaps brought ruin. This fear, the brooding expectation of disaster, led her to resort to rituals and spells in the hope of meshing with Fate, rather than being cruelly surprised by it.

This evening, as she and Fred return from the fried-fish shop with their Friday-night supper, Lucy is worrying over his tale of the terrible accident he'd witnessed that day. A stevedore had been crushed beneath the falling bale being unloaded from its sling.

Lucy crosses herself, without thinking. 'Don't let that happen to you, will you, Fred?'

'I 'ave no intention of walkin' under no greenacre, love.'

They stride along together for a while, Little Duke on Fred's shoulders. 'What you doin' – limpin' along like a free-legged dog?' He laughs, trying to match his stride to her strange gait over the pavement.

'Nothing.'

'Your ma's tryin' not to step on ve cracks!' he crows, digging Duke in the ribs to make him laugh.

'It does no harm,' she says defensively, trying to make her mismatched steps less obvious.

'If it keeps you 'appy.' He squeezes her hand for reassurance and then, holding it tighter, as though to steady her, ''Old on tight now, limp-along-Lucy!'

For which she gives him a slap.

If he only knew how obsessively this strong, protecting magic is woven into her everyday routines. Superstition even dictates how she pegs out the washing, always taking particular care to hang Duke's garments using closely matched pegs, strictly alternating each small item with something protective of her own. She uses every amulet and fetish endorsed by general use and some other personal magic of her own invention. For her, as in many other, more orthodox religions, careful and obedient housekeeping, the meticulous observance of the formulas laid down for living, eating, worshipping, is a way of placating the great, avenging unknown. But whereas for Lucy's neighbours the practice of their domestic and religious duties is public to the point of ostentation, her own rites and rituals are secret. To be effective they must stay hidden. She would rather die than acknowledge that she has a particular unshakeable way of doing everything to keep her family safe, from making sure to touch every third railing as she walks to replacing lids on empty pans so that bad spirits cannot occupy them in the night.

And 'lucky Fred' really has no notion. He knows only that Lucy is his tidy little woman, clean and punctilious in the kitchen. This sweet, gentle, magical catch, who was surely meant for great things, has ended up with him, cooking for him, sleeping with him. Buttons had broken all the rules and won his Cinderella. His happiness is grounded in the certainty that with Lucy in his home, Little Duke in his cradle and Big Duke in his stable all is right with the world and will ever remain so.

Comings and Goings

While Fred and Lucy's little family thrived, Beatrice too prospered. She thanked her lucky stars for that chance meeting in Burlington Arcade, which had been the making of her. Or the remaking of her, since she has been re-created as 'the depraved, veiled noblewoman'. This respectably dressed, near mute lady could pass without comment into the sets at Albany, the tearoom of the Ritz, the galleries of the Royal Academy. At first her reputation was made upon the rumour that this was a lady philanthropist gone to the bad. But as this gossip had receded so a more enduring fame, as one of the fabled institutions of a gentleman's London, had grown. It became a sport among certain undergraduates and second sons as to who might introduce Lady Georgina into the innermost enclaves of respectable society. One filbert took her to tea with his tutor, passing her off as a shy young aunt, which thrilling subterfuge made the lewd frolics that followed all the more satisfactory.

The real veiled noblewoman Georgina's work had not proceeded so satisfactorily. The strategy of distributing her subversive calling cards had caused a rift among the Fisher Folk. On one side ranged her devotees, a faction typified by the youthful hothead, half in love with the veiled young lady – the followers of Lady Georgina were mostly young men. On the other side stood gravitas, sobriety and Skipper Heever with the disapproving fold, quick to dismiss her as a squeaking false prophet, setting up her flimsy modern cards in opposition to his stone tablets of orthodoxy. And, of course, she unwittingly nursed a viper in her very bosom, for Carrie Flynn continued to supply the elders with information concerning her scandalous empire-building. However, despite their own misgivings and Carrie's poison, the elders equivocated for, at first, the bread Georgina cast upon those upper-middle-class waters brought money and converts to the mission. However, the tide began to turn when well-connected old patrons of the Fisher Folk appealed to the Skipper to staunch this bitter flow from gutter to drawing room. What was more, these wealthy supporters threatened to withdraw their names and, worse, their contributions. It was decided that the problem of what to do about Georgina could no longer be safely considered 'pending'. Lady Georgina, photographer and orator, had either to be put in hand or cut loose.

Skipper Heever knew she would be a slippery one: her reputation as a rousing orator was undeniable and she had the loyalty of certain key Fisher Folk, not least Albert Flynn. She might be as dangerous cast off as she was made fast. Rather than capsize, he decided that a sacrificial offering was called for to rid them of this turbulent young woman. Carrie and Albert were to be the small fish given up to snare the bigger one: they would be charged with founding a Fisher Folk mission in some colonial city, taking Lady Georgina and her photographic equipment with them.

The bait was swallowed and the Flynns and Georgina flung their energies into identifying a suitably godless, depraved and inequitable hole – where English was spoken. Lucky for them there was a surfeit of choice. Nearly a year was spent in excited correspondence between the three pioneers and Fisher Folk *émigrés*, gone before, who had been shocked and appalled as far afield as Melbourne, Australia. It had been decided that the right harbour was to be found in New York, USA, where there was already established a community of Fisher Folk in need of their own prophetess. Georgina was happy to oblige them and the Fisher Folk's founding fathers were overjoyed to let her go.

By the end of the second year Georgina and the Flynns were making their final arrangements to sail for America. They had been too busy to continue with the Work and the young saint had decided that the New World had a right to expect the most modern photographic equipment from her. She would have a Kodak – 'You press the button, we do the rest.' As she re-equipped and experimented with her new camera and lenses, the Flynns packed and Aurora and Teresa looked on as they prepared to desert.

Even for George these two years have measured a little outward voyage and homecoming. His uncle's attempts to kindle in him an appreciation for huntin', shootin', fishin' and escortin' the ladies, not to mention Harry's sly tutorials in the smoking of green cigars, have lit no spark in our dull boy. The time has come for the unimproved Fainhope heir to depart his uncle's mansion and travel the short distance back to his own. Perhaps because it is such a short distance and he has often been a visitor at the Hall, when he and Harry have ridden out with the hunt from there, he finds no glad reception awaiting him. Once there would have been Lucy to welcome him, take his coat and ask about his journey; now there is nobody. So he sidles round to the courtyard, following the sound of talk to the kitchen only for his sudden appearance to turn the lively colloquy into evasive throat-clearing.

Self-deprecatingly the young nobleman ducks apologetically back out through the door to mooch around in the stables where he surprises Miss Mantilla. Both stand transfixed until George takes an involuntary step towards her, as though he would embrace the guardian of his childhood days in greeting. Just as instinctively the governess takes an awkward step backwards and puts up a hand as though to keep him off. 'George! You gave me a fright.'

The boy, still seeking kindness, interprets the forbidding hand as one proffered in friendly welcome and shakes it.

Miss Mantilla reacts as though he has burned her: 'Goodness me, yes, yes, so you're home. Just in time to change your clothes and wait upon your mama, young man,' she says smartly, and hastens back to her duties at the Hall, although you might have suspected she was running away from him.

Late in the autumn of George's return, there comes an afternoon that finds the Duchess of Fainhope and Miss Mantilla sitting together over their handicraft of tapestry and basketwork. The two women have become accustomed to using the same room in the afternoons. Miss Mantilla has graduated from nursery floor to *piano nobile* and she has never felt so secure in her noble employer's estimation of her. Just as the Duchess had surmised it would, Miss Mantilla's grateful return to the Hall had affirmed her lasting assent to the ties that fasten each to the other. Such are the weighty chains of habit and expedience. Now they are discussing their projected departure for town and next year's Season, during which eighteen-year-old Euphemia will be launched.

'I hardly know how everything shall be arranged in time, Maria.'

'I could travel ahead and oversee preparations at the London house. It will need someone to distinguish between what may be simply cleaned or repaired and what must be replaced,' says trustworthy Miss Mantilla.

'And what of Miss Hart?'

'Isn't that lady better suited to closing up and dust-sheeting this house?' replies Miss Mantilla, decisively, a tone she would not have adopted before the two women became easy in their sorority.

The Duchess muses, 'It must be fifteen years since I was last there. No, sixteen. It was then that my husband took his last illness.'

'Do you think it may be unsafe – I mean, for the children?'

'Safe or unsafe, custom and fashion dictate that one should

deliver all unmarried daughters into this sink of contagion so that they may find for themselves a husband.'

Miss Mantilla smiles. 'Is a foul sink then the natural habitat of suitors?'

'I would say that the whole process is betrothal of the fittest. If Euphemia can stay up every night for weeks in a backless gown, subsisting solely on ices and night air, she'll prove herself worthy of matrimony.'

'Her settlement may be of advantage, of course,' says Miss Mantilla, with a raised eyebrow.

'She cannot expect riches, Maria. That man Gouch is determined to ruin us. I will launch her, and I will launch her well, but she will not bring with her a fortune. George's patrimony must be protected at all costs.'

There continues an amicable silence in which the governess draws a coloured yarn through her tapestry canvas and, thinking of the younger daughter, remembers that the elder, despite her play-elopement, remains unwed. But musing on Georgina-the-pariah brings back the jarring memory of her own long-abandoned home and causes her to pull the thread too tight and snag her work. 'What about Lady Georgina? Shouldn't she be presented first or, at least, together with her younger sister?' she asks, smoothing out the fabric.

Her mistress replies simply, 'The London house shall be Lady Euphemia's address alone. Georgina is of no further interest to me, Maria.'

Miss Mantilla does not pause to demur at this cool renunciation of a child but selects a lovely mauve wool for her next pansy.

'Georgina would have found a way to make the whole business into a farce. It is better she remains in obscurity,' continues the Duchess, snipping off the yarn and ending the matter. The two women work on for a while, tranquil over their needlework.

'Perhaps I could take George and his cousin with me to Town? George will need a new wardrobe,' suggests Miss Mantilla, after a few moments.

'I do not like George to be so far from the estate. His uncle's house was quite far enough,' states the Duchess, mildly.

'If I have him by I shall be better able to keep an eye on them both. You know they are a plague when they're left to their own devices.' The governess is now absorbed in stitch succeeding stitch.

'Take George and Harry in the brake with you, then. Let Stevens remove, with as many members of the household as you consider necessary, by the railway. You know that I trust only you in this. I know that in you I have someone who holds my personal interests as dearly as I would myself.'

'Your ambitions are mine, Your Grace,' replies Miss Mantilla.

Thus, quietly, we see how Miss Mantilla is irrevocably, willingly bound to her powerful patron.

Let us leave the two well-matched weavers to continue with their companion work.

Fate Slips In

Lucy is hurrying around Fred as he deliberately ties a knot in his neckerchief and seats his cap at the back of his head. She picks up Duke from the floor, where he has been playing with his pretty glass collection, and holds him up to Fred – both to exhort him to stay and to block him from going. He kisses the toddler's lips and steps into his boots. 'Luce, gal, I mus' go and stand wiv ve lads.'

'Oh, you can't. Fred, you'll never work again. Please stay here with Baby an' me.'

'Well, I can't work now. Not wivou' gettin' me 'ead caved in.' He sits, throttling the tops of his boots with the dangling ends of laces, which wind into their accustomed bright-rubbed grooves.

She stands, holding the struggling child, weighed with a terrible fear that neither careful husbandry of symbols, symmetry nor even his famous 'luck' can charm away. 'Oh, Fred, if you go I might never see you again!'

'Love, I'm only goin' where I go 'most every day,' he says complacently.

'But must you stand with the dockers? Isn't it their business?'

'Solidarity. Vat's what's needed to win the day, love. I *am* a striker as much as vem.'

'Can't you just wait until it's all over? It can't last much longer, can it, before the men get starved back to work?'

'Ten fousand men is somefink to reckon wiv, girl.'

'That's as maybe, but ten thousand without pay, let alone a tanner a shift, can't hold out for ever.'

'Neiver vey can, Luce.'

He goes to the door and Lucy hastily puts down the boy and runs to catch him. 'I'll just throw on a shawl and come with you. Duke can go to Mrs Campbell.'

'No, you don't. We don't want women at vem gates. You can bring me a can of tea, gal. An' bring the nipper along to see 'is dad. La'er.'

The door is open now and he stands half in half out, seeming to her on the edge of some terrible, self-chosen destiny, which she should have done more to prevent. 'But I worry so, Fred.'

'The on'y danger Is'll be in, is dyin' ov first. You come and fine me at ve dock gates. Vere's a girl.'

And he's gone.

Lucy moves around their attic room like an unquiet ghost, touching and retouching familiar things for reassurance: compulsively she follows a circuit of chairback, table, bedstead and the mirror above the fireplace, into which she looks as though to see whether it reflects the pale face of one condemned. All the while Duke plays on, unregarded. He is droning snatches of a nursery rhyme to himself, 'Fetch ve enjin, fetch ve enjin, fire, fire, fire, fire', heedless of the horrible, crushing thing that trembles, ready to drop into their lives. At midday she stokes up the fire and sets the kettle to boil for her man's tea, puts bread, cheese and an apple into a basket. She takes care to cut a neat first slice from the loaf, to clear away every crumb from the breadboard and let not even a single drop fall from the kettle as she pours hot water on to his tealeaves, even though she burns her hand on the handle. For Fred will be kept safe by these observances.

Duke continues to play quietly with a couple of wooden blocks, which he runs along the floor making chuffing noises. Lucy kneels down to him, looking away towards the door through which Fred had left. 'Duke, dear. You are to stay right here. Don't go out for anything. I'm just carrying Daddy his dinner. A'right?' Duke, busy with his railway engines, doesn't pause to look up. 'Say, "Yes, Mummy,"' she prompts.

''Es, 'Ummy,' he parrots back.

Still uncertain that he has understood properly, she picks him up to sit him in front of her on the kitchen table. 'Duke, Mummy'll be back soon. Jus' stay here quiet and play. Stay put, darling, and I'll bring you back a sweetie.' Lucy gives him a shake, for emphasis, kisses him and sets out, into the woods, carrying her little basket of provisions.

Even before Lucy turns the corner that will bring her to the dock gates she knows trouble has run on ahead and awaits her there. A huge crowd is listening to the speaker, John Burns. She notices there are some quite respectable-looking people, even some ladies and churchmen, near the plinth he is raised up on. She pushes forwards, in search of Fred, and is trapped within the mêlée. A rough man behind her yells, 'Yu 'spect me ta believe vem convicts is sendin' us money?'

'That's right, friend. Contributions from the colonies are expected any day!' replies one of the party below the plinth. Some in the crowd scoff at this prospect and others raise a cheer. Lucy is jostled further towards the front in a swell of bodies that presses from the back. It becomes apparent that a band of black-leg dock workers, many with covered faces, escorted by policemen, armed with batons, is forcing its way forwards. The already uneasy strikers begin to jeer and push. Lucy is swept along trying to stop her tea can slopping as she is hurried over cobbles between prisoning, pistoning elbows. As she is thrown towards them, she sees the strikers stiffen to action, many raising weapons of their own. Lucy's can is knocked, splashing, from her hands to be trodden into the street by the stampeding crowd. Now she is in the middle of the roaring strikers, black-legs and policemen. She has lost her shawl and her clothes have been ripped. A woman, on the sidelines, is cheering on the brawl. 'Giv 'im one, go on, 'it 'im!'

Lucy is too careful a mother to have left a light burning for Duke. When he looks up, at last, from his game with the wooden railway, he sees that the attic room is in shadows. He shuffles on his bottom until, back secured against a wall, there is no unobserved, undefended space behind. He calls, 'Mum?' but knows from the quiet and the dark that she is not there.

Lucy is in a police cell, with the heckler and some other women caught up in the heat of the riot. She says, over and over, to anyone who will listen, 'My little boy. I've got to get home to my little boy.' This fool's errand to save Fred has tricked her into turning her back on Duke. For as she closed the door on Duke the sly wolf slipped past unnoticed to be shut up with him.

As though governed by the same primal impulse that keeps fawn or leveret crouched, unmoving, in its hiding-place Duke waits for his mother to release him. But the cold of the evening and the fading light at last sets him bolting from cover across the dangerous spaces of the room to the big bed where he can tunnel beneath the covers and hide from the gathering night.

It is the morning silence that tells him she is still not there. And the coals that she, little cinder-grubber, has kept living in the grate since he was born are grown cold. He spends a long time in the bed, making his fingers walk the rumpled hills and valleys of the blanket. It is Big Duke's neighing, in the stable below, that makes him look up from this little world to the huge, cramped room where he has no dominion.

'Poor Duke,' he says.

By that evening he has emptied the kettle of its cooled water by tipping it towards him so that he can drink from the spout. He has reached the forbidden storecupboard by climbing on to a kitchen chair and managed to pull down upon himself a blizzard of incriminating flour and cocoa powder. But the deluge also brought with it a tin of treacle, the fall cracking ajar its gummy lid, like a hard nut dropped upon the forest floor, to let him into the sweet comfort inside.

Now, after a second night alone in the room, there is no more water and no more treacle. Thirst and loneliness are a louder imperative than the command in his head to stay put. The instinct to survive is stronger than his short training in obedience and it drives him out of the door, down the steps and into the yard, where Big Duke is kicking at his stable door for attention. He is still too small to reach the pump handle to fill the little cup he finds there. And since no one who might care notices him as he crosses the yard, he continues through the yard door and out into the street. As he walks his eyes are fixed on his tin cup, carried before him, carefully upright, as though it was already filled to overflowing.

When Lucy is at last released she hurries home although she already knows that the wolf has got there before her. She does not find her home empty, for Fred was turned out on to the street half an hour before her and has come back to light the lamp and set the kettle boiling. So around the huge black hole in her centre there is light and warmth, and kind, useless Fred.

The world did not stop turning: winter followed autumn, as it was accustomed to do, and the thoughtless sun continued to rise and set. The crack that split apart their little domestic sphere and let out all the warmth and light was only heard by Lucy and Fred. And they, too, seemed to carry on: Fred took his turn at the dock gates, as the strike staggered on, and scavenged for food and fuel where he could. Lucy haunted the streets looking for any sign of Duke. But this busy sham life, which left them numbed by physical exhaustion every night, was really only death animated.

A door had slammed within Lucy, shutting her off from the warm room where once she'd glimpsed a prospect of everyday bliss. Behind that door, in the life she had tried to sustain with spells and fetishes, lived on a Lucy who tended an eternal fire in the home hearth, a Fred who sat complacently taking off or putting on his boots and a Duke playing, forever safe, with other, more shadowy babies as yet unborn. But she had not been powerful enough to stop what was meant to be and could not step back inside that other charmed life. In losing Duke she had lost, too, the one key that would fit the lock and throw open once again this happy, ordinary room.

Her search for her boy had begun as a mantra fiercely repeated, as though she hoped to summon him to those familiar places in which she first sought him. 'Let him be at Mrs Kohn's, let him be at Mrs Kohn's, let him be at Mrs Kohn's . . .' This was her muscular tussle with the Fate that had hidden him from her, as though her strength of will alone could take the cruel thief by its throat and demand her darling's return. But when he was not at kind Mrs Kohn's, or trailing behind his friend the penny trinket seller, or hiding in the stable, she began to feel the psychic energy she expended in trying to make him be where she looked for him was merely dissipated. Worse, she feared that her futile attempt to force his return might muddy the clear, dispassionate pool of unknowing into which she must look to spot him. Gradually she began to bow down to a kind of Oriental fatalism: what must be, must be. She surrendered – like someone who realises that, whether a clock is looked at or not, time will continue its steady plod. For we know that however ardently we wish for the moment to be here right now, or postponed for ever, the indifferent hands will be exactly where they are appointed to be.

At last, as though in masochistic subjection, she turned away from the haunts where she hoped to discover him safe and sought him where she most feared to find him – the all-consuming river. Every day she slithered along its banks, like a mudlark looking for lost treasure, stopping everyone to ask after her lost boy – until people learnt, when they saw her coming, to hurry out of her way, repelled and embarrassed by her naked want.

Strange Meetings

The time has come for our worlds of town and country to be brought together: a collision that must surely multiply the possibilities of freakish encounters, mistaken identities and tragic missed opportunities.

It is early spring and Miss Mantilla has removed with her two male charges to open the Fainhope London address. Now quite the chatelaine, she walks around directing the opening of shutters and the removal of dust sheets, counting tablecloths and tutting over moth damage in blankets that date back to the reign of the late king's father.

The two scions of the houses of Fainhope are 'on the loose' for the first time in that tantalising metropolis, capital of the world. Twenty-year-old Harry has been quick to shake off his younger cousin and now parades the Strand, eager to see what the fashionable young men wear and carry this season. For Harry is inclined to dandification. Stuck in the country, he has had little opportunity to experiment with the modes illustrated in gentlemen's magazines and is, therefore, quite mad to spot a live aesthete during this little perambulation but so far the parade of smart London types has proved disappointing – a procession of cut-away morning and frock coats much as one would see in a largish market town; since the weather is only just mild, he is

225

reduced to entertaining himself by identifying the occasional 'Gladstone' or 'Albert'. There's not a sight to be had of indiscreet hue or pattern, no sign of velvet knee breeches or a wide-awake hat, and only one waistcoat with the power to astonish – and that mostly by virtue of the abdominal convexity of the gentleman who sported it. But the ladies, my, the ladies! Every one parading her Grecian bend: precarious, long-necked swans made to sway as they go with that beguiling duck-like walk below, which sets capacious skirts ringing. He's never seen more audacious bustles: he fancies he can hear the imprisoned creak of metal and the squeak of ingenious springs as each passes. There they parade, presenting their bobbing rumps to him, accentuated to ampleness by their back drapery, like a herd of stately buffalo, tiptoeing in tight-laced boots. And all for his pleasure.

It is the shock of recognition that cuts short this delectation of the enhanced female form. He sees Cousin Georgina, in her veil, looking into a shop window right before him. Harry approaches and touches her shoulder. 'Cousin Georgina, what a surprise. How many years has it been?'

Beatrice is startled; she hasn't been called 'cousin' before. She tilts her head modestly and indicates, with her umbrella, the hat shop where she has stopped.

'Georgina, it's Harry,' says Harry, and at the moment he takes hold of her elbow, he realises that this is not his cousin. 'Oh, excuse me. I thought I knew you . . .'

'You may know me better, sir,' says she, chancing her arm.

Harry looks around him, as though to check the sky has not fallen in. Just what he hoped for – a real live whore and one wearing a quite splendid costume. Again, his education in London life has been sorely lacking and he hasn't a clue what is the correct form in this circumstance. 'Well. Yes,' he says. 'Shall we find a tea-shop somewhere?'

Beatrice smiles beneath her veil. 'Wouldn't you like to have something more than a cup of tea with me?'

'Oh, yes, I most certainly would,' he replies hastily, as though he had committed a shaming social *faux pas*.

Beatrice lifts her veil and winks at him.

'What a pair of Langtries! You really shouldn't hide 'em away.'

'All the better to see you with, eh, love?' She tucks her arm into his, bending the elbow so that she may lean on him a little and firmly turns their steps towards Piccadilly Circus. 'Come along with me. Lady Georgina will see you sorted. We can think about cups of tea arter.'

'Cheesy!'

Lucy and her Fred are lying in bed; Lucy is holding him so tight that his ribs hurt.

'If I could just hold him again, just for one second of time.'

'I know, love.'

'It's like – if I could think really hard, so hard, about how he feels to hold I could get him back.' She squeezes again but it is not the crushable little body she finds in his too-substantial torso. 'I would know if he'd drowned, wouldn't I, Fred?'

But Lucy has no magical devices with which to read portents, unlike that Persian princess, of whom we heard tell in *The Arabian Nights*, whose knife would drip with blood, and whose necklace of a hundred pearls would lock tight. All that Lucy has is a pocketful of river-glass gems and Duke's first baby dress and they tell her nothing. Lucy must remain unknowing.

Restless, she holds Fred to her and they lie still, for a while. Then Lucy turns over so that she faces into the empty room, intent in the dark on sending forth her senses to uncover any leftover trace of him in this familiar room. She tries to breathe as quietly as she is able, drawing into herself the old air that might yet hold his scent. If she can only remember the smell of his hair and his knees and the back of his neck might she not summon him into being again? Her eager eyes scratch over the darkness for a glimpse of his shadow. She tries to dig under the familiar sounds – clock ticking, horses' hoofs on cobbles, calling from the street –

for an echo of him by which she may know that he is still alive. But all she can sense, coming from far away, is a baby crying alone in a dark room.

Now Fred turns to her, looking for her body in the dark. He lies close behind her, holding her, but she does not notice his strong arms. Instead he startles alive in her the memory of Duke's springy, slightly moist cheek upon her bare shoulder. Whenever she'd carried him on her back he'd pull down the top of her dress to feel the comfort of skin against his face rather than the rubbing of her dress. Even when Fred makes love to her, she does not feel him. He tries to pour all his love into her but it is like trying to fill a well. The only thing she feels is her loss, and that is such a huge, terrible, all-consuming thing that he can't share in it. He can only hide under its awful shadow to wait and watch.

He wants his boy back; he yearns and mourns for Little Duke but yet his loss seems an inferior, bottled-up thing in comparison to her huge need. Even if Duke had been his own, natural child he couldn't have loved him more but, he thinks, a child always belongs first to its mother. A child is not just a precious thing that she owns, a separate thing, for her, the child is *herself*. He goes with her when she questions lightermen, dockers' wives, crossing sweepers and their drabs, standing to the side, looking at his boots while she begs for signs. He follows her further and further away from their part of the river in pursuit of the cold trail that must lead them to him. He makes the fire and cooks the food, for Lucy has forgotten how. Lucy has forgotten him. So Fred hasn't just lost his boy but Lucy with him, and he waits for her to return. Sometimes he believes she never will – he can feel her, see her, smell her, but she has gone away down that dark tunnel, running, always running away from him and after disappeared Little Duke.

The Flynns have one final commission from Georgina the prophet: she has taken it into her head that she must make an iconographic picture of the old country before they blaze their trail in the new one. She has, in her mind, an image of a little boy, a street arab, in the usual garb of tatters, asleep over a grating for the warmth it might give. He has lain so still, so very still that, on looking longer at this familiar scene, it is possible to see the line of soft snow that has outlined the whorls of his ear. Every sweet, dirty toe has been dusted with its own snowcap, each drift so gently laid that should he only stir in his sleep they will be dusted away. If it is her fate to find only beauty in what she photographs, then so be it. Yet this must not be any ordinary scamp, but a neglected, sleeping angel. Adept as she is with slogans, Georgina will label him 'England, awake!'. The Flynns have brought back many urchins, in the Fisher Folk's care, for Georgina's approval – but she has yet to give it. She doesn't recognise in them the pathos she has in her mind's eye: those cheap tear-jerkers of filth and neglect will not do.

It is near to the time that they must depart for New York when the Flynns strike gold – they have identified a little boy, a mysterious little boy who seems to have come from nowhere and belong to no one. In the foundlings' home he is known as 'the aristocrat': the only part of his name that he can repeat appears to be the title Duke. Various ladies have made him their project, and claims have been made that there is a look of peculiar distinction to the brow. Unfortunately since the mite is too young to communicate anything beyond the fact of his nobility, the ladies have applied themselves to furnishing him with antecedents and history. They have assumed for him, according to the accepted tradition in these cases and since there has been no hue and cry for a lost, legitimate heir, a ridiculous, if romantic, history, and have woven for him a tale of concealed love, clandestine, if aristocratic, pregnancy and close-tongued retainers. However, even they could not contrive how he came to be lost, wandering an East End street with not so much as a monogrammed handkerchief or silver teaspoon to his name – in fact lacking in any of the props upon which a proper dénouement of reconciliation and restoration may turn. But with or without a curiously shaped birthmark, his inherent breeding, however diluted the blood, suits him to the Flynns' purposes. The little lost duke will personify the tragically beautiful Angel of Albion that Georgina seeks.

So the aristocratic pet of the foundling home is conveyed by them in an omnibus to be placed under Georgina's inquisitive lens. Upon his arrival, Aurora and Teresa put right, with bread and dripping and calming words, the unsettling experience of his first 'penny bumper' ride, aggravated by the ministrations of the accompanying Flynns. Then, while Teresa prepares the set and fetches props from the kitchen, Aurora sits the little noble on her knee and tries a couple of nursery rhymes to keep him quiet. As she sings, the influence of unaccustomed calories and the warmth of human contact cause him to relax and soften against her. She feels, for the first time in her life, a flood of maternal warmth. Pulling his cold little feet up to warm upon her leg she folds his knees in against her, and her body is hungry for the weight and feel of him, even though she is ashamed of the appetite and partakes as furtively as if she were stealing food from the mouth of another. At the end of the song, when Teresa returns, there is no need for the dose of Infant's Quietness with which they have equipped themselves to stop squalls. He remains gently asleep even as Aurora lowers him into position, and only settles himself more comfortably as they sift a glittering fall of icing sugar through a wire sieve to complete the tableau.

He is younger than Georgina imagined her 'Angel', but none the worse for that because he retains, under his London pallor, the freshness of innocence as yet untainted. As Aurora sets up the camera upon its tripod, she decides that, rather than risk startling him with an artificial flash exposure, it will be better to use what natural light comes through the large windows, and a very long exposure. Before she calls for Georgina she fits a plate and exposes it herself. Her first photograph.

Of course Georgina uses the magnesium flash for her picture, lit in a frying-pan, which startles the boy awake with the noise and flare and sets him bawling until he can be carried away, back to the East End, by the Flynns. But it is Aurora's technique that creates, in the finished print that she processes herself, an eerie image, hallowed by a suggestion of fuzzy iridescence from the crystalline sugar. And what she loses of the pinpoint detail of 'snow', she gains in a composition of texture, shadow and tone, which combines with something ineffably poignant and seems to show time itself, stilled in sleep.

At a more fashionable address Her Grace, the Duchess of Fainhope, and her younger daughter are exploring the long-neglected London house, which has been thrown open by Miss Mantilla, and the servants under her direction, with the violence of a small, tropical hurricane. The exemplary rigour of their airing, dusting, turning and beating has eliminated or displaced and made refugees of that arrogant multitude who, for countless generations, had assumed that this was their own quiet universe. Brooms and scrubbing brushes have worked, like Fate or avenging gods, to destroy the ancient citadels of spiders, black beetles and woodlice. The complacent and numberless fell before that dreadful, unpredicted Nemesis. Miss Mantilla was well satisfied with the massacre; the elimination of vermin, and the dirt and rot they made their home, was as good as absolution to her.

The eyes of Lady Euphemia and her mother, however, not having been dazzled by this miracle of transformation, note only that the now spotless furnishings are shamefully shabby, old and tired. Money, after all, must be laid out to create the proper setting against which Lady Euphemia will be best displayed.

The débutante, too, will be polished up ready for her presentation at Court, buffed and painted, padded with horsehair and stiffened with wire. Euphemia's long hair will be pinned up high above a lily-white face, she will be laced into a tight white gown and, since the Queen likes to 'see' her débutantes' feathers, will sport three impossibly tall ostrich plumes, fixed, somehow, slightly to the left of her head. She will be accoutred with the appropriate fans, furs, jewels, shoes, parasols, hats and underwear to complement the necessary morning, day, tea and evening dress. She will be trained in dancing a waltz, managing a full Court curtsy without toppling and the exacting deportment of exiting backwards from the royal presence while managing her ten-foot train. Only then will she be qualified and equipped for the twenty-five breakfasts, thirty dinners, fifty evening parties and sixty balls, as well as numberless rides, drives, tennis parties, teas, picnics, soirées, plays, concerts and operas that will see her successfully launched, exhibited and matched. A lovely white satin butterfly, by Worth, sumptuously mounted so that suitable men of taste may assess, admire and covet. That is, if all this exposure to Society doesn't kill her first – or the governess and the mother who must chaperone the lovely specimen at her every outing.

While her mother moves around the house deciding which furniture might be recovered, repositioned or just replaced, the young lady is watching her governess unpack the many pairs of long white kid evening gloves sent this morning from the makers. For Euphemia will be supplied with enough (their number multiplied by three as they may be changed that many times in an evening) to last from May to August.

'Oh, how too utterly utter!' says that modestly raised lady, eagerly thrusting her fists into the narrow sheaths of soft leather.

'Euphemia, do take care. You will stretch them.'

'I predict that all the men will fall quite violently,' she says, throwing one narrow pelt around her governess's waist to entrap her. 'I wouldn't be at all surprised if I bagged an earl.'

'Silly girl. The Season is just a wonderful opportunity for a young, quietly raised girl to introduce herself in Town – to dress beautifully and to be admired by suitable young men. It is not a marriage market,' lies Miss Mantilla.

'Well, I intend it to be. Since Mama spares no expense, I will take every advantage. I'll run ragged every couturier, milliner, furrier and shoemaker in Town. Flocks of rare birds will be plucked quite bare and hundreds and hundreds of needlewomen sent blind just to dress me marvellously. I shall be so spangly and fizzing and fine the Prince of Wales will wish he wasn't already taken. Not that I'd have him anyway, poor old tub. No, I'm going to have Prince Eddy or that other one – the sailor prince.'

'Prince Albert and Prince George will be looking for foreign princesses as their brides, no doubt. And I'm sure that the Prince and Princess of Wales do not want a badly behaved and thoughtless girl for their sons.'

'I bet the sons wouldn't mind a badly behaved girl!'

The involuntary start and compression of the governess's lips is sufficient stimulus for Euphemia to continue, 'Shan't I just throw myself at 'em? For I really don't care who I marry, so long as I shall take precedence over Mama.'

'You don't deserve to find a husband, ungrateful girl.'

Poor old spinster stick – hasn't an idea about men, Euphemia thinks. And, strangely, this is much the same conclusion that Miss Mantilla reaches about her charge.

Noble Visitors

Once sufficient numbers of birds have sacrificed their tails and needlewomen their eyes to enhance Euphemia's nubility, it is decided that she and George, the latter being a nuisance at home, should pay a call at the south London anchorage in which Georgina has been lodged. Brother and sister venture alone to that humble resort as Mama is disinclined to acknowledge a disgraced daughter in an unfashionable quarter, and Miss Mantilla is unwilling to chaperone her charges. Bothered by the forlorn sound of crying that haunts her last memory of home, she has taken a violent opposition to returning there.

Lady Euphemia, in particular, is motivated to reacquaint herself with the prodigal, believing that this will effect a nice opportunity both to provoke the Duchess, her mother, and shine by contrast with the drab and disappointed. It has been three years since Georgina left to find her fortune, and during that time Euphemia has hardly thought of her absconding sister and the reduced life that she might be living. But now that she stands upon the brink of a new and glittering existence away from Mama, as wife to some rich man, it strikes her as a diversion to swank and belittle. To this end she is wearing her finest jewels and palest colour, making herself appear a very young lady who has riffled unwisely among Mama's *papier poudre*, paste ornaments and shiniest cast-offs.

And as for George, well, Euphemia needs him for an audience: witness to the brilliant social *éclat* with which she will outsparkle her elder, unlaunched sister. George, ever the onlooker, is employed solely to observe the intended cruelty. For George is designed to be one of those wallflowers who line the walls and thus enhance the fun and frivolity of the exhibitionists engaged in the thick of the dance.

So, we find the young people: Ladies Euphemia and Georgina with the Duke of Fainhope seated together, knee against knee, in that shabby parlour, hemmed in by their hostess's luggage, readied for her impending departure overseas. There being no room and only three chairs, the two landladies have banished themselves to the back kitchen to hang over the kettle and both watch attentively for it to come to the boil. Outside, the splendid Fainhope landau and matched pair waits, blocking the way, its glossy paintwork and skittish carriage horses offering open incitement to under-employed boys to find sport in shying stones.

Euphemia, in her finery, seems to suck up space and light in the little room; Georgina is calm and commanding as a mother superior in plain robes and wimple. Seated between them, George shrinks back into himself, humming tunelessly and squinting at the ceiling, as though his only recourse in resisting the role of witness to the girls' rivalry is to absent himself as much as possible from the present moment. It's a strange reunion, which brings together the two sisters to fight over precedence, while sitting there, unremarked, is the heir to the Fainhope fortune. Unworldly George, by privilege of his sex alone, renders their contest pointless.

Georgina, having turned her back upon such surface effects as titles and fine clothes to embrace a future of lasting significance and meaning, bridles in the presence of all she now feels to be insubstantial and worthless, an affront to the bleak realities of life.

Euphemia, seeing her sister's broken-down boots and rough hands, finds in herself the courage to make Georgina understand that she is irrelevant in the real world of balls and splendid equipage. 'Do take off that horrid veil, Georgina, and show us your face. It's like talking to a sideshow.'

'We'd like to see you,' George says diplomatically.

'Now that she has no more use for her connections in Society, our sister must create the suspicion of a mystery to make herself important,' says Euphemia, emphasising the chasm that lies between her own brilliant success on the social scene and the laughable attempt by this nobody to aggrandise herself.

'Don't be ridiculous. George, of course you shall see me.' With this, Georgina throws back her veil to show her ravaged countenance. It is a kind of challenge to her siblings, like the deliberate use of some vile word spoken to startle refined ears. And even though they know that face, and have known it almost all their lives, there is still a shock at seeing again how disease may dig into and erode the soft clay of human features.

'Oh, the romance of keeping everyone guessing!' says Euphemia, glib to cover her discomfort at what the raising of that curtain reveals.

'But not for you, of course, sister,' retorts Georgina, 'for you are led a willing volunteer into the ring to be bargained over and gawked at.'

'Georgina, you have grown coarse!'

All Euphemia's finery and baubles are not succeeding in their job of showing Georgina that she is bested.

'Truth is coarse,' answers this implacable sister.

'That is like saying that delicacy and refinement are lies,' smirks Euphemia, flashing her eyes and rings.

Georgina, angry at the bumptious pronouncements of this eighteen-year-old innocent, brings out some of her *carte de visite* grotesques and deals them, one by one, on to her sister's knee. 'Here is truth, stupid girl, and this, and that.'

Euphemia affects a sigh and looks away. 'Do you expect that I know nothing, have seen nothing? These are oddities one might see every day, even in Grosvenor Square.'

'Quite, sister, but you do not see, even with your seasoned

eyes. Delicacy and refinement give you blinkers.' Georgina continues to lay out the photographs, one after another, each with a vindictive little snap, upon the side table, until she comes to the last, the one of Little Duke lying asleep under his dusting of snow.

'Who is this?' says George, who has been blankly looking out of the window at the infuriated coachman who entertains the idle quarter-hour by making violent feints with his whip at the nuisance children.

'This is my little noble, natural son of a duke, the symbol of all that is rotten in this state and among those parasites we call *Society*.'

'Duke. I don't believe it – look at his dirty feet,' snorts Euphemia, taking up the card to look more closely.

'He may not have been blessed with legitimacy, but despite his lack of fine clothes, his nobility is unmistakable,' answers Georgina, glad that she has squashed Euphemia's superiority.

'*Quelle scandale!*' is all that that sophisticated young lady can come back with.

'His face. His face is so beautiful and calm,' says George, looking too. 'I feel as though I've seen it before – in a dream.'

'He looks just like you, George, lying asleep on your bedroom floor with your knees hunched up. That proves it, I suppose – he must be the son of a duke since he is the spitting image of one. Either that, George, or it proves that you are no better than a ragamuffin!'

'Poor little thing, he looks so lonely. Was he abandoned by his mother?' asks the soft-hearted heir.

'I think he lost her,' supplies Georgina.

'Dead?' says Euphemia, indifferently, then adds, in a sing-song, 'She was poor, she was honest, victim of a rich man's whim . . .'

'No, not dead, lost. Really lost. He seems to have come from nowhere.'

'He's been wandering, lost, for years and years,' muses George to himself.

'Hardly years, you nizzy, he can't be more than three.'

Georgina gathers back her pack of cards, shuffling them so that her copies of Duke's picture shall lie at the top.

The sisters, having reached an armed stand-off in which neither can succeed in patronising the other into submission, fall silent.

'May I keep just one?' George says, surprising them both with his uncharacteristic animation.

'I'm sorry that you may not,' replies Georgina, the impulse to thwart and disappoint being wholly characteristic in her. 'There is not time to make another to replace it before our ship sails.'

George subsides back into passivity and the two sisters, seeing there is no more fun to be had in goading, bid each other an indifferent farewell and part, each to pursue her chosen destiny among the higher and the lower echelons. George ambles off, unconsidered, in search of the invisible householders to bid them farewell. He catches them out, dipping their fingers like naughty children into a pot of sugar plums, and Aurora is so disconcerted by this aristocratic head popping into her kitchen that she hands him a sticky plum before she can think better of it. George carefully wraps the sweet in his pocket-handkerchief. It is the nicest gift he has ever received and he will never forget it. The whip cracks, the horses' hoofs clash, and that glamorous conveyance departs westwards, thundering through the narrow streets, carrying one self-satisfied sister away from the other, never to meet again.

For now our two worlds, of town and country, will part too.

Book Three

Progress and Stasis

By the end of that whirligig Season, Lady Euphemia has indeed bagged herself a husband. Neither Prince Albert Victor nor Prince George Frederick had succumbed to her trappings or her vivacity, but she was mollified by the mobs of available young men, dressed like waiters, who thronged about her every evening to fill her dance card, and cheered by the full fervour of sisterly animosity that emanated from the passed-over young ladies of her acquaintance. However, when it came to the matter of her fortune she was found to be less tip-top than appearances had first suggested. Only an Irish knight was dazzled enough by her (borrowed) jewels and her connections to put in a bid. Lady Euphemia was carried off to discover for herself what it meant to be wife to a man who rather preferred his dogs and his horses.

The fashionable London address, having also served its purpose, was again 'put up' ready to be occupied by new spider, black beetle and woodlouse settlers. Having no tribal memory of the dreadful purge that had cleared this virgin territory for them, those first pioneers and every succeeding generation multiplied, among the gathering dust and rot, untroubled by the lessons of history. If, like them, yesterday could teach us nothing and, as a consequence, tomorrow held no fear, would not life be bliss?

⌐◦⌐

Unfortunate, sentient, Lucy knows herself all too well to be one of those little particles that are swirled involuntarily about, caught in the draughts made by bigger, more consequential bodies, people like her having no influence over bolts dropping out of blue skies. Her only comfort is to seek her lost boy. She cannot remain in the room above the stable while he must be out there, somewhere, calling for her.

Now Lucy's domestic routine is to throw her shawl over her shoulders and, taking her can of tea and basket of food, go out into the street or down to the riverbank to search for Duke. One day she comes upon a group of children, sifting through the mud with their bare feet for saleable items, which the youngest of them is sent to rinse off in the river. The pile of found objects is comprised mostly of broken clay pipes and shards of painted pottery but they dig away with their sticks ever hopeful of coals, copper nails, a coin or a whole bottle with a marble in its neck. Before they notice, she comes up behind them and, holding the smallest under his chin, tilts up his face so that she can look for Duke there.

'Oh, mi God, it's ve lady!'

'No, it ain't. Vis one ain't got no veil on 'er,' says a girl, turning back to her prospecting.

'Who d'you mean? Which lady?' asks Lucy.

'She steals children away. Her face is all mockered, vat's why she wears ve midge net,' says the girl.

'Vey do say she's a wommin what 'orribly murthered 'er own kid and now she walks at night, lookin' fer some more ta do in,' says the oldest boy, with relish.

'But is she real?' Lucy says.

'Course. Ain't you 'eard ve verse?'

The children momentarily stop their work and all, like good little children repeating a catechism in Sunday school, obediently recite:

'Hide-a-hood, baby snatcha,
A tanner if she ever catch ya.'

Lucy, who hardly remembers anything of her past beyond the lost time that still holds Duke, is transported back to a street where she once stood, long ago – surrounded by fish, she seems to recall. She looks down upon herself standing at the bottom of that high-walled canyon and hears the riddle again. These words must hold the secret of where he will be found – if she can only decipher them. She gives the biggest girl a coin (one must always reward an oracle, however unlikely) and hurries away, holding this precious clue close.

Before we leave that ancient riverside, we may spot another seeking figure similarly lured there by tales of the veiled lady. His descent into this hell has been a rake's progress of bawdy nights and unpaid bills, for Dr Oliver, too, is victim of an obsession. Neglecting work, society, friends, he is driven only to revenge himself upon the Duchess. To this end he must seduce and publicly humiliate the daughter of whose ruin he already stands accused. Even though he will gain nothing by it personally, there appears a perverse rightness in this course. And so he pursues the shadow of Georgina up and down the river and in and out of its pubs and lodging-houses.

But enough of stinking mud and motives: let us transport ourselves to the spanking new Apostle's Grove, in the district of St John's Wood, otherwise known as the 'Grove of the Evangelist', the respectable suburban preserve of many a well-set-up *demi-mondaine*. Here Beatrice in her playful veil, that other personification of Lady Georgina, and Harry are walking arm in arm and in delightful anticipation of love in a rented 'cot'. Harry will keep his canary in a villa, safe from temptation, to sing for his pleasure alone. Red brick and high hedges will screen his illicit nest of pleasure and keep his bit of nice game, his bird of paradise, snugly hid. Oh, the luxury of convenience.

He hands her, ostentatiously, to the front doorstep of number four Wellesley Villas, and feels in his pocket for the latch key – the first he's ever possessed. He almost laughs at the joke of it. Her hand follows his into the pocket, where she gives him a little squeeze. 'Jus' checkin' the cobbler's awls is still present and correct.'

'Wait till we're properly inside, my dear.'

'I can 'ardly wait till you're properly inside, darling,' she says, winking.

But when he has carried her over the threshold and they are in that properly equipped parlour, she seated on his knee, his sexual playfulness is blunted by the poky, claustrophobic, middle-classness of the place, hers dented by its splendour. He had thought to treat himself with a dainty little nest in which to sin, only to be suffocated by fabrics and furniture and other folderols – this being the very height of the stifling style of interior decoration.

'Look at the pair of china dogs on the mantel. No, I'm wrong – they're giraffes. Did you ever see anything like it?' He laughs, trying to ginger her up.

'Ain't they lovely?' she breathes back, overawed by his gift to her of all these accoutrements.

Nothing in the place has been left simple and complete unto itself but must be improved by drape or wreath or cushion. The boudoir is a sloshing sea of satin, velveteen and moquette, where appliqué lace foams and the larger items of furniture float as though cast adrift. She takes him in soft arms, compliant with gratitude and wonder, and hides her face in his neck and he feels, for the first time in their turbulent relationship, a nasty shift in dynamics. Have ornaments, mass-produced furniture and elaborate window adornments reformed the cheerful whore into a suburban housewife and made of him her unwilling redeemer? Harry, the philanthropist, experiences much less enthuzimuzzy for a game of in and out than would have Harry, the fast swell.

Beatrice, momentarily overwhelmed by the self-satisfied humility of the newly, and unexpectedly, exalted, lets drop a tear. 'Oh, Harry, you are ever so good to me.'

He finds her lips with his own and she half shrinks before submitting to the kiss, an unfamiliar gesture that provokes in Harry a new, manly sensation, not altogether unpleasant. However, their spooning is interrupted by a ring on the doorbell, which makes them leap guiltily apart – she replacing her veil, he smoothing his self-consciously naked chin. 'Blast it! That's the maid. I engaged her with the house,' says he.

'But Harry, what am I to do with her?' says Beatrice, in a panic.

'Tell her to do whatever it is that housemaids generally do. The secret is, show her who's mistress,' he says, drawing upon some half-remembered edict of servant-keeping lore.

'Who shall I be, Harry? I can't be me and 'ave servants.'

'Well, be someone else, then, if it will make you more comfortable. But, for heaven's sake, open the blasted door to her.'

On the short journey between front parlour and hall Beatrice rediscovers the connection of cousin that exists between herself and Harry. And by the time she opens the door to her new maid she is tragically widowed. All those swanky things in the front parlour have puffed up our little whore until even she wouldn't have recognised herself.

While Harry and his cousin played houses, the Flynns and Lady Georgina left, largely unmourned, for America. Carrie stowed away one extra for the voyage, her unborn son Zebulon – a secret even from her husband. And she would have hidden him longer, had she been able – a private thing of her own that she was not obliged to share with Sister Georgina.

Aurora and Teresa have been left with two empty bedrooms and an attic full of their former employer's discarded photographic equipment. They thought of taking in new lodgers to replace the ones who had escaped, but somehow the effort involved in advertising seemed too much and the matter was left to lapse. The sisters continued to share a bedroom, having turned the key on Papa's old room and its looming furniture. They traipsed in dust and slopped about in pots and pans. And where youth had excused domestic helplessness and lack of husbands, now that they had reached (and perhaps overstepped) maturity, their slovenliness and singleness were generally held to be despicable. Eventually their neighbours no longer bothered even to pass judgement on them. In just three years they had aged from giddy girls with future prospects to inconsequential spinsters with none.

Back again on his lonely rock, without even the human contact provided by Harry's teasing, or his uncle's bullying, George grew ever more silent and strange. With no Lucy to reach out to him, he retreated further within. The housemaid responsible for his bedroom knew that she would always find his bed just as she left it, sheets tucked in tight and pillow undented, but that there would be a pile of newspaper strips on the floor to sweep up. Not that he used even these to sleep upon, for it was known that he often wandered abroad at night, poking into corners, looking through windows. The amatory life that some of the servants had been used to conduct under cover of darkness was now curtailed for fear of being interrupted by the queer young Duke off on his perambulations. Nevertheless, life carried on around him: Mr Law died, the high-bred terrier bitch Harry left in his care surprised him with a mismatched litter of young giants and giantesses, Kathleen married the Boots and Stevens suffered an apoplexy. And George observed all, safely muffled and indistinct, as if he viewed the world through dusty glass.

Beatrice Gives Fate a Helping Shove

Having established that her gentleman relation Mr B. (B for Beatrice) has indeed two real female cousins – between whom he finds it hard to establish which is the bigger bitch – the mistress of number four Wellesley Villas elects to continue under the name of Georgina, or Gina, this being the female cousin Harry had first mistaken her for and the one Beatrice, in her elevation to kept woman, has grown to regard as a kind of patroness.

The fond gentleman cousin comes ever so often to console his widowed lady cousin, living on private means. They take tea, they take walks (she in her veil), they play cards. They generally amuse themselves, under the nose of the new maid, in ways that would not have disgraced the most unexceptional courting couple.

Now they sit in that nice, muffling parlour and wait upon the maid to light the spirit flame under the kettle and, finally, to leave them alone.

'Nosy cat,' says Gina after her. She comes and sits nearer to Harry. 'It's like me stays is done up too tight, livin' wiv 'er. I can't catch me breaf,' she says, gasping a little in this rarefied, smothering atmosphere.

Harry pulls her on to his lap and begins to fiddle with her fastenings. 'I'll soon see to that difficulty.'

'Leave off, love. I can 'ear 'er.'

He pushes her away. 'For God's sake, you're the mistress. You can do whatever you please.'

'But that's just it, Harry – I can't, now I'm respectable!' she says, in an agony of self-imposed constraint.

'If the damned maid don't suit, then send her packing!'

'D'you know 'ow difficult it is to find a good cook-general nowadays?' she replies, in the authentic voice of the lower-middle-class matron. She might only have added, 'What will the neighbours think?' to complete the transformation.

But she is not so far gone in propriety that she fails to notice the warning note in his reply: 'Are we to spend our time, now, in conversations about "the servant question"?'

Gina, maid or not, slips on to his knee and says, in her baby voice, 'Don't be angry with me, Harry. 'Ere am I, a poor li'le London sparra, stuck in a cage of canaries. I've got to try and at least look yeller to them, 'aven't I? An' I'm so lonely, Harry. Stuck 'ere waitin' for you to call, with none of me proper mates to keep me comp'ny. Jus' 'er snoopin' around, tryin' to catch me out.'

Had he only noticed how closely her coquettish trilling mimics that of the suburban canaries, Harry might have saved himself there and then. But he does not. Instead he is charmed by the idea of being lord and master even of this humdrum homestead. For though he is her lover, not her husband, and the son of a noble, Harry is a man after all and subject to a man's vanities. So, until they discover that the chair they are sharing is too small and unaccommodating to continue with what they are doing, they forget the disapproval of the housemaid.

But it is not the constrictions of the chair, or the prospect of cooling tea in the pot, that eventually sets Gina springing from her lover's arms, but a plan to save herself, once and for all, from this creeping refinement. 'I've a fine idea! I s'l get one a me old mates to come and act as maid. Then I shan't be lonesome no more and we can 'ave oursel's all the jolly times we like, wiv no worries.'

'That's the girl!' says he.

'I could get one ov 'em I was banged up wiv to 'elp out. Course, she might 'ave a kid in tow by now,' speculates Gina.

Harry is quick to scotch this doubting note. 'What could be more touching? The young widow, sole support of some relative's orphaned child.'

' 'Ow tragic.' She laughs, catching his playful tone. 'I'll go an' give the old cat the elbow right this minute.'

Gina jumps up and goes off to the kitchen to sack her servant – just in time to save her own job.

As his dirty little whore, Beatrice at least had the attraction of the unfamiliar for Harry: her language, habits and dress intrigued and excited him. But, like a foreign bride who loses her exotic allure once she is brought 'home', since Gina has aspired to becoming a domesticated species of the middle class Harry begins to suspect that she is merely vulgar. And drab vulgarity is not a dish he can relish.

Next day Gina, having regained some of her old bravado, goes in search of a maid for her and Harry's nest in the one place where she can guarantee that she will not be lied to about the girl's character. It is true that, dressed in her most genteel costume, she walks to and fro a couple of times past the door of the Fisher Folk's Home for Fallen Girls before she finds the courage to knock – but once past the threshold she revels in the topsy-turvy.

Any worries Gina might have that she will be recognised as a recidivist in that establishment, or sniffed out as an imposter, soon fade: it is sufficient to Mrs Flood, the matron, that she wears a veiled hat, sits, rather than stands, before her and speaks in a tone of equality. Apparently dress and demeanour have succeeded in raising her from her fallen state where weeks of prayer and laundring failed.

Mrs Flood opens a familiar ledger upon her desk and smiles at her visitor. 'We are sure to be able to find you a suitable girl somewhere in here. You see, every detail of a girl's background and history is set down when she first comes to us. Our Mrs Bentley does her very best to verify the information we are given, and then she records each step the girl takes along that steep climb to reform and salvation. So there is little risk that one of our girls will take you by surprise.'

'I ham willin' to take on any clean, 'ard-workin' girl – whatever her misfortunes may have been,' says Gina, piously, watching her pronunciation.

'We try our best to find suitable situations for all our girls. Of course, some are more difficult to place than others. But we never give up,' says Mrs Flood, looking up and smiling again.

Mrs Flood begins to scan the pages before her and reads, just audibly, from them: ' "Gypsy Rose . . . head a mass of vermin; Lottie Louisa . . . drink a great curse to her . . . sat as a model to artists . . . Alice Edith, moving regularly between the streets and service. Mary . . . manifesting a terrible aptitude for lying, gossip and giddiness." Not what we're looking for, eh?' She scans her lady guest's face for traces of disgust and, seeing none there, continues to search the pages until she calls out, 'Here! Here we have one who might suit. She has been trained in the home of one of our own Fisher Folk ladies. I'll read what it says. "Rebecca, aged eighteen years, originally from Essex, no living relations. Swore that she was honestly employed in service." Here, we come to the nub. "The circumstances of her fall were that her mistress's grown son kept his bicycle in her room, giving him free access. Although she pleaded with him to spare her, he would not be persuaded." '

Gina's smile is hidden behind her veil – bicycle, her eye! Still, if Miss Rebecca had got the old girl to swallow that one she couldn't be a hopeless case.

Mrs Flood continues, encouraged by the lady's attentive manner: 'I believe that she has come to perfect repentance and I understand that she is now thoroughly versed in all the domestic arts. It is our endeavour to train our girls to be sober, honest, truthful, trustworthy, punctual, quiet, orderly, clean and neat.'

'Oh, my!' says Gina, overwhelmed by this battalion of impossible virtues. She cannot quite conceal her dismay at this litany and asks, 'Ain't she got no vices? I wouldn't like to take one with no repentance left in 'er.'

Mrs Flood is gladdened to be able to supply the hastily scribbled note in the margin of the page: ' "Rebecca continues to make progress towards godliness. However, she is much addicted to cigarette smoking." There now, dear, you shall have ample opportunity to take her in hand for her tobacco habit.'

'When was this Rebecca brought into the home?' Gina asks disingenuously.

'Rebecca was fished from the streets eighteen months ago by our "cellar, gutter and garret" fleet,' calculates Mrs Flood.

So, this was not one of the inmates that she would have served time with – never mind, the girl had shown some spirit keeping up the coffin nails. She'd do. But Gina can't leave without daring a last risk. 'Mrs Flood, could you find news for me of a girl that my sister once hemployed what went to the bad? I believe she was brought 'ere in the wintertime, two years back. 'Er name was Beatrice Larkins. Poor thing.'

It takes the matron only a moment to find the month and year. She reads: ' "Beatrice, twenty-two, says she is from London although nothing she says may be counted the truth. She is a liar, a thief, a drunkard, has a vile temper, is very idle, shiftless and of a discontented spirit . . . well known to the police as a thoroughly bad character." ' Mrs Flood looks up from the ledger and shakes her head wearily over the last addendum: ' "Beatrice ran away from the home after having been delivered of a stillborn infant and has not been heard of since." ' Then she continues, 'The last detail we must look upon as only a blessing – Beatrice was not a fit person to have charge of a baby.'

Subdued, Gina simply comments, 'Poor little mite.' Then, rallying, 'I always knew that Bea Larkins would go to the bad.'

'Not what one would want in a good, plain maid-of-all-work,' concurs Mrs Flood. 'However, shall you take a look at our Rebecca?'

'Is there a hinfant surviving?'

Gina remains pensive as Mrs Flood searches again through her ledger. Her poor dead baby – a proper little shrimp of a boy, from what she'd seen of him. All of a sudden she comes over teary.

'I believe Rebecca's child died after a year,' says Mrs Flood.

Gina recalls Harry's complacency as to the point of an orphan child and her own need for some indoor diversion during the long hours between Harry's visits. 'I only ask because I, too, lost a dear child in hinfancy. Perhaps, as well as taking in Rebecca, I could offer some uvver muvverless child in the orphanage an 'ome. Then the wounded 'earts of two grievin' muvvers beref' may find solace.' The nip with which she'd fortified herself before knocking at the door has made her sentimental, as well as bold.

Mrs Flood, brimming with gratitude, starts to offer her thanks, when she happens to glance at the righteous lady's card to remind herself of the name. Having looked, there is a note of perplexity in her closing pleasantry: 'I'm sure Rebecca will suit you admirably, my dear . . . ?'

'Mrs Larkins,' confirms Gina, complacently, 'Mrs Georgina B. Larkins.'

'Mrs Larkins,' assents Mrs Flood, wisely biting her lip.

The women proceed blandly with the arrangements to dispatch the two unfortunates to Mrs Larkins's address. Why worry about the provenance of a common-or-garden stone if it is this missile, rather than one of flawless Carrara marble, that can pull down two birds at once?

Signs and Omens

Since she'd been slurred by the mudlarks, Lucy's reputation as the notorious 'child snatcher' never completely left her, but was to some extent supplanted by her new status as the river's occult hag, the giver of signs and omens. Perhaps this myth grew out of her habitual posture: that of the seeker-after-dropped-treasure. Her prematurely aged, bent form had become a familiar sight along her reach of the Thames, and the myth spread that she was a witch who could smell out valuables and Fate. She was trailed, for sport, by jeering children who threw stones, and so learnt to stuff her ears with cotton. But as she rummaged and raked she muttered torn phrases to herself, which, when anyone came near enough to hear, sounded like fortunes or warnings: 'Beware of the one with the black bag,' or 'A titled horse will bring riches,' or 'Keep the home fire always alight.'

This being a superstitious community, girls crossed the road to avoid grandmothers bearing handbags and believed themselves spared. Men bet indiscriminately on nags with noble names. Suggestible housewives burned their furniture rather than let the hearth go cold. And the girls were overtaken by disaster or not, the horses lost or won and the fires either warmed or consumed the household. In short, life continued as it ever had. Good luck and ill Fate befell the deserving and undeserving alike, although sometimes her inquisitors' lives matched the incoherent ramblings of the sad woman on the shore. And, perhaps, Lucy made those who chose to listen feel their destinies to be less random and formless. For signs and omens comfort by encouraging us to expect the worst, then confirm our belief that it was unavoidable. And predictions of good luck will always be welcome even if they are never fulfilled.

But what of Lucy's own future life, poor cinder-grubber? Her tale ran dry when she lost her child so she is fixed for ever, seeking along the margins, becalmed in the past, while the urgent narrative of other human lives flows past regardless. On and on run the stories of those who were born to bob, or be tossed and wrecked, or snagged, or pulled under, or to drift, or cruise along sublime, all borne upon an unstoppable current that brings us, every one, at last, to the same destination.

Just so, one day, our two spinster sisters awake from their dream of dust and decide to leap once more into life's turbulent race and let it carry them where it will. For Aurora opens the door on departed Georgina's photographic equipment and, rather than despairing about what to do with all this stuff, finds herself enlivened by the need to use it again.

This revelation provokes quite an orgy of activity. Other doors are flung open, furniture is polished and decisions made. The sisters strenuously remodel a corner of the attic as a photographic studio, complete with aspidistra in its art pot. And since they have no examples of their work suitable to be shown to prospective clients, the girls take photographic portraits of each other, Aurora finding something wistful and dreamy in Teresa, while Teresa gives her sister a double chin.

Having made this bold beginning the two maidens now sit on the *chaise-longue* that has been dragged upstairs from the parlour to discuss their new enterprise and how it shall be launched.

'No more of the Flynns' daily net load, thank goodness!' says Teresa, looking about herself with satisfaction.

'Absolutely not! We shall find a nook for ourselves among nice people who can pay for their portraits,' says Aurora.

'Not so different from our old line, really, quite respectable,' says Teresa, reassuring herself. 'Just a more modern way of making portraits, fixed on paper or metal plate rather than ivory and parchment.'

'Quite. But so much easier, don't you think? Cheap and easy—'

'But maybe a tiny bit common?' interrupts Teresa, dubiously.

'Not at all – and if we are to be business ladies we can't afford to be particular. Ordinary people want to commemorate themselves in pictures just as the rich and renowned have always done. And why shouldn't the common people be remembered by future generations?' reasons egalitarian Aurora.

'Pictures will never, and should never, replace tender memories of those who have gone before,' objects Teresa, squirming away from a direct confrontation with her sister about the rights of the lower classes to hand down their ugly countenances to posterity.

'Well, I don't think so. Consider Mama. Can you remember what she looked like – what she really looked like? And don't you wish that we had been old enough to paint her miniature portrait or, better still, take her photograph before she passed away?'

'I have something solid as a memento of her,' counters her sister, ducking Aurora's question. 'Gold cannot rust or decay,' she says, putting her hand piously to the brooch at her neck.

'It's not the same, though, is it? It tells one nothing about who she once was, the clothes she wore, her figure, how she dressed her hair, the grave look in her eyes. I consider pictures, not objects, to be a greater comfort and a truer repository of memories.'

Teresa has pause to consider that, in fact, she cannot truly remember Mama. And thirty years after her loss, it is indeed to a picture that she turns. However, this abiding image is the cheap colour representation of the Virgin Mary inside the front cover of her girlish missal, which has somehow become confused with and supplanted the saintly mother of memory. Now feeling outmanoeuvred, if only in her own head, she snaps back at Aurora, 'Well, I think that's rather an ungodly thing for you to say!' and holds on to her mother's brooch as though to shield her from the opinions of her youngest daughter. Teresa carries on, in a torrent of guilt and self-justification, 'Our existence on earth is fleeting and meaningless so we should really have no ambition to perpetuate images of ourselves here – that's just vanity and worldliness. And I won't hear another word!' She is on the verge of frustrated tears – fights with Aurora usually make her cry.

'Teresa, dear, I'm only talking about business, not life everlasting. We shall take the pictures and people shall pay for them because they want a memento for their family or just to show off their new gown. But we shan't care because we will live comfortably off the profits in the here and now.' She looks at her flushed sister and adds, 'In dreadful anticipation of the hereafter!'

So, as always, Aurora has her way and they place engraved advertising cards in local shop windows offering their services as lady photographers to prospective clients, thus:

The Wine of Life keeps oozing drop by drop,
The Leaves of Life keep falling one by one . . .

Two lady photographic artistes will take great pains to make natural likenesses of children and adults instantly, either at their own rooms or at private residences.
Secure the maiden's dewy loveliness, childhood's innocence, the family group happy and complete, ere time should fade or plunder there . . .

Please enquire within.

There must have been something particularly compelling in the threat implicit within this morbid sentiment that, combined with the promise that the process would be quick and painless, persuaded maidens, children and their families to seize the day. And for those who lacked either the money, or the inclination, to venture to the West End and into one of those imposing salons of portraiture on Regent Street, the Misses Mantilla became the first choice for memorialising fleeting lives.

Their first client was a young man who was that month departing for the Orient and, believing it only right that his absence should be insupportable to those he left behind, commissioned a compensatory *aide-memoire* to prick their grief. From this seed corn, there grew an abundant crop of heads, figures and groups arranged at christenings, engagements, marriages and funerals.

Teresa laboured at this, the unglamorous coal face of photography, chronicling those little lives and little events that to the participants meant so much yet remained so trivial to anyone beyond that particular family circle. She recorded diligently, by the thousand, those unremarkable moments that give us, the anonymous and ordinary, a heritage to hold on to. At all those important occasions when new clothes were worn and family history made, Teresa was sure to be present with her tripod and measuring-tape. She told lives in pictures, made storybooks out of hundreds of those bourgeois albums in which every family tells much the same tale.

What brought her relief from the tedium of repetition, and occasionally delight, was the element of the unconsidered or accidental, in short the unconventional. She relished the killingly old-fashioned hat that some aunt wore to frighten the baby, the ugly adolescent who was stood at the back so his pimples might be obscured by a parlour palm, or the little dog scratching itself indelicately in the corner, which she took care to include. But such diversions aside, her pictures usually represented an idealised image of orthodox family life. She never recorded the row that had raged a minute before everyone had assembled in the garden and put on their holiday faces. She, not her camera, was observer of these things, sensitive to the nuance and atmosphere of tension, rivalry and fear. It took Teresa, not the camera, to tell you that the happy bride was hiding a five-month pregnancy and the proud father fell down dead drunk a minute after the flash went off.

Teresa also cultivated for herself a particular genre in this trade of official recorder. She began to specialise in photographing the families of soldiers and sailors posted overseas. When a papa was a long time away, this yearly ritual of showing *how they have all grown* provided a nice bit of repeat business. One family of six mixed infants, in particular, could have been tracked through her series of portraits. The original image shows the matron sitting, with a babe in arms, toddling twins confined in a miniature hay-cart, her serious girl and two further boys flanking her. As years passed – and still no sign of Papa – the ranking and distribution of this group changed. The twins graduated from skirts to sailor suits, the big girl lost her plaits and grew discreet breasts and, most striking of all, the baby leapt from its place upon the chair to stand beside it and then, in a series of remarkable progressions, having bolted ever upwards into an aetiolated adolescence, at last, supported himself by it. Who knows what became of absent Papa? It seemed probable to Teresa, since the family group was never augmented by a little seventh or eighth, that he was only ever after acquainted with the postcard family, conveniently portable inside his Bible. In some hot Indian cantonment he would have watched as, by degrees, the children grew up, then exited the tableau until, by the last known photograph, we find left only shrunken Mother, the constant in this time-lapse portrait of the rise and fall of the family unit. Who was this woman? What were the names of her children and what became of them? Nothing survives of them but photographs. All those forgotten faces, looking out bravely into a future that belongs to us.

The 'naval and military' side of the business was wholly Teresa's responsibility and she exercised some ingenuity in tracking down prospective clients through the army lists. She offered competitive rates for a three-year contract with, as an introductory offer, a portrait of Papa in full uniform – to stare, judgemental *in absentia*, from the mantelpiece upon his progeny.

If Teresa's was the documentary branch of their photographic enterprise, then Aurora was to claim the artistic high ground. Hers was an urgent, somewhat clandestine speciality, which tracked her down and found her out like a fellow conspirator in a crime. Post-mortem photography, or mourning memorials: the modern mechanism by which the living may hold on to the dead became her business.

It had been her old reputation as a portrait painter that had brought to her the first discreet enquiry from a parent who had lost his baby to a gastric disease and had no portrait with which to preserve her memory. The original commission had been to photograph the dead infant and upon this quick, realistic representation base a memorial portrait. However, Aurora produced a tintype of the dead baby of such delicacy and naturalness, even though the poor subject was somewhat wasted by her illness, that the bereaved parents settled for the permanent, and realistic, reminder of the photograph instead. So Aurora gained her reputation as a sympathetic practitioner of this genre of photography for which there was huge demand, particularly after a hard winter or hot summer.

After her accidental introduction to this shadowy craft, Aurora made a little study into the conventions by looking through others' representations of the dear deceased. She soon understood that in order to arrange her subjects in a manner as agreeable and satisfactory as their bereft relations could wish some beautification was generally required. Long exposure to Lady Georgina's loathsome, if living, models meant that Aurora could calmly close eyelids, wipe faces of any nasty fluids that the dying process might have left there, comb hair and arrange stiffened limbs without succumbing to fits of the vapours. She grew skilled at removing death's sting by presenting her clients, as near as possible, in attitudes of harmonious sleep, often tucked up in their deathbeds. Women she attired in white, and posed to hold flowers: morning glories, which wither in a day, or a rose held downward or by a broken stem to indicate a life cut short. Her men she had dressed prosaically in their day clothes with hands laid on a Bible. But seated poses were also called for, particularly when the dear one had been snatched away prematurely, leaving behind no other picture to fit inside a memorial locket, or to display in a draped frame on the mantel. For just as Aurora had predicted, people needed the image, not the possessions, of the dead to remember them by. In these cases Aurora had taught herself how to use hidden props and ties to create a relaxed pose suggestive of life interrupted rather than ended. She grew especially skilled at finding ways to mimic this painless slip from waking to post-prandial snoozing despite the conundrum of how stiffened feet might be fitted back into shoes, or a casual newspaper slotted into hands clenched like claws by the death spasm.

Apart from perfecting the natural and unambiguous representation of death, Aurora also offered a style of quite theatrical sumptuousness. Just then becoming fashionable for the portrayal of a maiden's mortal remains was the Sleeping Beauty style, in which the lovely corpse was shown, side view, draped in white and often so smothered in flowers that it was hard immediately to locate the 'beauty' in the midst of them. These icy virgins lay, like Juliet upon her catafalque, as though upon their bridal beds, potent symbols for the contemplation of that tragic trinity: death, youth and chaste beauty.

However, Aurora found the staple of her mortuary trade to be children. For children will persist in being carried off with such rapidity and by such a variety of apparently trivial causes that there is often no opportunity to preserve their features in a happier manifestation than that of their premature death.

Just as with the adults her dead children were usually laid out upon a bed or contained within their tiny coffins. Sometimes she posed siblings nearby in cautionary contemplation of the awful absolute; often, and most tenderly, she showed the child supported in the arms of its grieving mama as though she were still able to nurture and soothe. It seemed to childless Aurora that some of these hollow-eyed mothers were so young and their infant's death so untimely that her photographs were evidence of their having given birth as much as a record of the life that had been snatched away. They appeared, in their grief, as startled at having had a child as they did bewildered at having so soon lost it again, and looked upon these stiff, baby bundles as though taken by surprise at what they found propped awkwardly in their arms. Some parents wanted the useless medicine bottles that had failed to save their darling one included, as though in warning, beside the corpse. Many wanted the trappings of childhood to be shown – toys and games, like tomb goods for the afterlife, were laid within still hands. Once Aurora was asked to frame a carved rocking-horse in the photograph, leaving the little body of its owner annexed to one side and dominated by the apparently vital, snorting horse, as though *it* were the subject of the picture. And there was a particular little girl who, Aurora considered, Mama had dressed up like a birthday present, such were the ruffles and ringlets and bows. On the hard bed next to the child was laid out a rigid, wax-faced, same-sized doll, dressed just alike, so that they seemed twin children or twin dolls, one with eyes shut, the other's wide open. But which was which? Were they sleeping or waking? Living or dead? Aurora squirmed at the nasty ambiguity.

Often the child's death had been so swift and unexpected that Aurora would notice its fingernails were dirty from play or the little worn shoes kicked off at bedtime were still under the deathbed. But the parents would always attempt to make angelic corpses. Like good children readied for church, their hair, often lank from illness, was wetted, parted, combed and curled. They were dressed in best clothes: starched white frocks and stiff collars. And they *were* beautiful. The pale, calm faces were grave, with solemn eyes that seemed to behold the ineffable, beyond mortal suffering. Even if the illness had been a wasting one, which had stretched the skin over the skull, childish hands remained plump and smooth, innocent of the marks that longer life and hardship leave there.

And though the circumstances of each mourning tableau would

one day be lost, their power remained undiminished. For these inward stories of a particular death became emblematic of all death that is buried in life. Death gave Aurora's pictures a significance and a resonance that Teresa's carefully posed celebrations of the living would never achieve. And in her most mature and skilful mourning portraits, Aurora found such depth of meaning and emotion that they conferred a kind of immortality upon her subjects, who seemed to exist for ever in a place of stillness and thought. Beside them, Teresa's images seemed bathetic or banal.

Occasionally the two entrepreneurs worried that Georgina would send for her old equipment. But less so since the only word they had had from her had been to inform them of her and the Flynns' removal to a new address in Australia. Where, apparently, God's call to disseminate shock and alarm was even more urgent than it was in America.

East End Legends

It is time for us to decide about Lucy. Shall she continue to be sucked into the mythology of the London underclass, a sad spirit in a cloak haunting the margin of the story, or shall we be kind and restore her to her life?

In and out the piers of London Bridge she slips, searching in those alcoves where shelter the destitute and dispossessed. Investigating among the tramps' nests and the children's lays, she looks particularly into the faces of the children, coiled like oily ropes. In this grotesques' gallery there are many whose physical oddities would qualify them for an anatomist's display. One such is a woman squatted asleep but still holding herself almost upright, so that she may support the half-grown baby laid across her lap, his legs and arms hanging loose. Although the narrow, undernourished body is as undeveloped as a girl's, her face has the thickened and seamed look of something made from ancient leather. This girl has the inward-looking, time-folded face of one long preserved in some airless place. She might be the sacrificial offering of a great dead civilisation, left to travel on alone with their message down the long, lonely road of time. Or perhaps she's the triumphant product of their immortalising skill and ceremony: its carefully mummified, now nameless, queen.

But when Lucy comes closer she sees that what is timeless in that enduring face has been etched there by living. In that face is every mortal mother's limitless acceptance of the pain and loss there must be in having and loving a child. For Lucy, this mother and child, the heavy boy borne upon that untiring lap, is the very image of love's sad sacrifice of self. It's a love that makes her ordinary and divine, beautiful and debased. And vulnerable, how vulnerable. Perhaps it is safer for the human heart not to invest in love for a child: the bloody ties of that love cannot be loosened without damage. When Lucy looks into the still unwrecked face of the beloved, she finds there the detached beauty of George's burning boy, of Aurora's chilled angel, of her own lost baby. An unmarked face, complete unto itself, viewed as though it lay just beneath calm water. The embodiment of new hope; the 'blithe spirit' that is as yet ignorant of pain, as yet untainted by sin or the knowledge of selfless love. With a simple gesture of unselfconscious fellow feeling, Lucy takes off her cloak and lays it over them both. So that when the woman does awake, she will be doubly warmed: by the cloak and by the knowledge that some kind person gave without asking. Then she turns towards Fred and home.

That same night another is seeking in that quarter, for Dr Oliver may be glimpsed among the more wakeful denizens of 'outcast London' still in pursuit of his vanished lady. Here we find him washed up at the Ten Bells pub, a shabby-genteel figure in a slouch hat, carrying the tools of his trade that remain unpawned in his shiny black bag.

'Yu come out on a skirt 'unt, dearie? Do the 'andsome an' stand a girl a drink, eh?' says a florid woman, assuming him to be one of those middle-class thrill-seekers who are drawn as prurient tourists to that notorious neighbourhood.

A man standing nearby good-naturedly addresses her mark: 'I'd stay away frem Queenie, squire. She'll pross off of you all evenin' an' you won't get a sniff at the end of it.'

'Don' yu lissen to 'im. I only wants ta cheer meself,' says she, trying to shove away the warning man with her elbow. ' 'Onest, love. I'd be ever so obliged to yu, for I'm that down in the dumps seein' as me dear 'usband 'as turned me out a doors an' only give me the key to the street.'

'My dear madam, I wouldn't touch you with the fire tongs,' says he, with the precise enunciation of the very drunk.

At this last there is some derisive laughter and, on seeing that he is a hopeless case, the part-time harlot calls him 'Dr Draw-fart' and slams out of the pub door. However, her parting words have an electrifying effect upon the rest of the rowdy party: one can't have lived in this particular part of London these last couple of years without having been infected by the hysteria that has made Whitechapel a synonym for the most bloody and notorious of crimes. The effect of eighty thousand handbills, and it would seem as many newspaper articles and wrongful arrests, has inflated the exploits of that nimble Jack, who taunts his pursuers with boastful letters 'from hell' and continues to evade capture some eleven gory murders on, until he verges upon the mythological. For Jack's a slippery one, who wears the changing face of those we fear most, as public enemies always do, being devils suited to their times.

Because the papers declare London is menaced by Eastern European Jews who, we are told, infest our slums, bringing crime and horrific rituals, the beast wears the badge of his tribe, the expressive countenance, saffron beard and talon nails of the sly Hebraic. Because the press is similarly alarmed by those ranting middle-class religionists, apparently sent demented by the insuperable sin they find on the streets, he is made to wear the mask of an open-air evangelist. Because the people hate the nobs, he is a corrupt blueblood. But perhaps he's a mason, an anarchist, a foreigner or even a vengeful woman – whoever is an anathema to good, ordinary, decent folk such as ourselves. Or does the evidence that he knows how to wield a very sharp knife point to slaughterman, butcher, boot-maker, or even doctor?

Thus Dr Oliver, with his black bag, a moment ago the butt of ribald remarks, becomes quarry for the vigilant bloodhounds who have set themselves up to do the chief inspector's job for him. He is chased from the place on unsteady legs, slipping over greasy cobbles and colliding with walls until he is run to the very edge of the river where the howling mob press him until his only recourse is to plunge away into the mash of mud, leaving his shoes and his pursuers behind.

Who knows what became of him then? There will be no further sighting of this suspicious gentleman. However, a black doctor's bag is found next morning choked with mud upon the foreshore together with a pair of water-logged shoes. These last are refreshed and find themselves among others of their ilk, clumsy of make and ancient of date, in Petticoat Lane market. Likewise the bag is made Christian again: washed, patched with cardboard, blackened over with boot polish and sold on, before a heavy shower melts its refurbished parts and it falls to pieces in the new owner's hands.

The sun is rising as Lucy arrives home, at the place where she is loved without giving herself over completely to the man who loves her. She returns to Fred, shivering without her cloak, to find him sitting glumly at the table. He hardly bothers to look up when he hears her enter the room for the only conversation they can have nowadays is one that is exhausted with overuse.

'I've come back, dear,' she says, sitting down beside him.

'You should git some sleep.'

'I should.' She turns sadly away from him as though to climb into their bed, then comes back to Fred and, taking his heavy hand, lifts it to her face to make him look at her. 'Fred, he's gone, he's really gone from me. I know I'll never see him no more.' She starts to sob. Fred encircles her with his arms and holds her close. 'But, Fred, it's as though now that I've let him go I really feel him come again – inside of me. A life's inside here, moving and growing.' She takes his hands and puts them on her belly.

He stays stock still, as though he were struck blind and was listening hard with his hands. 'Is it true, Luce?'

'Yes. I think he's come back to me. Only this time I shall be a better mother.'

He holds her close again round the waist, groaning with the agony of their old pain and this new promise.

'And, Fred, I'm going to hold on to this baby so hard. I won't never let it go,' she says fiercely, crushing his face against her and pulling his hair in her passion. 'I'll just hold him and hold him and squeeze him and keep him. This baby'll belong just to you and me, Fred. No one else shall claim him.'

They stay, holding tight to each other like shipwrecked sailors who cleave to the timely flotsam that will save them.

'Now, then, here's a turn-up! Here's a jolly turn-up!' says Fred, standing so that he may embrace her better. 'A new life for both on us, eh? Shall you and me begin agen, my dear?' But Lucy is too full of sad happiness to reply so he just holds her tight and wonders that he should be so blessed. 'Brave gal. There's my brave gal.'

And she is brave. For it is the bravest, blindest leap of all leaps of faith to knit again those cords that attach us to our children. But children are hope. They affirm the courageous choice that humanity makes to carry on into that precarious future life and to live it. Death's only remedy.

And although, upon the little journey they started together, Lucy will go one way and Duke another, their paths never to cross again, down the years Lucy will always carry him with her and he the lasting imprint of her love.

Domestic Bliss

Since last we called at four, Wellesley Villas, that household has been augmented by ex-inmates of the Fisher Folk: by Rebecca, the housemaid with a past, and Duke, a boy with none. Lucy's lost boy has now no memory of a mama other than Mrs Georgina Larkins – a widowed lady, grown fat and fond on lace curtains and porcelain ornaments in her billet in the suburbs.

On this day we find Rebecca enjoying a cigarette in the kitchen, Georgina in her parlour with 'baby Duke', as he is known, at play upon the carpet with his Noah's Ark and wooden animal couples. At the doorbell's ring Rebecca hastily curtails her spit and a drag, extinguishing the lighted end of the cigarette with dampened fingertips and hiding it in her apron pocket before she hurries up the passage to open the door to her master, Mr B.

Having handed her his hat and gloves, Harry looks at himself in the ugly hall mirror and strokes the waxed ends of his moustache. He wears a Malmaison carnation in his buttonhole, his inexpressibles are fawn-coloured and he smells agreeably of 'Jockey Club', like every other lounging Johnnie who frequents the stalls of the Limelight. He is grown to be rather a fine dog. The fine dog, distracted from self-admiration, sniffs before entering the parlour and says, irritably, to its mistress, 'That girl's on fire again. I wish you'd do something about it, Gina.'

'Don't I know it! She's costin' me a fortune in cotton lawn for new pinnies,' she replies, without standing.

'Don't go on about household expenses. My head won't stand it.'

'Well, if I don't manage the accounts, I don't know who will. Really, Harry, dear, I 'ave quite a job of keepin' this house comfortable for your calls. Whenever they might be,' says Gina sulkily.

'Come and give your cousin a kiss if you expect any allowance at all this month, you little tart,' he says, and she is not so sunk in domestic complaisance that she dawdles in obeying him.

'And you never take me out no more,' she wheedles. 'Can't we take a little trip to the Alhambra or the Philharmonic, or even a penny gaff, Harry, love?'

'I do believe yellow feathers are sprouting from your rump, Gina. Look, there they are! I see them most distinct. Canary-yellow ones.'

She has strained to look behind herself before she understands his allusion and whacks him on the shoulder, saying, 'Leave orf!' and smooths down her skirts.

'What I want to know is, if there's a tidy, penny-pinching little housewife inside every street whore, then d'you think it works t'other way? Is there a tart inside every nice girl, struggling to get out?' he says, pinching her behind.

She struggles free, saying warningly, 'Harry, *pas devant l'enfant!*'

'So, it's chirruping in French now, is it?' He sits down, putting his feet provocatively upon a little side table. But Gina ignores this in the face of her more urgent concern. She has learnt how to employ the accent and pronunciation of her middle-class neighbours now when she has serious things to say.

'That's another thing, dear. Baby really ought to begin his eddication.' To press home her point, she picks up the protesting boy and says, this time in mock baby language, apparently for his benefit, 'Ifn he wants to be a fine gen'leman, he needs to learn a fine fist and his nine times threes, and I don't know what else.'

'Now I'm to be the fond uncle of an aspiring bank clerk, am I? How the family expectations do grow!'

'Harry, it's just ordinary, respectable life. You owe it to your family, really you do,' she replies earnestly, without noticing the way 'ordinary' and 'respectable' toll a death knell around that little cluttered room.

If Gina but knew it, she is playing with fire as surely as her recalcitrant maid. Harry is no longer the sexually ignorant beardless boy and she, it has to be said, is no longer the spicy little piece who had the educating of him. Harry, up to his eyes in debts – incurred on the expectations of his father's demise – and now as well used to picking up a whore as he is a taxi cab, has begun to weary of his fat-arsed little cuckoo sitting, beak open, in the alien nest in which he placed her. And the idea that he should take responsibility is like the clang of a prison door to him. For Harry wearies of all that is ordinary, unexceptionable and nice. Now Gina only makes him feel like a husband. So what if the maid could be depended on to turn an indifferent eye during their romps, if the only thing that distinguishes him from their neighbours is having it in the afternoon when respectable men should be at their business? Sex with Gina in her frilly bedroom is as unerotic as making love in a curio shop. It feels like a poor form of timid, middle-class sinning. It feels like habit or, worse, duty.

Gina's misfortune is that she has fallen in love with all that is ordinary, unexceptional and nice. She is a well-satisfied wife who sets sex, on demand, in the balance against being comfortably kept. And she has her 'baby' to play with when Harry is away. All that distinguishes her from her lady neighbours is that she is only 'married on the carpet and the banns up the chimney'. But what a difference that is. For if Gina had been able to see beyond the charm of playing at husbands and wives she might have known that her status was as secure and enduring as that of an inconvenient, ageing household pet. A pet whose fickle master had outgrown it. Of course, cunning alley-cat Beatrice had claws and teeth sharp enough to hold him. But docile Gina is grown so accustomed to being kept that she turns her soft belly to him, claws sheathed and teeth rotted with too much sugar, and purrs obediently under his hand. Gina, with as little foreboding as the house-cat for the sack she will be drowned in, now looks at her hubby and fondly imagines them promenading together, the boy running ahead with an Eton collar round his little neck.

Harry jumps up from the domestic hearth, as though resolving that he can no longer neglect his family responsibilities. He has shirked his duty as an honourable man, but now he knows that he must face up to it: he should go back to the country and look for a rich wife. But not quite yet. Not while there is life in the young dog. How true those words of Bacon: 'He that hath wife and children hath given hostages to fortune; for they are impediments to great enterprises, either of virtue or of mischief.' Harry, being decidedly in favour of the latter enterprise for himself, is off to Paris to pique a palate dulled by the bland diet to be had at his suburban bolt-hole.

A Fairy Tale

Surely man must have a mate or, more particularly, a wife if he is to lead a continent life, beget legal heirs or please his family. Where else will he find his domestic comfort, his helpmeet, his fruitful vine, his spur to virtue? But no: a man will always be running off and discovering continents or writing plays or leading armies with no thought for his social responsibilities. For all that he overflows with every eligible virtue of fortune, youth and availability as to be quite embarrassed by the numbers of girls applying for the role of wife, he will not consider himself 'in want' of one. Perversity! And even though society accepts that it becomes a man to be romantic – for love in a man is a civilising ideal – he may still honourably dodge marriage. He may worship at the shrine of feminine beauty, compose sonnets on his beloved's collar-bone or make an awful ass of himself and still die a respected bachelor. Such aberrations merely demonstrate a noble frailty of the mind. For it is understood that marriage, let alone love, will never be a man's be-all and end-all, his ultimate purpose in life. It is even whispered that, 'One wife is too much for one husband to bear.'

Yet it is certain that no husband is too much for many a maiden to bear – although, having landed him, she may well prefer to throw him back. For what shackles him seems to her a liberation.

And while he may love extravagantly before, she may do so only after she is safely married. Perversity! For women marriage is the one delightful cure for the shameful spinster state, a glad surrender into strong, protective arms that brings the happy ending every woman deserves. However, both well-married duchesses and insecurely hitched whores might advise alike that, for a woman, marriage is best looked upon with open eyes as a strategic alliance made between self-interested parties, and recognised by the Church and the law. But which is nearer to the truth: bed of roses or business arrangement?

Our idealistic Teresa is intoxicated only with the thought of roses. At the age of forty we find her trembling at last on the brink of finding or being found by that obscure 'prospect of delight' for which she has waited half a lifetime.

The photographic business of our two entrepreneurs continued to thrive in their little backwater of south London. It did so well, indeed, that they were for the first time not only financially secure but able to see a way of arresting their slide into genteel indigence. They even considered launching themselves as a business proper by renting a shop in which to house their studio and darkroom and receive clients.

Teresa made a point of looking for suitable premises wherever she walked – something on a busy street and with a picture window in which they might display their wares. It was when she was enquiring about a grocer's shop that had gone bankrupt and smelt of the dirt from old potatoes that she had met Mr Murphy, commercial letting agent.

To start with their relationship had been based wholly upon square footage and westerly aspects. And, like scouts after spoor, they had thrilled together in pursuit of suitable premises. They even tracked down a few and would enthusiastically talk up the possibilities of partition walls and new paint. However, they never seemed to come quite to the point of landing one. Then, by degrees, the talk they shared shifted away from retail premises to themselves. Mr Murphy, product of a charitable education, had raised himself up in his profession by hard work and self-denial. He lived with his old parents in three rooms on two floors of a rented house, and he saved. He was an honourable man, careful with his money and steady in his ways. The evidence was there that he was dependable, moral, clean and cautiously ambitious to improve himself. However, it was the fact that he said he admired her that made Teresa's heart spin.

From this point on their friendship stopped being based upon business and instead floated high, full of the heady gas of romance. Their meetings in high-street tearooms became assignations, their walks along hard thoroughfares and through dusty parks intimate perambulations.

Now, the evening drawing in, they are sitting together on a park bench and too tired to continue walking – that sole respectable resort of the urban poor when courting, besides filling their bladders fit to burst with shop-bought tea.

'Are you cold, dear? Give me your little hands and I'll hold them,' he says, lifting her knuckles up to his lips to blow warm breath on them.

Teresa is touched by this tender gesture, and even more to see how his gloves are worn thin with age but meticulously darned. She notices that everything about him personally and everything he possesses is worn and thin and yet, at least from a distance, he always contrives to appear neat and well dressed. Only since she moved in close has she noticed the effort he makes to keep his attire whole and clean. This noble struggle to keep his head up moves her inexpressibly. 'Thomas, darling.' She squeezes his hand and is ashamed of her own, rather nice, new kid gloves.

'Shall we go on? The evening is chilly. There's a stall where we may get a mug of beef tea by the bridge. Would you like one?'

'Thomas, won't you come to my home? We could be so cosy tucked up there, just you and me and . . .'

'I can't compromise you, Teresa. A younger sister isn't a suitable chaperone – no, you must come to my place first and meet my parents.'

This fruitless conversation is one they have had on several other weary evenings. She knows that he is right and that, even if she had told her sister of his existence, Aurora would not make a chaperone. But having proposed to introduce her to his parents in his own home, he has never made a firm arrangement with her to do so.

They go on, arms linked, feet beating the lovers' tattoo: 'nowhere to go, nowhere to go'.

Down the darkening alleys of trees they march, so close that he imagines he feels her whole body moving, rustling under its clothes, as she walks beside him. How to kiss her and when? Should he ask first but, then, what was the proper way to do so? He wants to be romantic, not formal and correct – it is a burden to him to be the one who must take the risk, make the first approach. 'They say there's a fine view of the Chelsea Hospital from this point,' he says desperately, leading her away from the path and towards a stand of trees.

'Thomas, I can't see my feet, I don't know where I'm stepping. Isn't the river over in that direction?'

'I believe you're right. Oh, just one other thing . . .' he says inconsequentially, turning towards her. Before he knows what he intends to do, he has taken off his hat and kissed her on the lips.

It is as though she has been waiting for this all her life. She doesn't yell, she doesn't weep, or run, or rebuke, she just holds on tight and kisses him and kisses him back, full on the lips. What a lovely sensation, so warm and true. Those kisses make all the conversation that went before, however intimate and friendly, seem paltry, time-wasting, when they might have been doing something else so much more significant. This physical connection is a rich, new dialogue, in which his awareness that she has newer and nicer clothes than he, speaks without having to watch her accent and can afford the rent on a whole house is meaningless.

He is a man, she is a woman, and they are both made essential and absolute by this generous pleasure.

Now that she has been kissed by a man for the first time, with passion, Teresa discovers that the sensation is so utterly lovely and absorbing that she can't imagine why, having started, one would ever choose to stop. All her senses are dominated by her highly sensitised mouth. Her eyeballs turn back into her head (no need for sight) and, since she apparently has no further use for her legs either, she has to hold him tight to stop herself falling.

When they do stop because, after all, they are standing in the middle of a London park in the late afternoon, they both laugh as though with relief and look candidly into each other's eyes. Neither feels awkward or bashful. Like every other couple in the history of time they are the first ever to have felt exactly how this feels, the first to have discovered this delicious pursuit – fellow conspirators in pleasure, they are not a little self-satisfied in contrasting themselves with those other drab individuals who walk politely about and are not them.

From that first kiss Teresa is giddy with the delight of Thomas and romance. She privately calls him her *secret lover*, holding their passion close to herself, safe from her sister. Now that they have got over that huge obstacle of the first embrace, every time they meet they concern themselves urgently with finding a secluded place in which to practise and improve the art of kissing – hardly talking to each other as they hurry to the more shadowy areas of the park to indulge. However, love *en plein air* is neither respectable nor comfortable. They find that other couples crowd out the same secluded spots as themselves, making their love seem a common, sordid thing, or that the nasty smells that meet them down alleyways, or the leers of rough men, chase them away. So their love takes on a rather wretched character, desperate rather than tragic romantic.

Tonight while tramping down some long, anonymous red-brick road Teresa leads her lover quick through the gate of one of the houses and behind the sheltering privet hedge, coated with warm dust from the street. No lights show from within and the narrow space between bay window and hedge is as discreet as anywhere else that a spooning couple might chance to find. They have been seeking somewhere all that evening and so it is with reckless abandon that they launch themselves at each other, impatient to squeeze what pleasure they can, standing up in someone else's front garden, in the dusk.

This night Teresa is reckless. Perhaps, having decisively led him into trespass, she is emboldened to tempt him into other profligacy. Whether it is desperation, despair or simply sexual frustration, Teresa kisses Thomas, here in the garden, with such violence and presses herself against him with such unmistakable need that she has him backed up against the house wall, breathless. A passer-by, glancing beyond the front gate, would suppose that these two bodies are locked in mortal combat – the repressed gasps of effort, the shambling, stumbling wrestlers' hold, the urgent struggle to prevail. And within their combatants' clench, Teresa and Thomas are as intent upon forcing pleasure on and from each other as fighters are to dominate through giving and taking pain.

This is not airy, dreamy kissing, it is not respectful, modest kissing, it is not romantic, or sentimental or comforting. This is something hungry and carnal and vicious. But exciting, so exciting. Teresa cannot stop her shameless hands exploring him – they mirror his own, which are running over her armoured breasts, fumbling for some fastening among the ornamental bows that he might loose to gain access. She pants as his hands slither over her surface, blindly nosing for any unprotected part of her body. Hers thrust between buttons, bursting studs to find the final, woollen layer that will reveal his body. As she fiddles and flaps inside his jacket, she releases a musky smell of his sweat and his stale, warmed clothes that she drinks in with her nostrils, adding this new depravity to the abandon of her thirsty lips and hands. Then her hands slip down over his belly towards the importunate coat-peg that props up the front of his trousers.

Thomas springs back from her as though the touch of her hands will scald him. 'Don't,' he gasps. 'Don't. Not there.' He falls away from her, bent over that sore, hard thing, which, she senses, pulses with agony, trying to protect it from her dangerous hands. But it is too late. Whatever damage he feared from her is done – he gasps and turns away from her to lay his forehead on the cool brick of the house wall.

'Thomas, what have I done? Did I hurt you? Oh, darling, let me kiss you better.' What has happened? Is he ashamed of her and of what she has done to him? The fine celebratory feeling that they had once shared seems to have been curdled by her shamelessness.

'Oh dear, I've disgraced myself,' he says at last, blushing.

Teresa cannot tell what he means, but guesses, with relief, that it must be something to do with his compromising her honour. She looks down at herself and notices that he has half ripped off one of her decorative bows. 'It's nothing. I can sew it back on,' she says, smiling and glad that he does not blame her. 'Really, there's no disgrace.' She takes his hand for reassurance.

At that moment someone enters the front room of the house, carrying a lamp, and the two middle-aged lovers outside the window start out of the front gate and hurry away down the street as though they had been caught in a game of Knock Down Ginger.

No such drab, limiting pleasures for our absconding Harry: the taste for high times bred by low life has led him to seek Eros with another accent. The last, positively the last, of his bachelor spoils before that final snap of the married man's shackles. So, we find Harry where Gina may not even begin to imagine him, in that quarter where windmills creak and at that interval known as *l'heure verte*. For Harry is being entertained by the wicked 'green fairy' who lends this hour her name. A French coquette on one knee, he charges his perforated spoon with its sugar cube, places it above the glass and lets iced water trickle from his absinthe fountain upon the place below so that the sugar water may fill it up to its marker. Five to one, the beautiful distillation, green like a peridot, is diluted and, as that miraculous chlorophyllic green turns cloudy, Harry and the genuine French tart, connoisseurs both, lean into the bumper to breathe the floral bouquet of aromatic fennel, *anise* and wormwood.

Harry has truly learnt now to press hard pleasure's grape against his palate until it bursts.

Lost Sons

Back in Harry's native country, a month after he'd bailed out of his north London hubby-and-pa routine, his own gov'nor and illustrious aunt are in conversation in her private sitting room.

'My apologies for this hurried visit,' says Lord John Harpur, sitting down suddenly. 'I call only to inform you that the passage is settled for tomorrow night. I will engage a carriage to carry me to Paris and . . . collect the body. My poor boy's body. You are to expect us within the week.'

'Poor John, I could not have wished for this,' she says, taking his hand in her cold one. Even this meagre gesture of sympathy releases the tears he cannot contain. 'You shall take the brake. It can be spared for as long as you shall need it. It can await your return in Dover.'

'Thank you. Perhaps you could give me your boy also. I need someone who speaks the language and will not be bamboozled by these Frenchmen.'

The Duchess of Fainhope is a little unsettled at the idea of letting her captive leave his rock for such a long journey, but she cannot think that this booby could mean him harm. 'George? His accent is quite dreadful – it sounds more like Chinese to my ear. However, you may make such use of him as you can,' she concedes.

'You should not be so hard on George. He's a good enough lad. And now he's all that's left to both our poor houses,' says Lord John, again letting slip his insipid tears.

The Duchess cannot suppress her own welling emotion at this, which emerges in the form of an acid little smile and the gnomic remark, 'He is his father's son.'

While this interview is being conducted, all is in turmoil at number four. Gina is in her bedroom, gathering up clothes to throw them down again upon the bed. It is hard to know if this erratic behaviour derives most from her being distraught or drunk, for she is both.

Impassive Rebecca is standing, leaning in the doorway, openly smoking a cigarette. Woken by this familiar, domestic whirlwind, 'baby Duke' ducks around her and comes into the room, causing Gina to drop what she is doing and bury his head in her impassioned bosom. 'What are we to do, Dukey? What are we to do?' she exclaims.

Rebecca taps out her cold ash into a cupped hand and takes another draw.

'My poor, fatherless boy! How could he desert *you*? Leave you penniless?'

'Penniless? Di'n't I allus say you should 'ave been saltin' it away?' says Rebecca, in her uninflected told-you-so voice.

'Shut up, you 'eartless bitch! Can't you see the poor li'le man misses 'is father?' shouts Gina, trying to hold on to the squirming boy.

Rebecca gives a slow shrug and says matter-of-factly, 'Only if it's penniless we are now, mebbe I should fink about slingin' me 'ook an' all.'

Duke pulls his smothered head sufficiently free to breathe and, when he has achieved this first necessity, embarks upon the second, which is to yell for her to stop crushing his face. The fond mama abruptly loosens her grip and says sharply, 'An' you can shut up an' all if you don't want a blisterin'.' She lets go of him altogether and gives him a little shove out of the door. The two women watch as he traipses back to bed. 'I'll be in in just a minute. Just let Mama and Rebecca talk in peace, won't you?' Gina calls after him, more kindly.

This eruption seems to have taken the edge off her frenzy and she uses the moment of calm to swig from her gin bottle, then says to her servant, with some of the indomitable candour of the old Beatrice, 'Look, it's serious this time. 'E's really gone an' left us in the lurch. 'E's obviously found 'imself some cheap little piece to join giblets with up over Town.'

Rebecca lets this pass, then says sympathetically, 'Can't you go round there wiv the figlia homey an' shame 'im into a pay-off?'

'The boy's only a 'doption, and 'e was never that bothered.'

'A standin' prick 'as no conscience, as they say,' concedes Rebecca flatly.

Gina walks around the room, picking up and putting down ornaments and baubles. 'And where exactly am I supposed to take 'im "round" to? 'Is people live somewhere in 'Ertfordshire. An' God knows where 'is digs in Town are. I never bothered to ask. Stupid cow.' She sits on the bed, letting her shoulders droop, and Rebecca, coming to sit beside her, pinches out the stub of her fag and lets it drop on to the floor.

' 'Ow much tin you got left, girl?'

'To be honest, Becs, we've been livin' on our "expectations" these last coupla monfs and I ain't got no more than what's left in me purse.'

'You got lots you can fiddle or fence,' says Rebecca, looking appraisingly around the overstuffed room.

'Not so much before people will start to notice and talk. I'll 'ave the landlord sniffin' around *and* all the tradesmen I owe. And that dressmaker!'

'Go on, you got them pearls, and what abou' the fevver fans he brung you? I can get rid of them fer you, no problem. That'll give us some actual to live on. And when you're ready, we can do a flit wiv what we can get on an 'andcart – bolt ve moon.'

'All my beautiful things! I couldn't,' whimpers Gina.

'Most on 'em "Made in Germany" and not worth the trouble,' supplies practical Rebecca. 'You got to get what you can fer vem, while you can. There ain't eny choice left, love.' Rebecca puts her arm around her mistress's shoulders while she cries.

'What will become of me?'

'Buck up. Somefink'll turn up. You're still a good-lookin' woman and you've got some lovely clothes,' Rebecca encourages Gina, giving her a squeeze.

But Gina cannot metamorphose back into Beatrice. Her transformation, if imperfect, has been complete. Having adapted to her stunted butterfly wings, she cannot contemplate life, once more, as a grub. 'I can't go back. I can't never go back. Not now!' she wails.

'Come on, it wouldn't be 'awkin' it on the streets. Now you'd be lookin' at a 'igh style of West End sin!' says Rebecca, with the *élan* of a salesman talking up seconds.

The Banquet Years

So George escaped his desert island at last, by paddle-steamer. This journey was the first that had released him from the vast duchy of Fainhope estates and taken him beyond the watchful custodianship of either mother or governess, into the sole care of his negligent uncle John. And we have seen how butter-fingered that gentleman can be. However, the enchantment of Fainhope Hall was bred so deep in him that, even when he broke free of the place, George was not roused from that dream of passivity to the bright consciousness of his own youth, sudden liberty and the possibility of happiness. Far from being excited and seduced by what that city might have to offer, George followed Lord John about like a semi-sensible sleepwalker, baffled and a little afraid to find himself in some place other than where he last fell asleep, and he was of very little use to that gentleman, indeed.

On their arrival in the corrupt French capital the two follow directions for the *hôtel de passe*, where rooms are available at an hourly rental, from which the obscure letter informing his father of Harry's probable demise had been sent. They discover that this place is located in one of those inner, sunless arcades that are called *passages*. Lined by low shops and offices, they are paved below by slimy flags, which leak the smell of new-dug graves, and lidded above by blackened glass roofs. These gas-lit corridors are let between buildings to link street to street, making a crepuscular labyrinth along which one may follow the way down to the very heart of that underworld of illicit pleasures and unlawful professions.

The two Englishmen dismiss their cab and turn off the bright and populous boulevard into the obscure entrance of that corridor where Harry, the *flâneur*, had gone before them to meet his death among gamblers, drunkards, occultists and, worse, poets and artists. The two pass into this Stygian realm where the flash of bared flesh, a face, a leg, a breast, is as suddenly lurid in the murk as though they swam all together in some human aquarium of the dead. On every side those sirens and harpies, the birds they call *hirondelles de passage*, have found vantage at first- and second-floor windows from which love nests they spy passing men and sing to bewitch and wreck them. It is like a walk down into death or hell where one may encounter every species of dangerous temptation, from the *fille publique*, or the consumptive *grisette*, to the *cousette*, the *ouvrier* or simple, pickpocketing *jeune fille* pattering on her way to or from school in innocent sabots.

Having followed each other into this vault, they identify the address they seek, a mean little entrance from which spills the oily smell of anchovies. Lord John, holding protectively tight to his purse as though it were his testicles, prods George over the threshold to negotiate with the toad-woman they find deep within her little concierge's cage, boiling potatoes in a coffee pot. George's governess-bred French is confounded by her wheedling and prevaricating until eventually it becomes clear, through elaborate mime and exasperated exhortation, that the earthly remains of the young 'milord' are no longer on the premises. It is only after Lord John relieves the weight on his purse that the sibyl in her cave is able to deliver the second part of her poisoned truth. It transpires that the body, not having been formally identified or claimed, with no money about it and being bad for trade, was conveyed to the *salle d'exposition* of the city mortuary on the other side of the river, at the Quai Notre Dame. There, the unidentified suicides, victims of murder and accidental death are displayed. Lord John, distinguishing the French for 'suicide' among the fog of the old woman's words, would have wrung her presumptuous neck had not George taken his arm, like a nervous child, to lead him blundering away from the air of the tomb to the sunshine of the upper world, into which they pop, like startled, blinking rabbits from an earthy burrow.

Had they been tourists in that pleasure-seeking city, they might have availed themselves of one of those tours organised for English travellers by the Thomas Cook company, which include a stop at the infamous mortuary chamber on their itinerary of notable sights of the capital. Instead Lord John and George join the queues of indifferent idlers, anxious relatives, lascivious ghouls, thrill-seekers, those ladies and gents, men and women, boys and girls for whose edification or delectation the recently and long dead are daily exhibited.

Now they enter upon another long passage, this one better lit, airier, and filled with the respectable and well dressed as well as the poor, with waist-high barriers running all along one side upon which lounge the curious. Near enough to touch, beyond the barrier fence, the large plate-glass windows of a department store run the whole length of the chamber. Some of the nonchalant crowd glance in as though they merely check the artistic effect of the display as they amble by. Others stand transfixed before a particularly choice item within, perhaps considering whether to enter and buy. But what manner of goods does this window reveal? For what the customers see there causes some to turn away in revulsion or tears, just as it provokes others to hoot and beckon delightedly for their companions to come close and gawp. George notices a respectable-looking matron, who leans into the window only to stagger backwards, half collapsing, into the arms of her pale young son, while other window-shoppers pass by. She cries, '*Oh! Ma fille, ma pauvre fille!*' and he struggles to locate his pocket-handkerchief into which to retch.

George moves closer to the window to witness for himself

what provokes such shock and indifference. But his perplexed, jumping eye can make no sense of the wares exhibited behind the shop window. At first his confused brain tells him that this is the butchery department for, laid on stone slabs, kept cool by trickling water, are the blue, red and white of flesh and bone – joints, cuts, ribs, sides, whole carcasses. When he looks more steadily, this meat resolves itself into the forms of men and women, drab or lurid, whole or in subsiding parts that lie, heads tilted forwards a little, genitals covered by strategic half-screens. They are naked and grey as fish on their cold, wet slabs, and the clothes that should have covered their shame are hung up on rails above them.

Sure enough, Lord John finds his boy there. He is led to him by the beautiful brushed-silk top hat perched atop evening clothes on the rail above, like a signifier of quality. That expensive hat calls to him from between the dripping rags of one pulled from the river and the death-stained costume of a suicide. Here lies Harry, beneath his jaunty hat, water drip, drip, dripping upon his sad face, soaking into his moustache, trickling from the corners of his sensualist's mouth and filmy eyes. At first Lord John is transfixed by pity and he presses close to the glass as though to comfort his boy, yet he struggles to control an opposite impulse to flee from death.

For George, who has found his comfort standing outside windows and looking in, this is the peep-show that will cure him of that furtive pleasure: he is glutted by looking and looking at that unknowable and unknowing thing, death. He turns away.

But Lord John looks on, trying to make clear within his foggy head the difference he sees here between Harry now and Harry then, Harry living and Harry dead. Lord John looks at the long white body of his one and only child, trying to understand that the very presence of his son behind the window tells of his absence. Lying across the pale forehead is still his mother's curling hair, and still his father's fine eyes weep their artificial tears . . . and yet it is not Harry. He can never be Harry again. Then Lord John realises he might have loved his son, he might have loved him simply for who he was, not for whom, or what, he might have become. And he understands at last that Harry is now placed for ever beyond reach behind the impenetrable window. And all the ambition and hope in his soul is turned to cinders and dust.

One cannot face sights such as these without a sense of awe at the mystery of death, which takes away a person and leaves behind a thing.

Arranging for the body to be conveyed back to England, and thence to the family seat, exhausts both men. They are complicit in a knowledge of terrible things that means neither will ever be comfortable in the other's company again.

Courting

After the incident in the garden Teresa and Thomas's courtship is less blithe and uninhibited. They continue to meet in steamy tearooms and to tramp the streets but, having bitten from the apple of knowledge behind that sooty London hedge, their love can never be quite the same again.

They still kiss, but never as wantonly, and Teresa continues to worry that she had committed some shameful act behind the hedge that had shocked him into this respectful formality. As autumn begins to approach she realises that she must either win him back or lose him to the creeping chill of gentlemanly manners and evenings closing in. At last she persuades him to invite her to meet his parents – a ploy that she hopes might jolt their relationship into its next delightful phase: the marriage proposal.

So, we find her in the parlour/bedroom of her prospective parents, the Murphys.

'Will you tek a thair, Mith Manty?' asks Ma–in–law, who has seated herself on the bed/sofa beside her husband to free the solitary chair for the guest.

'Mother, I told you, it's Miss Teresa Mantilla,' says Thomas, impatiently.

'What d'you say?'

'Man*tilla*,' Thomas repeats, with emphasis.

'Man-tay-yer, d'you say? What kynd of a name is dat?' shouts back the deaf old pa-in-law.

'My father was originally from Spain,' she explains and then, aware that further justification for this irregularity in her parentage is expected, goes on, 'He served as a British officer . . .' and, on seeing this has not done the trick, adds, '. . . in the British army. He fought in the Crimean campaign, in Russia, and received a wound there.'

'What does she say?' shouts old Mr Murphy, at his wife.

'The thayth the'th from Roothia,' replies Mrs Murphy complacently.

'Oh, no, I'm English. I was born in England. My mother's people are from the West Country,' says Teresa, nodding and smiling, trying to present her credentials so that they may be understood and passed as acceptable by these ignorant Irish peasants.

'Whath religion are dey in Roothia, pet?' mumbles Mrs Murphy, through her slack and toothless mouth.

'Roossian Ortodox, ya idyet, dey're Roossian Ortodox, any fool knows dat,' shouts her husband, with a slap of the knee and a wink of triumph at Teresa. 'Aren't you, nahy?'

'Catholic, she's a Roman Catholic!' Thomas is exasperated into jumping up from his stool by the fireplace. The two old people sit in reverie for a while, Mrs Murphy compulsively chewing her gums. It seems as though the grotesque couple have lapsed into malevolent silence, the custom of their every lonely day spent together: like two smelly, resentful old dogs that had once mated, sitting either side of the fire, twitching with old memories and occasionally snapping at fleas.

'Her mynd is gone!' bellows Mr Murphy suddenly, poking his old wife so that she is pushed over, lopsided. She remains in this off-centre position and Teresa notices that her moist eyes are grown wetter with unshed tears. 'Ol' fule!' he says, cheerfully, gesturing at his wife with his thumb.

'We only ever had juth the one thon, oar Tommy.' She pauses, as though to let them digest this incontrovertible fact. 'And he wath borned on a Mond'y, half patht twelve of the arternun. And he weighed 'leven poundth, tho he did!' she says, smiling at him.

'Mother, don't!' warns Thomas, like a petulant schoolboy.

She smiles inanely back, and continues with the well-worn recitation of her master work. ''Leven poundth, tink on that, young lady! 'Leven poundth, tink a forcin' tat grea' lump outh into de worl'!' She cackles with mirth at the very idea of that town-bred, dried-up virgin being capable of such a thing and her eyes water again, perhaps in sympathetic remembrance of that great effort. 'Only iver had juth de one.'

'She . . .' Mr Murphy again gestures at his old wife, as though she would not hear his shouted confidence. 'It was hor, the ol' cock-chafer, niver wanted na more chil'run!'

She clamps her gums and turns from him in a huff. At this point in the dreadful, interminable ordeal, Teresa feels like shouting or crying or running from the room in confusion. But she sits still, her face clenched in a rictus of embarrassment, and waits for Thomas to rescue her. He, however, says nothing, just sits on his stool, knees near his ears in a kind of pent, adolescent fury. She sees that it is left to her to restart the conversation upon safer, more conventional lines. 'Oh, well . . . it must be a comfort to have a son to care for you . . .'

' 'Deed he doth care for uth, mith. 'Deed he doth! Tommy ith a goo' boy to hith por mammy,' replies Mrs Murphy, her spirits apparently rallied by this invitation to sentiment.

Teresa notices, although he does not, that some beads of her fond spittle have landed on the arm of his jacket.

'Nottin' less dan his bounden dooty, young lady,' abruptly adds Mr Murphy, as though he were accusing her of something.

'Of course.' Teresa tries hard not to be belittled by the old bully. 'My sister and I spent the last twenty years of our own dear father's life nursing him,' she puts in demurely.

'Army pension went wid him, I'm supposin'!' he shoots back, raising a huge, black eyebrow for emphasis.

'Miss Mantilla and her sister have their own little business. She is quite independent,' says Thomas, sullenly.

'Does she, hindeed? Dere own little business, is it?' he answers, with a deliberation that sounds like heavy irony.

'Yu than't be tekkin' me babby away from me, will yu?' Ma Murphy turns her bleary eyes on Teresa, and tries to take Thomas's hand in her own; he withholds it.

'Oh, no!' she is shamed into replying, desperate to get away from the dreadful pair.

'So long as we may onderstond each odder, nahy. Mammy dere, and me, hov put everyting intay the raising o' the lad and nahy he has a doody tay us, his old y'uns. D'yu cutch me druft?'

'Mr Murphy, I am no fortune-hunter!' she says melodramatically, and almost laughs at the unreality of the situation. Who, in their right mind, would think of seeking a fortune in this smelly apartment with its landing kitchen and shared WC? Having parried the old devil, surely the only appropriate follow-up gesture should be to rise dramatically, turn on her heel and exit? However, his bombast has confounded meek Teresa with a kind of social paralysis. She lowers her eyes to her lap, noticing that the spittle is still drying upon Thomas's jacket arm, and waits for him to rouse to fury, defend her, sweep her away from this humiliation – and yet Thomas says and does nothing!

'He-he, now he'th in a way!' lisps the old lady, delightedly. 'Look on y'm, red ath a girl!'

'Will ya shod up, ya ol' pot hid?'

'Don'th yu lithen ta y'm, ma dear. He'th a terr'ble ol' man, tho he ith,' and now she wipes her watery eyes again and looks reproachfully at her flaring husband beside her on the bed.

'Tear an' ages, woman, will ya feel de back o' me hond?'

She lapses again into aggrieved docility, mumbling her empty gums and giving Teresa hurt, conspiratorial looks.

'Is she to make yu a tenant fer loyf, son? Is dat de woy of it?' he wheedles, addressing Thomas, who is himself now red as a London stock.

'I cannot stand this!' Thomas jumps to his feet and, taking Teresa's hand, gallops her away from mother, father and that grubby room.

When they reach the street, Thomas leaves go of her hand and rushes away headlong so that she is obliged to trot after him or be left behind in his wake. 'Thomas, Thomas, stop, slow down! Thomas, it doesn't matter. None of it matters to me . . .'

Still he hurtles onwards as though trying to shake her off. He makes her run so fast to keep up that she no longer has the breath to speak and scurries along after him, the hair at her temples wet with the tears swept off her cheeks by running. He comes to a stop so suddenly, turning to her, that she runs into him and seems to bounce off his hard chest.

'Teresa, it should be you running from me. And from them. Oh, God, I am sorry to have let you see – let you see who I am and what I come from . . .'

'My dear,' she says simply.

'To think that they accuse you of fortune-seeking when it is I . . . Oh, God. I don't deserve you. I never shall!'

She takes his hand in her own forgivingly, and smiles at him a brave, trusting smile, but the smell of the malevolent old dog and his bitch sits still in her nostrils.

Mr Murphy Comes to Visit

Unfortunately passion is not best nourished upon embarrassment and gratitude. Nor are these the sentiments that a woman looks for in her lover. They may make him respectful but they also elevate her beyond his unworthy reach, and a venerated woman is a disappointed one. After the horrible interview with his parents, Teresa beheld herself to have been cordoned off within this rarefied, undangerous zone and could have cried with the frustration of it. There is nothing for it but to use her unwanted ascendancy over Thomas to persuade him to come back home with her and there show him that she would welcome some tarnishing. Clearly she has no choice but to draft Aurora as chaperone, but how to curb her? Teresa dithers and flusters, saying nothing for fear of the sharp beak that will rip her sorry little love story into shreds of derision. So when the afternoon arrives upon which he is appointed to call, Teresa still has not told Aurora, but instead displaced her anxiety in dabbing at dust and fidgeting with mops.

When he does appear she is in such a state of high fret that she has to sit down and Aurora answers the door to him, and takes him, noting the dejected, downturned eyes, for a prospective client. 'Do come through,' she says, matching her tone to his sombre look. 'Beloved infant?' she guesses. He has the strained, out-at-elbow look of a husband harried by domestic responsibilities.

'I am an only child,' he replies, startled that his mother's pride in her one and only should be so apparent.

They reach the parlour, conveyed there upon this conversational impasse, and find, just behind the door, eager Teresa who by no means clarifies the situation: 'Ah, Mr Murphy. Do come in. You have met my sister, Aurora? Aurora, this is Mr Thomas Murphy, of whom I have told you so much.'

Since Aurora is silenced, for once, by this untruth, Teresa has the opportunity to aim at her sister a gagging glare, so that when they sit down together they find that further conversation has died on their lips. Teresa rushes from the room on restless legs and rushes back with tea and cakes, and they remember themselves enough to eat and drink and talk of this and that. At last they even laugh about Aurora's mistaken assumption that bachelor Thomas was led to their doorstep by a dead baby.

And all the while Teresa watches Aurora for the reptilian look that fixes in the eye of a bird of prey when it has identified its next victim. She knows Aurora well enough not to fall into the trap of distracting techniques: the desperate artifice of the mother bird, pretending a broken wing to draw away the cruel beak. She tries not to be too chirpy, too placatory, too quick with the subtle words Thomas lacks to keep the conversation going, and all the while Aurora is as nice as pie.

When it has grown dark enough for Teresa to talk about lighting the lamps, Thomas slaps his knees decisively and takes his leave, promising that he will return. He gives a civil farewell to Aurora and squeezes Teresa's hand before disappearing down the front path more jauntily than he came up it.

When his footsteps can no longer be heard, Teresa turns her bright, expectant face to her sister. 'Did you like him?' is her unwise question.

'I dote on him! I shall always call him "the beloved infant"!' Aurora takes her hand, saying piously, 'He's his mammy's precious

boy, so he is.' Then, throwing her eyes around the room in imitation
of a perplexed calf, 'And did you see the way he looked around,
like he was making an inventory?' She collapses backwards on to
the sofa, in giggles, pulling Teresa down beside her. 'You don't care
for him, do you?' she says, lightly dismissing the unrealistic
possibility.

'Oh, no. Not at all,' replies Teresa, miserably.

The 'infant' himself has no understanding of how close he came
to losing the status of 'beloved'. On the contrary, he is feeling like
a well-set-up fellow as he swings down the road, mentally totting
up the number of rooms in the house. He calculates: parlours,
front and back, kitchen with washroom, south-west-facing garden,
two good-sized bedrooms on the first landing and a boxroom on
the half-landing (suited to being fitted out as an indoor bathroom?),
with a head-height attic room at the top. A good residential area
with a brand-new Underground connection to Town. Very
desirable.

The next time the lovers conspire to meet, Thomas is not at all
shy about suggesting another rendezvous at Teresa's home. She is
a little disappointed that he makes it sound quite so much like an
'appointment to view' rather than a tryst.

So now they wander around the empty afternoon house, tense
with the knowledge that they are alone, together, with access to
items of furniture upon which they might be comfortably
recumbent. He does not, exactly, calculate the dimensions of the
rooms as they pass through them, but he casually checks, from the
window of the boxroom, the location of exterior plumbing
pipework.

They reach the last room in the house: the attic/studio, with its
rolled canvas backcloths, tripod, aspidistra in an art pot and mad
assortment of props: chairs, small tables and the mustard-yellow
velvet, button-back *chaise-longue*, covered by a dust-sheet and
pushed back against the wall. At last, something they may sit down
upon to kiss, which is not as blatant as a bed. The moment is

heavy with expectation, like an unasked question in a tightening throat.

So they sit there together, among the bric-à-brac and tools of the photographic business, with no lamp to brighten the gathering gloom, no domestic fire to warm the air, and are lifted out of themselves. In this room, like a stage set, they are no longer an ordinary courting couple sensible of their duty to God and society. They feel raffish, giddy, liberated. They feel like actors who have licence to be and do and say what ordinary people must not. Their gestures are extravagant, their joy comes in naughty giggles and their kissing is self-consciously abandoned. Finally, Teresa will remember thinking, This is delight.

When they pull away from each other even the darkness and the cold in the room does not bring them back to themselves. Without speaking, both hurriedly complete the undressing that the other had begun, backs turned on each other, half shy, half impatient to be quickly rid of these mufflers. They finish together and hide themselves in a plunging embrace that topples them on to the *chaise-longue*, legs in the air, laughing at their own wickedness.

Teresa and Thomas's warm, naked skin touches at last. Apart from her sister's, his are the only eyes that have ever beheld her naked, adult form. And no other hands have ever touched or mouth kissed as his do now. She keeps her shameless eyes wide open so that the memory of this first time that she was loved by a man will be recorded for ever in pictures. But all her senses are alive to him: she feels the unexpected scrape of his bristly chin on her face, smells again that intoxicating musk his body gives off, tastes tobacco in his mouth and hears the soft grunts of satisfaction he makes, like an infant nursing. All these will make memories.

Then Teresa notices the hard 'coat-peg' nose her in the belly and is surprised that it seems to be ill-attached on its base – sprung, mobile and sinewy, it feels like something skinned and gristly from the butcher's. If her senses had not been overwhelmed, more particularly if she had sneaked a glance downwards, her rational mind might have been revolted. What he does next, pushing the peg up into her vitals, would have made her scream with fright and pain had not this seemed like the most natural place for it to go. It fits. Fastened, groin to groin, by this simple device of tenon into mortise, they are finished, complete. His shape, fitting hers, fills the blind cavity, deep inside, which she had not even suspected was there. Now he begins to saw, using a careful rhythm, easing up and down, in and out. His sawing strokes grow harder and faster, the job is nearly finished, and she knows when it is done, because something within her surrenders and falls apart. Or she falls apart. Or she falls. Falls.

They catch each other in the fall and hold on tight so that they may land together, hot where their bodies touch and chilled where they are exposed.

'Teresa, my love, I'm sorry, sorry. Unforgivable. Disgraceful behaviour,' he mumbles into her hair.

She is momentarily stunned. Why should he apologise? Has she done something wrong, again, something revolting? He is suddenly heavy on top of her and she is aware that their feet are extending uncomfortably beyond the end of the *chaise-longue*. Thomas springs up and begins to struggle into his cooling clothes. 'Really, I can't tell you how much I regret . . .' he says, not looking at her.

Lying there, exposed and abandoned, Teresa notices that something is leaking from her and guesses what the disgrace might be. She pulls the dust-sheet, stained with her shameful blood, from off the *chaise-longue*, wraps it round her and bolts from the room, saying, 'I must attend to . . .' and trying not to look at his nakedness. And miserable Thomas is left to find his discarded clothes in the dark.

Home to Roost

Now, after months of searching, a shrouded figure flies from London to Hertfordshire, like a poisoned arrow directed at the heart, to bring the intrigue back to its source. But who is this? She, for it is a woman, presents herself at the gatehouse that guards the entrance to that dripping alley of sweet chestnuts. This is the last stage in a journey that began that morning, in a London pop shop where, in exchange for an artificial-ivory brush set, she'd managed to get enough money for a single railway ticket. She'd spent the change, put aside for the cab from the station, on a small reviving bottle of gin, and so is forced to walk, in the dark, between these wet and whispering trees; a walk that seems to her to lead through a haunted forest to the ogre's lair.

But the gin, at least, makes her resolute, and she braves the horrific country sounds of unseen birds settling themselves for the night and the heavy taps of raindrops on her head to reach the ogre's house, where his human retainer opens the door to her.

That same evening, her return journey back along the gloomy avenue and over the muddy lane down which she'd toiled on foot is effected in minutes in Lord John Harpur's dog-cart. This female Hermes (who, quite apart from being the bearer of prophecy, also shares the god's gift for cunning) has whipped Lord John into such a lather with her insinuations and allusions that he cannot delay rushing to gabble the 'news' to his powerful neighbour.

By the time they reach Fainhope Hall his incautious assertions and assumptions have schooled the messenger most thoroughly in the potentially profitable nature of her news. Indeed, he runs on, in his eagerness, somewhat in advance of her: letting drop that his son is dead and that he had been unmarried and was his sole heir. So that when they reach the Duchess of Fainhope's private sitting room to find that lady and her companion, Miss Mantilla, the female Hermes stands back judiciously to allow him to deliver the nicely elaborated and coherent whole, so that she can observe which is the best way to play it. And he obliges beautifully, without a breath of cautious restraint, saying to his sister-in-law, 'The most astounding news – or, at least, it might be. Might it not, Miss . . . ?'

'Call me "friend",' the messenger replies, judging it safest to keep her powder dry.

'Our friend here has brought me some wonderful intelligence. It really is as though she brought Harry, or at least a part of him, back from beyond the grave,' he says, addressing himself to Her Grace this time.

'John, you are to leave off talking in riddles. That is, if you hope for a response informed by any kind of understanding.'

'A ladies' maid – this woman – comes with news of a grandson,' he replies, looking her full in the face, as though this would better communicate the seriousness of the message.

'Is this the usual way of receiving such news, outside the pages of a shilling shocker – from a mysterious stranger in the night?' she asks simply.

The introduction of this speck of doubt takes Lord John somewhat aback so that his reply comes more haltingly: 'All I say is, he may be my grandson. If I could only be sure . . .'

'I think that our "friend" should excuse us for a minute while you take the opportunity to compose yourself, John,' she continues, nodding the messenger outside. 'How much money has she asked for, John?' she says, as soon as they are alone, with the eye-opening candour of the sceptic.

'None. As such,' he says, the chill of doubt now beginning to dissipate the lovely warm fug of self-delusion.

'What is her story, then?'

'She says she was maid to a gentlewoman and her young son, who lived quietly in London. The boy's father would visit, although he pretended to be a gentleman cousin of the lady. When the unfortunate mother died, the father, as she believed, having disappeared, her first thought was to trace him, not knowing my boy to be already dead. And so she found us.'

'Why did you even let this gypsy across your threshold, John? What possible link is there to Harry in all this?'

'Well, that's just it. There is a link, d'you see? Here,' he says, holding out to her a cheap gold wedding ring, upon which is engraved the family crest.

'Do you recognise this ring as Harry's?' she says, slipping it easily on to her own finger.

'Well, no, it is a lady's ring, I see that. But how does it come to have the crest inside? Harry must have married the lady with this ring,' he supplies, encouraged.

'Before he went off filly-hunting in Paris and drank himself to death? How honourable, how domesticated of the dear boy.' Evidently he is determined to hear only what he wants to hear and disregard the rest. But a little logic will clearly show him that, like a mesmerist upon the stage, this woman is only luring out his hidden desires to re-present them to him as though they were fact. 'Really, John, think. Can this be the only explanation?' she says sharply, to bring him back to his senses.

When he makes no reply, she sees that she must deal with the conniving woman herself. She opens the door to her and invites her back in to face a proper interrogation.

The woman repeats, without adding anything substantially, the bones of the story she told Lord John Harpur, apart from larding on her tragic, and onerous, role in tracing the poor little one's natural relations after his parents' sad demise. And the Duchess perceives that although the wolfish woman is nervous, as she would have expected, there is also a brazenness about her communication that suggests she knows she has the kernel of the truth, and understands how to use it. She concludes her tale dolefully, 'All I knowed was 'is nearest family lives in 'Ertfordshire and 'is ma give me 'er ring, wiv the fam'ly crest, afore she went and died. So as to provide for her dear Duke.'

'What a strange name for a boy,' comments Miss Mantilla, speaking for the first time.

'Could it be Harry's boy?' asks Lord John, plaintively, of his sister-in-law.

'How old is this boy?' she continues, ignoring him, trying to winkle out the worm of deceit at the heart of this untrustworthy woman's words.

'I can't be absolutely sure, ma'am,' and here the Duchess gives a grim smile of triumph, before the woman goes on, 'I shou' calculate 'e must be five, or six, or seven, near 'nough,' she says, evidently trying to gauge the right reply. 'It's 'ard to say, 'im bein' so quick and rare for 'is schoolin'.'

Lord John eagerly endorses her: 'Five, would fit, eh? Isn't it six years since Harry went up to London for your girl's Season?'

The Duchess chooses not to reply, but the messenger is emboldened to continue, 'Vat's 'im! An' di'n't my mistress dote on ve lad, couldn't abide the fought of lettin' 'im leave 'er side. An' 'im too, ve real farver,' she goes on, warming to her theme, ''e couldn't niver do enough for 'is fine little fellow, used to jog 'im on 'is knee somefink chronic. And dress 'im up, my, you shoulda seen the weskits vat little chap 'ad to 'is name—'

Lord John, seeing that the Duchess is preparing to cut short the beautiful clarity of the message with more questioning, interrupts, 'Doesn't her description of the father fit my Harry to a T? And he has chestnut hair, just like his papa, wouldn't you say?'

The Duchess of Fainhope sees that, if she is to stop this woman feeding back to him the corroborative crumbs he conveniently scatters before her, she must take over the interrogation. 'By what name did the gentleman call himself?' She blocks his last question.

'I only knew 'im as Mr B. 'Er name was Georgina Larkins, though I niver believed vat was 'er right name.'

Now the Duchess of Fainhope suddenly discovers a real interest in this aspect of the story. In her surprise, at hearing that name, she lets slip her own leading question: 'Georgina? Did this lady cover her face at all?'

To which the mesmerist, perceiving a potential advantage, is quick to reply, 'Oh, yes, ma'am. She used ta wear a veil whenever she went outa doors.'

'Was this lady's face marked?' asks the Duchess, beginning to fall under the spell of that dangerous inclination to find more meaning here than there actually is.

'Terrible mockered she was, ma'am. Face like a crumpet, poor lady.' Rebecca now switches her efforts to enchanting this grander personage: the supreme manipulator is herself manipulated.

And Miss Mantilla, too, is tricked into co-operating with the Svengali: 'Seven,' she interrupts. 'That would certainly fit with the unpleasantness with Mr Briggs.'

'Georgina the mama, and mysterious Mr B. the papa,' says the Duchess.

'Just like him to insist on the family crest. Always the snob,' adds Miss Mantilla.

Lord John, mouth agape with consternation at this ambush of his message, can only interject, 'Dear God, sister! My only boy is dead. Are we to battle now over a grandson?'

Rebecca senses that now all she need do is let them argue themselves into accepting her story, convinced that they have freely arrived at their own conclusions.

'If he is really Georgina's then I must know him. If he belonged to Harry, then you shall claim him. The boy must be sent for and the thing thoroughly tested,' says the Duchess, judicially. 'You,' she continues, addressing herself to the vile message-bearer, 'must bring the boy to us. What is his name? Of course: the Duke.

Curious that the boy has only part of a name. How like Georgina to snub family honour and tradition in that way.'

'It shows that she – or he – had expectations for the son,' sniffs Miss Mantilla.

'Or might not it show that Harry had expectations for his own boy?' says Lord John, miserably.

'Half made and awaiting only the family name,' continues Her Grace, ignoring her brother-in-law. 'Still, he must be brought so that we may judge whether that part-name is his due.'

Rebecca, realising too late that her lady gull is a tough-minded one, counters this speculation: 'Not so fast. 'Ow do I know you'll be kind to the poor li'le mite what I've 'ad the sole care of these six monfs? An' what abou' ve expense I bin put to, keepin' 'im nice?'

'You must tell us where he is lodged so he may be sent for,' says Her Grace, without looking at the woman.

'I'm on the straight, sir. You believe me, don't you? All I'm askin' fer is a little sub to cover me expenses an' somefing fer me trouble.' She appeals to the gentleman, seeing that she is losing the lady's co-operation. 'You know I only do it in memory of 'is poor dead mama. An' I wouldn' never give 'im up lessen I was sure 'e went to a kind 'ome,' says she, turning on the waterworks.

'John, we may send this woman to collect the boy in the carriage,' the Duchess directs.

'Oh, ma'am, I couldn' turn 'im over jus' like vat. 'E's a delicate boy. Very aristocratic in 'is ways. Only ever eats the blandest food and I keep 'im from any coarseness an' shocks – which 'as been a terrible draw on me purse.'

'Enough,' commands the Duchess. 'When I have the boy and can vouch for myself you may expect a consideration for your "expenses". If I am not satisfied then you shall find yourself in gaol for kidnap and attempted deception. Mind me, madam.'

She's been too quick for Rebecca and Lord John, both.

'Really,' he blusters, 'I must go with her in the carriage. I must see for myself!'

'John, you are a fool. If it were a question of your heir alone then, of course, you would be free to go. But if he is mine, then I cannot risk losing him through your incompetence.'

'But we might lose her. How can we know she'll bring him to us?' he cajoles, without pursuing the slippery issue of his own worthlessness. If he has learnt nothing else from being a brother-in-law it is to concede that point to her.

'Why not send George with her, as Your Grace's family representative? You remember what a help he was in Paris,' says Miss Mantilla. And since she is worth listening to, George is sent for.

And the wonted puppet mistress finds herself well and truly tangled in her own strings.

Love's April Fools

Let us hurry back to London in advance of George and conniving Becs. For there we left our sisters suspended, poor Teresa wrapped, like a sacrificial victim, in her bloodied dust-sheet and Aurora still hunting out the newly dead. The most unexceptional couple of docile middle-class ladies one could hope to meet.

That evening, when last we saw him, shivering Thomas had gathered up his clothes to creep from the attic room like a thief in the night. He hadn't known whether to call out for Teresa, to kneel before her in apology or simply run away home. He had cleared his throat before her closed bedroom door and then, when no answer came, had descended the stairs and walked guiltily away from the desirable property.

When Aurora came home she'd found her sister, wrapped in her dressing-gown, her feet tucked underneath her, staring dreamily into the fire. 'Are you ill?'

'Do I look ill?' she'd answered, startled that something of the change in her might show.

'Why are you undressed like that, then?'

'I am a little unwell. My flow has arrived.'

'Has it?' Aurora had said, rather indifferently. 'Isn't it usually the same week as mine?'

'I don't always have to do everything the same as you, do I?' Teresa had replied, surprising her sister with this misplaced passion. 'I'm different, you know. I can be different from you.'

'Of course you can. I didn't say you couldn't be, did I?' Aurora had shot back, stamping out to find some food. Teresa was always impossible at that time of the month, she'd thought sourly.

The first month had passed and no word from Thomas. Teresa had remembered to herself the fierce rhythmic action of his hips, the feeling inside when he had inexorably sawed through the last strand that separated knowing from unknowing in her. Whereas all experience of that delicious coupling had been concentrated into physical sensation, now it seemed as though her eyes had been opened by it so that she truly saw for the first time. Suddenly she beheld everything around her with the eye of an initiate. She had seen that dogs mated on the street, that horses' rumps were indecent in their nakedness, had been transfixed by the suggestive rise and fall of the railway engine's well-oiled pistons and had blushed to see the muscled back of the coalman as he heaved sacks from his cart. If the whole world thrummed with sex, why was it that she had never seen it before?

The second month had passed and Teresa had not been able to escape the torment of undressed animals, men sawing wood, of pistons turning and labourers' sweaty skin. So she had sent him a picture postcard. It had shown a rather dull view of the Houses of Parliament and the message on the front read, 'Dear Mr Murphy, My sister and I have missed you. Will you come to visit, Sunday next? T. M.' Perhaps unconsciously, she had made the 'I' stand out like an exclamation mark: bolder, blacker and more upright than the rest of her tentative scrawl.

He replied with a postcard, this one showing a kitten in a pickle jar. The communication read: 'Dear Miss M., Shall be delighted to call, Sunday. What time suits best? Yrs wth r'spt, T.

Murphy.' She had not been able to detect personal loathing in either message or style.

He arrives, as requested, at three o'clock, looking sheepish and carrying a bunch of flowers. Conversation is not easy, being mostly hurried into the advantageous periods when Aurora is out of the room. The rest of the time exchanges between the three are faultlessly conventional and dull.

'How do your parents do, Mr Murphy?' Aurora asks, looking at her hands.

'They are getting older,' he replies, at a loss for what he might add to this unassailable fact.

'They do not suffer with this cold, damp spell we have been having?'

'Oh, no. No more than we all must. My father is still a fine specimen.'

'His eyebrows are still very black?' Teresa says, recalling those exclamatory monstrosities.

'Indeed they are.'

'Shall I pop the kettle on?' Aurora offers, desperate to escape their dreary pleasantries. She leaves Teresa to her 'beloved' and stands in the kitchen, where she looks vacantly out into the garden, eating handfuls of currants from the jar.

Somebody had to say something. 'Oh, Thomas . . .' Teresa blurts. 'My dear, I worried that I should never see you again.'

Blushing Thomas falls before her, bending his head so that she sees the pale creases open on the sun-reddened skin of his neck, the serried crop rows of his tight-growing orange curls. 'I know that I committed an outrage. I cannot express how bad it makes me feel to think I did you an injury.'

'Oh, Thomas, you did not,' Teresa replies, remembering all that blood on the bundled dust-sheet. 'It is just a women's thing,' she falters, embarrassed. 'But, Thomas, I did not . . . I do not personally revolt you?'

'My love, how could you? It was so . . . I know that what we did together was wrong but I cannot think that anything so fine could be. It was so . . .'

'Yes,' she says simply. 'Yes, it was.' And she places her hands on either side of his face, still downturned to the floor, and tilts it to hers so that she can kiss him.

Upon returning with her tea tray, Aurora finds the courting couple grown even more insufferable. They hardly speak again but roll their eyes at each other, like a couple of lovesick sheep. They simper and titter and blush until she could knock their heads together. On seeing that there is no more conversation, however pedestrian, to be had from them, she abandons her role as chaperone and goes off to read a book.

By the fourth month, billets-doux passed between them with the measured regularity of a pendulum clock. They employed picture postcards for their jaunty messages of relief and reassurance – the language of symbols, even though mostly unconscious, in their choice of these cards corresponding to their attitude towards or, perhaps, expectations of each other. She sent him unequivocally masculine subjects: lofty buildings of national importance, the statues of famous men and their horses, raised up upon plinths, and impressive feats of modern engineering in bridge, railway station and tall-chimneyed steamship. In every one the viewer was made to feel small and awed by the priapic perspective of the subject matter.

He answered with piles of fluffy kittens – oh, those kittens. Kittens singly, in pairs and family groupings. Kittens by the dozen. For him kittens seemed to have been expressly invented to embody the trite sentiment suited to the penny picture-postcard. Kittens sat baffled in wooden clogs, plaintive on tea trays, squatted unhappily before puddles of milk, '*I never cry over spilled milk!*', peeped from straw boaters, '*Oh, my hat!*', and china bowls. Pansy-faced kittens disguised themselves among bouquets and contemplated themselves in looking-glasses; they mewed, hissed, slept and played, and all to tell Teresa that she was beloved, a dear fluffy little thing.

Five months after the first, they contrive another rendezvous, this time under cover of an envelope, but even then not quite naming what they are meeting to do. When she opens the door to him, neither of the nervous lovers can quite meet the other's eyes. Recalling those times when their *al fresco* passion had forced them to take urgent recourse to smelly alleys or dark groves, the door is hardly closed before they fall upon each other. He hurries her from door to door of the six rooms of the house and at each threshold she falters, until they reach the attic again, and the mustard-yellow, button-backed *chaise-longue*, which is still pushed up against the wall.

'Darling, will you?' he says, his face buried in her warm neck.

She kisses his hot red ear. 'Shall I light the paraffin stove, this time? And we can get the bearskin rug and be really warm and comfy.'

Teresa disengages herself from her lover and goes about hauling the stove and the rug to their service before she takes him in her arms again and pulls him down beside her. This time, in the soft light of the stove, side by side upon the rough fur of the rug, they undress for each other, bold and unblinking. This time his eyes look steadily into hers, as he raises himself above her on his pale, freckled arms, and plunges them both over the brink to fall, clinging together.

This time they are quiet and still afterwards, lying snug in the fur cocoon she has made.

'I love you,' Thomas says.

'I love you, too,' Teresa replies, and she feels a surge of glad energy run through her so that she wants to jump up and run madly around the room, whooping with joy. But instead she remains lying cramped within his arms, warm fur against her skin, her unseen smile ripening in the half-light.

'I shall tell Father tonight. He'll be talked round, don't you think? He and Mother will love you as much as I do, darling Teresa. A good Catholic girl. And once they see this house . . .'

Teresa says nothing, but the smile has dried, dead.

'We can make them a very comfortable apartment, up here in the attic. They shall bring all their old furniture from home and they'll hardly know the difference. Although I'll be taking that big ol' double bed for us,' he says, squeezing her unresisting bones tight against his lean side. 'We shan't be doing with a smelly stove and a mangy rug to cover us, shall we now?'

A Letter

In the sixth month of their courtship, they corresponded using grown-up and responsible writing-paper. Aurora, having steamed open one of his letters, was more entertained by the discovery that he needed ruled pencil lines upon which to write, obliterating the evidence with an india-rubber afterwards, than by the schoolboy sentiments he strung along them. She only saw that Teresa's relationship with the 'beloved infant' was a dangerous one when her sister began anxiously to try to win her approval of him.

'Thomas is such a good handyman. Thomas knows a shop where we might get it half price. Don't you think Thomas would look well in such a cravat?'

She bided her time and kept her tongue, waiting for this unfortunate infection of calf-love to pass, but alert to the possibility that the contagion might prove fatal. Teresa certainly seemed to be suffering from something. She seemed simultaneously to thrive and sicken, pink and bustling one moment, lethargic and weepy the next. And she was forever rearranging furniture – Aurora heard her, overhead in their attic studio, pushing chairs around as though she were clearing floor space for dancing at a party.

Since the growth in the specialist provision of the commercial funeral parlour where the deceased were displayed before burial, rather than privately in their own home, and the general availability of easy-to-operate box cameras, both branches of their photographic business had suffered a recession. But the attic room with its jumble of props still represented a stake in their financial future. Teresa felt that she could sacrifice it to him – it would be like surrendering her desultory spinster life in exchange for his masculine protection and ratification. And she did so want to surrender and sleep safe under his wing. She was so tired of the worry of finding a living in this uncertain world, but what would she do without her little business? Nurse his garrulous old parents, that was what. It always came back to that dreary certainty: she could subordinate herself to him, the man she loved, the man to whom she had given her body, but could she as cheerfully subordinate herself and loan her body out in service of that ungrateful pair? Teresa had had quite enough experience of being stifled by the needs of old age with her own beloved papa.

Teresa twittered, dithered and doubted. Her correspondence with Thomas blew hot and cold: one letter would coyly enquire whether he thought orange blossom might be considered inappropriate in a middle-aged bridal bouquet and the next would plead that she was not ready for marriage: was too old, too young, too fixed in her ways, too flighty.

In the end, as always, it was Aurora, the artist of the pair, who, like an authoress with a predilection for melancholy outcomes, stepped in and decided the path the tale should take. Seven months from their first kiss in the park, a letter arrived from the 'beloved infant', which Aurora plucked from the doormat and steamed open by that morning's breakfast kettle. She structured the dramatic scenario upon which she would turn her sister's story into a little tragedy before Teresa had even come downstairs for her toast.

And so Teresa never had her happy ending. And yet would marriage, that most conventional of conclusions, have been the idealised final act she had hoped for? Given that the union was to include Mr and Mrs Murphy, perhaps her fate was not such an unlucky one. But how did Aurora contrive to make Teresa's common-or-garden romance into a tale of love disappointed? She simply tucked away his ultimatum in her pocket.

Thomas waited with his engagement ring in the outdoor café by the bandstand all the next Saturday afternoon. He waited until the band stopped playing, the folding chairs were folded and the waiter, tired of waiting, had passed and repassed his lonely table, ostentatiously totting up his tips. Then he moved to a park bench, under a plane tree, and waited longer. Then, in an excess of activity, antidote to enforced inertia, he jumped up and slashed at the bench with a fallen branch, grimly repeating, 'Damn you, damn you, damn you!'

The other side of the story, Teresa's, was not to be played out as conclusively as was Thomas's moment of dramatic disillusionment. Her wait was to be stretched over long weeks, bringing her one and only love affair to its end within a year of her first kiss. Like all heroines of romance gone wrong she cried herself into fits, turned from food as though it were poison and alternated between blaming herself and blaming him. At last she gathered up all the reminders of him, his sheaves of kittens, all that cheap paper covered by his charity-school hand, flowers pressed in her Bible, the lock of his wiry red hair. Then, crying as she wrapped, she bound them up in tissue paper and hid them away in a drawer.

From that moment on Teresa was to employ the mode of the *demi-tragedienne*. She found that sudden discreet tears and languid looks suited her and even began to relish her status as a lady disappointed in love, not least because it made her feel superior to Aurora who (she well knew) had never been kissed – in that way. The stroke of pistons, muscular shoulders and red hair continued to bother her but, ever one to treasure a secret, she took comfort in nursing the amazing truth about sex and keeping her knowledge jealously hidden.

A Stranger in a Strange Land

Bloody Gina! Stupid whore!

That night when they had realised Gina's Cupid wouldn't be coming home, Rebecca had done her best to sort through what could be pawned, sold or liberated from the house. They had had to work fast as the landlord's patience with his late-paying lady tenant was already exhausted. For a couple of days she had carried small, valuable items to the pawn shop under her clothing. That had raised enough to rent a couple of rooms in Town and the hire of a cart and driver to remove them there. And one night they had flown the nest with the best sticks of furniture and a great many hatboxes.

For the first week, all the mistress had done was cry and bewail the cruel Fate that had brought her to this low ebb. A shipwrecked queen, she sat weeping among her possessions – the flotsam and jetsam left behind when her life had foundered – pathetic remnants of what she had once been. Life with a washed-up bag-lady was not easy – you would have thought she was being murdered alive, the fuss she made when she found a couple of the heavy cavalry in her bed! Like she'd never before been bitten on the bum by a louse. However much she bewailed the hard times they had fallen upon it wasn't as though Gina'd only known a life of comfort. In fact, Rebecca began increasingly to suspect that her mistress had

had an even lowlier upbringing than her own. However, Gina would not surrender her unsteady place atop the diminishing pile of bric-à-brac and bibelots she had built for herself. So they sat tight, living extravagantly on four ale and fried fish, while Rebecca nibbled away at the bulwarks of baubles, raided the ramparts, converting all that could be into eatables, drinkables and rent, until they reached low-water mark and had to pike off again to even lowlier lodgings.

Then they were forced to contemplate other, more sustainable means for getting their living. And once the only saleable object they had left (since she wouldn't part with her clothes) was Gina herself, before long she was put back on the market. Like dwindling Alice, grown small enough to swim about in her own salty tears, Gina had suddenly snapped back to the reality of their situation and started to paddle desperately to stay afloat. Lucky she hadn't let go of all her lovely costumes as they were valuable tools of her trade and, indeed, brought in a higher class of client.

Of course she was older and stouter than she had been in her manifestation as the 'veiled lady', but the genteel look reassured customers that she was disease-free, and her rooms were conveniently situated for a gentleman about town and after his greens.

Rebecca had continued as the maid and dresser. And even though her mistress was, if anything, more autocratic and exacting, the job of maid to a common whore felt like a demotion. Apart from being bossed around in a confined space by this disappointed *demi-mondaine* there was also the problem of the boy. Since she'd been fired as a wife, Gina seemed to have forgotten that she'd once been a mother too. That game was over as soon as she'd taken up again as a freelance tart. He'd stopped being her 'baby Duke' double quick – no more sugar cubes and cuddles for that young man. She'd even suggested to Rebecca that she might take him out for an omnibus ride and lose him somewhere.

However, Rebecca had not been put to that inconvenience as, shortly after, she'd returned to the rooms from some fool's errand

Gina had sent her on to find madam had flitted off, leaving behind her only son and heir, crouched terrified on the bed. Rebecca had tried to find her. She'd asked around, with the boy in tow, fuelled by rage; that she should be left in the lurch after all she'd done for that conniving madam!

True, she could have cut his nibs loose and made the best of things. However, Rebecca was too clever for that. She remembered that one of the last items of jewellery to be hocked had been a cheap little 'wedding' ring Gina'd had his family crest engraved upon when she was a play-wife. She'd reckoned that, if she could work it right, it must be as good as money in the bank. Her only problem had been in finding the pawn ticket and, that located, the money to redeem it.

After she had the ring, and with no ready coming in, Rebecca had but little time to track down the illustrious family whose crest appeared inside the band. She could not read, nor had she any notion of libraries or records offices. But she wasn't green as duckweed. At last she hit on the idea of making up to the doormen of London's gentlemen's clubs and asking them to help identify it. And, bingo, she'd tracked him down – the slippy bastard: the crest of the dukes of Fainhope, family name Harpur, family seat Hertfordshire. Rich as stink.

So the bad fairy had set off to buy the railway ticket that would spur on the dance again. The ring in her pocket, she was ready to make the most of what this interview would bring, having tied the boy to the bed and menaced him with threats into lying quiet.

Now, having grabbed the main chance, she is spinning along in the Duchess of Fainhope's own crested landau, back to London, giddy at the pace that events have taken. The silent George (passive as a child, even though this is the very year of his majority) sits back in the shadows of his corner of the carriage. He had been woken from his habitual bed on the floor by Miss Mantilla, then bustled into clothes and this carriage with instructions to bring back a lost boy – whosoever he might be.

For several rocking miles the two passengers remain in silence, him on the edge of sleep, her uncomfortably fermenting stratagems. Watching his nodding head, Rebecca mutters under her breath: 'What a bloody tangle. Which way do you jump now, Becs?'

'What do you say?' George's response startles her, until she sees that this is an idiot son, of no real danger. She might as well risk a few exploratory questions.

'I don't spec' your sister Georgina used to pass 'erself orf as a tart going by the name of Beatrice?' she speculates, conversationally.

George blushes. 'No one has heard anything from my elder sister for years. But she was never very fond of her family. And, I believe, she got in with some rather strange friends.'

At which Rebecca snorts, then moves on to her other line of enquiry. 'And your cousin, vat Lord 'Arpur's son, did 'e ever talk to you abou' 'is life in London – where 'e lived and what 'e did up vere?'

'I can't help you with any information about Harry. I rarely saw him after he went up to London to live.'

Rebecca decides to let it drop. The boy is obviously kept banged up in the countryside to stop him causing or coming to harm. She gambles on having better luck with her last shot: 'You ain't got a smoke, then, 'ave you, love?'

By now dawn is not far off and, as they travel nearer to London, they begin to pass the laden fruit and vegetables carts that lumber up from the market gardens of the country suburbs like slow beasts bringing their tribute to be tipped into that ever-hungry maw. They reach the indeterminate land that has left off being the countryside but has not quite become the town.

Looking out of his window, George sees that they pass through a land of shadowed fields into which London has unfurled tendrils. Streets, roads, avenues, terraces and high streets nose their way into the countryside looking for space. Like tributaries that must escape the main, swollen current, they flow first along the lines of least resistance, carved out by railway, road or canal, then find their own way round the contours of the land, bursting upon those villages and hamlets that had stood, sufficient unto themselves, for centuries to pool around the central indent made by an old coaching inn or a village green. What centuries of agriculture have shaped and adapted is now swallowed by modern urban needs, the tumbled farms, labourers' cottages all drowned, annexed or swept away by the tide of red brick that races out to meet and encircle them. Straight out of the builders' pattern books, whatever style you could fancy – from baroque to cut-price Venetian, new homes are the crop grown in these brickfields.

Just as George hates the raw look of these new suburbs, Rebecca hates the countryside. Like most Londoners, she is an economic migrant from that hopeless, hungry life on the land. For her London, even with all its stinks and dangers, is the place where there is a chance of making your fortune – or, at very least, living a life different from that of your parents. In Essex, surrounded by potato fields, she had known with an absolute certainty that no one ever could or did. Rebecca understands the reality of bucolic bliss: never anything new to eat, drink, do or see. She knows that the charming simplicity of country life is merely the exchange of brute labour for food to keep the body working. And if supply and demand is the rule that drives the city too, and one may as easily end up in the workhouse here or there, at least existence in the city is exciting, anonymous, and so much riper with possibilities. Rebecca, resourceful and bold, aspires to be predator rather than prey.

It may comfort Rebecca to see all trace of dreary nature disappearing as they enter London proper, but strip away that man-made sediment of roads and buildings and you will find still the accidents of geology and topography that brought those first enterprising incomers to town – the twin gravel hills (of Cornhill and St Paul's) that stand above the marshy plain of that lazy, tidal river where it narrows to the lowest convenient bridging place. For geography makes history. The uneasy epochs of eruptions and erosions – the tropical forests where woolly rhino grazed, the clamp of ice a mile thick – a long story carved in the landscape, made that bridging place. What came after the Roman survey that identified this providential toehold, in just two quicksilver millennia, were the busy markings of men – a history of military occupation, trade and industry that has been scribbled and scribbled again over that plain face.

The bold, improving hand of modern engineers – from the illustrious Bazalgette and Cubitt, the Brunels and the Dances, fathers and sons, to the most obscure road-planning civil servant – has tight laced the river and scored above and below. Rulers now leave their triumphal mark across the busy page of the London map. Vicky and her Albert and the heroes of Empire who have flung their names across these new, straight-as-a-die thoroughfares, running through the devious medieval knottings of alleys and courts, close-packed, wooden streets that themselves were scrawled across rational Roman roads just as *their* 'work of giants', the garrison, fort, temple, baths and markets, had bisected the most ancient, tribal thoroughfares worn by feet. And even though every succeeding generation's page has been rubbed away by barbarians, famine, plague, war, fire or fashion, still it is possible to uncover past centuries, in the sly seepage of the ancient marsh into city basements, in the tessellated floors of the merchants of that other imperial age uncovered by nameless navvies of our own day. Here, too, in the anarchic medieval traditions and secrets that survive within the halls of the City Livery Companies.

But it is in the naming of places that we can best read the lives of those other Londoners: 'What London hath been of ancient time men may here see . . .' or hear. For those other generations that went before us clamour still to be heard and remembered. Like life itself, which comes from water, London's earliest history starts with the story of the Thames, oldest surviving place name after Kent. In Fenchurch and Finsbury and Moorgate there is the memory of the drained fen that once the river wallowed through. And, if you listen, you can hear its long-buried tributaries still flowing in Fleet, in the -bourne of Holebourne, now Holborn, in Walbrook, where the Britons made their settlement, and in the ancient Sho Well that has become Shoe Lane. And the foul work that men make water do is also named: in the stinking moat that became Houndsditch and the open sewer, or Latin *cloaca*, that is Cloak Lane.

As well as watering men, the sweet Thames grew commercial crops – for food, cures and flavourings – and nourished private pleasure gardens. In Pear Tree, Mulberry and Camomile Streets and on Garlick and Saffron Hills there is left a breath of those times when the country came more to town. And in Baldwin's Gardens, that notorious slum and sanctuary of criminals known today, in the last decade of our Queen Victoria's century, as the Thieves' Kitchen, Richard Baldwin, Queen Elizabeth's gardener, laid out Fulke Greville's famous garden. Lost under streets for twenty years now is the original of Draper's Gardens, where the long-dead gardener once complained his herbs were destroyed by the drips from drying and bleaching clothes.

Craft and industry found a foothold on those two gravel hills, served by bridge, wharf and river; the thriving neighbourhoods of those past artisans still chime out in Fetter Lane (where the armourers to the Knights Templar had their workshops), in Goldsmith Street, Billiter Square (home of bell-founders) and in Hart Street, where hearths were made. There is the sweet smell of trade that brought the world to London and London to the world in Sugar Quay, Ivory House and America Square, the clink of finance in Old Change and Lombard Street where those subtle Lombardy merchants settled. Home manufacturing made its name in Cartwright and Ropemaker Streets, in Masons Avenue and Cooper's Row. The city fed itself from Oat and Honey Lanes and Milk Street and from the hogs kept in their *hoggene* on Huggin Hill and, on the appointed day, from fish brought from the Friday Street market. The markets of Cheapside, *Smoothfield* or Smithfield, Billingsgate and Poultry, with the grocer-pepperers of Sopers Lane, supplied the rest. As for the staff of life, London got its grain from the ancient market of Corn Hill, traded it in the Corn Exchange, was made to itch from all the chaff that floated down Seething Lane, baked it in Bread Street, using wood from High Timber Street or charcoal made by the charcoal-burners of Coleman Street, and carried it away in baskets made in Panyer Alley.

The populace was shod from Leather Lane and by the soft, Córdoban leather of the Cordwainers' Guild; they brought their wool for homespinning from the *distaff* displays of Little Distaff Lane. They were hosed by Hosier Lane and clothed in Rag Fair – now cleared away to make the entrance to that new 'Wonder Bridge' under construction by the Tower. And, at last, they lit themselves to bed by the light of candles from Cannon, or Candlewick Street.

Buried within this busy world of work and commerce is the history of other needs met – in the lively menagerie of Eagles and Falcons, Cocks, Swans, Boars, Lions and Tygers, Horses, Elephants and Mermaids, which named the thousand taverns and inns; in the coy come-on of Love Lane and the bolder signal of Cock Lane where prostitutes were licensed to walk. And in that other indulgence of a comfortably off civilisation, literature – which is here among the text writers of Paternoster Row, thundering in Printing House Square and, everywhere, in the casual commemorations of Spencer, Shakespeare, Pepys, Johnson and Dickens that make this London the London of words.

Even before Wren's familiar churches rang out in the children's rhyme of 'Oranges and Lemons' our ancient city chimed with worship. When water was holy the Romans built their temple to Mithras here, and in Bridewell for St Bride the Celts worshipped their watery goddess of fertility. The sound of holy waters runs still, in Holywell Lane, and the Clarke's Well, or *fons clericorum* of Clerkenwell and the lost parsonage well of Well Street. And just as London was ever host to the dispossessed, so has she given shelter to alien faiths and theological offshoots. Hear how Old Jewry, Ave Maria Lane, Quaker, Calvin and Carthusian Streets, the Temple

Church of the dispossessed Knights Templar in Pilgrim Street, and Mincing Lane (which recalls the fastidious black-clad nuns of St Helen's), all tell the tale of religious miscellany.

Here, then, is a city heavy with its own history, where the sediment of the lives of all those past Londoners, who ate and shat and ate, lived and died and lived, made and destroyed to make and destroy again, is laid down, each generation on top of the last, to build the super metropolis. For the biography of London is made by man and man's works, and recorded, if you have ears to hear it, in man's casual, practical naming of places.

George and Rebecca, who look vacantly out of their chariot window, are entering this capital of the world at the height of its confidence. They enter as many have done before, and will do after, with the sensation of coming home.

Rebecca feels enlivened just to breathe its soot, and even poor, dull George perhaps smells the whiff of freedom. For here true, or truish, fairy stories are begun: a vagrant boy and his companion cat, called by bells to a glorious destiny; the daughter of a king, branded illegitimate and imprisoned in a place of execution, who survived to be a faery queene. And even for less exalted heroes and heroines London breeds stories as devious as its own medieval alleys.

By the time George and Rebecca's coach has burrowed through the city's outer membrane to its dense, impacted core, the moment has come that will engender new beginnings. Before dopy George might detain her, Rebecca calls for the carriage to stop and leaps down into the teeming anonymity of London Bridge, having half achieved her mission of cashing in her capital. 'I must go to me lodgin's an' fetch back the boy. Wait fer me, sir. I'll not take long,' she calls, as she runs off.

George sits in the carriage and watches as the sun comes up red, filtered through smoke and steam, so that it seems to blur rather than reveal the city. Even at this early hour the traffic over the bridge is getting heavy, with vehicles and people walking to their work, while below him dingy figures embark and disembark from the steamboats that slop at their moorings among the barges, wherries, skiffs, tugs and penny boats. Upriver, rattling over the railway bridge, come trains of the South Eastern Railway bringing hundreds more into the Cannon Street Shed to be gobbled up by factories, warehouses, mills, works, banks, offices, markets, shops. Traffic between the City and the Borough is dragging over Southwark Bridge, too, and the pearly dome of St Paul's is lit by this sullen, early light as though from within. Downriver, he sees the near-completed structure of the new bridge, next to the Tower, which will carry some of the multitude, now squeezing itself to file from one side of London to the other through this narrow stone gap let across the river.

Two hours pass and, having sat silently watching this lively stage set through the carriage window, George feels that he, too, should be active in some way. He is mindful that he has been charged to take control of the situation, and since he cannot think what he should be doing, he gets out and walks about energetically for a minute, ostentatiously slapping his sides as though he were numbed by cold. Outside, the noise of nine-a.m. London joins the assault on his senses: dirty men, filthy women and squalid children hawking their wares, from the monotonous 'Ole clo's' of the Jewish rag-dealer to the pleas of the matchgirl, calling, 'Two 'undred an' fif'y wax 'uns fer a penny, two boxes ov flamers, the best a-goin'.' And this is only the top line of a cacophonous symphony of London sounds. The groom, who expects no sensible instruction from the young man looking stupidly about him, calls down that he must move the carriage out of the way and find water for the horses. George, frightened that the ghastly woman will miss them when she brings the mysterious boy, says he will wait here on the bridge for the coach to return in half an hour or so.

And so George stands upon London Bridge, intermittently waving off the coach for another half-hour's wait. He leans over the parapet and watches the broad brown water swirl underneath until the sun is high and his own hatted shape stands proud on the bulky shadow of the bridge. As he stands, in familiar, blank idleness, he becomes aware that another dark figure trembles next to his own watery reflection.

George remembers that other shade cast upon his night wall, when he was a child, and knows that at last he has returned and must be standing quietly by his shoulder. Without turning, George says, in a measured voice, 'You have come again. I knew you would.'

'Is that you, Uncle George?' Duke would have run at this moment had not Rebecca been standing sentinel close behind, trying to overhear the interview. He continues, with the line he has been tutored in all the breathless way from his bed to this strange rendezvous: 'It is I – your own dear nephew, Duke.'

'Nephew?' says George, turning to look at the corporeal boy standing beside him.

At this point Rebecca hurries forward. 'You sayin' 'e ain't yer nephew?' She slaps Duke briefly around the head in her exasperation. 'I knew it! Lyin', rotten bitch! Just like 'er ter leave me in ve lurch.'

George and Duke are repulsed by this female passion. As she stamps and spits, George turns to Duke and, taking his hand, says simply, 'Let us jump together this time.'

Caught between the strange man's calm certainty and Rebecca's all-too-familiar ranting rage, Duke follows George on to the parapet and allows himself to topple forwards to meet the shadowy reflections of a man and a boy, head on.

Rebecca doesn't hear the distant splash as their bodies hit the water. For her, they simply vanish. But for an instant her astonished face can be seen poking out over the side of the bridge to scan the slop and swell of the river for any sign of them. Seeing none, having apparently mislaid her potential money-spinner, and being aware that the future prospects for a swindling procuress-childsnatcher are not bright, she legs it, to sink without trace into the arms of that consuming metropolis. London now closes over her insignificant head for us, as surely as the Thames has over George and his celestial twin.

Lost

By that evening, when the coachman at last returns home, without a single scion of the house of Fainhope, the Duchess recognises that her walls are breached. She should never have let her captive from her sight. But long years of unchallenged supremacy have given her the misplaced confidence that she truly has control over her own destiny. And now, without him, her hostage against convention, her talisman, what is she but a widow without a son? Powerless.

Miss Mantilla is anxious, too; perhaps a little more anxious than her mistress about George's personal well-being. She cannot stop herself checking his bedroom that evening, as though she expects him to have flown back in through the window, unremarked. And she sleeps that night with the old pillowcase stuffed with the winding rags that still hold faint comfort in their iron odour of old blood.

Now the two women are in Her Grace's private sitting room, the scene of many a previous war council. But this one is marked by an unusual infirmity of purpose in the commanding officer.

'Perhaps I could travel to London and make enquiries?' hazards Miss Mantilla, vaguely.

'Don't be ridiculous. Who knows what vile rookery spawned

that woman?' dismisses the general, slapping the padded back of an armchair, as though with a military swagger-stick.

'We might deputise Lord John to engage a detective, a lady detective, to search for us,' Miss Mantilla responds, an attempt at tougher reasoning that the supreme strategist does not dismiss.

'At the least, that might give that idiot, Harpur, something to occupy his empty mind. But can we trust him even with that?'

'I really think we must do something. And soon,' says Miss Mantilla, again slipping into nervous indecision.

'Be assured, I will *do* something. I will not be cheated of two heirs, Maria. He or the other will be found, you may depend upon that,' concludes the Duchess, splendid in her absolute impartiality. Victory in this latest battle of a long campaign requires a legitimising male, and a legitimising male she will have – it matters little which. Miss Mantilla leaves the war cabinet to cry over George's lonely pillowcase in her own room.

Where is George and the putative substitute heir? Deep within the anonymous waters of the eternal Thames, keeper of secrets, their bodies having bobbed and sunk and bobbed again, to sink for ever? Or were they hooked out by a waterman, along with the other slimy offerings that people cast upon the river? Or rescued by those same outcasts Lucy had once visited, as they slept, between the piers of London Bridge? All we can know of them is that they are lost. The rest is imagining.

Twice now Duke has disappeared into that impenetrable void of unknowing where first mother and now rival grandparents may not locate him. Lost. Of course, within the black hole that consumed him all appears as normal. For he is not lost to himself. In this parallel world the sun continues to shine for him and the birds to sing. Or, equally, the bees to sting and the hail to fall. He continues to be. For all their urgency the telepathic messages sent to seek him do not find their mark.

We know that Lucy has never forgotten him. He still exists for her, mostly now as a memory of touch and smell, although when, in her mind's eye, she does catch a glimpse of him he is a much younger Duke than the toddler she lost. Even though every morning she wakes with the knowledge in her heart of how old he is on this particular day of his life he has stayed a baby. For a brief couple of years he was her oldest child, then the middle of three and soon he will be her youngest. Her last-born darling. Those other two will grow up and away and yet the one who is truly lost will stay with her for ever.

As for George, in losing himself, he is found. His lifelong spell is broken by the sudden, baptismal kiss of cold water. So, no longer the somnambulist, he awakes and starts swimming strongly. Not all the healthful training he underwent at his uncle's mansion was wasted. And that was what happened within the black hole: George started swimming. Vitalised by the cold and the freedom, he pulls young Duke after him until they reach the slimy shore where they step out into their new lives. George, reunited with his shadow. Complete at last. Of course, what really happens next, which we may observe with our privileged access to the land of the lost, is unexceptional: they slip and stagger and shiver, cough and gasp and laugh. They wander in their begrimed and watery state; are accosted, pointed and stared at, and offered a cup of hot coffee by a vendor who is used to this kind of thing. Then, finding no trace of the carriage, George asks directions to the only address in London he knows, other than the shut-up family mansion, remembering that there had been a kind welcome there when he had called to visit his sister Georgina.

When George and Duke appear on Alonso's doorstep and read the small brass plate upon which is advertised the sisters' trade as 'lady photographic artistes' they are away from home about that business. The gatekeeper, who interrogates them upon the doorstep, is doubtful about letting in this odd, shivering pair to spoil her clean hall floor. This seneschal is neither mythical three-headed dog nor sly riddler. She is something altogether fiercer and more sophistical: the new maid-of-all-work. However,

George's nice speaking manner and Duke's pathetic sneezing persuade her to accept their story and let them in – only to drip dry in the back kitchen, mind. Meek George is quite content not to be ushered into the parlour as honoured guest, and Duke has no remaining memory of having sat in that kitchen before to eat bread and dripping.

And that was how it happened: twenty-one years after his own mother shut him out from home and family, George found his own way back from the cold to reclaim his bartered life.

What Shall Become of Us?

W e must now be patient before returning to that anonymous London suburb to discover what next became
of Duke and George after the decisive moment when they
disappeared down their rabbit-hole to pop up again living different
lives.

Let us beguile the time by discovering how the anxious relations
passed this interval. And, indeed, they were not idle: the Criminal
Investigation Department of New Scotland Yard, finest and
foremost detectives in the world, was contacted only a day after
George's failure to return. The detectives took the disappearance
of a noble son so seriously that a sketch-portrait of the young
man, as he appeared at present, was requested to aid them with
their investigation. However, the sketch that artistic Miss Mantilla
supplied, showing a half-grown boy without any expression
whatever, as if she had never properly looked at him, did not
facilitate a satisfactory identification of the missing aristocrat. The
only piece of information that the London police force has so far
reported is based on the questionable evidence of a matchgirl,
who claimed to have seen a young man and a boy fall, or jump,
into the Thames. And there the trail has ended, doused in cold
water.

In her war room, Her Grace, the Duchess, has called a meeting with her subordinates, Lord John and Miss Mantilla, over tea. She will not allow George or the mysterious boy to swim out of her grasp without a mighty effort to haul them back to her. She turns to her brother-in-law, who has been sent for to present his parallel intelligence report into the background and possible whereabouts of the back-up 'grandson', as supplied by the female detective.

'Not a bad return on two guineas,' says he, taking up his teacup.

'And what did your investment buy us?' answers Her Grace, looking again at the document he has set before her.

'An address, at least.'

'An address of a rented house in a place called St John's Wood, which was vacated in a hurry eight months previously. And that appears to be our only definite information on the ménage that might or might not have included my daughter, or your son, and a possible grandchild. Useless!'

'No, not at all, according to my reckoning. Since we know, *de facto*, that my own boy is dead our best chance is to pursue the Georgina lead, and that's exactly what I set her on to. For if we find your girl alive then we may disprove her involvement . . .'

'Ah, yes, disprove Georgina's maternity and so allow the field clear for Harry's paternity. And what have we further learnt from that rich seam?' She consults the document. 'Georgina is in Australia or, conversely, running around the streets of London, frightening children or, most inconveniently for me, dead.'

'One of 'em's bound to be right,' he replies nervously. 'Pretty good for a first trawl, I'd say. *Cherchez la femme*, and all that. Find her and all will follow after. No?'

'It's not my unfortunate daughter I'm looking for,' is her short reply.

'It's a process of elimination, d'you see?' he persists.

'Shall you be going to Australia on that supposition, then, brother?'

'Oh, I don't think that can be necessary. I suggest we ask our woman to make further enquiries in London first,' he says, with the bravado that is his sole defence against the forensic interrogation that passes as conversation with her.

'Dripping away. Don't you see that time is dripping away from me and you achieve nothing?'

'We have the police on the trail of your boy, and my detective is like a bloodhound on the trail of the other. Between us we're bound to close in,' says he, demonstrating the inevitable success of this pincer movement with his hands.

'Where is he? Damn him!' the Duchess sobs, with ill-repressed passion. 'What shall become of me?'

Miss Mantilla is surprised by that sob into gabbling, 'We might advertise in the papers for news of an orphaned little boy called Duke and put in some message in code that only that dreadful woman would understand.'

Lord John, too, is rattled by this disturbing sign of impotent despair in the phenomenon that is his formidable sister-in-law. 'Well, quite, there's the difficulty, for we have no way of knowing what name she goes by. And that's why I have to start with the known facts of the case—'

'Oh, you might as well. I really do not know what else we can do,' cuts in the Duchess, answering Miss Mantilla and ignoring the irrelevant man. 'I feel as though I should be able to see where George is, if only I could know where to focus my attention.' She looks with eyes so black and intense that one might easily believe that they pierce straight through the bubbles to the cauldron bottom and read the future there. 'The battle is not lost. The battle is never lost!' she concludes fiercely.

Miss Mantilla, emboldened by her vehemence, starts up, 'There are some ladies, the Misses Timms. Oh, but it is years and years ago, they are most probably now dead . . .'

Deputised to investigate the supernatural route, there being no more concrete paths to follow at present, Miss Mantilla employs her morning constitutional to cross the park to the village, which serves the railway station, where the Misses Timms dwell in their carefully kept charnel-house. However, even as she enters upon their lane, she sees from the washing whipping upon the line in the front garden – collarless workman's shirts and the innumerable worn garments of a family of children – that her quest will be in vain. Life and fertility have come to that virgin shrine to the dead. She doesn't even stop to enquire further, being wary of the strong-armed woman she sees at the open door mopping the Timmses' erstwhile doorstep. Most probably dead, then. But both? She'd thought that the bovine Miss Timms wasn't much older than herself. What became of respectable women of dwindling means with no visible male support? The workhouse? Miss Mantilla's mind recoils from exploring this possibility. Living as the unwelcome dependants of grudging relations, then? More possible, but no less horrible a prospect. Again she thinks grimly of those other insecure spinster ladies burning holes in milk pans and letting the meat go off. Long ago she had stopped sending her weekly letters; there seemed to be no point now that Papa was gone. She continued to post her remittance, though, year after year – her tithe.

Miss Mantilla turns her back upon these speculations and strides home to the Hall and security – or dependency, at least. Ahead is the prospect of well-mended fires, plentiful food, repose and companionship; behind, the horror of self-reliance in a cold world. Miss Mantilla's footsteps are certain for, unlike the average wife or servant, she knows that her protector's motivation in supplying fires, food and comfort is their mutual concern. They are bound by more than legal ties. For the contract she has with another woman, based upon sisterly partisanship, she feels to be a more dependable thing than those founded upon the usual, more precarious arrangement between men and women. Compare that bendy reed Briggs with her own resolute duchess. But if Miss Mantilla's security is fastened upon the rock of the Duchess's ambition, then on what is Her Grace's future anchored? Why, on the shifting sands of a man, of course, for a woman must always be some man's daughter, sister, wife, mother or, even, aunt. With a man she may contrive, if she is clever like the Duchess, to run her own life; without one she is horribly exposed. Her Grace would not vanish from the face of the earth like the poor Misses Timms but she could not properly continue to exist in this unnatural estate. The dowager Duchess of Fainhope needs her self-manufactured heir back. For there will always be a man at bottom.

Time's Fleeting River

But what of the maidens of modest means and their burnt-bottomed pans? Having narrowly escaped the excitements and changes that matrimony would have wreaked, that precarious female household had continued to trudge along in much the same higgledy-piggledy way as ever was. Until the Thames spewed up the two castaways and reduced them to more of a muddle than usual.

For having experienced a period of relative, if dwindling, financial independence as businesswomen, the arrival of George and Duke backed them once more into the condition of drudging landladies. Worse, their two new incumbents were, evidently, *non-paying* guests. At first Aurora and Teresa had been mortified that His Grace, the Duke of Fainhope, had been shooed on to a rag rug in their kitchen by their fourteen-year-old maid. They were not, however, much surprised, since Maria might take it into her head to land on them with no notice any assortment of her noble charges, it seemed. They were anxious, though, that their handling of the last one might not have been a success. And they were further flustered to learn that George had neither letter of authorisation nor sensible explanation as to the purpose of his visit. In fact, he gave no account of how he came to be there, and who the mysterious little boy accompanying him might be. He could divulge, though, that they were wet from having come via the river.

Once their initial exclamations of surprised embarrassment, apology and demur, interrogation and obfuscation were exhausted, rather than allowing everyone to stand around and gape at each other, as all seemed inclined to, Aurora seized upon a sterling way forward endorsed by literature. For characters in books made cold and wet (particularly accidentally and out of doors) inevitably succumb to chills and possibly even death if they are not quickly and vigorously made warm and dry again. Even then it's a close thing. So rushing about boiling water and pulling off bedsheets to wrap their guests in gave everyone a role either as nurse or patient, and nobody the opportunity to consider what should sensibly be done next. When they were dry and warmed (both within and without) all that remained was to bundle them into beds and so out of the way. Alonso's daughters, having learnt never again to sacrifice their own bed to visitors, installed them in their father's room; George, since he was the senior party, in his huge bed, and Duke on a camp bed by his side. Then the sisters crept away to whisper in the back parlour, repressed by the sensation of something weighty on the floor above that lay heavy on their minds as a guilty conscience or undischarged responsibility.

It is during that night, in their shared room, Duke now in the bed and George having removed himself to the floor, cosy in the cold, that they at last have the opportunity to talk to each other. The long night through they tell their tale, try to make sense of their lost lives. And if their stories are not as fantastic as those from *The Arabian Nights*, they seem to be as well populated by symbols, magical beasts, sorceresses and genies.

'I don't think that I ever had a real mother. There was a fat lady who said she was my adopted mother and I used to think that that woman, Becs, might've been one but now I don't think she can. Then I have a sort of memory that I once had a lot of brothers and sisters and we were all looked after by ladies in crossover pinnies. But far, far back I have the idea that there was something before even that life. I seem to remember a room that was like a tree-house with a ladder and wooden walls, and in it a safe, soft mother who kept the fire burning bright.'

'Do you think you were stolen from your real mother?' says George, as well versed in romances as those benevolent ladies from the Fisher Folk's Home had been. 'Try to remember back to your very earliest days.'

'It's so hard. I don't know whether it was a dream or real, but I seem to think that I was abandoned in a white cave in a cold, lonely wood where there were wolves or something else ready to bite, and told to wait there for her. And I waited and waited.'

'You are a young Romulus!' says George. Then, on seeing that Duke knows nothing of Roman myth, he adds, 'You know, raised by wolves.'

'I don't think so. The strangest thing is, I have a notion that my father was a horse.'

They talk, too, of George's childhood, and although he is all too secure in his background and relations there is always the mystery of the bright twin who leapt from the cupboard. Duke loves this story and asks for it again as soon as it reaches its conclusion. 'Did you really think that I was him?' he clamours, anxious for reassurance.

'You know I did. That's the first thing I said to you, if you remember. "You have come again."'

Duke whispers the mantra along with George. The spell that binds them. 'Perhaps I really was him. We must be somewhere while we're waiting to be born, mustn't we? Or perhaps it was a sort of ghost you saw – of a lovely twin who died?'

'Perhaps,' says George, kindly.

'But now I have found you, my brother, and you have found me and we may live together happy ever after,' says Duke, reaching out his small, dry hand to take George's in the dark. The first kind and mutual contact George has had with another human being since Lucy left him.

The next morning, still wrapped in bedsheets while their clothes dry on the line, George finally states his expectations: 'I'd like to stay. Duke and I would like to stay on with you. I mean, if we may?' he says, diffidently but firmly.

'Of course you may, Your Grace,' responds Teresa, with a curtsy. She feels she is in no position to deny a peer of the realm, even if he is wrapped in her flannel undersheet.

'Well, that's civil of you, Miss Mantilla. I say, may I call you Teresa and Aurora? *Miss Mantilla* means someone else in my mind.'

'Of course, Your Grace. Shall you write and say what has become of you or would you prefer us to communicate with my sister, or perhaps your mother?' risks Aurora.

'Oh, I'd rather not, and please call me George. Duke and I will just carry on here for the present. Quietly.'

Perhaps noticing the look of repressed panic on Teresa's face, George propitiates: 'Of course, we'd expect to make ourselves useful. Is there any silver you need polishing, perhaps? I'm really very good at polishing silver. I used to go through the whole canteen sometimes when I had nothing else to do and Mama wanted me out of the way.' And that is how they are obliged to leave things.

Since George and Duke have no plans to return home and it doesn't appear to bother them that they contribute no payment, the sisters decide pragmatically that Maria's disbursement should cover his and the boy's expenses for the moment. Confronting Maria with a bill for lodgings and food would be an unpleasantness they would tackle only when need be.

And so they continued for that first month, the women not raising the courage to ask and George never feeling the need to establish quite what the arrangement between them should be. Both George and Duke, well used to having their lives organised and directed by women, were strangely inert in the face of busy domestic reorganisation, there being no silver to speak of that needed polishing. They idled inoffensively, stagnant while all around them the everyday business of domestic life flowed on. Aurora had at first taken George's inertia for arrogance and had bridled at his easy, masculine assumption that they would be fed and cared for by the women. This lackadaisical behaviour would certainly 'butter no parsnips'. However, when she had angrily remarked that the washing wouldn't bring itself in, she had been surprised that George had sallied out to pull the linen inexpertly off the line (sending the clothes-pegs snapping over the garden fence) like the biddable beast he was. Having discovered that he did not lounge but only awaited orders, the pent fury at having had to serve the useless article had, at first, expended itself in making him 'jump to'. There was something of the novelty of making a bear dance, ridiculous and emasculated on lumbering legs. But neither Teresa nor Aurora was a martinet, particularly about household arrangements, and they shared a growing affection for their strange visitors.

And so they blundered on day by day, in this way gradually slipping into those little habits and routines that ease the passage of time and make us forgetful of that we would prefer not to confront.

Waiting

Equally at Fainhope Hall there are no plans for the future – for the future was suspended when George was let to slip through Her Grace's fingers. The September of the year he was spirited away he reached his majority and, *in absentia*, became eligible to take control of his inheritance. Since Her Grace insisted that she believed him to be still alive, and would not allow the estate to pass to her brother-in-law, circumstances in the Hall, its lands, farms, tied cottages and other dependencies had reached an impasse. The nitwit and the booby who had been engaged to administer the eleventh Duke of Fainhope's future inheritance at his birth, having complacently warmed their bottoms for the last twenty-one years, decided that action was urgently called for. It was agreed, in mimicry of the spirit of stasis at the Hall, that George's deeds, titles and monies should be frozen until he should be incontrovertibly proved dead or should return to claim them. The dowager Duchess was allowed a stipend, drawn from the capital, to maintain herself and a skeleton staff. It had been suggested to her that she might more economically remove her household to the dower house, but she had been magnificent in her refusal.

It was during this first year of waiting that Her Grace, the Duchess, came upon the *carte de visite* that showed young Duke in his snow-dusted rags, which Euphemia had smuggled away from her last visit to Georgina. She stood, with the picture in her hand, and felt as though her heart must stop beating. It was like a sign. For here he was, her son and yet . . . how could this beggar child be her son? But who was her son? That dead bundle she'd carried in tired arms or the blank, faceless thing she had called by that name these twenty-one years? But no door into that empty chamber, her heart, was thrown open to maternal feeling by the sudden apparition of this poor lost boy. She held the card before her and spoke to it sharply: 'You must come back, you must come back from there. I have need of you.'

During this season of stasis, Lord John Harpur somehow couldn't rouse himself to rejoice much at this possible fulfilment of his ancient ambition to topple his sister-in-law. Since Harry had died he didn't seem to have the stomach for the fight any more. He reflected gloomily that the whole shebang would end up with some dismal Shropshire cousins, when the old girl finally gave up the ghost of George and pulled her talons out.

She squatted in her sonless pile and he in his. But whereas he had been used to dull his discontent in his brandy and his dogs, a change had been effected in that stolid squire since his return from France. The rumour of his boy's boy had briefly revived him and he had clung on for a week or more in the expectation that the 'bloodhound' would triumph, bringing home George with a curly-haired lad in an embroidered waistcoat. A little chap he could sit on his own knee and even, perhaps, learn to love. When this had not been, he had taken to wandering the house at night with a candle, his illuminated face floating past the window-panes like a drowned man's. So now, husband and wife, unquiet and mournful ghosts both, took turns by day and by night to haunt the passages. And when he did not wander, Lord John would sit in his favourite library chair with Harry's silk top hat on his knee, stroking and stroking along its grain until the nap was quite worn away.

A Flask of Wine and
A Book of Verse

Back in south London more months pass and what started as an enforced accommodation evolves by degrees into a comfortable, domestic arrangement between the visitors and their hostesses. And so time runs on, smoothing away the niggling worry that something really ought to be done or said about their guests. But nothing is done or said as Duke and George are first accepted, then beloved.

That other occupant of the female household, ancient Mrs Evans, the household cat, has been replaced by a sweeter version of the original. Prudence, the kitten, not having inherited the matrimonial sobriquet of her predecessor, is now the darling pet in the spinster and bachelor establishment. She is imputed with all manner of saucy opinions, which she expresses, in the third person, through the medium of her doting 'mamas'. These days, it seems to Aurora that she no longer directly addresses her sister, or her sister her, but all conversation is conducted as though it were the infantile monologue of this sly little madam. Perhaps ventrilo-quising Prudence allows them to continue to talk together, and to George, as unself-conscious girls when they know themselves only to be awkward adults. The other purpose the cat serves is as the object of their displaced affections. Teresa could brush until Prudence crackles with the unspent electricity of her sensuous need to touch and love another.

When their guests first came to stay, the sisters had been bashful of exposing Prudence's shocking bad manners to a wider circle. But the liberation of putting things into the cat's mouth that somehow shouldn't have come from their own was a habit hard to break. What's more, once they began to forget and let Prudence express herself, George, too, found that he could speak his mind when the cat had got his tongue.

So, in the earliest days of their cohabitation, there exists a curious situation when all three stand around the cat, while she unaffectedly washes or daydreams or sleeps, and conduct animated, three-way conversations all in the voice of a small, petulant girl.

'She says, "Did you see the look Mrs Next Door shot over the fence at George putting out the washing?" ' says Aurora, smiling at George.

'She shall go right over there and scratch up her seedlings,' replies George.

'And then, she says, "I shall do worse – and right on top!" ' puts in Aurora, huffily.

'Prudence says, "Nasty old trout, no better than she thinks she is, with her husband who drinks and only one pair of sheets to her name," ' snaps Teresa.

'But first she must attend to her toilet, says she: there's a flea that needs hunting out and putting down,' adds Aurora, as Prudence twitches violently and begins to bite methodically through the hair at the base of her tail.

' "Excuse me," Prudence says. She doesn't know where she learnt to be so vulgar!' ventures George, his affected impression of affronted gentility making the other two laugh. George proves a quick learner in this game, working hard to adopt just the right tone of light mockery the girls enjoy.

Gradually, having served her purpose in allowing them to talk freely among themselves, Prudence is a less vital prop in their growing trust and friendship until they notice that she is, in fact, nothing more than a cat. It is Duke who displaces Prudence to assume his rightful place as the child at the centre of this curious analogue of family life and conversation, as is the habit among parents, soon revolves exclusively around him.

During this allocation of familiar roles it breaks upon unfledged George that he is the senior male of the household and that he could learn to relish walking around in big man's shoes. However, manly shoes denote manly duties: in order to fit perfectly this newly elevated status as *man of the house* George must have an occupation. However, irretrievably bashful and indifferently educated, he is quite horrified at the idea of stomping about in office, shop or counting house. George resolves to start up on his own account. After a few false steps – his small-scale scheme for curing the skins of rabbits and making them into gloves having resulted in a lot of maggoty, stiffened pelts and his home-made ginger beer having excitingly exploded – George realises that it would be better to relinquish the part of masculine provider and simply make himself more useful around the house. He begins by taking over the marketing and becomes quite obsessive about stretching the domestic budget: he travels miles on the twopenny omnibus to save a penny on flour; struggles home with a cheap, but aged truckle of Cheddar that yields, from its stinking heart, just enough to make a Welsh rarebit. Exasperated with the cost of potatoes, he starts a vegetable patch in the sooty little garden to provide them with crops of their own potatoes, rhubarb, cabbages and sweet peas in season. Then, in order to make the most of what he produces there, he teaches himself to cook plain family dinners by looking into W. B. Tegetmeier's book, *The Scholar's Handbook of Household Management and Cookery*. And thus, little by little, George takes over the running of the house and garden, and the sisters gladly let him. Although George is not a perfect housewife he finds contentment in it, and his application and enthusiasm are much admired by those whose only culinary achievement has been with a kettle. And once he has taken on every domestic responsibility in their domain, the sisters are able, oh, liberation, to let go the last and final maid-of-all-work.

With no maid to worry them into being 'proper' ladies and lodgers, they subside into a routine that suits and occupies them all. George's economies, if erratic, nevertheless allow them to subsist on the tiny allowance that Maria continues to send every month. And Alonso's girls find delight in being middle-aged mothers to sweet Duke.

On first coming into their home the child had been shy and anxious to please, frightened that he would be smacked or banished to his room for dropping crumbs. But over the months, he has grown to be a happy, sunny child, encircled, supported and protected by his loving aunties/mothers and kind brother. It is as though the germ first nurtured by his real mother needed only the reminder of what it was to be beloved to spring back to life.

Aurora loves to empty her sewing-bag on to the parlour floor and watch him unselfconsciously humming to himself as he plays with cotton bobbins, glass-headed pins, ribbons and buttons, a crust spread with jam close to hand beside him on the carpet. Sometimes they make rival armies together, he chief commander of the thimble-men who ride on bobbins and wield needle swords, she ranging her partisan force of odds and ends led by the bold and indefatigable darning mushroom.

Teresa loves to sit the boy on her knee to sing to him and tell him the stories that her Spanish papa had told her when she was a girl. She looks out for him the old painting materials, put away years before in the attic, so that they may sit for hours splashing the walls and dripping the floors with their paint-water. George teaches him how to grow vegetables under glass, make a sweet omelette and get out stains with borax.

We all discover that the poignant season of our youth is soon past, but Aurora and Teresa never were allowed even this brief interval of foolish hopes and egotism. For what chance do these have, set against an invalid father's need? All their lives they have cared for somebody, and even when this care and love are given, as they are now to Duke, gladly, willingly, still there remains a nostalgia for the life that got away. So real, to Aurora, is that betrayed girlhood promise that she seems to glimpse the running figure of herself in her springtime, with bouncing black plait, forever just ahead, disappearing down corridors.

But she knows when she looks, with a kind of perverse fascination, into her glass that she will not see the face of that ambitious girl. Instead, looking back, framed in mahogany, she finds the living memento of Mother, just as she had appeared in her middle years, before death had removed her. The hair of *her* head is grown meagre and fine, just as Mother's had, and her eyebrows are as thick and bushy black. And she hardly recognises her hands as her own any longer: they are now so completely her mother's.

Having made no mark with her own life is she then merely the earthly repository for all those mute generations of women that went before, who now look out through her own disappointed eyes?

The anniversary of George and Duke's homecoming finds Aurora and Teresa lying side by side in their shared bed whispering in the dark, as they have done all their long lives.

'Do you have recurring dreams?' asks Aurora and, before her sister can reply, continues, 'I do. Often I dream of discovering lost places in the house. Sometimes it's only a room hidden behind a forgotten door, sometimes a whole wing that's been there all the time, shut up and neglected but, somehow, never noticed.'

'How very odd,' says Teresa, without animation.

'What's more,' says Aurora, annoyed by her sister's apparent indifference, 'I always come across something precious hidden away in the rooms – although I can never remember by morning what I found. But I wake up in floods of tears knowing that I've let it slip, whatever it was, through my hands again.' As she lies there, the tears running silently over her cheeks and on to the pillow, she feels Teresa take her hand and give it a squeeze.

Sometimes the sadness of these dreams, the sensation of loss, or of time lost, and the brooding guilt that she hadn't properly occupied those closed-up, imaginary rooms stuffed with unfulfilled promise, is more real to her than the life she wakes up to, again and again.

Knowing that her sister is crying, Teresa comforts her with a soothing, jocular tone: 'Dear, I just remembered, I do sometimes dream the same dream. It started when Duke arrived. I run around the place, seeking out squalling babies who are roaring to be fed and changed. And there are hundreds of them tucked away all over the house: behind cushions, inside basins, up the chimney, under the bed and I don't know where else! I do so much running about after the little tyrants that by morning I'm exhausted!'

She gives her sister another reassuring squeeze and, before she drops off, wonders whether this dream could be about Duke. It could hardly be so, for he brings such fulfilment and joy into their lives and is such an easy and accommodating little boy. She smiles in the dark at the thought of their darling. That Duke has become the mainspring of the house, the chief source of every action taken, every decision made, every anxiety suffered, is gladly conceded. Nowadays it is sufficient to their happiness that he is happy. Sufficient to their future hopes that his will be bright.

Aurora gently weeps and lets the girl with the bouncing plait run on and away.

Thus relations within this curious family balance at last. The happy toils of devoting themselves to the care and love of one another let those who had been lost find roots, and those who had been grounded by their sex and circumstances grow wings.

For with love there are no rules. It is the heart that decides who will be our real family.

Ozymandias, King of Kings

Back at bleak Fainhope Hall we find Her Grace, the Duchess of Fainhope, and Maria Mantilla together in the private sitting room, which has been at the white hot centre of the Duchess's long, blazing reign. It now lies, the last ember, at the very centre of a dying and darkened Empire. 'Maria, will you ring for a housemaid?'

'I think she is away from the kitchen at present. I saw her, with a broom, passing by just this minute.'

' "Her". Have we only the one?' says the dowager Duchess, sniffing.

'Since Betty went, it is so hard to find anyone suitable to replace her. And I'm concerned that Cook must soon follow.'

'More fool her, then. We shall engage another.'

'I don't imagine that we can easily find one willing to work for what Mrs Beam is paid.'

'Well, I am quite satisfied that there are any number of young women ready to jump at the chance of serving in a grand establishment such as this,' she says, with the authority of lofty ignorance.

Miss Mantilla gives a cough of demur at this assumption.

'I think that I may be allowed to assume that the "poor" continue, as ever, to be with us, Miss Mantilla?' the dowager lady admonishes. 'As you well know, the world outside is a cold and inhospitable place for women who must work. Your class will always need my class to batten upon.'

Shorn of her power and influence, Her Grace, the Duchess of Fainhope, has grown ever more autocratic in her opinions. Miss Mantilla bows her head and lets the remark pass. She has begun to understand that a subtle exchange has been effected in their relationship. It is now she who must contrive and scheme to keep their heads above water. Like a marriage in which the virile partner has fallen on hard times and is pathetic in his insistence that he continues master of the house and undisputed provider, she, the little wifey, knows what it is to awake from a long sleep of dependency and find that only her carefully hidden economies will keep the wolf from the door.

So she swallows the torrent of worries about servants leaving for factory and shop work, of damp plaster in the ceilings, mice in the pantry, rust in the water cisterns. She bites back the suspicion that the new farm manager is robbing them blind, that *all* the chimneys need sweeping and goes out herself to see about tea and bread and butter.

So the briars begin to grow up around Fainhope Hall. The great steam engine that had thundered through every day, greased by money, shudders to a halt; going nowhere, seized upon its rails. The magnificent liner of wasteful comfort stands grandly shabby, obsolete in dry dock. How quickly this great gobbling monument to the high art of extravagant living becomes defunct and derelict.

It is as though, when not constantly fixed in their purpose by the touch and use of humans, the protean nature of all the materials that went into the making of that magnificent artifact, the grand house, reasserts itself. It is a stealthy process of inevitable decay and growth, death and rebirth, that neglect and the simple passage of time release in house and garden both. So slow at first that you might not even notice that the process of unmaking had begun. Within the house, wood, metal and stone begin to unlearn the ingenious man-made forms in which they had been unnaturally set. For without that vigilant army of servant conservators the quiet work of decomposition, rot and rust allows the artifacts to forget themselves. It is the large effects of the elements that first assert themselves upon the fatally exposed house. The heavy bombardment of the sun exploits neglected defences: without housemaids to pull down prophylactic blinds, the edges of curtains are bled of colour and grow brittle, their fibres unknit. Without men to strip and fill and paint, exterior woodwork is peeled bare to be dried out and cracked open, ready for further attack. Next in the assault come the rain and the wind, working in concert to tease and worry at the house, seeking weak points at which they might enter. The wind tears off a roof slate, the better to let in the rain, wobbles a chimney to crack its mortar, rattles a pane loose in its shrunken putty. Then the sly damp goes to work inside the house, unchallenged. The dry, dead wood of a roof beam is made a host to new life: moulds and fungi, the feeders on damp death. The plaster of the ceiling, below the beam, blooms with a spreading stain, drinking up the damp until it bulges heavy with unspent water. Now the rain finds its route from the distended plaster, like the slow drips of whey through a cheese-maker's muslin, to the bed in the room below. Dust-sheeted long before, it receives each patient drop and blots them up in its ancient horsehair body until it is burdened with rot. After seasons of being wetted, dried out and wetted again, the bed dribbles its heavy, fermented load into a spreading pool below, to percolate through the next stratum of floorboard, ceiling beam and plaster.

Even the silverware, locked away safe from harm, cannot escape the reverse alchemy of air that converts bright to black. Dry air parches and warps the once-saturated wooden draining-board by the side of departed Kathleen's scullery sink. Damp night air rusts together the housekeeper's keys, left hanging, long ago, by the ill-fitting kitchen door.

And outside the gardeners' perpetual battle to halt Nature for ever in pleasing shapes and submissive productivity is lost to the aggressive dominion of weeds and seeds. So the formal gardens surrender themselves to rampant growth. And the wild wood of whippy hawthorn and brambles, which once defended the outermost perimeter of the park, turns inwards to face the house and advances, year by year, in an ever-tightening ring. Like encircling bandits creeping up to look in through the windows, the wild wood gathers, waiting its chance to invade when the house shall finally be cracked open. Harbingers are dispatched to find a foothold in crumbled chimney mortar, thrusting down roots to prise apart and weaken. Grass grows thick in the clogged gutters and moss throws spongy runners along paths and window-sills.

There is an indecent explosion of vegetable fecundity in the once tame gardens. Plants riot and disport where once they had stayed put, obedient in their beds. In an accelerated model of Mr Darwin's theories, the fit thrive and multiply with greedy green vitality and bully the weak into extinction. The lawn becomes a field, busy with yellow grasshoppers, yielding a bumper crop of uncut autumn hay full of tough-stalked, small-flowered weeds. The crystalline fountain is a ripe green pond bubbling with frog spawn. The carriage drive is rutted and muddy as a farm track, where birds bathe in and drink from puddles. All that was once made and controlled by human effort is unmade and unleashed by time's unstoppable twin engines of change: decay and new life. Creation and destruction.

Now when Maria Mantilla goes into the ruins of the vegetable garden to cut salad leaves, she must search beneath and between huge, spiny alien plants. She finds tiny dark-skinned tomatoes – the last clingers-on of their breed, a colony of cannibalistic marrows sprung from the dead, rotted body of their giant parent, pea vines that scramble towards the sun and have forgotten that their pods could contain anything other than dry little seeds from which to grow the next generation. Only a few years of running wild and these civilised food plants have reverted to the forms of their uncultivated ancestors. Selfish with their energy and driven to reproduce, they grow small and tough around their precious seeds. No longer are they bred to please, with expensive refinements like taste, or juice, or colour.

Even as the floodgates are breached and the depredations in house and garden advance with increasing insolence, the dispossessed Duchess will permit no lifting of her self-imposed purdah. All around is growth and change, birth and death. Had she looked, she might have seen seventy species of birds from the window of her private sitting room. Every spring they re-enact the yearly rite of fierce, territorial mating songs and the desperate toil of raising fledglings to repeat the urgent task next spring and every spring after. Unremarked by her, thousands of flowers open and fade all the summer days, yielding up to the bee their one brief chance of consummation. The giant cedar of Lebanon loses a bough and then, like the house, begins to rot secretly from the inside out. It is the busy battlefield of warring insects, whose bloody conflicts and countless casualties are of no concern to the woman who sits and waits within the Hall.

Secluded from the noise and hurry of the natural world outside, it seems that she alone is immune to change. Her hair is a defiant black; no need to disguise contrary silver with walnut juice. Her face is unlined and unmarked, without benefit of enamelling; she dresses according to the fashion, she never neglects her toilette. Unlike Lucy, she does not long for yesterday and lost happiness. Neither does she wait passively for tomorrow in a mouldering bridal dress, grown grotesque with her need. The last Duchess has too much strength of purpose to submit to that state of sad, mad dependency. No, from the day that George disappeared she simply stopped. She fixed herself at the dead centre of the wheeling world, cold and unchanged, hands folded, to focus her will upon forcing his return. When her ascendancy comes again, as she knows it must, she will pick up the dropped threads of her interrupted life and let it run on again. Her ambition is not dead, just sleeping.

Across the park, confined in his own morgue, Lord John also waits. He waits without hope of consolation since his own son is dead and his grandson evidently a mirage sent to torment a neglectful father whose thirst to love is now unquenchable. All that is left him is to attend upon death, the grave his only goal. But death does not call. His own wife, Caroline, has already gone before, seeming to find it no effort to slip through that side door and off down the endless corridor. And yet he cannot seem to do the same, has not the courage to step into the cold, dark, narrow place and leave behind life's burdens and disappointments, perhaps because there is no child of his own to continue when he leaves off the dance.

Time's Wingèd Chariot

As Nature gained the upper hand in Fainhope Hall, the inner London suburb where Aurora and Teresa led their new family life was marked more and more by the hand of man. What undeveloped green patches, unfelled trees, unplumbed cottages and urban cattle sheds supplying sweet, unpasteurised milk, brimming with tubercular bacilli survived from the old queen's century would not last long in the next. The quaint, unhygienic or obsolete gave way to modern efficiency and accountability. However, behind the closed doors of Alonso's old place, the topsy-turvy household of aunts and nephews remained content to live lives at once antiquated and verging on the squalid. The two women apprenticed their beloved Duke in the defunct processes of the dry collodion photographic method. Not for them the universal box camera, which any fool could point at a family group and increasingly did, stuffing his family album with the convenient postcard photos the Browning company would return, processed and ready-printed, in the post. The business of formal portraiture of both the animate and the extinct did not thrive.

When Duke had finished his brief formal education, his two aunts/mothers had been full of anxious expectations for him to make something of himself in the working world. But somehow, between his own disinclination to try and their unwillingness to let him, they lapsed into the myth that he was a rising young buck in the family business, biding his time before he seized hold of the reins and dashed ahead on his own account.

Notwithstanding, the larger world came and found him. One day, in 1914, Duke went to buy fish and a lady passer-by dropped a white feather into his basket. He'd gone straight to the recruiting office and volunteered. So they lost their boy for a soldier in the Great War. It was the start of anxious years when, once again, letters and picture postcards from the absent one were cached on the top of Papa's wardrobe. At first Aurora, Teresa and George had been cheered by Duke's descriptions of the beauties of the French countryside, the scarlet poppies and blue cornflowers in the fields; reassured by news of bread, bacon and onions shared with pals, a farmer who'd let them bivouac in his apple orchard, the little brown and white dog that attached itself to his brigade. It had seemed a jolly holiday war, bound to be done by Christmas. Time passed and the boy in the letters seemed to grow coarser and his conditions harder, he often referred to wet feet and made blasé comments about the size and cunning of the ferocious trench rats. But because censorship, both official and self-imposed, spared them reports of battles, bullets and bloody death, it was impossible to learn from his letters what they really wanted to know: the truth. It was during this uncertain time that George had finally surrendered to his barely suppressed obsession with newspapers. Under cover of following the course of the war he had begun to cocoon himself in Alonso's old room, with bundles and bundles of newsprint. He built it into ragged ziggurats, turned it into uncertain standing pillars, marched it up the stairs, step by step, and lined every wall right up to the ceiling with it, progressively eating up the interior space of the house with his bundles and bales. Finally, it was newspapers that provided the information they sought, but never wanted to hear. Just as his letters dried up, George calculated from the lists of the dead and wounded that dear Duke's regiment must have taken part in the Passchendaele offensive. And then they dreaded the news that the knock of the telegram boy must bring.

In Fainhope Hall, too, the spasms of history that upset human lives could not pass unnoticed. The old Duchess of Fainhope was approached by a War Office man with orders for her to surrender the house as a convalescent hospital for returned soldiers. Though he flattered with the promise that the soldiers would be only officers, and threatened with the power to requisition, somehow the dowager-in-waiting and her home escaped this call to the cause. Perhaps it was the conspicuous fall of plaster while they wrangled over ranked iron bedsteads in the ballroom, which she, raised to be above such things, affected not to notice. However, the official man, being only the son of a banker, did – the plaster and the unavoidable smell of mice.

If it had been hard to hang on to housemaids before, in those times when nearly every girl found employment in service, now that women were needed for war work, had cut their hair, shortened their skirts and even earned a man's wage, what hope did rotting Fainhope Hall stand of attracting biddable slaveys?

For convenience's sake, the two ageing women had moved their lives closer to the source of heat and food, retreating before encroaching ruination. They now lived mostly in the butler's shabby old quarters, near the kitchen. Her Grace was persuaded to invest in a new gas-operated stove but Miss Mantilla was not able to force a single additional penny out of her mistress to go towards other comforts, like plumbing a bathroom for them or installing an indoor lavatory. They squatted in the servants' quarters and lived a life of hand-to-mouth shabbiness that would never have been tolerated among its original tenants.

And the unruly outside world, kept off by money for so long, now advanced, insolent and greedy. The first forays were tentative but, when the felled tyrant did not stir, the once cowed were emboldened to commit outrages. Her Grace had flinched on hearing the tall windows of the ballroom smashed in, one by one. The governess had surprised a ruffian on the stairs. And both had glimpsed the flares carried through the gardens to light the way of trespassers. Easily portable things disappeared and their loss was not remarked upon. It was only when they saw a group of laughing, straining men cheerfully removing the harpsichord piano that Her Grace was roused to action. The Duchess ordered the lower-floor windows and doors to be boarded up and she herself and Miss Mantilla personally removed all the smaller valuable items and pieces of furniture to the drier attics. Henceforward, only the few windows of the servants' quarters were left unboarded, occasionally to frame the bleary, grinning faces of those devils whose sport was to torment the two old witches holed up in their dreary castle.

The only time that the dowager Duchess was to leave her citadel before she left it for the family mausoleum was when Lord John Harpur was on his deathbed. This, too, was the only time that she was to ride in a motor vehicle – *her* hearse would be correctly drawn by smart, black Belgian horses. On this notable occasion, she sat looking neither to left nor right in splendid denial of the wreckage of garden and park around her: the unharmonious gaps let into the avenue by toppled giants, the uncomfortable ruts in the unmended drive, the busy brambles that choked the banks of the ha–ha. She was indifferent to the decay of the old, the springing up of the new. 'All which it shall inherit shall dissolve' signified nothing for her: her destiny was a larger, grander and more enduring matter than mere bricks and mortar and ancient trees.

That lane, muddy in the rain, dusty in the dry, was now convenient, smooth tarmacadam down which other motor vehicles roared, incurious at her stately passage. When they turned off she saw that the coupled rows of sweet chestnuts had survived into the new century, despite Lord John's loss of patience with them, but that the house they had screened for a hundred years was looking nearly as shabby and untenanted as her own. This alone made her raise a grim smile.

The idiot is lying in his room, the bed covered with elderly dogs. The squandering fool has put in electricity, she notices. It is cheering a lamp on the bedside table and warming a little contraption of glowing rods that sits on the floor.

'How d'ye do, brother Harpur?' she says, shoving a worn velveteen spaniel off the chair from which she intends to reprove him.

'Oh, it's you. I heard you never left the Hall, these days. Got a new broomstick, did you?'

'Heard you were dying,' she replies. She prefers to season her exchanges with unequivocal cruelty: spite or teasing she considers rather weak and common.

' 'Deed I am.' He coughs to himself sadly.

'Can't be helped. How old are you?'

'Same age as you, or have you chosen to forget that?'

She nods in assent and slides her feet nearer to the comforting little red beast squatting on the floor.

'Our birthdays are in the same damn month,' he continues, as though there hasn't been a gap in the conversation of a minute or more. 'You met your husband, my brother the duke, at my blasted birthday ball. Or have you forgotten him too?'

'Oh, no,' she says. 'How could I? My knight in shining armour. The one who rescued me from a life of penury and left me in the lap of luxury.'

'Convenient of him quietly going off and dying, eh?'

'As I say, he couldn't have been a better husband to me.'

So accustomed are they to their mutual antipathy that their conversation mimics the genial exchange of conventional pleasantries. The visit already bores her. She looks round the room again, noticing the silver-framed photographs of dandified Harry displayed on his mantel.

'I wonder, now that she is at rest, whether I might not have been a better husband to my wife?'

'It seems to be a characteristic of the human heart to value most that which has been taken from us,' she replies, softened, perhaps, as much in contemplation of her own loss as in sympathy for his. She notices, with distaste, that his expression is collapsing into that look of sly, trusting imbecility that warns of a sentimental confession.

'Both to lose a spouse and an only son . . .' he continues, rubbing a dachshund's sateen ear between finger and thumb, '. . . should be reason enough to bury the hatchet now. Don't you say?'

Just as she had thought: the booby is frightened of death and is going to demand that she make it all better by saying that she is sorry for him, that she loves him, really. She'll be damned if she will. 'I shall never surrender, John. Never.'

'I'm not asking you to surrender, damn you, always so melodramatic. I'm only saying can't we two call it a truce and just be old fools with no spite left between us, just some shared regrets?'

'He's not dead until I say he is! And that I will never acknowledge.'

'Can't you just leave go, woman? There's nothing left for us to fight over. All gone. The boy's dead – he's been dead for years! Look at you – you're dead too, nothing but a corpse holed up in that rotting mausoleum of yours. Let the poor boy rest and yourself with him.'

'I can't. I won't.'

'Why hold on to the house? I wouldn't want it – not now. No one can afford to run a place like that properly nowadays, so let it go. Move somewhere smaller, enjoy some comfort. You're a long time dead . . .' He puffs with the exertion of his emotion.

'I do not consider dying.'

'Quite right, it's a fool's game,' he answers, defeated by breathlessness, red in the face, with the effort of speaking. 'But I was ever the fool, eh, sister?'

He chuckles between gasps. Still trying to shame her into drinking his draught of sickly sweet reconciliation, then. A tonic poisoned with self-pity and imposed forgiveness. She makes no reply. And then, as though he read her mind, 'You'll take a glass of something with me? Toast me a last toast. Can't do any harm.'

'You are kind to offer . . .'

'Then accept. Can you ring for Hipgrove?'

While they drink from none-too-clean crystal Lord John slips into a reverie, his breathing still noisy and irregular even at rest. Had you apprehended them at this moment you might have perceived an old couple, at ease in this kindly setting of dogs, dusk and unforced silence.

'Shall we forgive each other? Come now,' he persists, rallying with the rest and the whisky. He reaches an importuning hand towards her, upright on her chair. She is unsettled to see that his old eyes are swimming with bogus, postulant tears. 'Shall we call it a day and make friends? Let bygones be bygones?'

'I have no time for this . . .' she says brusquely, trying to scorch his seeping sentimentality.

'No time. That's the thing, now. No time but to forgive and forget. Said yourself, we always regret the word left unsaid.'

He extends his hand once more towards her, as though he is offering her something rather than trying to take, take, take. He reaches so far that he almost causes himself to topple over the side of the bed.

'What do you want from me?'

'Damnation, woman, nothing but your hand in friendship before I die! Just that, no deeds, no settlements, no codicils . . . just that.'

Standing, the last Duchess goes towards him, her hands hidden among the folds of her long dark skirt as though she conceals a knife there. She smiles down upon him and he looks back, trusting as the child who has never yet been smacked.

'For our sons,' he says, reaching again for her.

'You must propose another toast for I never had a son. At least, I never had a son who lived an hour beyond his birth,' she says, smiling still that ironical smile. 'You should say "for my own sons". Both of them.'

'Harry . . . ?'

'Harry . . . and George.' She taps him sharply on the nose with her finger, just as she had done all those years before. 'Nasty timely little afterthought George.'

'He could not be. We never . . .'

She laughs at that. 'No. You surely might have remembered and I'm positive I would have! No, your bastard, with my dead husband's name, had a less well-bred dam.'

'Who – which was it?'

'So many to choose between? Who were you diverting yourself with early in the new year before he was born? Whose season was it then?'

'You know, my wife was always so ailing at that time of year . . .'

'Quite. So you let yourself be seduced by the governess. How weak men are in the face of these voracious household predators. Such an old, old story it makes me want to yawn . . .'

'He was Maria's?'

'He was. Before I made him mine.'

'You're a devil!' he cries, trying to back his heavy body away from her towards the bedhead.

'I'm nothing but a tidy hen, gathering in a stray chick.'

'You stole my son's inheritance.'

'Not me. Nothing to do with me. No, it was you, John, you did it all by yourself. It was you who stole away your own son's birthright. You men really should consider the consequences of where you choose to sow your wild oats. It was your slip and my sleight of hand that did for you. You are weak and I am strong. You are the subject of Fate, I am its mistress. You, my husband, my father and all of you men who celebrate your selfishness, lack of imagination and negligence have taught me to be daring, quick and ruthless. My male masters! *I* should bend the filial knee to one who sold me into marriage? *I* should honour a husband who valued me only as a brood mare? If marriage and motherhood are where my worth lies then I shall have them on my own terms. So, brother, you should not condemn me, for 'twas your kind who had the making of me.'

She leaves the room with as proud a deportment as ever she had at that birthday ball, never looking again at the man on the bed, who is shouting, between his sobs and his coughs, 'You lose, you bitch! You lose! You lose in the end . . .'

Leavings

Then Her Grace, the last Duchess of Fainhope returned, satisfied, to that hard-won fortress, the Hall. Hollowed out by rot, worthless and abandoned, nevertheless she claimed it as her prize. She had won it, despite them all. To spite them all.

Next morning, her old companion found her, still as stone, sitting upright, in the armchair that had been drawn up close to the cold kitchen range, as though she had been dead for centuries. The long enchantment was broken. They told Lord John Harpur that his old adversary was finally defeated, that the battle was fought and won, and he sent for his solicitor and his will. There would be one, last, posthumous blow that he could strike against her, with his pen.

He outlived her by just four weeks. And that bitter, dying month was to be his only spoil in their weary conflict; anticipation of the trick he set in place to be activated by his death. He relished that tit for tat: now, he would steal back what she had thought to have robbed him of. It was a revenge that could neither be actively enjoyed by the perpetrator nor suffered by its intended victim, but it seemed a fitting addition to the litany of posthumously played jokes that had shaped their miserable lives.

If Maria Mantilla had expected that she might be a beneficiary in her mistress's will, then she was to be disappointed. Her mistress died intestate. Perhaps she really had intended to live for ever. Perhaps she just didn't care: in life, she had never felt it necessary to cultivate anyone who would not be useful to her and since she did not believe in the needs of the dead, why bother buying gratitude and remembrance from the living with bequests and trinkets? The matter of her missing will was of little consequence to the wider world: there remained almost nothing, exclusively in her own name, of which to dispose. Once she had 'let go', the inheritance proper – that over-ripened cornucopia of properties, titles and estates, which should have been settled somewhere upon the death of her husband but had been held in abeyance, while she lived, apparently by force of personality alone – became the real feast upon which family feuds and lawyers' fees would grow. As with other tyrants, her awful reputation did not endure beyond her death. Just as their faces will stop appearing on every banknote and postage stamp, their proud statuary is smashed, and mention of their name no longer strikes fear, so her influence lapsed and she was soon forgotten.

Notices advertising a reward for information leading to the discovery of George, Duke of Fainhope (or his fate), were printed in newspapers and a detective was engaged to examine again the files of muddled theories and false leads that had been gathered when last he was sought. No one thought it necessary to enquire after lost Georgina. During this time, somewhere in south London, George himself had unwittingly folded and stacked a good twenty broadsheets in which his name was emboldened in an inside back page.

The story of the search for a lost heir stirred up a slurry of imposters and mountebanks who tried their luck in the resulting talent show, affecting accents, wigs and amnesia in the game of winning a real live dukedom. Miss Mantilla, his former governess, had been invaluable in telling the fake from the genuine. Of course there had been no genuine candidates – she saw them all for what they were: vile imposters. After all, a real duke was born to it not manufactured, wasn't he?

Since the eldest daughter, Georgina, was, like George, misplaced, it was left to Euphemia alone to mourn the passing of her parent. She had come howling across the Irish Sea and passed, like a fury, through the Hall, gathering up and shipping out anything of value that could be moved before the executors could stop her. Having first raved about plots and forgeries, when she discovered that there was no inheritance to be had, she had taken the pragmatic course of willing herself two complete dinner services, an ormolu clock and a canteen of Georgian silver cutlery (badly tarnished), by which to honour and remember her parents. Lady Euphemia thus proved herself to have been, beyond dispute, her mother's child, inheritance or none. Of the fine furniture and furnishings that had once graced the Hall, that which had not been already stolen was now made worthless by neglect or changed fashion. So, having informed her old governess that she could no longer expect to stay on, she felt that her filial duty, if not her entitlements, had been fully discharged and left before the funeral.

Unlike Lady Euphemia, who had, after all, been provided with a rich husband, Maria Mantilla had genuine cause to be bitter about the lack of a will. She might have expected some little pension or annuity in return for more than fifty years of fidelity and discretion. However, in the midst of worrying about how she would live and where she might go, she learnt that she was indeed to be recognised from beyond the grave. For this was Lord John Harpur's little time bomb. In a codicil added to his will on the very day her mistress had last visited him, Lord John Harpur had claimed and acknowledged George Henry Frederick, Duke of Fainhope, as his own illegitimate son and heir and named her, Maria Isobel Mason Mantilla, as the mother. What was more, he had left her a lump sum that, carefully invested, would provide an income of one hundred pounds per annum and in addition humbly invoked his executors to allow her to remain living at the Hall, as its caretaker.

What legal confusion ensued after this confession? Did the claim made in this will overturn the legitimacy of the other, that of his more illustrious brother? And which, where and who now was the rightful heir? This tangle, and the fact that they never were to track down a genuine George – whether legitimate or illegitimate – resulted in those undeserving Shropshire cousins getting the whole shebang. Much good it was to do them. By that time, half a fortune had already been diverted into the coffers of the legal profession and three sets of death duties, all in a row, had been levied (by those same gentlemen) on the remainder – that of the old duke, the young duke (now, officially recorded as dead) and Lord John Harpur.

The consequence of these deaths and that will was a hard pill for Maria Mantilla to swallow. It was to be her own and her mistress's unmasking that brought her this livelihood. In order to survive, she must accept this imposition of exposure and humiliation. This was not the secret sorority of mutual self-interest that had tied their lives together with a blood pact and ensured they could live independently in the world of men. This was public exposure and humiliation.

The Shropshire relations, having inspected the white elephant that was now the Hall, neglected farmland above and no mineral riches to be had below, cut their losses and sold off as much of the estate as they could, keeping the best of the shooting and the title, but let her stay on in the mouldering pile: a kind of human watchdog and fire alarm. She did not consider that there was any other home for her, certainly not that house in south London where the lost thing cried, where her sin was buried. No, her home was here, where she must continue to wait, for she had been set to wait, only to wait, for the homecoming that would never come. And there, barricaded in the kitchen, she hid her shame and eked out her allowance on twice-brewed tealeaves and broken biscuits, deter-mined that she should not touch the lucre that had come from that betraying man. So the house of Fainhope was all gone, eaten up and scattered to the winds. Perhaps the Duchess of Fainhope really had cast a sleeping spell over them all, and it was only when she was dead that they had woken to find nothing left but dust.

Fortune's Buffets and Rewards

We left that modest home in south London all shrouded in loss. But news of missing Duke did eventually find the sad aunts and brother who waited there. And when it came it was to tell them that their boy lived.

Duke had become a casualty in that other insuperable war, the one waged against body lice, which infested the soldiers' underclothes and caused that illness the lads in the trenches had learned to call five-day fever. All the hours spent soaping along inside seams, removing the blighters by hand or burning them off with lighted candles were largely ineffective in preventing trench fever; nevertheless, it was a way back from the front line even if, like the trench foot which turned to gangrene or the funk in the face of the enemy that got you shot, it was one that might see you dead anyway. So fever, paralysis and pains in the shins took Duke off to the convalescent camp in Rouen the day before the confusion of the Passchendaele offensive did for so many of his regiment with bullets, shells and bayonets. So saved he was, but only just. At Rouen he'd gone down with an infected throat, swiftly followed by rheumatic fever which irreversibly affected the heart muscle. Finally well enough to be shipped back to England, they'd enquired where he wanted to be returned to and, having requested London, he was dispatched to Leith to recuperate in a poor house fitted out as a hospital. At last he'd been able to write home that he was alive, and returning to them.

So their boy was given back to them in 1919 with a damaged heart. Teresa, Aurora and George thanked God and began the nursing. But it wasn't just a physical problem that they had to cure: there were the nightmare memories that could not be committed to words, let alone letters – the comrades he'd shared sentry duty and a cup of tea with who later became part of the stinking fabric of trench walls. The sight of that poor pet dog, loyal to the last, who had lain and died at the bottom of the trench with his paws over his nose, trying to escape the gas. The man he'd seen cut off at the thighs by flying metal who'd carried on for a few stumbling steps on his stumps before he fell. The screams of horses.

Every night, for many years, George had to hold Duke down in his bed while he raved, shooting spittle into his kind old face. This was when George began to sleep in the same bed as his broken brother. One below the sheet, the other above, hand in hand so that poor Duke would know and feel (even in his sleep) that he was not alone, that there was always one close by who loved him.

Now George sought out the comfort and protection of lost and discarded things without let. He roamed the streets to redeem the lumber that others threw out: this salvage made him feel safe, provided for, anchored. Like the millionaire who collects hundreds of pairs of shoes in memory of having gone shoeless in his penniless childhood, refuse was George's insurance against future want, compensation for the emptiness that had filled his privileged past. And apart from the household's own leavings, the newspapers, used tealeaves and egg shells that he rescued from the bin, he compulsively preserved everything that belonged to Duke. George was the sailor who takes possession of his love's shed sealskin so that she may never again slip into it and return to that other life in the mysterious sea. Worn toothbrushes, holed boots, ragged clothes, even his clippings, combings and trimmings were hoarded, as though by retaining everything of Duke, George held tight to Duke himself. And between his preserving and his scavenging, at last, George stuffed the narrow house to its rafters, wrapping himself and Duke and the old aunts up, tight and safe, at its very core.

Thus they lived on in each other's company and care. So fragile was Duke's health, there was no question he would ever again be called upon to earn a wage, or bring home a bride. The means-test man would never catch him out, despite his periodic visits.

The years of Duke's convalescence passed. The sight of old soldiers selling matches on street corners grew rarer, motor cars more common, and George and Duke, Aurora and Teresa carried on much the same. But even in uneventful lives the passage of time is measured out in aging and death. Far away, and unmourned, the last lady of the Hall took her final leave of it ten years after her mistress. Unlike the Duchess she had made a will, leaving her small nest egg to her sisters. Then, hugely regretted and missed, the two old aunts left Duke and George, Teresa unassumingly following Aurora's lead to the grave, second in death as she had been always in life. The momentous fact that one had loved and been loved by a man and the other had not was not recorded upon their gravestones, and went otherwise unremarked. Their two boys were to be the last beneficiaries of the money that had been made over to Miss Mantilla by Lord John, so with that little tainted crumb of the feast that had been the Fainhope inheritance, George was finally made the heir to both his natural parents. More than half a century after that blood pact was made, George at last fulfilled his born duty, and inherited. But to him and Duke the little bit of money meant no more than that they could continue on in the old house and occupy themselves in preserving everything their dear aunts had owned, or indeed touched. George, and his assistant Duke, became recorders and keepers of those two lives, annotating and filing every letter, postcard and photograph left behind by Alonso's girls.

George, on his scavenging rounds, was often trailed by little boys who occasionally would ring the doorbell and run away. Once, after Duke had wheezed his way to open it, he surprised a boy who stood forward and asked, 'Got any empty bottles we can 'ave?' Didn't their eyes shine with the treasure trove of redeemable pop bottles and jam jars, collected over decades, that the curious pair were able to load in to their old pram? Soon the neighbourhood kids began to call regularly to take the bottles off George's hands, returning with a share of the profits, or to pay in kind with old newspapers. And in time the exchange developed into a friendship with the two old chaps.

Now there were often a few kids sitting in the garden on the stray items of furniture which had overflowed from the house, drinking George's homemade lemonade while, knees wrapped in a rug, Duke rested his poorly heart and George pottered and gardened. In the winter they moved their deck chairs inside to the warmth of the range, a cat on either lap, while children came and went to read the funnies or learn how to make swords from tightly rolled paper spills, or fold paper hats. And when Duke looked across, there he would see George and when George looked there he would see Duke. They had found perfect contentment surrounded by the junk that was the sole testament of four lives lived – their proper inheritance.

Endings

So now we have arrived at the final chapter and must, therefore, contrive a proper conclusion for our story. And it is surely required that we aim high at this point, rounding all (the deserving, at least) with happy endings, as secrets are revealed, the lost found and the parted reunited. And if such loose-end-tying should be considered banal, then at the very least we should stoop to a more general moral: a satisfactory ending should leave the reader with a sensation of either well-being, all's right with the world, or hope, all's potentially right with the world. However, woefully, we find our conclusion to be in the long, uneventful years of our principal characters' aging and exits which only seem to confirm the futility of life, the inevitability of death, and, greatest betrayal, remind us, the heroes and heroines of our own stories, that we too must exit the book at last when all the pith and juice has been squeezed out of our tale. Is the last chapter, then, to be just the final snapping shut of the door upon our dancers after their jig is done?

Lucy died, Frederick died, and they left nothing tangible behind them but what they had made flesh – a huge East End clan of washerwomen and carters, and the fading family memory of a lost or stolen boy. Fred's broad shoulders and way with animals, and Lucy's kind heart and blue eyes continued to be replicated down the generations. For them, their descendants were the eternal souvenirs of what they had once been.

Georgina distinguished herself by dying of a spider's bite, instead of quietly, from old age – but then she had ever delighted in snubbing convention and drawing attention to herself. And even if she did not become the Fisher Folk's most renowned spokes-woman, she was to achieve an immortality of sorts through her art.'The Angel of Albion' (the photograph that Aurora had actually taken) came to define her as artist rather than as merely an eccentric social chronicler. Mistakenly attributed, this was the one photograph, with its depth of warmth and human sympathy absent from her otherwise dispassionate, if lurid representations, that spoke to posterity. It was this picture, reproduced in anthologies and entitled 'Lost Boy' (which you may buy as a sepia-tinted poster) that would bring her a little, posthumous, celebrity. In a curious way it brought Duke a fame of sorts too. Even though he lived out his days anonymously, this often-reproduced image would be his everlasting memorial – without his having known that this remainder of his lost childhood existed.

Zebulon Flynn inherited his godmother's mission and was to spend the remainder of his life writing social history by meddling in other people's lives. He made a speciality of fishing for aboriginal children and placing them for adoption with pious white folk, so that they could be reprogrammed to forget their ancestors' dreams and be raised up instead on poems about English springtime, stories concerning chimney-sweeps and parables from the Bible. His memorial would be whole tribes of stolen boys and girls, severed from parents and culture alike.

And we know that George and Duke died too, together in old Alonso's bed on an early summer's day in 1944. What quiet lives they lived, lives that encompassed an empire's zenith and its decline, revolutions, innovations and two world wars, to make so little impact of their own. Their beginning in a nineteenth-century melodrama of ambition, secrets and lies, their ending in the modern age lying hand in hand, in their pyjamas. Just two old men who simply loved and understood each other, if not brothers in the flesh then conjoined by that spark of love lit in them both by Lucy, and sustained by substitute mothers Aurora and Teresa.

Once the old men's bodies were secured on stretchers and lowered down to be carried away to the morgue, the navvies set to work dismantling the dangerous ruin that the doodle-bug had left behind. Unique in the street, the house remained standing: George had crammed it so full that the walls could not topple. They went at the still-standing brickwork with their pickaxes like barbarian wreckers. Ever-changing London would never look the same again: one house in every five damaged and every one in a thousand destroyed. Shovels scraped up a pile of ceiling plaster and splintered glass and deposited it in the gutter, where it would wait eighteen months for a lorry to fetch it away. Shattered wood cracked under heels. Fragments of marble mantlepiece and shards of vitreous china from the smashed WC, still with the painted flowers on it, were flung into a heap.

Their London, that overwritten narrative, was blown open; all the certainties of development and growth exploded by war. Yet all will heal and reinvent itself. Bomb craters will be filled in, Anderson shelters removed from gardens to leave only a footprint in the undernourished grass that will grow back where once they stood. The names of the dead will be carved upon the war memorials in every village and town square beneath those engraved only a quarter-century before. And succeeding generations will remember little and eventually nothing of what and who passed before. They will forget that every age, however self-confident, must pass and live and die in the expectation that each little individual life has point and purpose, and that momentous events shall not overwhelm them. And perhaps they will be lucky, and will measure their span within those quiet intervals that exist between the upheavals of history.

But whether we die poor and miserable or laden with wealth and contentment, in the end all will be dross, all will be forgotten.

For a while mementoes – a name, a house, possessions, pictures, descendants – may show that we once lived and breathed. We might endure in a kind of half-life in the memory of how we walked or talked or laughed. And the distinctive little things associated with us, a battered volume of often read poems, a walking-stick with a hand-worn handle, may be dearer memorials than all the pomp of a chilly portrait that hangs for centuries upon an ancestral wall. Reputations made in the wider world by monarchs, dictators or saints will resound longer still. And the works of great artists claim nothing less than the prize of immortality itself. But truly the only souvenir that can survive for ever, the only sure way of killing death is, as Lucy knew, in our children and their children: lamps lit by mankind's experience and knowledge which are handed on from generation to generation to illuminate the dark and fearful way mankind must march to the end of time itself.

How then can we be sure of maintaining that trembling flame age after age? Consider the child of the century: in him is personified the triumph and shame of our times. Look, he is a poor and neglected thing, beaten, starved and uneducated. His name is Ignorance, he got it from his father and, like him, will grow to be a ruffian who hands down only blows. Consider that other, Neglect, a chill little being who, frozen, freezes all that come after. And here is Cruelty, who breeds true to his name. Shadowy beings that engender shadows. But here are also Love, Nurture, Peace and Justice, shining and bright. Let them spill only a little of their healing light upon their ugly brothers and see how even they may grow to a more pleasing human shape. But when they turn away their brightness, from disgust or fear, the misshapen ones grow uglier and plot to destroy those who loathe them. Only let the generous flame catch everywhere and what a blaze! Then will the full force of humanity shine down the generations and eternity shall be lit by the one thing that ennobles and immortalises us all, love.

Just as Vic worried it would, a discarded cigarette stub finds the sniff of escaping gas from a smashed pipe and an explosion finishes for them the job of toppling the chimney. One man is injured by the blast, loses a hand, and a fire is started. All those piles and piles of newspapers, all those letters and postcards, all those photographic prints make a big, warm blaze in the dying light. Shreds and scraps of scorched paper fly and swirl on the thermals made by the consuming flames to blow streets and streets away. The half-burnt shreds land to make sooty smudges on people's washing, drying on lines. Half-consumed photographs of whole departed families, their dead children, their wedding parties are picked up and contemplated for the first time in fifty years. Time and the fire have lent them a kind of poignant significance: the ghost of lives gone before.

Perhaps it is a good thing, this fire – the pomp of a funeral pyre a fitting way for a story to find its conclusion. It is as though all the potential energy and emotion, the hopes and fears and expectations that were locked up in those scraps of paper, those words and images, are finally released in a blast of heat. Vic stands back and watches as the firemen spray down the last embers. Barry comes up behind him.

'You won't believe what I've just found!'

Vic turns to him, certain that nothing could surprise him now. 'Go on, then.'

'Only an abandoned baby. Lewis found it, crying fit to bust, not a stitch on it and all bundled up in an old suitcase. Would you credit it?'

Vic can. War seems to make unwed mothers of young girls as quick as it uses up their brothers and fathers. Nature's way of righting the damage, he supposes. Still, no cause to abandon the little tyke.

Vic stoops to pick up a flame-browned photo of a poor boy lying asleep on a grate, tucks it into his pocket and follows behind Barry to see the foundling child.

'Poor little blighter. What a beginning.'